THE DAMNED

"All hell breaks loose—literally—in the complex sixth install-ment. . . . stunning."

—*Publishers Weekly*

"In [*The Damned*], relationships are defined, while a dark energy threatens to destroy the entire squad. Banks's method of bringing Damali and Carlos back together is done with utmost sincerity and integrity. They have a love that can weather any storm, even when dire circumstances seem utterly overwhelming. Fans of this series will love *The Damned* and, no doubt, will eagerly await the next book."

—*Romantic Times BOOKreviews*

THE FORBIDDEN

"Passion, mythology, war and love that lasts till the grave—and be-yond. . . . fans should relish this new chapter in a promising series."

—*Publishers Weekly*

"Superior vampire fiction."

—*Booklist*

THE BITTEN

"Seductive . . . mixing religion with erotic horror dosed with a funky African-American beat, Banks blithely piles on layer after layer of densely detailed plot . . . will delight established fans. Banks creates smokin' sex scenes that easily out-vamp Laurell K. Hamilton's."

—*Publishers Weekly*

"The stakes have never been higher, and the excitement and tension are palpable in this installment of Banks's complex, sexy series."

—*Booklist*

MORE . . .

"L. A. Banks has taken . . . the fourth book in the Vampire Huntress series to another level. [She] has crested another realm to her writing, as she unleashes a battle between the topside master vampires so intense it alters the stasis between good and evil. With the skill of a veteran, Ms. Banks takes this horrific storyline and evolves it into a classic love story without losing the power or the intrigue of the world of darkness. In awe at the depth of this story, and the intensity with which Ms. Banks approaches this series, I anxiously await Book Five. *The Bitten* is not for the faint of spirit; it will cater to those who love to embrace the forbidden. At one point I was tempted to lower my collar and offer my neck. Kudos to L. A. Banks for another masterful link in this arduous chain. Outstanding!"

—*RAWSISTAZ*

"The storyline and the action are intense, and this book is a page-turner that showcases Ms. Banks's writing to perfection. While the storyline is fascinating, the characters make this series one of the most enjoyable I have ever read . . . unforgettable, toe-curling love scenes . . . an excellent read. Ms. Banks has written a book of passion, romance, action, horror, and intrigue. Sit back, hold on, and enjoy the ride!"

—*Romance in Color*

"Duties, pain, responsibilities—what this duo does in the name of love is amazing."

—*Romantic Times BOOKreviews*

THE HUNTED

"A terrifying roller-coaster ride of a book."

—Charlaine Harris

"A spellbinding thrill ride."

—Zane

"The well-conceived and intricate rules of Banks's vampire-inhabited world provide endless opportunities for riffs on the meaning of power and sex that will please lovers of similar . . . philosophical musings found in the vampire tales of Anne Rice and Laurell K. Hamilton."

—*Publishers Weekly*

"In this third adventure, Banks fleshes out the rich world Damali and her friends and enemies inhabit, making it an even more exciting place to visit. Another thrilling tale."

—Booklist

"Hip, fresh, and fantastic."

—Sherrilyn Kenyon, New York Times bestselling
author of Dark Side of the Moon

THE AWAKENING

"An intriguing portrait of vampiric society, reminiscent of Anne Rice and Laurell K. Hamilton."

—Library Journal

"L. A. Banks has taken her Huntress series to another level; the action, adventure, and romance have readers tingling with anticipation. I am not normally into science fiction or the vampire genre, but I find myself addicted to this series. The characters are strong and compelling, and following them throughout this series is a thrill. I highly recommend this book to others."

—Book-remarks.com

"With <i>The Awakening</i>, Banks solidifies her intriguing, dark series as a project worth watching."

—Booklist

"Again, Banks brilliantly combines spirituality, vampires, and demons (and hip-hop music) into a fast-paced tale that is sure to leave fans of her first novel, <i>Minion</i>, panting for more, but nothing seems quite as hot as the steamy, often tense, relationship between Damali and Carlos . . . a newcomer to the vampire genre . . . [Banks] lends a fresh and contemporary voice."

—Columbus Dispatch

"Banks's mastery of character creation shines through in the strong-willed Damali . . . a sure-fire hit . . . pretty dramatic fiction."
—*Philadelphia Daily News*

"[*Minion*] literally rocks the reader into the action-packed underworld power struggle between vampire rivals with a little demon juice thrown in. Nothing less than the future state of the universe lies in the balance . . . it furthermore blasts open the door of the vampire huntress theme to future African American writers . . . [a] groundbreaking concept . . . *Minion* is the first appetizer setting up the next course. As in any delectable meal, it is the savory morsels of each bite that count. So fasten your seatbelt and enjoy a ride littered with holy water, vamp ooze, and a layered web of political intrigue ingeniously woven from the mind of Banks. Cutting-edge wit and plenty of urban heat fly from the pages of this quick read."
—*Philadelphia Sunday Sun*

"*Minion* is arguably superior to the *Buffy* franchise . . . while Banks relies on an established vampire-slayer mythos for part of her story, she is also wildly creative and invents a totally new and refreshing milieu. Its social hierarchy and politics are fascinating, and the author's reinterpretation of the seven levels of hell is brilliant. Another inspired detail is her explanation for how some otherwise 'normal' humans end up as cannibalistic serial killers. *Minion* is an entirely delicious read, leaving the reader licking one's lips and wanting more, cursing the cliffhanger ending. Luckily, this book is the beginning of the Vampire Huntress series, so there's more to look forward to."
—*Fangoria*

"[A] tough, sexy new vampire huntress challenges the dominance of Anita Blake and *Buffy* . . . Damali is an appealing heroine, the concept is intriguing, and the series promising."
—Amazon.com

THE DAMNED

A VAMPIRE HUNTRESS LEGEND

L. A. BANKS

St. Martin's Paperbacks

This is a work of fiction. All of the characters, organizations and events portrayed in this novel are either products of the author's imagination or are used fictitiously.

THE DAMNED

Copyright © 2006 by Leslie Esdaile Banks.
Excerpt from *The Forsaken* copyright © 2006 by Leslie Esdaile Banks.

Library of Congress Catalog Card Number: 2005044593

ISBN: 0-312-93443-2
EAN: 978-0-312-93443-9

Printed in the United States of America

St. Martin's Griffin trade paperback edition / January 2006
St. Martin's Paperbacks edition / January 2007

St. Martin's Paperbacks are published by St. Martin's Press, 175 Fifth Avenue, New York, NY 10010.

10 9 8 7 6 5 4 3 2 1

Always, every gift is given from the Most High and protected by the angels, thus all that I have and am is because of the beneficence of the Creator. Therefore, I am deeply grateful.

Psalm 91, verse 7 . . .

A thousand shall fall at my side, and ten thousand at my right hand; but it shall not come near me.

This book is dedicated to all those who keep hope alive, move with faith, and who work in the Light spreading love. Let your Light shine!

ACKNOWLEDGMENTS

Special acknowledgment goes to: The VHL Street Teams that constantly spread the word about this series, who keep a lively and fantastic community of readers going, online, off-line, bus stops, in the subways (LOL)—wherever they are! You folks have shown so much support that it is hard to describe. Your selfless giving and positive energy is beyond wonderful!

Bless you for the love: Zulma, who is the backbone of the danged fan club and who reminds me of Marlene in so many ways! Tina, our promo czar and my girl from waaaay back! Candace, a sister writer/artist and so efficient that I'ma start calling *her* Wizard—girlfriend's got Post-it tabs in the books, okaaaaay. Glenn, a.k.a. "the slogan master," holding it down in NYC and taking mad-crazy photos. Kenyetta, another Marlene who has my back—feisty, funny, sexy, cool—from Philly, too! Then Roshida, with her quiet, behind-the-scenes moves that are the team's glue . . . plus Gudrun, moderating and handling thangs on the forum board and working Hotlanta down to a nub!

Plus, special thanks to our honorary Carlos Rivera, good minister of the Word, and Tyesha, Quick/LaShonda, and Charlee, who are just blowing up cyberspace! Chantay is holding it down in SC, and is always moving with a "can-do" spirit, Sisters of the Word SidneyBlue Heeler/Michelle and Shaboogie/Shauna got GA on lock, with Lisa up in the Big Apple—y'all are deep! Much love! And I didn't forget about Brother Craig, Kemetic, and Nique in D.C., and our sister Leone out in L.A., plus Rene, a deep analytical brother who is always on point; Alicia, holding it down in Detroit; and Sandra, an international sistah in Australia. . . . Y'all betta work. We've got Ray Jones, who is handlin' the streets like a campaign manager, LOL—go brutha. Barbara Keaton, sister author, who is da bomb, and Lissa Woodson and her talented prodigy, Jeremy, plus Bonnie DeShang's positive vibe—all of y'all holding down Chi-town for a sistah!

FAMILY. Guardians is da houze!

However, no acknowledgment would be complete without speaking on the folks who provide phenomenal Covenant-level infrastructure and support, and who deal with my crazy concepts: my family, especially my husband, Al; Monique Patterson, my editor extraordinaire, with her dream team at St. Martin's—Vicki, Harriet, Emily, Elizabeth, Gina, Christine, Joarvonia, Michael, Matthew, and Sally (wink); Manie Barron, my agent, who makes things happen like magic; Eric Battle—Lawdy—who brought the characters to life in graphic arts; baaaad azz Web master Chris Bonelli; and Vince Natale, who always brings my covers to life. Then came Lauretta Black Pierce, a great publicist, and all was right in my universe. Thank you, all!

PROLOGUE

LaShawna left the house early in the morning, just as her aunt expected, but instead of getting on the bus to school, she waited until she knew Aunt Belle would be on her way to work, and she doubled back. What was the use of school these days? School hadn't kept her momma from dying from a crack overdose. It hadn't kept her brothers from selling it out of their momma's house with her mother's boyfriend after Momma was gone. Now she was living with tired old women who wrung their hands and called on Jesus. Grandma and Aunt Belle didn't know her world. School and church didn't keep nobody safe.

Today she would go back home—her *real* home—and find something that hadn't been stolen or broken, then she was out of her momma's. Maybe she would go live with her boyfriend, or wherever. It didn't matter, as long as she didn't have to answer to people always asking her if she was all right. That was a stupid question anyway—who could be all right after their momma just up and died a month ago?

She trudged around the corner, hoping that her brothers would be asleep. Worse than worrying about them, she just hoped Sylvester wouldn't be home. Her mother's boyfriend had started the whole thing anyway—first getting her momma high, then getting her brothers to help him with his *business*. They were the last ones who could tell her anything about anything.

She peered up at the dilapidated aluminum-sided house,

and tears slid down her face. "I ain't even get to see you before you died," she whispered. She went up the steps and inserted the key in the door.

In her heart, given the way her brothers and Sly rolled, she knew it was dangerous to enter while they were asleep. If they woke up startled, a shotgun blast would end her life. But that wasn't altogether a bad thing, either.

Steadying her nerves, she pushed on, half hoping to die, half hoping to find some peace, and knowing full well that anything her mother might have had, had already been picked over by Sly, her brothers, crack buzzards, her aunts, family—and maybe sold. But that was just it. She wasn't looking for anything of value. What she'd set in her heart as a treasure to find was something not sentimental or valuable to anyone but her.

LaShawna headed for the kitchen, a place that her mother once occupied when times had been good. A place that had seen laughter and good cooking once. The place where her aunts would gather—before her momma got caught up in the madness. Before Sly moved in.

But as she crossed the threshold to the tiny kitchen, LaShawna froze. A scream lodged in her throat and made her chest tight. A warm trickle of urine wet her jeans. She couldn't move or breathe.

Her mother stood at the sink looking out the window. The back of her baby blue burial dress was slit from the neck to the hem where the undertaker had dressed her. Every disk in her mother's frail, knotted spine pushed up beneath her ashen brown skin. Her hair was flattened in the back as though she'd been lying down for a month. Dirt stained the dress. Patches of light danced across LaShawna's eyes as she wobbled and grasped the doorframe and began backing away slowly.

"Baby, don't be scared. It's Momma," her mother said in a rasp without turning around. "Came home to see my only girl. Can't nobody raise you but me. 'Sides . . . your brothers didn't have what I needed, neither did Sly. But that's okay. You here now, honey."

Silent horror transformed into bleating sobs, and the young girl remained paralyzed between bolting for the door and going to what had to be a ghost. Everything in her told her to run, but her legs wouldn't cooperate. Yet, it was her mother's voice. It was her! What if her momma had come back with a message in a vision, like her grandmother always prophesized about?

"Momma, I missed you so much . . . but you supposed to be in Heaven!" LaShawna cried out, covering her face.

A groan and a thud made her jerk her attention behind her. She stumbled backward until her spine hit the adjacent wall as she watched Sylvester's body collide with the post at the top of the steps, catch the banister, and tumble over it, leaving a tangle of entrails from his slashed-open stomach behind him. Her eldest brother crawled to the top of the steps and simply slid down them. No face. He just left a bloody streak in the stair carpet.

This time LaShawna screamed. At the same time, her dead mother turned, bulbous eyes glowing black-green, twisted teeth distending her gaunt, worn face. LaShawna pivoted and dashed for an escape. Claws snatched her arm, spun her around, and pinned her against the shut door. Putrid breath covered her, and she escalated her futile screams. Dogs barked and howled in neighbors' yards, but she'd gone deaf from the fever pitch of her own shrill voice.

"I didn't go to Heaven, baby," a deep, demonic voice rasped. "I went to Hell instead."

The local newspapers said that a horrible family butchering probably occurred due to drug affiliations the family had. The police said the assailants were still at large. The community held a candlelight vigil to end the violence. But old folks and preachers who knew better whispered on porches about the devil and his damned.

THE GULLAH ISLANDS OFF THE SOUTH CAROLINA COAST.
PRESENT DAY.

The nightmares were back. Running hard and long to Marlene's old safe house path proved worthless, as far as improved sleep went. Damali sat up in bed with a jolt, her nightgown damp and clinging to her body. Her breath was ragged as she sucked air in through her mouth, shuddered, and placed her hand over her heart. She peered down at Carlos, who hadn't moved. It was odd the way he slept like the dead whenever she had these dreams. Other times, he slept like a cat; always ready to spring awake. The Sankofa tattoo on her back tingled eerily.

She glanced at Carlos's neck, where he'd received the invisible marking of a male Neteru. There was an identical one at the base of his manhood. Neither had glowed silver since Philadelphia, not even when they made love. Hers never came alive anymore, either.

It also no longer sent guiding messages through her system. Now it only throbbed vaguely or tingled like a pinched nerve when the night terrors swept through her, as if struggling to communicate with her chakra system to no avail. She wondered if either of their marks would keep her from conceiving when lit . . . not that that was an issue, it seemed, given the infrequency of their lovemaking these days. Latex had been a temporary, disappointing answer. She wasn't about to tempt fate.

Damali touched the small of her back, feeling for the tattoo, hoping that it would rise beneath her skin as it should, would move to let her know that it was still alive. But her hand touched the smooth, flat surface of her damp skin. It was as though all that was Neteru within her was slowly dying.

Why was this happening? She'd even helped Raven into the Light in a quiet parting that now allowed Marlene to sleep peacefully. Damali ran her fingers through her locks, searching for some task left unfinished. Commissioning Raven into the Light had been swift, merciful; within an embrace—semivamp style, one quick hug laced with a point-blank stab from the baby Isis dagger, her mother watching ether turn into light, a prayer on both women's lips, and then it was over. The purging was private, the heavy soul transfer done neatly. She'd keep her word. It was an act of kindness, and it delivered a tortured soul that Heaven wanted back where it truly belonged. So why the nightmares?

Suddenly, there wasn't enough air in the room.

Full daylight filtered through the windows, but didn't chase away the lingering shadow of terror. The sensations evaporated so slowly that she could almost reach out and touch them. The nightmare was always the same.

The ground near her feet would yawn wide, allowing Lilith to slither away and escape. Then billowing black clouds would gather beneath the hem of the Chairman's robe, where Lilith had descended back into the pit. It would crawl up his body as though a living entity, caressing his face and entering his nose. He would breathe it in and gasp. Blood gurgled in the opened, fanged, black hole in his face, bubbling, spilling over his thin lips and chin, coursing down his throat and the front of his robe as though there were an endless fountain of the thick crimson substance within him.

She would raise her Isis blade, but it always felt too heavy, requiring her to grip it with both hands. Moonlight would glint off the silver. The Chairman would smile. She would try to rush forward, but it felt like she was standing in waist-high water, wearing concrete boots. She moved in slow motion, but she would not be stopped until his head rolled.

Damali looked down at Carlos and stroked his tousled hair. New tears rose to her eyes, and she shut them tightly as she remembered the dream.

She would raise the blade, swinging the heavy metal until it connected with demon flesh, bone, gristle, cartilage, sending a black-blood geyser into the air, on her, spraying the terrain until she almost couldn't see. The Chairman would laugh as the last of the tissue was severed, then he'd wink, and his face would become Carlos's stunned, dead, glassy eyes . . . flickering silver, then going brown, a haunting question of *why* left in them.

Another horrible shudder ran through her. Marlene and Father Patrick had said it was posttraumatic stress syndrome—something all warriors dealt with—and it would pass. Big Mike and Berkfield, who had been to 'Nam, confirmed the diagnosis, and the others admitted having similar after-battle nightmares, too. She could only tell Carlos about the first half of the dream; the last part felt so frighteningly real that she couldn't speak of it to him while looking into those same questioning eyes. He'd told her that he still had sleep terrors from time to time, taking him back to his old vampire existence or his torture, but it would soon pass . . . just like her nightmare of the Chairman would.

He no longer woke up screaming, wiping nonexistent blood from his mouth or cringing at whatever sunlight had filtered into the room. So, why was she still so freaked out? Why was the dream the same, over and over and over again, as if her mind was a CD with a nick on it? And why did it take her so long to warm up in her man's arms? Why did this horror she experienced while sleeping always feel so real?

She had to get the team to the Native American lands Jose owned. Sanctuary, hallowed earth. It was also the only safe place left for them. However, it wouldn't help with the dreams. The dreams still attacked her, whether in a cathedral or hotel bed. As long as Carlos slept beside her, she was tortured to near hysteria day or night. When she slept alone, peace swaddled her mind.

What did this mean? *Dear God, what did this all mean?*

Just as day broke, Carlos watched Damali finally drift off into a fitful slumber; then he silently crept into the bathroom. He shut the door with care and latched it behind him. Why did Father Patrick have to choose now to go back to Rome? He needed someone to confide in, a man of the cloth, the one who took him to his heart like a son.

A stability factor was needed. Father Pat was definitely

that. But every man had his limits; maybe Father Pat found his after Lopez bought it. And who could blame him? The shit they'd all gone through was more than anybody should have had to deal with at any age. It was ridiculous.

But he couldn't escape the fact that every man who had been a force in his life had walked when he'd needed him most. Besides the aged cleric, who'd been a ground wire for a while, who had ever really been around to guide him? He wasn't complaining about it, wasn't crying. That was just a fact. All his life lessons came from the school of hard knocks. The way of the world, alive or dead.

He ran his palms down his face and breathed in deeply, then let the air out of his lungs in a resigned rush.

Weary of the thoughts that besieged his mind, Carlos sat down on the closed toilet seat, hung his head, and shut his eyes to the blue-gray dawn.

"Forgive me, Father, for I have sinned," he whispered to the elderly priest in absentia. "It's been who knows how long since my last confession."

Carlos kept his voice to a low murmur, battling for composure and using slow, deep inhalations and exhalations to steady his voice as his thoughts raged. "I can't get Padre Lopez's death out of my mind. I'm so sorry about that, I don't know what to say. They were seeking my essence, my vamp line . . . and Lopez had it in him, as well as that . . . image of Juanita I'd poisoned him with, before I knew better." Carlos swallowed hard.

"If I hadn't, then maybe . . . he was just a kid, really. They didn't come after Jose like that, so there had to be a reason, a cause, a link with more juice than Jose had in him, so you can't tell me it wasn't my fault. I got serious debt behind that. I know it. And they honed in on that foul shit, thought he might have been me because of the heart chakra connection he and I shared, and they"—Carlos choked and he made the sign of the cross over his chest—"they took his heart, man. How am I gonna live with that?"

A silence interrupted only by a slow drip from the sink

faucet was his answer. Two huge tears rolled down Carlos's cheeks, and he let them fall, splashing his thighs as he leaned forward with his face in his hands. "Father Pat, I know you said it was fate, he had fulfilled his purpose without breaking his vows to the Covenant, which was eminent, but how come that don't make me feel it's okay?"

Again, silence. It pounded in his ears and added to the ever-present throbbing headache he was constantly nursing these days. Drawing a shaky breath, he pressed on with his complaint in the eerie quiet, hoping Father Patrick would hear him in his mind and send a sign, something, anything, maybe a little salvation for him to cling to.

"Everything is falling apart, Father. The team is in disarray. My claw of Heru ain't working no more than Damali's stones can give up a charge so she can do a shift; none of our powers are stable, and our reaction time is slow. Bad position for everybody to be in."

He breathed out hard and pulled his fingers through his hair as his voice faltered. "Father Pat, this is too much shit going on at the same time with all the newbies to train when I ain't even ready for whatever myself."

Carlos drew in another shuddering, ragged breath and let out a rushed exhalation of frustration. He took his time, framing his next statement. There was something he had to get off his chest that he could never tell another living soul, could never tell another man . . . but Father Patrick was somehow different, in a different category than a Guardian brother, or a friend. But even sitting alone in the privacy of the bathroom, which had been turned into his tiled confessional, just forming the words in his mind gave him a chill. Saying it out loud would give it energy and reality, and then he wouldn't be able to tuck it neatly away and ignore it. It had gnawed away at his brain so long that it nearly bled. He had to get it out.

"Father Pat," he whispered, his voice barely audible to his own ears. "I'm scared, man. I can't lead this team. What

if I fail? What if I really fuck it up this time and get somebody else killed? My powers ain't fully back, been dwin-
dling since the battle in Philly."

The words had come out in a panicked rush of emotion. A
repressed sob held back more of the truth for a moment as
Carlos began rocking and speaking to the cold bathroom
floor. "I know this ain't your department, but, even with my
woman . . . you know what I'm saying . . . things ain't
right." He clutched his hands together as his forearms rested
on his thighs, studying the blurring mortar between the tiles.

I can't sync up with her, he murmured within his mind,
unable to verbalize this deeply personal pain. "I hope you
can hear this part, man," Carlos whispered, talking as much
to the absent Father Patrick as to himself. "I can't even say
it." He glanced toward the window, as the walls in the bathroom felt like they were closing in on him. Just thinking
about it, much less mentally stating it, made him want to get
up and go take a long walk. He needed fresh air. "I'm a
Scorpio, what do you want from me, hombre?" he muttered
with a sad smile, trying to joke it off. It didn't work; it just
made him feel worse and made the truth barrel into the forefront of his mind.

"All right." Carlos sighed. "No games." He focused on
the small clerical cot and wooden chair that used to be the
only furniture in the old safe house room where he and Father Pat had some of their deepest discussions. Then he
jarred the lid to his very personal thoughts, the real dark and
scary portions that he shared with no one, and mentally told
the truth.

*At first, when I got marked by Ausar . . . I thought I'd
been, you know, messed up—permanent. Then I found out I
wasn't. And I'm not, but it's complicated. My silver ain't firing on all cylinders.* Comprende?

Carlos let his shoulders drop and intensely studied a single tile on the floor.

When I go to touch her, she pulls back, almost like she's

afraid of me or doesn't want . . . There's no heat, you know
what I'm saying? Half the time I don't even feel like it, when
we . . . There was a time when I'd give my eyeteeth just to get
with her, and could get a mind lock going to make her hit
high notes in three-part harmony. Now . . . I can't explain it.
We don't even lock anymore. It's like we're just roommates.

Carlos stopped breathing for a moment, and then pulled
in another hard breath through his nose and let it out quickly
through his mouth. He closed his eyes and allowed his head
to hang back. "What's wrong with me, man? I've never dealt
with nothing like this in my life." *Me, I could always count*
on, if I couldn't count on nothing else . . . now . . .

He looked at the door, wishing his vision could bore
through it to see Damali like before. Good memory was a
bitch, and he knew he was nursing the past like an old drunk
nursed a drink in a run-down bar . . . thinking back on the
good old days or nights and mentally editing out the twisted
parts about it. Yeah, he knew that's what he was doing, but
that still didn't make it any better. His past was a complicated blend of the horrible and awesome. Bitter irony. Perhaps karma, as Shabazz would say. But he'd never breathe
any of this to his seasoned Guardian brother. The shit
sounded weak, pitiful. Soft.

He wasn't about to divulge to another man beyond a
priest that all he had left was his hard outer shell, and some
of his pride—illusion caster that he'd once been. It was the
law of the jungle; you never showed anyone or anything your
soft underbelly, lest you get it ripped open . . . and that
wasn't an option in the joint, in the 'hood, or in Hell. Never.
And no woman wanted a soft man. Forget that. Natural law.
Yeah, he'd suck it up and figure this out alone. Father Patrick
didn't have advice for something like this.

"I'm not feelin' this shit at all, man," Carlos whispered.
Out of reflex, Carlos ran his tongue over his teeth—
something he still did when thinking hard or pissed or both.
"Old habits die hard," he said with a crisp tsk of his tongue

against a normal canine, and then stared at his hands. "Fuck it."

He didn't miss the blood, the torture, or the foul darkness, but there were some things he secretly had to admit his soul ached for. He tried to tuck all that away and into his mental black box before he left the bathroom to go back to bed; he couldn't even tell Father Patrick about that part, or about missing his old power, even if it did come from the dark side. He was a priest and definitely wouldn't understand.

But strangely, all the stuff he'd pulled out of the box seemed to mysteriously expand on its own and didn't go back into it as neatly after it had fallen out. Nothing was crisp and folded as it spilled out.

Carlos stood and stared in the mirror and set his jaw hard. "Show me something, then," he said quietly through his teeth, "that'll make me know what to do from this point forward, 'cause right now, I don't know. All I know, that works, to get the job done, is power. And so far, it's only been shown to me, for real, from a throne that had a lineage arc to it that was no joke. Serious kick. Feel me?"

The bathroom was silent. Now, so was he. Dawn fully crested. He was too disgusted for words. The good old nights had to go back where they belonged, inside his mental black box. He'd let them stay there until they begged for another private review with a nonjudgmental audience—him. Carlos closed his eyes and steadied himself for a Joe-normal day. The old nights whispered good-bye like an unhappy lover and slipped back into the shadows of his thoughts. It had been real.

Quiet as he kept, he missed *all* of that.

CHAPTER ONE

She didn't need to look into Carlos's eyes or try to go inside his head to know he was pissed. The pulsing muscle in his jaw was always a dead giveaway. So was the attitude.

Damali watched him stare into the distance as she said her good-byes to the team at the front screen door. There wasn't even a flicker of silver in his irises. That hurt, but she'd live.

"Okay, listen, guys—I'm only five minutes down the road, so it's cool." Her smile was forced, her concerns about her man's mood growing as hugs got passed out on the front porch of Jose's grandfather's house.

"Call us in the mornings, though, D. You ain't gotta be longwinded," Shabazz said, fussing as he ran his palm across Sleeping Beauty. "All a brother wants to know is that you made it through the night. After that, we're cool."

"I will, I will," Damali said, kissing his cheek quickly.

"Any problems, we 'round the corner," Big Mike added, nodding toward Rider. "I'm gonna be in Houston with Inez to visit the baby at her momma's, but still call somebody."

"You send up a flare," Rider said, "and you know your crazy brother, Mike, if he's here, will launch a rocket-propelled grenade from his bedroom window to wake up the neighborhood, if he has to. If he ain't, I got whatever in rifle range. Jack Daniel's or not, I can still nail a target with my eyes closed."

"Sho' you right," Mike said giving Rider a pound.

Damali smiled. Way too much testosterone was flowing in the house this morning.

"Now, if you need anything, baby, you let me and Marj know, and we'll be sure you're stocked at the new place." Marlene sighed, gave Damali a defeated hug, and let her go slowly.

"I will," Damali said, wondering why this was so hard to do and why everyone was so worried at this point. It didn't make sense. She was grown, and had shown them she could hold her own in battle, but she knew some things were just instinct. It was always hard for mother birds to watch one of their own fly away—even if it was just around the corner. She squeezed Marlene's hand and let it go when the older woman smiled.

"You need anything, *you call*," Marlene repeated, gently placing a finger on her third eye.

The group seemed to be holding its breath, as though Marlene might say something at the last minute to get Damali to reconsider. But when Marlene nodded and moved away from Damali, shoulders slumped.

"That's right," Marj said with emphasis, picking up the mild guilt trip where Marlene had left off. "Towels, blankets, you have everything, right?"

"I'm well stocked," Damali affirmed, attempting to swallow a big smile without much success.

"How about some more rounds?" Berkfield said with skepticism in his voice. He looked at Jose, J.L., and Dan. "Her weapons room is righteous?"

"Yeah," J.L. said, stepping forward on the porch. "It's tight."

"I ain't just concerned about the realms," Jose hedged, glancing at the others. "You know, escaped convicts, crazy SOBs from off *America's Most Wanted,* and shit like that might not show up on radar."

"See, that's what I mean," Dan said, nodding emphatically. "She's a celeb, too. Somebody could snatch and ransom her, happens every day."

"I ain't worried about that," Shabazz said with a grudging smile. "Bastard will get his heart cut out first. It's nightfall that concerns me."

"We do have a coupla team members who specialize in

night work," Damali reminded them, but without saying any names. Speaking of Tara in front of Rider, especially in the same breath with Yonnie, was taboo.

"You ain't scared?" Inez said, reaching for Damali's hand and clasping it. "Girl, I ain't trying to be funny, but—"

"Yeah," Bobby said, glancing at his sister. "Me and Kris could be over there with you as an extra pair of eyes and ears, especially on the computers. All you have to do is say the word, D."

"We could take shifts," Kristen offered eagerly. "It would be fun."

"Uh, that would be no," Damali said, laughing and ignoring their dejected expressions. "You two have to go into heavy training with the seasoned brothers. Nice try."

Juanita folded her arms and leaned against the doorframe. "If the Covenant brothers said she'd be fine and left this house, then I see no reason to worry." Her cool statement delivered with a frosty bite made everyone stop clamoring around Damali for a moment.

Damali ignored her, laughed, and kissed them all again, semiavoiding Jose, but offering him a quick peck on the cheek and then she stepped back. She didn't even approach Juanita or look at her, but quietly served Juanita her ass to kiss. "I'm just around the corner, dang," Damali said as gently as possible, making her tone upbeat. "I'll be fine."

Carlos cut her a sidelong glance from his position away from the group and near the steps. "She always is." He walked farther away from the group and walked down the steps to stand by the driver's side of her black Hummer.

If he didn't get out of here soon, his head was gonna explode. He understood where the brothers were coming from, but it was also the height of disrespect. *Before,* she didn't need no serious artillery—she had *him* as her weapon. *He* had been her night security system, locked and loaded. Fuck Yonnie and Tara being that. Now she needed some old motherfuckers to blow something up or shoot a target from their windows? Mike and Rider needed to step off. Even the young bucks were talking about going over to Damali's as a defense system? *Right.* The only one who had said anything that made sense had been Juanita. And if Damali called anybody on second-sight impulse, it, by rights, shoulda been him—her man!

Carlos walked a hot path toward her vehicle, his back straight. With that, everybody nervously waved and went into the house, but stood huddled just inside the screen door.

Damali took her time meeting Carlos by her vehicle. She had known he'd take it pretty bad when the day finally came, but she'd expected him to be cooler about it in front of the team. "It's gonna be all right," she said, trying to extend an olive branch of peace. "Your place will be finished in a couple of weeks, they said, and then you'll—"

"It's cool," he said, cutting her off and yanking open her Hummer door. "I'll see you around."

Damn. No kiss, no hug, muscle in his jaw still jumping, no effort to even act like—

"Act like what?" he said evenly, not hiding the fact that he'd read her surface thoughts. "Act like I'm okay with this bullshit? You oughta know me better than that, D. The one thing I don't do is front."

"All right," she said calmly. "I feel you. No problem." She got into her Hummer, casually closed the door, and started the engine. "I'll call you later. *On the phone.*"

Carlos tilted his head. A nonverbal, "Say what?" passed between them. He lifted his chin, turned on his heels, and stormed back into the house. A screen door slamming was his answer.

Her Hummer took to the road as though on autopilot, kicking up dust as she leisurely drove to her destination. Her thoughts were miles away, the scene behind her competing for attention with the perfunctory motor skills required to drive. She wasn't angry, just annoyed. It was what it was. Instant marriage was out. Shacking still meant having a man and his dirty laundry and drama in her space. After what she'd just been through, she wasn't trying to have a baby anytime soon, anyway . . . and living with him 24–7 increased the odds that one day or night she might be moved to forget all about lighting her Sankofa.

Damali quietly laughed to herself. She knew how Carlos rolled. Not to mention, he still had a lot of inner personal development to do. By all indicators, the Light wasn't finished with him yet, and as wild as Carlos's ass was, she didn't need to be in lightning-strike range while they honed him. His mild apex in Philly had been rushed and temporary, spiked like a flux, just by seeing Lilith. If he fluxed and started trailing aphrodisiac to draw out lower levels, Tara would be near to protect him; if Yonnie bulked on him, there were enough brothers in the house to cope to make Yonnie stand down . . . and Carlos needed to learn how to work with that weapon, too. She couldn't teach him that. The Neteru Queens had intimated as much. This was his battle, not hers.

Naw. Carlos Rivera needed to get his head together, deal with his new circumstances on his own, before bringing that baggage to her door. Uh-uh. Plus, after the heat in bed cooled, *and it had,* she had enough sense to know that it got real basic—Marlene and Marjorie hadn't needed to tell her that. They were living examples.

Carlos would either get over it, or not. He'd better recognize that the Light worked in mysterious ways, and needed to stop challenging the Father for all the gifts he'd been given. Did the man *realize* that he was alive, had all body parts accounted for, with a for-real second chance, and had been elevated to Neteru status? Incredulous, she could only shake her head as she drove. "Carlos better stop, y'all. My name is Bennit, and I ain't in-it. Okaaaay."

Shoot, the way he was acting, thunder and freakin' lightning from the sky was likely—and she'd go into the pit for the brother, but wasn't *even* trying to get in trouble with the Most High. Nope. Not hardly. Especially not over some male ego yang. Puhlease. Hold the line, stay the course, handle her business as the female Neteru, that was it. They already took her long blade behind the nonsense, and she'd gone through too many changes to get back the baby Isis dagger. She'd learned her lesson, and had learned it well. She wasn't going backward, not for love nor money. Uh-uh. He had to step up to her level, this time.

She smiled wider. Live with him while he was challenging the Light's blessings? Hell no. Not until they were evenly yoked. When he got his head right, *then* she'd consider it. She needed time to breathe and assess. The whole meeting with the Neteru Council had given her serious pause, and before she made another rash move, she wanted to be sure the timing was right.

It wasn't about communal living arrangements any longer, either. Too much water had run under that particular bridge. If Juanita stepped to her wrong one more time . . . See, that was the problem; she couldn't just drag her narrow behind out into the front yard and kick her ass old-school style. That would be irresponsible as the Neteru, would have repercussions if the girl got seriously injured, and . . . no. Moving out solved a lot of problems, beyond Carlos's mess. A sister needed space, time, privacy, and room for all the thoughts tumbling around in her head.

Damali turned off the engine and hopped out of her vehicle, crossing the dusty driveway and listening to gravel crunch under her feet. What was there to fear, really? She'd literally been to Hell and back already and wasn't even twenty-five years old yet. She'd have her own place, not far from the others, just like Carlos would. But that whole thing of everybody living under one roof was beyond tired. It was better this way—much better.

She leaned on the porch rail, not ready to go inside the house, just staring at the pretty desert flowers and cacti in her front yard. Yeah, after doing the Philadelphia job, it was time to fly the coop . . . Even though, truth be told, settling in Chinle was a far cry from usual for a sister from around the way. However, once they'd all seen the majesty of Jose's people's land, all the arguing had stopped. The only one still opposed to the hallowed location had been Rider, who eventually relented. But she could understand that now, too.

Damali sent her gaze across the sheer sandstone canyon walls that towered some six to eight hundred feet above the wide expanse beyond Jose's grandfather's land. Sunlight played with the shadows, turning the layered rocks pink, orange, and red, depending upon its mood. As the sun danced with the wind, it cast vermilion stripes and pastel hues on the porch furniture. Here, in this sacred land, the light was alive, different, a living entity.

In the distance she could make out the sunbaked clay, multistoried, cliff-side dwellings left by the Anasazi people. Canyon de Chelly, *tsegi*, meaning rock canyon, in Navajo, held more than two thousand years of quiet, mystical wonders and rock art . . . profound spirituality within its panoramic vistas. Yes, this was where she and her team needed to be.

The grumbling about being so far from city life, access to modern conveniences, airports, and so-called civilization had ceased the moment they'd set foot upon the land. Spellbound, the group had reached consensus immediately and had squashed the bickering. Yet, deciding where to go had been a delicate balancing act indeed. There were many issues to consider. Some of those worries still lived in her soul.

Without the compound, they'd needed to be somewhere safe while the new construction was underway. They'd needed hallowed ground, but that would have made it virtually impossible for two of the team's valuable members to seek shelter in an emergency. It wasn't like Tara and Yonnie could just blow into a church or temple with the rest of the squad to take cover. But to leave them ass out in a firefight was unacceptable, even to Rider.

What it had come down to was access. Jose had tribal access to thirty-three pristine acres of land deeded to him from his Creek grandfather, who had married a Navajo woman. Under carefully written wills, the land went to his father when his mother passed first, and now eventually to him— something that all of her and Carlos's money combined couldn't buy. It wasn't for sale; birthright dictated reservation and nation acceptance status. Sure, the rest of the team could tag along as Jose's family, but the position of the Navajo nation was clear; if you weren't from the nation, forget real estate development.

Damali smiled as she leaned on the porch rail of her small ranch dwelling. The negotiations to build a couple of cottages and expand upon a simple house made of pine had seemed harder than bargaining for all the world territories she'd temporarily amassed in the Australian master's parlor. Jose's family's house had fallen into disrepair while abandoned, and was currently more shack than house. But to build anything new required a long, drawn-out process of permits and talks.

Perhaps it was the architectural drawings that had freaked them out. The significant technology and barriers, along with a helipad, had gone against the tribal council's sensibilities. They'd been aesthetically offended, so her team had to go back and redraft everything to look as natural a fit to the landscape on the outside as possible. Gone were the exterior, ultramodern-looking cement walls. Good riddance. She agreed with the tribal council on that.

Working with Jose and a good designer from the nation as go-between had finally rendered a concept that was both environmentally and politically correct, while doing what it had to do—namely, serve as a fortress for her Guardians. If it hadn't been for the respectful adherence to prophecy, they still might not have been able to get the deal done. The downside was that everyone who sat at the table knew who they were; their cover was blown within the Navajo community. Soon, that would spread like wildfire to other communities, but it didn't matter. You couldn't just roll up on Navajo reservation lands without permission like that, and the eyes of the people were everywhere to protect their own. Very cool arrangement.

Damali let her breath out hard, but refused to let her

thoughts grow dark, even though her squad was holed up in
a wood-frame structure with rickety old windows, with only
shotguns and artillery, in case it got hectic, like the freakin'
OK Corral. She hoped it wouldn't come to that, because the
greatest thing they had going for them beyond skills and fire-
power was an old man and lady's very old prayer. Ancestral
shaman guarded the joint.

Until all that was put to rest, she hadn't been able to just
up and move out, and never in a million years would she
leave her team unprotected, anyway. The big problem that
had haunted them all had been where to go during the rebuilding, where to rebuild period? She was so glad once that
nonsense had been settled that she'd almost praise-danced in
the streets.

Months of living from pillar to post had given them all a
case of raw nerves along with persistent headaches that
made tempers flare at the slightest provocation. Peace was
just beginning to be theirs, and she cherished it as she stared
out at the sublime majesty.

Hotels required being constantly on the move to avoid
night hazards and the media. There were new, uninitiated
members, like Berkfield's kids and wife, to worry about,
Inez . . . Juanita . . . plus the old guard was busted up pretty
badly and on the mend. Shabazz was still walking slow, like
Big Mike. Marlene's shoulder still wasn't right, and Rider's
heart was broken. And until her small ranch was built down
the road a piece, in the opposite direction from Carlos's, all
of them had to cozy up in a one-bathroom, four-bedroom
dwelling when night fell. Pure drama.

During the wait, she knew if they didn't kill each other
while the compound was being constructed, then they'd survive. Vampires and werewolves were the least of her concerns.
Damali nearly laughed out loud, just thinking about it. Everybody was snarling and barking at each other by now. The slow
advance toward more room and freedom had seemed interminable, but she'd learned patience along the way.

Tara's grandmother, although Cherokee and not a Navajo, also had an impact on their decision to locate in Arizona. She took comfort in that. Despite the fact that the woman was long gone, when she'd moved in with Jose's grandfather, she'd made quiet magic . . . a path in the hallowed grounds to the house that only her granddaughter could cross . . . along with a male with a good heart.

Damali pushed away from the porch rail and went back into the apartment-size house. *Her house.* It felt good to say that, even in her own mind. The screen door softly clattered shut behind her; she liked the sound of that. It was *her* door. A regular door, not a hotel door. No compound grates and security-thick steel that made her feel like she was entering a federal lockup.

A persistent smile was on her face as she walked through the spartan sandstone-colored rooms filled with light pouring in from endless windows and skylights. The sun practically somersaulted off the oak flooring and then embraced the bright Native American hues trapped in handmade rugs, blankets, and wall art. When she hit the electronic hall panel, mellow instrumental music from the new CD she was crafting greeted her as she made her way toward her kitchen for a cool iced tea.

Yeah, the old girl was so wise. Tara's grandma had it right; a man with a good heart . . . on this land, that would be Rider, and truthfully, any of the guys on her squad, even Yonnie. She'd have to lay down her own barrier on the new joint like that, only letting the good ones in. Mischief crept into Damali's thoughts. Most assuredly Carlos was a good man. *Jesus* was he good . . . maybe Jose, too. She immediately straightened and banished the thought, swigging the iced tea right from the pitcher.

"It's *my* house," she said to the nothingness around her. "My thoughts. And it's my crazy-ass dreams," she said with more emphasis while laughing at herself. "Don't worry—a sister can think about stuff while alone in her *own* house,

can't she?" Damali took another satisfying swig of sweet tea.
"And in her *own* house, she can drink from the pitcher, no
brothers or mommas in the joint! I don't have to share—*yes*."

She became still for a moment, realizing that for the first time
in her natural-born life, she was living somewhere alone. She
glanced around the cozy little nook of a kitchen and set the iced
tea down slowly on the counter. Marlene and Marjorie had hovered in her space like worried mother hens, primping and fixing
it up as the builders vacuumed their way out the door. Oh, no,
the first order of business was to redecorate and organize things
to *her* liking. She had to remember that this was *her* house.

Shabazz, Rider, and Big Mike had made her crazy with
checking and double-checking the construction and door
locks she didn't use or need. They'd loaded her minibase
station room down with enough firearms and explosives to
blow up half the state. Berkfield offered her rounds and set
up a target range behind the house, while Marjorie cleaned
and recleaned everything in sight, making sure her plates
and cups matched in the process. Martha Stewart, watch out.
Marj had even matched linens and towels with the curtains!
Had Damali been left up to her own devices, some of those
fine points of housekeeping might have been overlooked.

Damali shook her head, thinking about Marlene freneti-
cally adjusting furniture in the most cosmically advanta-
geous position, then doing her mojo thing after Marj
cleaned. Those two were a trip. They'd wrung their hands
like she was a freshman going off to college, and she loved
them dearly for that. Damali hesitated. Maybe she would do
that one day . . . something normal. "Wow, I never really
thought about that," she whispered. She'd done a lot, but
there were still so many things yet to explore. "College."

As annoying as the whole ordeal of trying to get away
from them had been, she couldn't blame her two surrogate
moms. Everyone had been displaced, needed to nest, and her
new dwelling was the haven where they could vicariously
take out their homemaking urges.

But the best part of it all was that soon they'd descend on Carlos—she *couldn't wait* to see how he'd cope. Her plan was to lean against the wall, an Inez-made pie in hand to gain her admission to the show, and to laugh till she cried as the feathers flew. Damali bent over and hollered: *"Lord, let the compound get built soon so everybody can go nest in their own space!"*

J.L. and Dan had retrofitted her office with so much computer and stereo equipment that she could probably talk down a NASA flight from that room. Her Guardian brothers had acted like she was moving to Siberia, but this afternoon was the first time that she'd been in her own space all alone.

Oddly, her girl Inez had only fallen by once, with Big Mike in tow—but girlfriend had left her the greatest gift of all. Food. *Inez knew what time it was.* Sister had come in there with trays of mac and cheese from scratch, lemon butter pound cake, candied yams, collards—it was clear that she'd already slaughtered Big Mike through his stomach. Probably the rest of the house, too. Brotherman almost seemed jealous that Inez had thrown down for her the way she did.

A rippling laugh came up from Damali's belly and filled the room. But she wasn't mad at Inez for being scarce; a brand-new love-jones was an all-consuming thing. She wasn't studdin' Carlos's ornery ass, though. Just because she refused to move in with him . . . whateva. He'd get over it. She needed her own space. He needed his own space. It wasn't about doing 24–7 with a brother going through new Neteru mood swings, transitional drama, and what have you. She put the iced tea back in the ivory-colored fridge with more force than was necessary, slamming the door. Good thing the Covenant brothers had blessed and anointed the joint up before they'd gone home!

The Berkfield kids had practically begged her for sanctuary, using poster art and CD donations as their offerings to get in her door. Damali laughed out loud again, shifting away from her attitude with Carlos to lighter thoughts. Poor Robert and Kristin, she could dig it. Stuck in an old grandparent-type home with all those edgy adults, now *that* was hell for any teenager. But she was sorry that Jose had only popped by once. It was such a strange visit, too . . . quiet, short, ended on a slow parting, then came what seemed like pure avoidance.

She walked down the hall thinking, chewing her bottom lip. Maybe she should take the blanket he gave her off the bed and put it on the sofa? It meant the world to her, as it came from his grandfather's cedar chest and had been in their family for generations. Juanita had been the only one that hadn't fallen by. Good. She didn't need Carlos's ex-woman to be bringing bad vibes through her door.

Everyone had brought something of themselves and left it as a good omen . . . except Carlos and Juanita. Tara had given her a small medicine wheel and further access to the land; she knew Yonnie would fall by with a bottle of bubbly sooner or later, that was hombre's style. But what was up with Carlos and his old flame? The thought nagged at her and she poked and pushed at it like a mental blister while staring at her bed. She would not go there. Nope.

Her gaze traveled along the edge of the rough-hewn, high, four-posted ponderosa pine. It was clear what Carlos could bring and leave . . . A sly smiled crossed her mouth and then turned into a pout. If the brother ever decided to stop being salty about her decision, he could bring plenty.

The scent of fresh-cut juniper branches called out to her from the open-air hearth across the room. Maybe she'd just drive to Sedona for the weekend, but after rock watching and art-gallery hopping, then what? Metaphysical classes and treks to vortexes were out. She wasn't a tourist, and anyway, she could teach enough to turn any participant's hair white.

While the group trip to the Grand Canyon had been awe-inspiring, true, doing some things alone wasn't all that it was cracked up to be. Rider's words followed her around the room as she went to the wide picture window and stared out at the landscape. Sunset would be like watching Heaven paint on a canvas of sky. Maybe she should have made her point to Carlos less bluntly?

She fought not to open her third eye to hone in on Carlos's whereabouts. She'd been firm, said she wanted to be alone this first weekend, and brother was done. Okay. Fine. It didn't have to be all that, though.

But dang . . . her new place was all feng shui correct, romantic, weapon-ready, and he hadn't been there to really appreciate it—or her. Yeah, yeah, part of that was her choice, but still. Lake Powell's surreal red rock spires and jewel-green waters set against rose-colored sand had insinuated themselves into the color scheme of her home, just as what the Navajos called "the rainbow turned to stone" bridge had influenced the delicate stone design of the fireplace mantle. But lighting that with a glass of wine and curled up in bed listening to music suddenly seemed such a waste all by herself. Sitting on her porch for the entire weekend, rocking in a wicker chair, and contemplating the vortexes of the universe wasn't gonna cut it, either. Maybe she'd work on some new music.

Personal space was one thing, but now that all the postbattle drama had settled down, she was out of her element. The fast pace of city life was making this new sanctuary feel more like they'd moved to another planet. L.A. clubs were calling her name. A good vamp fight was, too, even without her long blade. A game of poker, house music, a good party, maybe?

She'd never been the TV-watching type, and sitting still to write music wasn't what inspired her muse. Artistry came from living life and then getting so filled with emotion that it spilled out of her heart and mind onto a page. Again, Rider had been right on that score. It was going to be six more months before the compound was complete, and she was already rethinking the location. She had to chill.

They had everything in the world they needed out here. Money was not a problem. Maybe when the guys were fully healed, Dan could book a tour. Something? Anything!

Damali placed her hand on the window and imagined heat from its surface fanning out to rim her fingers, then snatched it away. Too powerful a memory. Yeah, she had to chill.

How miraculously strange, she thought, staring out at the natural beauty that surrounded her, that for all their current assets, the things they needed most came from the ancestors, the elders, people who'd gone on to glory seemingly poor but indeed very rich.

She could feel the small Sankofa symbol on her spine tingle as the reality entered her mind. Waves of awareness slid between her boredom to visit like a friend and kept quiet company with her. It whispered deep truths: The ancient ones had spilled good spirit onto the earth, making it hallowed and impervious to demon inhabitation. By lineage, they had offered sanctuary and had baptized each of them with wisdom through experience. Every one of their past actions had created a bond, linking the fate of each team member, intertwining it with the subtlety of a spider's web, but it was a healing connection like the multicolored threads of Tara's medicine wheel. Now she understood that, too.

Damali nodded and wrapped her arms about herself. "Okay, y'all, I got it," she said softly and closed her eyes.

They'd indeed been graced by many blessings too profound to name. They were family. They were somewhat injured, but still alive. They were all half-crazy, but they'd mellowed. They loved one another, even though they all got on one another's nerves. They all wondered what the others were doing when apart. They all got in each other's business, constantly. They all fought over the bathroom. They argued and cussed each other out with regularity, but they all needed each other and wouldn't dream of having it any other way.

However, as she glanced around her house with a sly chuckle, she was still glad to finally have her own space.

Damali could do whatever. Always did, always would. Carlos jumped into his Jeep and pulled out of the driveway, headed in the opposite direction from her place down the road. He swerved into his driveway three minutes later, making dust fly, and got out of the vehicle to stand before the partially finished structure. A ranch. Aboveground. Wood, drywall, windows . . . shit. He might as well have been living in a papier-mâché box.

Yeah, cool. Be thankful for the many blessings. He was alive, she was alive, and his whole squad, except one, had made it through the worst. But the drama with Damali rubbed him the wrong way. What was all that "Baby I need my space" bull about? *They* needed space. *Together.* They hadn't been able to get busy since they'd all moved into the one big happy family vibe *for months.* Last time was all quiet—like in a hotel on the sneak tip, all because she didn't want anybody hearing anything down the damned hall . . . like they were kids and whatnot. And now girlfriend was talking about being alone the first weekend. Forget her nonsense. If it wasn't important to her, it *damned sure* wasn't important to him.

Carlos walked up the path with purpose and stood in the unfinished doorframe. The hair on the back of his neck was raised. He didn't do Navajo art, colors, and whatnot. This wasn't him at all!

He needed a place that he could truly funk out—surfaces needed to be solid. Whatever happened to marble, Spanish tile, real stone masonry that might give a man twenty seconds of reaction time before something mad-crazy blew through the room?

"Huh? What about that, D!" he yelled, his voice echoing through the empty space.

Living with kids, a band of big brothers, two mommas . . . he might as well have been back in the barrios of East L.A. A hundred fucking million dollars in the bank, and he was gonna be living in a tiny ranch down a dusty road in no-man's land. Carlos wiped his palms down his face and tried to regain a sense of calm. He was not gonna lose it out here. Yeah, yeah, yeah, he remembered all the Zen crap that Shabazz had taught him, and the old ones had shown him. "Okay, fine!" This was a new level of hell.

None of this was what he'd envisioned. A mad joint off the California cliffs, access to the clubs, transpo, real security, the family hooked up in lovely Beverly Hills, far enough away to miss, close enough to get to in a jam; but he and his woman together, under one roof, in the same bed at night—or day. Not this campground bullshit! Driving a bloodred Lamborghini, tricked the fuck out with bulletproof glass, his boy, Yonnie, able to fall by and go hang out at will. Handlin' their bizness, like men. Training day was about to be over, *por favor*. What the hell was on D's mind?

Carlos pushed off a wall and walked straight through the house to the back deck. Yeah, all right, the mountains were impressive. Beautiful view. Cool. A natural cathedral. So what? After the places he'd been and the things he'd seen, it wasn't about merely surviving. "If you're gonna be alive," he shouted, opening his arms wide toward the canyon, "then, dammit, you might as well live! What is this bull*shit*!"

Plus, right around the corner, his ex was pushing up on his house brother—and why that shit disturbed him so much made him question his sanity. Jose was cool, though. Carlos folded his arms and shook his head in disgust. Jose was walking on eggshells—but why was Damali? If girlfriend had acted right, had gotten with him, then Jose coulda hooked up with Juanita without any drama and everything woulda been smooth. But this tiptoeing around the subject at hand about who used to get with whom, was working his nerves.

It was too much madness under one roof, especially with Mike sighing every time he passed Inez's big behind and got damned wood every time she put a plate in front of him; and Shabazz all tight in the jaws because Marlene was keeping her distance; plus Berkfield snapping and barking; and goddamned Rider drinking like a fish and all edgy, while J.L.'s ass was so damned horny waiting for Berkfield's daughter to turn eighteen, he was about to put a bullet in the brother's skull himself to end it with the quickness before the girl's daddy did! And Juanita's crazy ass, hanging on Jose every time he passed them by, trying to stir the jealousy pot that didn't exist, but making Damali bristle—and why was that?

Crazy-ass Marj running around like Suzy homemaker, making sure everybody had something green on their plates; her kids following him foot-to-foot all day long; Marlene whispering and praying like a storm was coming, fucking chanting in the kitchen like a crazy, old witch; Dan begging him to tell him stories of the underworld for vicarious thrills . . . Yeah, next time Yonnie passed through, he was out, and might take Dan to the clubs just to get the newbie laid so he could chill. At least somebody would walk back through that screen door with their head on straight. "Oh, shit—I cannot live with these people another day!"

His voice bounced back from the hills as though it were laughing at him. As he stared out at the sky, he knew it was all going to come to a head. Juanita and Damali weren't feeling each other. Never had. Sooner or later he and Juanita had to really talk. They couldn't get this raggedy-assed little house built fast enough. But that also meant that, sooner or later, Jose and D were gonna have to have a serious conversation—and that was really getting on his last nerve.

His head jerked up and he spun to stare toward the direction of Damali's new home. "Aw, hell no!" He began walking and tore through his half-completed house, making his way to his car. Oh, so she was trying to play him—after all they'd been through? She wanted time and space to have that conversation with his house brother? Alone? Why couldn't girlfriend just say what she had to say on the back steps or in the yard out of earshot, huh? That's what he wanted to know!

Then it hit him, and he stopped short. *Oh shit . . . Jose had been more of a provider than him.* This was Jose's people's land. Jose was the one going to the tribal council, sealing the deals, getting the permits in order, was handling his business. Carlos spat on the ground as he walked across his front yard, shaking his head.

He wasn't having it. The way this shoulda gone down, if

nothing was up, he and Damali were supposed to be together this weekend, then get some transpo over to L.A., or Vegas, or whatever, hang out, be where the action was, not solo communing with the freakin' universe, old flames, or any of that other twisted we-are-the-world bull. He'd had it, had followed all the rules, gotten a second chance, delivered as promised, and was not doing another tour of duty in Hell, whether dictated by the Light or the Darkness!

If there was a problem, and they needed another Neteru to step up, they had his digits, and could blow up his cell phone. And if the Chairman was topside and wanted to bring it, then he was ready to go. He'd step to his punk ass, too, but on *his* own terms. Squash the plans to build here. Rider could take this joint—now *he* was a man who needed and deserved some headspace. He was going to Cali, might crash in Yonnie's lair until he got a new place and had it funked-out and furnished, security doors and shit put on. If not there, sheeit . . . Gabrielle had a place to his liking, if she kept her girls outta his face.

Carlos slammed the Jeep door with such force it made his ears ring as he drove away. By the time he pulled into the driveway of Jose's grandfather's house, he was breathing hard. He jumped out of the Jeep, his gaze tearing around the front yard. But when he saw Jose through the screen, he waited a beat, took a few deep breaths, and kicked gravel away from his tires.

But first, he needed to chill. This didn't make no sense.

Chapter two

As soon as the sun kissed the horizon, Yonnie's black transport cloud began to form in the pathway leading to Carlos's semibuilt house. Carlos leapt up from the steps and almost ran to meet him.

"Yo, *holmes*, you ain't forget about a brother!"

"Naw, dawg," Yonnie said, laughing, as the two men pounded fists and returned bear hugs.

"Get me the fuck outta here, man," Carlos said, raking his hands through his hair. "You have no idea!"

"C'mon, now," Yonnie said, laughing harder. He held Carlos by his arms and surveyed his black T-shirt and leather pants. "This ain't you, nerves fried and shit, brother."

"Stop fucking with me, man," Carlos said, play-boxing Yonnie. "See, how you gonna do me like that? I thought we was boyz?"

It felt so good to be in nonhousehold company that tears almost came to Carlos's eyes. He laughed from deep within his chest as a sense of pure freedom filled him.

"You know I gotchure back, man," Yonnie said, straightening the lapels of his suit jacket. "I was just laying low, trying to stay out of a married man's way, can't have D coming for me. The sister might cut my heart out, some of the places I had in mind to take you, boss."

Carlos pointed at Yonnie and walked away from him, smiling. "You ain't right, motherfucker. First of all, I ain't married."

"Like hell," Yonnie scoffed, teasing Carlos without

mercy. "You're married right here," he said, slapping his chest. "Y'all mighta had a little spat, but at the end of the night, I'm dragging your ass home. Don't front."

"That's cold. See, you done got brand new on me and left a brother at the hands of old ladies, broke down Guardians, and a buncha kids. You *wrong,* man. Damali ain't the one you gotta worry about, no way."

"I know," Yonnie said with a wink, offering Carlos a hint of fang. "Rider's still got an itchy trigger finger, broke-down or not. So, I figured, why rub salt in the wound? We men. Shit happens. I stay on my side of town, he can stay on his."

"But meanwhile," Carlos said, folding his arms over his chest, "you need to get a brother outta here."

"Damn, this is smooth," Carlos said with deep appreciation, running his hand down the side of Yonnie's black Alfa Romeo 8C. The bloodred interior felt like a kid glove against his palm, but the chrome grill was off da chain.

"We can't be rollin' up to no club raggedy, my brutha," Yonnie said, pleased that Carlos liked his ride. "Need to get you suited up right, too." He waited until Carlos nodded and smiled.

"Hook a brother up, then," Carlos said, opening his arms wide.

"Don't get used to this, though," Yonnie cautioned, losing his smile. "For real, man. Not like this."

"You worry too much." Carlos let his breath out hard.

"Yeah, I do," Yonnie said in a serious tone. "I'm not playing, man. Later on, when I gotta go eat, you gotta go home. Feel me?"

"Yeah, yeah, yeah, I feel you, man. But that's later, this is now. Relax."

When she heard a Jeep pull into her driveway, Damali ran for the door. She was all prepared to do battle about saying what she meant and meaning what she said, but when Rider staggered out of the vehicle, she stood very still on the porch.

"Yo, *que pasa?*" he said, laughing and stumbling once,

and holding out a bottle of Jack Daniel's toward her. "Housewarming present. I forgot to leave it earlier."

She smiled through the worry. "How about if I go get two glasses and we—"

"Glasses?" Rider said, making a face and then grinning. "Sis, why stand on ceremony? This is a new-house party, right?"

She didn't answer, but simply walked over to the wicker slider and flopped down. She didn't know what to say to Rider, hadn't since Tara went off with Yonnie in a cloud of smoke months ago. Rather than speak, she watched her Guardian brother unscrew the top with care, but declined the first swig from the bottle. This was not how she'd planned to spend the first weekend in her place—dead drunk on the front steps.

"Aw, c'mon, D," Rider said in a wistful tone and plopped down beside her. "It's just me and you here, kiddo."

She begrudgingly nodded, accepted a small sip, and handed the bottle back to Rider. "I think you should slow down," she said gently, watching him turn the bottle up and guzzle almost a pint of its contents.

"Yeah, maybe you're right," he said, wiping his mouth on his jacket sleeve. "I've already slowed down in every other way, so, yeah." He proceeded to take another liberal swig of booze and gave her a jaunty smile. "But not tonight."

"What's on your mind, big brother?" she asked softly.

He looked out at the stars and nodded in the direction of Carlos's property a half mile away. "Can't you smell it?"

Damali cocked her head to the side and sniffed. The slight hint of burning ash filled her nostrils. She knew Yonnie's signature blind. "Vamp transport."

"Wasn't Tara's."

Damali fell mute for a moment as Rider took a more careful sip of Jack Daniel's and set the bottle down on the porch floor. "I know."

"Yep."

"I'm sorry."

"Yep." Rider's gaze went back to the horizon.

"He just probably came to visit Carlos . . . since Carlos's spot is almost finished."

"Makes sense. Can't begrudge a man for checking in on his best hombre."

"I'm sure that's all it was."

Only the sounds of night responded as strained silence fell between them.

"Do you know how hard it was for me to come back here after all these years?" Rider said quietly, closing his eyes as he spoke. "This is where I brought her, hoping for a miracle that never happened. I buried my heart here, D. This is sacred ground for me in more ways than one, and the fact that this bastard has access to it, is like him walking over my grave. I gotta get off this land."

Rider had spoken so softly but with such intensity that she touched his arm. "I'm so sorry," she said in a tight whisper. "Listen, I'll tell Carlos not to—"

"Only under emergency conditions, D," Rider said flatly, no emotion in his tone. "We're in a firefight, then his homeboy crosses the line to save his ass. But just to stop on by and do a pop-call visit, can't tolerate it."

"I'll let Carlos know," she said, watching Rider stand slowly and straighten his back.

Rider thrust his chin up with unwavering dignity, even though he was as drunk as Cooter Brown.

"You need to have that conversation, as well as the one with Jose—soon."

She stared at Rider, and a pair of bloodshot eyes stared back at her without blinking.

"Soon, D," he repeated, holding her gaze until she nodded.

Finally, she looked away. She knew what Rider meant, and that was one of the many things she loved about him, he was always straight, no chaser, about things.

"I miss you, darlin'," he murmured. "The house ain't the same without you . . . but, can't stay in the nest forever. We got new chickadees to feed and train, and gotta start this bullshit cycle all over again." He sighed and hitched up his jeans, then took out a pack of Marlboro reds and tapped the back of it, extracting a butt.

Damali watched him strike a stick match with his thumbnail and inhale slowly. "You gotta take care of yourself, Rider."

"So everybody tells me." He motioned toward the bottle on the porch with his chin, and lifted an imaginary cowboy hat from his head, saluting her and adding a sad smile. "Ma'am, it's time for this old gunslinger to go on back to the ponderosa."

"Want me to drive you home?" she said, standing, deeply concerned about him getting behind the wheel of a car in his condition. If the alcohol didn't send him into a tree, his state of mind surely would.

"Nah, I've crawled out of bars on my hands and knees. This is nothing but a little nightcap," he said, weaving down her front steps, holding on to the rail. "If you don't smell smoke in the distance, then I made it back just fine."

She was down the steps and leaning on his driver's side door before he even got to the walkway. "Rider, for real, now. Give me your keys. I'll—"

"Baby girl, I've let go," he said, kissing her forehead and gently moving her aside. "Now *you* let go. Okay? We can't watch you twenty-four–seven anymore, and you can't be all up in our house drama, either. Fair?"

Damali nodded and conceded. The man had a point, but still. "I love you," she said quietly, holding his arm.

"I love you, too," he murmured as she filled his arms. He hugged her tightly and laid his cheek on the crown of her head. "Some crew, huh?"

"Yeah. Some crew."

They stood that way in her front yard for a long time, saying nothing, but allowing the comfort of human touch to transmit all that was necessary. When he let her go, she placed her hand over his heart. He shook his head and covered her hand briefly, but then removed it.

"You can't put the healing balm on this man with a supposedly good heart, baby. Not even Marlene could do that." He tweaked her nose and got into his vehicle. "Only a soul mate can do that for you. But I appreciate the attempt."

She folded her arms and stepped away from his Jeep, fighting tears. Damn, damn, damn, it was not supposed to go down like this.

"You think you oughta slow down on that Remy?" Yonnie said as he watched Carlos pour another drink at the bar. He gave Carlos a glance from the corner of his eye and then sipped his drink to finish it slowly.

Carlos leaned forward on his forearms, propping himself up. "I'm cool, man. We supposed to be out in the world tonight, right?"

"True dat," Yonnie said, pouring himself a splash of Remy Martin from Carlos's bottle, then adding a bit of color from the gold flask he carried in the breast pocket of his suit.

"See, that's what I'm talking 'bout," Carlos said, referring to Yonnie's flask. "A man's gotta do what a man's gotta do." He weaved a bit on his bar stool and leaned closer to Yonnie. "But you didn't have to go civilian just for me. We coulda did a vamp club, whateva, man."

Yonnie let out a long breath through his nose and studied his drink. "First of all," he said quietly, "your system is so squeaky clean, right about through here, your ass is drunk. You been eating holistic, no red meat and shit, for months. That first bottle of Remy behind several martinis has your ass lit; the second one you're working on will probably make you pass out. Not advisable to be out of your element and in a zone like that. Sloppy."

"Man, I'm—"

"Second of all," Yonnie said, not allowing him to finish the slurred comment, "like I told you, there *are no more* openly vamp joints."

"Oh, yeah . . . you're right," Carlos bumped his glass

against Yonnie's and then laughed. "Damn. What has the world come to?"

"Anybody left is in lair or underground," Yonnie said, not finding the humor in Carlos's comment. "A few scattered Thirds, maybe some Fourth gens and lower. Even the weres are keeping a low profile, since y'all blew up New York and Philly. No turns have been authorized while every seat at council is vacant, especially the Chairman's, but you can still get your ass beat down or killed." Yonnie straightened and tossed down the remainder of his new drink. "So, on that note, I think it's time for you to go home and sleep this night off."

"Man, the night is young," Carlos complained, glancing around the club. The music had become his pulse, even though it gave him a headache. Booty was everywhere, the joint was jumping, and the last place he wanted to go was back to the shack with the team.

"You're married. That's all I'ma say." Yonnie rubbed his chin and folded his arms over his chest.

"Like you ain't?" Carlos smiled.

"That's different," Yonnie said, reaching for his flask. "You and D are heart-to-heart; me and Tara have an arrangement."

"You with her every night, then—"

"You got it all wrong," Yonnie said, easing his flask next to his empty glass. "Only when necessary." He stared at Carlos.

"C'mon, man," Carlos said, abandoning his drink. "Be serious."

"I am serious," Yonnie said, his voice so low that it was hard to hear it. "She only comes to me when it gets like that, when she's missing him real bad . . . you know what I mean?" Yonnie shook his head. "She can't actually be with him anymore, since I elevated her to a strong second—it's not like when she was a Fourth-gen. Her bite is lethal, liter-ally, since no turns are authorized. This time he won't even come back with fangs, and I can't make any new friends so I can leave her alone. The broads at Gabrielle's . . . hey. They ain't her." Yonnie looked at the dark liquid in his short rocks glass. "The more she stays away from him, the more she misses him, the more she blames me. Catch-22."

"Damn, man . . ." Carlos raked his fingers through his hair and allowed his shoulders to slump. "Ain't how I envisioned things."

"Is it ever the way we think it's gonna be? That's true in life, and is so true in death. You know that." Yonnie stared down into his drink. "Sometimes she tries to make me feel like I'm the one. But, it ain't like that—won't be till Rider crosses over, until he's dead and buried. All I asked her to do was not put it in my face if she goes to see him . . . that's part of the reason you ain't seen me. Last thing I wanted to do was come on the property and pick up her trail right to that motherfucker's door."

"Whatchu gonna do, man?" Carlos said. Eerily, he was half intrigued, remembering the vampire code of snatching a heart out if one's territory was breached, but the other half of him really wanted to know how his best friend planned to handle a situation that vaguely paralleled his own. Carlos shook the strange combination of thoughts and focused. He needed to understand where Yonnie was coming from to avoid having something crazy happen to Rider.

"Look," Carlos finally admitted. "I'm in a fucked-up Catch-22, myself. Y'all are both my boyz, and I'm not trying to see either one of you iced over a woman. Seriously, man."

"If *I* kill him, I lose, if I let him live, *I lose*," Yonnie said without emotion. "Most times, I go stay with Gabby, until I miss Tara so much that . . . you understand what I'm saying."

Carlos only nodded. The conversation was sobering.

"Tara keeps a separate lair at the edge of the canyon, sometimes when needing her gets bad, I might blow through . . . she might be inclined. A few times, even when she wasn't, she cast a good enough illusion that I didn't care. You know how it is when you're having one of those nights when you're over the top. You'll lie to yourself and blow your own mind. Tara's cool, won't leave a brother strung all the way out. We're friends, and friends do shit like that for friends, right? Even vanishing point." Yonnie stared at Carlos, hurt shimmering in his eyes so clearly that Carlos looked away.

"Yeah, man," Carlos finally said, extending his fist to Yonnie, and softly pounding his. "She's good people."

"Real respectful, too," Yonnie said, as though talking to himself. "I ain't smelled him on her yet. Not sure how I'll react. Time will tell. As you know, women are complex." He opened his flask and took a healthy swig directly from it. "But I knew I was walking into this situation, so that's cool."

"That's fucked up, man," Carlos said, shaking his head and going back for his drink. "I'm seriously sorry to hear this, man. I don't know what else to say."

"Like I said, it's cool. I stop by Gabrielle's from time to time; Tara don't ask me my business, I don't ask her hers. Everybody is respectful, discreet. Every now and then, she comes to me and offers her throat and all that goes with it— we cool like that with each other. Then, we don't speak on it. No more, no less. It's all good." Yonnie stretched and glanced around the club with disdain. "That's why I'm taking your ass home before you mess up, do some irreversible shit, and then be caught up in the madness like me."

Carlos lifted his glass as Yonnie reached for his flask to put it back into his breast pocket. "Hit me with some color, and let's hang. You don't seem in the right frame of mind to be going back to Arizona right now."

Yonnie held his flask midair. "What did you say?"

"Look, man," Carlos said, letting his breath out hard. "This is me and you talking. If you—"

"You asked me to color your drink." Yonnie's eyes held fear, and he quickly put the blood flask away.

"I did not, man," Carlos said, chuckling. "Your ass is the one who's drunk."

Yonnie's eyes widened and his glance went from Carlos

to the mirror behind the bar and back. "You've got a reflection, but you are serving a quarter inch of fang!" His whisper was so intense that the bartender briefly looked up.

"Get the fuck out of here," Carlos said laughing nervously, but his line of vision shot straight to the mirror. Sure enough, he was sitting on the stool; Yonnie wasn't, as he studied his reflection through blurry eyes. He couldn't see any fangs. But as his tongue slid over his teeth, a short fang nicked it, putting the distinctive, salty taste of blood into his mouth. He felt his jaw, and as casually as possible, allowed his thumb to graze his incisors. "Well, I'll just be damned," he murmured.

"My point exactly," Yonnie said and stood. "You're cut off, time for you to go home."

Carlos spun around slowly on his stool, but didn't stand. "Maybe I'm just going through some crazy flux . . ." Awed, his voice was reverent, but he couldn't shake how secretly pleased he was.

"I don't know what it is, man, but I ain't being a party to a relapse. Not on my watch. The only reason I can cross into some places to avoid the Chairman is because you elevated up and out of Hell. *They ain't got you no more.* Not even the *Chairman* could fuck with that. *Think.*" Yonnie spoke through his teeth, his incisors lengthening slowly as his agitation progressed. "You can't just throw away an opportunity like that behind some—"

"I know what I'm doing, man, and I'm not re—"

"You *don't* know what you're doing," Yonnie said, leaning in close enough to Carlos that his cool breath crept along Carlos's throat. "You are in here considering stray tail when you got D, something you didn't even do when you was at council level, motherfucker." He poked Carlos in the chest as he spoke in fast, nervous bursts. "You're in here jonesing for a hit of blood like a damned crack addict. And shit, I don't like it. Talking crazy about hanging out all night and switching your whole body clock from daylight to dawn. No, man, I'm taking you home. That's the end of it."

◆ ◆ ◆

Crickets and owls created a symphony outside. The stars were stage lights, an occasional coyote howl added treble to the bullfrogs' bass. Jackrabbits made shaker sounds as they dashed through the brush. Damali's mind composed on the fly as she sat on the darkened porch, only a candle for light—the floodlights just brought mosquitoes, gnats, and moths. She wanted to sit very still without having to swat anything. But she gave up that desire the moment a dark cloud began to form on her bottom step.

Burnt ash filled her nose, Yonnie's signature was in it, but one could never be too sure. Damali stood and picked up the Glock nine that had shared the wicker rocker with her. "Friend or foe?" she said in a mild but tight voice. "Talk to me."

"Friend," Yonnie said, dumping Carlos on her steps.

Damali relaxed as Carlos caught his balance and held on to the stair rail.

"You ain't right, man," Carlos said, disgusted as his clothing changed back to what he'd been wearing when Yonnie had picked him up earlier. "You could have at least taken me back to my place."

"Take yourself, and talk to your woman," Yonnie grumbled, and began walking away. "Hey, D," he added, without turning around. "Y'all have a good night."

She watched Yonnie vanish. "Bye, Yonnie. You have a, uh, safe night, too." Her gaze immediately went to Carlos, who was halfway down her front path headed toward the road. "Hold up. What's going on?"

"Nothing," Carlos said, totally outdone. "I'm going home."

"Wait," she shouted, catching up to him. "What was all that about?"

"Nothing." He kept walking.

"Yonnie doesn't just make pop calls. And what's with the attitude?" She held his arm; he snatched it away and resumed a slightly wobbly path toward his unfinished house.

She was on him and in front of him in two seconds. He rounded her. She reached to grab his arm again, but he snatched it away.

"Get off me, D, I'm not playing."

She lowered her hand slowly and let him forge ahead of her. Was she losing her mind, or did she see a flicker of gold in his eyes, not silver?

"Yo, yo, yo—wait a minute, Carlos Rivera," she said, running to come beside him when he refused to slow down. "What was your boy, Yonnie, talking about—talk to your woman? About what! Where did he take you? What did he do to you?"

"Aside from getting me nice, nothing," Carlos muttered, "but you are totally blowing my nice."

"Your eyes."

"What about 'em?" He stopped and glared at her. "You need space, I need space. That's how you—"

"Oh . . . shit . . ." Damali whispered and covered her mouth with her hand.

"What D? Stop trippin' out here!"

"Baby, run your tongue over your teeth," she said quietly, backing away.

He let out his breath hard and did as she asked, then stopped and stared at her.

"Yeah," she said. *"That."*

"It ain't nothin'," he said, trying to be cool. "It's only a minor flux . . . a quarter inch ain't shit to be—"

"Carlos, *listen to yourself*. Tonight, it's a quarter inch. Tomorrow night—"

"Aw, girl, I've still got a reflection. Chill." He resumed walking, but with less confidence in his stride. "It happened to you, a while back, and you came out of it. This Neteru shit is—"

"I had never been fully turned, never died, brother," she said, not following him into the darkness.

He stopped, but didn't turn around. "You think that could make a difference?"

"Maybe," she said quietly. It was hard to find her voice, but she finally moved toward him. "We should tell Marlene."

"No . . . I mean, not yet." He turned to face her in the moonlight. "If it's just a flux thing, or because I was out drinking and my system wasn't used to that for a while, you know, it was probably just jacking with my body chemistry—like when I temporarily apexed in Philly but it didn't hold, and . . ." His voice trailed off as he ruffled his fingers through his hair, annoyed. "D, you know what I'm dealing with over at the house. There's no room to quarantine a brother, the kids in there will freak, Marjorie and Berkfield will have Glocks to my temple until daybreak, then they'll be all in my face about some shit that's just passing through my system. You've been there. So, just let me go sit on my own front steps, sleep off the buzz, and in the morning things will be fine."

She stepped closer to him, one hand on her hip while the other held the gun down at her side. Yeah, she'd been there, all right. The team didn't play that. But if he was on hallowed ground, only showing a few passing signs, and a vamp had brought him home to pull himself together . . . She immediately opened her mental radar to scan him.

"Don't be going through my pockets without asking me! What about trust, Damali? Huh!"

"You're standing here drunk as a damned skunk, and you're asking me to trust you with fangs in your mouth? What did you do, ask Yonnie to nick you and—"

"Are you crazy?" he shouted. "That would be a step *down*. He's a master; I'd be a second, if I didn't go straight to ash. I was a fucking councilman, D! I was *never* a lieutenant! Ever! Was never second in command, you got that?" Carlos walked in a haphazard circle, stopping intermittently to point at Damali. "I had a throne, woman. Do you know what that means, how much power that was? Let my own elevated master nick me? I was made by the Chairman himself? I'm so fucking offended I don't know what to say to you! Just because I ain't number one on this fucked-up, so-called Neteru team don't mean I don't have no pride and would go for sloppy seconds in my old yard. I used to run that shit—so be clear!"

"I'm going to ask you some questions, and if you give it to me straight, then I won't have any doubts in my mind," she said carefully, pulling back her mental scan to bring the argument down a notch. "I don't like the sentimental references to your old life. Period. Be clear about that, because *that's* why I'm worried. *Not* to get in your business, but, like you said, I *have* been there."

Carlos closed his eyes, leaned his head back, and jammed his hands in his pants pockets. "Fine. Go 'head."

Damali circled him slowly, talking as she inspected him, her questions sounding detached and medical.

"When did you first notice this change?"

"Me and my boy was sipping Remy, talking, and suddenly they were in my mouth."

"Be honest," she shot back. "When you felt the change in your mouth, what was running through your mind?"

"Aw, D, I don't—"

"What," she said emphatically, "was on your mind?"

He sighed hard. "A lot of things, D."

"Like?"

"Like how messed up my boy's situation really is, for one." He was not about to divulge Yonnie's deepest secrets. Some things were between men, and only men.

"Okay," she said, standing in front of him. "That's good. Compassion is a feature of the Light. What else?"

Carlos opened his eyes and stared at her. "I was angry."

Damali cocked her head to the side. "Somebody in the club piss you off? You pick up a trail that set you off? Blood-lust will make a new Neteru system haywire like that," she said, snapping her fingers.

He slowly removed his hands from his pockets and folded his arms in front of him. "No. Nobody in the club pissed me off. I was mad at you."

She swallowed a smile. "Oh."

"Yeah. Oh." He shook his head. This was getting nowhere.

"Okay, so you were pissed off at me because we weren't spending the weekend together, but that—"

"Is precisely what you don't get," he shouted, and began walking. "How fucking off-the-hook mad I am about having to endure your endless rules and regulations and family and the way it always has to be your way!" He stopped, opened his arms, and glanced around at the tumbleweeds and sparse cactus foliage. "I am not a desert dweller! I hate this place. This is not me, Damali. I ain't trying to live here under any circumstances—but I was ready to come out here to be with *you*, then your ass doesn't wanna be with me! All of a sudden, you need your space. That's enough to make a man drop fang!"

"But you never said how much you didn't—"

"I didn't say all that because what was the point? We had people bleeding, banged up, had barely made it out of that Philly shit alive. I've never been this Neteru thing I am, my ass just got out, you were driving this thing so fast I wasn't sure what was going on, and every time I protested, people were telling me about some three phases of seven that I had to deal with, security precautions of hallowed ground—aw, kiss my ass!" He stomped his foot and let out a primal yell. "I'm tired! I've been cooped up, and me and my boy was just going out for a minute."

He was breathing hard. She smiled and allowed her gaze to slide down his abdomen.

"My bad," she said quietly. "Yeah, I remember that first real flux. Another month and—"

"Don't fuck with me, D. I can't take it."

"You're gonna be all right," she said, and turned and walked back toward her house.

"How you know?" he said, not moving but very concerned.

"'Cause along with fangs, you have an erection that won't quit." She released a sly laugh and looked over her shoulder at him.

"Something like that can make a brother crazy if left un-attended too long," she said with a wink.

He still didn't move.

She turned around and faced him, a wide smile gracing her lush mouth. "I asked you what had been on your mind . . . the real underlying emotion, and you started talking all this rhetoric about everything *but* what was really on your mind."

"This past coupla days . . . girl, it's been real bad all of a sudden . . . like before—almost as bad as the old blood hunger." That's as much as he was willing to tell her at the moment. He could feel her attempt to lock with his mind, but blocked it, not wanting the invasion into his personal thoughts.

"I remember those days," Damali said, smiling. "Okay, stay mad."

"You wanted your space, sis—you got it." He would not be moved.

She inhaled sharply. "You smell real good, too. Remy, bar smoke, and all. I'll be up for a while, if you change your mind." She gave him a sly grin. "I never said I never wanted to see you again . . . I just didn't want to live together, right through here."

He closed his eyes as another hard shudder of desire passed through him. He ran his tongue against his teeth, but the fangs were gone. The only evidence left of the aberrant spike was the throb in his groin. He wasn't sure which pissed him off more—the loss of fangs, the throb, or her. "Listen," he finally said. "That still don't change the fact that I hate Arizona."

"Never said it did," she said in a husky voice. "I ain't too partial to the location, but it is what it is—can't be too far from the team, and they're sitting ducks out in the cities off hallowed ground, especially Yonnie and Tara, who can't cross—"

"I know, I know," he said, holding up his hands, defeated. "I need to go somewhere and lay down." He rubbed his abdomen as the slurry of Remy Martin chasing martinis on an empty stomach began to gurgle within it.

"Walk me back to my house and I'll give you a lift."

"Don't bother. I need air, anyway." Carlos shook his head, held it high, and resumed his broken path down the dark road. Pride had a stranglehold on him, even when he was half drunk. He was not going to be led around by his dick, no matter how much he wanted to be with her. Those days were over. There were just some things that he wasn't going for, and being told what to do all the time by her was one of them. If he couldn't make it to his house, he'd sleep on the porch swing at the family house and call it a night.

"Back there in Philly," she said, calling out into the darkness behind him, "that was an early apex spike brought on by your birthday and the battle of your life."

"So what! It'll pass! Just like everything else!" he yelled back, each footfall stomping the road harder.

"Come May or June, I'll hunt you down myself for a hit, mad at me or not, baby . . . damn, if that's what you're trailing now."

Her warm laughter sent another shudder through him, but he kept walking.

CHAPTER THREE

Damali sighed with frustration as she went back into her house. She paced through the small dwelling and slid her gun across the weapons room table. This whole life was crazy. She peered around what should have been a cozy den or family room. A daggone crossbow was mounted near the door, hand grenades and semis on a desk. An Isis dagger held by a wooden stand lay in wait where a letter opener should have been if things were normal. Every man on the team was bugging in one way or another. The sisters seemed to be holding their own for now, but she wondered how long that would last.

The only male who had a perpetually sunny disposition was Big Mike—but that was probably because he'd figured out how to be AWOL 80 percent of the time, regularly claiming he had to escort Inez to Houston to visit her child. While that was true, she also knew that the getaways doubled as conjugal visits, since Mike was supersensitive to sound traveling and his business being public.

Damali lifted her hair off her neck and laughed sadly. She could definitely identify. What she wouldn't give right now to let her voice rent the place . . . or hear Carlos's deep, low-decibel thunder.

She shuddered, nearly feeling the vibration as she remembered it. Didn't he know by now what he meant to her? If after all they'd been through he didn't get it, then what could she tell him that would make a damned difference? He'd have to figure it out on his own.

But in the meanwhile, *whew*. Just seeing him all messed

up and fluxing . . . maybe she would call him. Pride goeth before a fall, and her man was *fine*. It had been too long since they'd been in sync. Privacy had been a hard commodity to obtain. Now she had that and he was squandering the gift. Damali glanced around the room and left it, seeking something to munch on.

She opened the fridge and stood in the dim light it cast within the darkened kitchen, hoping something good would strike her, as though just looking at the shelves might materialize whatever her palate craved. What did she want? Her hands were on her hips, her brow knit in thought. What did she want, what was good in here? She had a refrigerator full of food, and didn't want a danged thing in it.

Damali left the refrigerator door open as she went to the back door and flung it open wide. Fresh air, for one thing. The room was too warm, and she hated air conditioning. She went back to the fridge to study the shelves. She smiled and closed her eyes. Carlos, naked, in bed, right now, no drama, no attitude, not drunk, vaporizing her one cell at a time. Yeah, that was definitely what she wanted. She licked her lips as her mouth went dry from the mental sight of his lit second tattoo on his base, one of his sweet spots, and therefore hers. Caramel. She laughed. *Oh, yeah,* she practically breathed out, *that tasted real good.*

A shiver swept through her as the vivid image made her moisten and swell. She wasn't sure if it was the cool air that wafted from the opened refrigerator door, or just her thoughts of him that produced gooseflesh. Her hardened nipples strained against her tank top as remembered what his warm, wet mouth felt like . . . what the tip of his tongue did to them, when he was so inclined. Damn, she missed that man . . . why'd he have to flux with a hint of fang and then get salty!

She hadn't felt intense arousal like this in months. And he'd picked this night of all nights to act stupid. Men. If he woulda allowed a mind lock, she could have sensed what was running through his brain, sent him some serious Balm of Gilead for whatever ailed him and sobered him up . . . shoot, they might not have even made it back to the house. But, noooo.

Damali wrapped her arms around her waist when her Sankofa at the base of her spine lit and nearly screamed up each vertebra. Her head dropped back as the old puncture wounds on her throat began to taunt her. One by one, she could feel each bite he'd ever laid down begin to burn hot with memory. Aw, man . . . forget pride, she was going over to his house in a minute. Whatever was wrong with him and jacking with his head, he was still her pleasure master as far as she was concerned.

Didn't he know that his touch simply dissolved her? Just thinking about his mouth made her bud throb. And his voice . . . dayum. When he got all into it and lost himself . . . started that Spanglish in her ear, rolling *r*'s till her womb contracted . . . and when he'd finally put it in . . . *umph, umph, umph.* Yeah, she was gonna call him. *Had to* now. Had messed herself up just remembering. Open transmission: *Baby, I'm sorry—whatever I did.*

She inhaled deeply and dabbed her forehead with the back of her wrist. If this was a prelude to his real apex, then she would probably burn to ash when he went there to the max. Her baby was awesome in that department, not to mention all the other cool shit he could do. Why was he trippin' so hard, though? His other powers were coming in, just like new shoots came up from the dirt in the spring. It would be all right. He was still da man. *Baby, I'm sorry. Let's talk about it. Okay?*

No answer. Shit. He was gonna make her beg and just say it. She let her breath out hard, deciding. Memory sent a hard contraction through her canal and the sensation squeezed more hot liquid want into her panties. "Aw, c'mon, baby, I'm sorry, for real," she whispered out loud. He was the one, the only one who could make her feel this way.

All right. I admit it. I've been acting funny for months. I'm sorry. I don't know why I've been feeling out of sorts. But tonight, I promise you, by tomorrow we won't remember why

we were arguing. I've got this new place to christen . . . fire-
place ready and waiting, just for you. You don't have to be all
subdued and quiet, neither do I—nobody's within earshot;
Big Mike's in Houston, and even he can't hear that far.

She laughed quietly as desire tears began to wet her
lashes. Suddenly she wanted Carlos so badly it actually hurt.
This is a nine-one-one. Come home, and answer this emer-
gency, stat . . . okay, papi? All right, you call the shots. Cool?

No answer. Fine, then. Damali shook it off, and slammed
the refrigerator door. She caught a glimpse of something flash
past the deck and smiled. *Stop playing and come inside, Carlos.*

She paced out to the back of the house, stared up at the
moon, completely understanding why werewolves howled.
Her focus was singular as she briefly closed her eyes again
and inhaled sharply. Carlos was still in her nose. His near
apex scent haunting, teasing, making her hands tremble . . .
and he was three sheets to the wind, out here acting crazy.

She opened her eyes and a tall, dark male form was in the
shadows just beyond the house lights. She placed her hand
over her heart and held on to the deck rail. "Oh, wow, baby,
I thought . . ."

Damali sniffed again, and the stench of rotting flesh hit her
just before the shadowy figure moved like lightning from behind a cactus and toward her. Gangrene-pitted flesh hung from
a contorted, skeletal face. Eyes too big for the sockets glowed
something blackish green, like withered, rotten olives. Half of
the creature's head looked like it had been bashed in, the other
half was gone, and tattered, filthy clothing hung from his grue-
some body. But the claws at the ends of his long, gnarled fingers, along with the twisted fangs protruding from his hideous
mouth, made her know he was deadly and a demon. What the
hell . . . Damali felt herself go from aroused to pissed in two
seconds flat. Damn! Couldn't a sister get a moment's peace?

She whirled around and ran into the house, glimpsing
over her shoulder once. Her peripheral vision caught something rushing, fast behind her. The weapons room the guys

had created was her destination. There was a heavy thud on
the deck porch. He was coming into her house!

The crossbow by the door was the closest thing to her. She
grabbed it, cocked it, and leveled it toward the window. The
moment she went deeper into the room to go for a nine millimeter, she saw him speed by the main open window in
a blur.

Damali's gaze shot around the room, following the sound
to get a bead on the creature's current location.

She heard a thump overhead and jumped. He was on the
roof. Shit! Damali stayed in the center of the house in the
hallway, watching as he scampered across her skylight.

Damali dashed back to her weapons room, but the thing
leered at her through the secondary bulletproof glass-block
window and screeched. Screw going near the window for the
Glock. The Isis dagger was closer. In one deft swipe it went
into her back jeans pocket as she backed away from the window and readied the crossbow.

A few seconds was long enough for her to see that the
creature's face was mangled, dripping red flesh, skinless—
as though an Amanthra serpent had swallowed him whole
and puked him back up. She'd seen those half-eaten, soul-
damned humans before in Hell's feeding zones. The chest
and abdomen were also torn open, and he stunk of sulfur.
He presented yellowish green dripping fangs, upper and
low canines. The were-demon signature of foul sulfur
stench combined with the heavy wet-dog odor was as
strong as the Amanthra on him. His head had been half
blown off, obviously by a shotgun cartridge, and the sucker
moved way too fast.

Damali stalked along the corridor leading to the kitchen,
hugging the wall, her weapon before her. Why hadn't he
come in? The prayer barriers and sea-salt lines over thresh-
olds and windowsills had to be the reason. They'd done the
interior of the new house, not the perimeter, assuming the
hallowed ground around it was enough. It should have been!
What was this thing?

It didn't matter what he was. This creature couldn't be allowed to escape. The fact that she hadn't felt him before he manifested really worried her.

As she crept toward the back door, she could sense him waiting for her. She kicked the screen door open; he rushed the door. She fired her crossbow, dead aim in the thing's chest. He just looked at her and scooted to the left side of the house. She glanced at the crossbow and set it down slowly. Okaaay. No response to a silver stake in his chest? Her mind quickly scavenged for information. Demon food—the heart was the first thing eaten out. No heart meant nothing to stake. But he still had flesh, open wounds, where purified, prayed-over sea salt could catch and burn him—ignite that sucker.

No time to lose, she rushed to her cabinets, grabbed a bag of anointed Red Sea salt—shrapnel to slow him down—then dashed to her weapons room, snatched up a semiautomatic filled with hallowed earth rounds, and went hunting.

As she ran through the house, the creature's ugly face popped into each window, following her moves. She ran out onto the back deck, unafraid. This low-level, wannabe demon thing had actually tried her, the Neteru! Didn't he know she'd smoked master vamps and had been to Hell and back? The bitch had actually tried to break into her house! She was too angry to feel fear.

She waited, on guard, Red Sea salt in one hand, semi in the other. He leaped down from the roof to the ground just beyond the deck rail, and she hurled the opened bag to strew holding salt at his feet, instantly lowering her weapon and squeezing off death rounds.

Damali yanked her weapon upright as the thing squealed and began to smolder. But she noticed the bullets hadn't affected him. The creature was melting from his feet up, turning into a puddle of black liquid ooze as he screeched. Then she saw his face in earnest as he began to transform back into what he looked like before he had died and had been fed upon in the lower realms.

She stumbled back until her spine hit the house wall. Her foster father? "I thought you were dead, you child-molesting bastard!" she screamed, running forward and blowing off the creature's head. "Inez's family saw your ass in Hell! Time to go back!"

Raw emotion kept her weapon firing even after the thing had no head. Gaining her wits quickly, she saw that the head she'd blown off just rolled around in an angry circle, snapping and snarling, while the body went into a black puddle and within moments, disappeared into the ground.

Damali dashed back into her house, grabbed another handful of salt, and flung it at the spinning head. Oddly, it began to smoke and disintegrate, too, but not before looking her squarely in the eyes.

"You can't keep us down there," the head hissed. "We're all coming back!" Then it dissolved into black muck and was gone.

Shaken, Damali's attention jerked to the distance. The Guardians were scrambling. Gunfire had alerted everyone. *Stay home. I'm coming to you!* she mentally shouted to Marlene. *I don't know how many more are out here. Find Carlos, and bring him into the house—now!*

Furious at the invasion, Damali was down the steps standing near the spot that had withered the already dry grass. The crude oil-like stench still lingered. She squatted, the Isis dagger now in one hand, at the ready.

She splayed her other hand wide over the black sludge. This didn't make sense. She could feel subterranean movement, quick dashes like things fleeing, moving between levels that they should have been blocked to. Demon food was on the move, but their captors were not? From everything she'd been taught and had seen down below with her own eyes, all original demons, the ODs as Carlos called them, Lilith's spawn, the Lilim, or Lucifer's direct-made entities, fed on scum souls like her foster father's on every level and had them on lock within carefully guarded zones. The Damned made up 30 percent of Hell's furnaces, and their rot fed the Lilim like fossil fuel. It kept the ODs fed and able to stay subterranean out of harm's way. Why would their food be topside? How did the Damned get loose?

Damali stood and jogged around the side of the house toward her Hummer. It was time to have a meeting.

"Well, wake his ass up!" Damali shouted. She shook Carlos hard again, but he only groaned and rolled over onto his stomach.

Rider shrugged and peered over at Carlos on the porch swing. "Not possible, sis. He's passed out cold. I caught him before he fell in the yard. That's what was taking us all so long. Half the team was arguing about leaving Carlos to go help you; who would go, who had to stay to protect the newbies, in the event this was an all-out—"

"All right, Rider. I hear you," Damali said, holding both her hands up. She was too disgusted to go down that particular rat hole right now. She could not believe she was standing out on a porch even having this conversation.

"But all that shit you told us, D, is crazy," Jose said. "You sure he couldn't come into the house?"

"No," Damali said, glancing around the nervous eyes that watched her every move. "Haul Rivera's ass into the house. Put a salt ring around the borders in the morning. I want Father Patrick on the phone, stat."

Damali began pacing. "All right, people. Listen up. J.L., get Mike on a cell phone. Tell him to come home ASAP with Inez."

"We've been trying to raise him and Inez since we heard gunfire," J.L. said, glancing around.

"I told J.L. not to leave a specific voice message, since we know who runs the airwaves," Shabazz said coolly. "I ain't sensing brotherman is in no imminent danger, he's just AWOL." Shabazz looked at the clock. "This time of night, he ain't taking no calls, but if I know Mike, he'll surface in the morning."

Damali let her breath out hard. "We take this convo inside."

"Sho' you right. Everybody's got salt on 'em, except Yonnie and Tara," Shabazz said evenly. "Why don't you, uh, let them stay outside with our boy, while he sleeps it off on the swing, and we handle this family bizness inside under the prayer vibe so family business stays family business?"

Damali glanced at Yonnie and then Rider. Both had non-verbally squared off. Tara was the stalemate breaker. Shabazz was wise. Yonnie couldn't be invited to cross the threshold as a male master vamp . . . not with Rider in the house, because one night that might be her Guardian brother's only retreat defense if it got crazy between them. Plus, Marjorie had gone pale at the suggestion, which made sense. If Yonnie and Tara had a rift, with young, nubile females in the house, and Carlos not available to talk reason on an unreasonable night . . .

"I'll stay with him," Tara said. She stooped down and placed her hand on Carlos's chest. "I understand how serious this is."

Damali almost nodded until she saw a slight red flicker momentarily form inside Tara's irises. Big problem. Carlos was definitely trailing something damned near irresistible. Yonnie bristled, but stood downwind in the yard. Rider fingered the trigger on his pump shotgun.

"How about if y'all leave the door open so I can hear and add my two cents, and I stay out here with her and Carlos. I'd hate to see Rivera wake up in the morning a Third gen. I don't think he'd like the demotion." Rider glared at Tara and then looked down at Carlos.

"If she goes there, he wouldn't wake up," Yonnie said through his instantly lowered incisors. "Put money on that, even though that's my boy."

"I didn't deserve that," Tara hissed, glancing at Rider, then Yonnie. She stood. "He hasn't fully apexed, and even if he had," she snapped, walking to the edge of the porch, "Damali is my friend."

Rider put the safety back on his weapon and cast his hard gaze out toward the moon. Yonnie normalized and folded his arms, staring out toward the horizon.

"I got the yard," Yonnie said in a begrudging mutter.

The rest of the team filed inside. Damali waited as edgy Guardians filed into the dining room behind her. Marlene looked at her.

Mar, how could he be dead drunk at a time like this!

Not, now, baby. He's seen the Light, but hasn't found the Light within himself yet. Give him time.

Screw that! His ass is worthless in this condition. This is—

Focus on the task at hand.

She took a deep breath. *All right, say a prayer and let's do this.*

Damali raked her locks and dropped the private connection to Marlene and waited for her to seal the room against Yonnie and Tara's ears. She placed both hands on the table and closed her eyes to keep from screaming.

"Listen," Damali said as she let her breath out hard. "I've explained how these things seem to roll, how fast they move, and what liquefies them—so stay sharp. From what I sensed, they're on the move."

"If they're tortured demon remains and still have enough negative energy to have them in feeding zones," Marlene said as she lifted the sweat-damped hair off her neck, "then they're probably coming back to where they were killed or had a grudge." She looked at Damali and a silent understanding passed between them. "We know demons, like ghosts, are location-locked. Raven had vampire in her, so she could trail you and me wherever. But your foster father wasn't a vamp, so if he moved past the location where he was killed as one of the undead to find you here, then it stands to reason that he had to be following negative grudge energy."

"Good enough theory to work with for now, Mar. That bastard was definitely a demon while alive," Damali said, her line of vision going toward J.L. and Krissy. "Let's go with that hunch and see if we can get something to confirm it. Fire up a computer, get on the Net, and see if you can pick up any weird news services, crazy sighting reports, anything that sounds like what I just saw. I wanna know when the sightings began, regions, anything. Check the spook nets and paranormal watchdog sites in cyberspace."

Krissy and J.L. almost bumped into each other as they both snagged laptops and sat next to each other, their eyes intermittently glancing at their screens and Damali.

"I know you're the bomb, but how'd you pick all that up? The thing about the grudge," Dan asked, his gaze flitting to Marlene for confirmation, but paying way too much attention to J.L. and Krissy.

"Because, like I said, it was her foster father and he didn't die on this land," Marlene muttered.

"Yeah," Damali agreed, her voice tight. "The one who tried to molest me when I was living with Inez. He got smoked by some people who knew some people, and he probably came back from the realms where I suppose his bestial ass should have gone. Amanthra revenge level and were-demon realms— Levels Four and Five. The signature scents were all over him."

For a moment, no one spoke. She'd never openly admitted the private violation to anyone but Inez. Now, like all the other humiliations in her life, this, too, was out on the table for family inspection. Jose's eyes met hers and held such empathy that she had to glance away. When Marjorie covered her mouth, Damali began to pace. "All right. So, that means demon food, the Damned, is getting spit back up topside."

"Lilith's open portals," Marlene said quietly, seeming deep in thought. "When you injured her, maybe she didn't have enough energy to seal them behind her?"

"Or maybe none of the entities on any level had enough balls, or juice, to go behind a Level-Seven sister?" Shabazz folded his arms over his chest. "The thing that's fucking me up is, nobody on the team felt it—even though we'd run the portals checks by the numbers after the Philly job . . . which means we're slipping."

"The bigger question is," Rider said, clearing his sinuses, "*why* are we slipping? How'd the hell we miss that?"

"Yeah, unfortunately, the person I could ask for sure about the portals or our senses being off is out cold," Damali said flatly. "Lilith was on the run, like the Chairman. I doubt either one of them went home to face Poppa on Level Seven and tell him they'd been bad children. If that's who opened the portals, then that would be the only entity that had enough juice to close them off . . . but I'm with Rider. How come *we* didn't feel it? Even Tara and Yonnie didn't pick that up."

Damali walked back and forth between the table and the wall, as though trapped. "We need to know what this fleeing food can do, besides kill innocent people. Do they turn people? If so, what do they become, where do they come up from, what's the gestation if a human gets injured by one, but lives? I want to know everything about this madness. Get Father Pat on the phone, and ask him to do whatever he can to secure the convo from the Vatican, if that's where he is. Something tells me we need a double layer of protection on this discussion."

They waited as J.L. left his laptop and tried to raise the aging cleric by a landline.

"Hold it," Krissy said, standing with her system and rushing over to Damali. "Look. Woman eats boyfriend's heart in hotel. Police still looking for the weapon that opened his rib cage. Entrails everywhere. A month earlier, assailant had tried to file a report and obtain a restraining order, claiming her ex-husband had come back from the dead and beat her. Assailant was subdued and taken into police custody. Defense attorney's seeking insanity plea. Assailant awaits trial in Mississippi facility for the criminally insane." Krissy shoved the laptop into Damali's hands, seeming both proud of her work and scared.

"Dear God," Marjorie whispered.

"What's the date on that?" Damali muttered, visually scanning the article and then shoving the laptop back toward Krissy to grab.

"Not quite a month ago," Krissy said, and then looked at J.L.

For a moment Damali didn't speak. Krissy and J.L. were supposed to be constantly monitoring all the crazy news sources, and had been off the job. What was up with that?

What had those two been doing all this time! Scratch the question; her ears were ringing with fury. She let out a slow but impatient breath and tried to keep her focus on the immediate need for information. Later, she'd address the critical lapse.

"You done good, Kris," J.L. said, nodding, his gaze holding hers.

"J.L., you mind getting that landline to Father Pat?" Damali said, growing more peevish. They didn't have time for this. When Carlos got back up, she'd knock his ass out cold for leaving her in the middle of this mayhem.

Finally, after fifteen tense minutes, J.L. got through to the senior cleric and everybody almost shouted at once.

"I cannot speak this over the airwaves, but it is why we were all called back to our respective headquarters," Father Patrick said once the commotion died down. "Damali, with Marlene, to boost the mental transmission, I have to send this to you directly. All right?"

"Do it," Damali said, closing her eyes and waiting for Marlene's hand to fill hers. She could feel how weak the elderly man's signal had become, but had to shunt aside that concern about his oddly fatigued condition. Marlene's quiet prayers enveloped them as Father Patrick's message came through in fits and starts.

Look at the news reports online. The tabloids. Mainstream media is not broadcasting this; the world governments are keeping a lid on public panic. Infection is rampant. It passes by touch, not bite. One touch. Then that person touches another, and another.

Father Pat, Damali said, alarmed, *why didn't you alert us immediately?*

Since the appearance of Lilith and the Chairman's abandoned throne, we have been in cloistered conference to keep all information within our clerical units until we knew more. Initially, the sightings seemed like normal demon activity, which all Guardian teams are well versed in and can handle. But our research took us to The Book of the Damned.

Something didn't sit right within Damali's gut. If the clerics knew something was up, they should have immediately alerted the Neterus and the Guardian squad. There was more to this, and she could feel the tension in Father Patrick's silence. She took her time responding to his statement.

What is The Book of the Damned? Damali could feel the older cleric's lock weakening, his age, the distance, and level of his fatigue wearing him down.

"Okay, nix the question," she said aloud into the speakerphone, trying to preserve his psychic energy so she could learn more. Clearly, even in the extremely private mental exchange, he wasn't ready to divulge everything. That really troubled her, and she knew it had to be bad if the old man was even shielding portions of a Neteru-to-Covenant telepathic transmission. Fine. Then she'd pose a more generic question for the sake of the team; her squad needed to know what they were up against without any additional bullshit getting in the way. "Just tell me what we're looking for."

We have been in meetings debating the cause, he said in mental fits and sputters, as though his brain needed to rest, and ignoring her attempt to give the team more data to go on. *All that we know is these creatures make normal humans begin to manifest demonic behaviors. Regular people who have been infected begin acting like those entities from the realms of the undead carrier that touched them. Normal people are becoming cannibals, bearing super strength. Whatever level the infected entity came from, and whenever it touches but doesn't kill a living human, that person takes on the demon characteristics from that level.*

"I don't understand," Damali said, speaking out loud for the benefit of the team, too annoyed with the Covenant's decision to keep her and her squad in the blind for something as major as this. She felt a sense of betrayal that made her defiant.

I know how you feel, Father Pat said gently, trying to send healing balm into her mind with his thoughts. *For instance, exorcisms are on the rise, as possessions mount from incubi- and succubae-like inhabitations. Living people are slither- ing up the walls of their homes, attacking those closest to them. Deviant behaviors from those realms are epidemic. It seems to have a twenty-eight- to thirty-day gestation period, like the phases of the moon. But the humans infected by these entities come out during the daylight hours as well.*

How do you know it's only twenty-eight days? Damali shot back, squeezing Marlene's hand.

"Because the normal person drops dead," Father Patrick said aloud, saving his mental fuel. "Then they get back up and walk after they're buried. But not only do they sustain every death wound they'd received; they've been eaten by the creatures of the realms their souls have been sent to. When you see them, what they are is unmistakable."

Shabazz raked his locks as the rest of the team slowly found something to sit down on.

"If we kill the carrier, do the rest of the ones they've touched bite the dust?" Damali waited. This time Marlene gripped her hand more tightly.

"No," Father Patrick said after a moment. "It is exponen- tial. You can kill the carrier, but it keeps spreading from the next infected and so on. We are working on a cure as we speak, because for those that haven't died or killed another living soul, there may be hope."

Damali squeezed Marlene's hands. *You've gotta talk to Kamal as soon as possible.*

Tears stood in Marlene's eyes, and she released Damali's palms and wrapped her arms around herself to gather composure. It was pure reflex, but the physical break caused further signal dropout between Damali and Father Patrick.

Damali gave Marlene a firm but gentle gaze. *I know you're dying, but not now. Hold my hands, we'll finish this. You tell Shabazz straight up that a conversation is necessary—*

no bullshit. Kamal is a Guardian, and if his men are out there fighting hand-to-hand combat, like they do, they might run into a problem.

Marlene nodded and clasped Damali's hands tightly; her eyes wild, her lips pursed shut. *Oh, Jesus . . .*

Breathe, Damali ordered, compassion making her chest tight. *We ain't letting him go out like that. Kamal is one of ours, too. Center, and breathe, so we can talk to Father Pat.*

"Everything all right, Mar?" Shabazz asked, standing.

Rider poked his head in the door and glanced at Marlene then Shabazz.

"She's cool," Damali said. "But this mess we're hearing ain't no joke. Stand down, big brother, and let us work."

Shabazz cocked his head to the side, gave them both a skeptical glare, but eventually fell back and leaned with a thud against the wall.

Once Marlene finally focused, Damali lit right into Father Pat's mind with hard questions. *How do we seal the weak portals to keep more demon food from spilling out?*

Kill Lilith, Father Patrick said. *As long as she's topside they will leech into the gray zone.*

Done. Anybody got a location on her?

Not yet. Our most highly trained seers have never been able to find her. Even in the dawn of days, Adam couldn't, nor could Eve. She's very shrewd. Three angels sought her, and they couldn't find her.

The Chairman is after her, so we follow him, then, Damali said. *We're pros at finding vamps.*

Where is Carlos?

For the first time since the conversation began, Damali hesitated. "Dead drunk," she said aloud with enough emphasis that the team members' worried gazes immediately shot toward the porch in unison.

"That's not good," Father Patrick said over the speakerphone. "Not at a time like this."

"You're telling me?" Damali replied, her voice oozing with sarcasm. "Try irresponsible, stupid, totally . . ." She closed her eyes and took a deep, cleansing breath.

"What if he accidentally got bitten by one of those things?" Dan offered, defending Carlos. "Maybe that's why he's out there asleep and nobody can get him up, you know? I mean, we've never seen him outta control like this. What if he's really hurt?"

"The Damned cannot infect a Neteru," Father Patrick said bluntly. "Just like Neterus are impervious to the other demon bites."

"Oh," Dan said quietly and looked out the window.

If you know it can't pass to a Neteru, then you've dealt with this before? Damali waited. The elderly cleric had slipped and told her more than he'd intended. Her tattoo was tingling. She knew what was said next would hold the answer to why the Covenant was being so cagey.

Father Patrick sighed. "Drop Marlene's hand. Only me and you."

Damali glanced at Marlene as their hands parted but their gaze held each other's intensely.

Adam went after several Lilim. I'm sure you can understand why, Father Pat said. *The Amanthras thought they could claim him through vengeance . . . given what happened with Lilith, then subsequently, Eve. They allowed one of their damned out of the Amanthra feeding nests to attack him, given that it was too risky for a demon in that era to show themselves topside with the Almighty's wrath still at an all-time high. Remember, these were the old biblical days and forgiveness was nigh. Eden had been breached.*

Damali ran her palms over her face, better understanding why the Covenant was trippin' so hard. If this mess went back to Adam, and he'd been attacked . . .

Quite right, Father Patrick said. *He conquered the creature much as you instinctively did, using Red Sea salts. Adam used what the angels that sought Lilith and her Lilim used, crystalline tracker that had her energy in it to hold her, but with something so much more in the crystallized element of salt. Adam was injured by one when he fought it, but never carried the infection, or passed it to his family or others, even though it had touched him. So, we know Neterus aren't carriers.*

What's with the salt, why that more than any of our other weapons? I mean, my on-the-fly theory worked—burn it to temporarily disable it, but you guys seem to know—

Crystallized natural minerals from the sea that was much-later parted by the Hand of God, from the holy region near Eden. Crystals hold a charge. Light infused from the Almighty's creation lightning arc . . . and it worked for you because it had been charged again from the waters parting during Moses' time.

'Nuff said. I got it. Salt from the water parted by the Hand of God . . .

Yes, Damali. We know that something as simple as salt, but as profound as the Creator's touch, stops the Damned. But the damage they can do once they are topside is enormous. Even if we get them all, who they've infected is an anathema to us until those people start exhibiting clear signs of the infection. We have been making combinations of saline solution to try to use as an antidote, to no avail thus far. There is also the problem of how to quickly distribute it, how to know who was infected, and how to inoculate anyone who hasn't been yet. We just don't know, and time is of the essence.

Damali's thoughts whirled. If Adam had seen this, so had Eve. Which meant her Neteru queen would know what they did not. There had to be an antidote. And if Carlos could get his act together, maybe he could ask his ancestral Council of Neteru kings a thing or two as well. But that was a conversation for another day.

All right, Father Pat. We find the Chairman, use him as bait to get to Lilith, and put them both to sleep. That should close the portals. Sounds like we've got thirty days or less, given we don't know how many actually came up right after the battle in Philly. They could have just started coming up a month or two ago, or maybe more. Problem is we just don't know how many humans have been infected.

Temporary silence waited between them. Damali couldn't tear her mind away from thinking about all the people riding the buses, folks bumping into each other on the streets in a crowd, standing in elevators, kids hugging their parents, or greeting friends with an embrace or handshake, brothers high-fiving after a game, lovers touching . . . even down to somebody handing another person change for a dollar . . .

The spread of this is unquantifiable until the infection finally manifests itself, Father Patrick said in a weary tone. *And we cannot just take innocent human lives on a hunch that they've been touched. Each person who dies and comes back adds to the legions of the Damned, and each is a loss from the Light. Of course, with this surge in dark energy, there has been a breakdown in normal human behavior as well.*

Damali paused. *Like anything already deep and dark slithering inside a person's head is given more energy?*

Yes. Tell Carlos to call me as soon as he can. I'm concerned. Even those of us within the Covenant are being affected. I will not speak of my other brethren's issues, but I'm sure you can understand why each of us was called home.

Hold up, Damali said. *You said Neterus can't—*

Adam couldn't be infected, but he wasn't impervious to the energies and neither was Eve. It was at that time that Adam and Eve made that fateful choice in the Garden.

Wait, Damali nearly shouted and folded her arms. *Then, who released the Damned the first time around? Lilith?*

The Chairman, Father Patrick said flatly. *Lilith was on the run and didn't dare cross her new husband, Lucifer. He'd provided her amnesty. But remember, in that era, the Chairman was also a Level-Seven entity. He had not been banished to the weaker Level Six and made a vampire. That's why we initially discounted him and thought that with Lilith on the run, she wouldn't attempt such a stunt that would allow her enraged husband to find her. Until we began to see the same manifestations that had been reported in the ancient Dead Sea Scrolls, we weren't sure if the Damned had surfaced again. We now believe that she was simply too weakened to close the portals she'd opened, and has fled. The issue is we cannot confirm that theory.*

Damali allowed her arms to fall away from her body and covered her mouth. She mentally blotted out Marlene's stricken expression. *Oh, my God . . . that's why the ancient Neterus have been quiet on this one.*

Yes, Father Patrick said quietly. *This shames the heads of both Councils, to some degree. But if a direct request is made, maybe they would give some guidance within their own ranks. They have heard our entreaties and said they would take it under advisement. No one wants to touch this matter with a ten-foot pole. Every layer On High is debating personal choice, not wanting to breach that human option as they assist and potentially draw the Wrath. The current living Neterus, you and Carlos, have to make clear decisions, defeat this the old way, for reasons the angels have not yet made clear to even us. Each time we've asked, we've been told to have faith, patience, and to back off. Ausar and Aset inquired and were told to wait and watch and that they would be given a sign, so their hands are tied.*

What! Damali mentally shouted. *But what if the dark side has been perfecting this biohazard weapon since they ran the test on Adam? What if it's not an accidental energy leak and there's more to this? What if they're working on some new Neteru-compromising infection—*

Yes. It's thoroughly documented that they will stop at nothing to be able to render a Neteru ineffective. We just hope this isn't it. We've all been discussing whether or not they needed larger populations to see if it worked, because the first time they tried it, Adam contained it. Then they targeted major biblical cities—I take it you remember Sodom and Gomorrah? What was the Light's answer? Total wipeout. Noah's flood . . . wipeout of the contagion.

Damali's breath hitched, and Marlene offered her a full-body hug. *But why didn't we know about this before? We should have been warned and—*

We were! It's in all the scriptures across every religion telling humanity to brace themselves for visceral spiritual attacks and to stand firm in their choices before the sea spews back her dead and—

I know! But, specifically, why didn't—

Because, child, after the sacrifice of the Lamb, there was enough heat in the system . . . enough Light to keep the portals closed. Lilith dared not come to the surface, and Level Seven was lying in wait for the right hour. But when she thought she had a sure-fire plan, she acted prematurely and opened a way for the Damned to escape. Don't you understand? The only thing keeping this somewhat manageable is that this all occurred while Hell was in leadership chaos. These infected souls, the Lilim's food, are slipping out of each realm and sporadically escaping. They have not been harnessed as a direct weapon, yet. The power drain on Level Six is making it difficult for them to properly align. But if anything galvanizes them at that strongest strategic level above the Seventh . . . like if the Chairman gets reinstated, or a replacement is found—

Not on my watch.

We hope not. We have faith, and it is only because of what you and Carlos did together to ransack Level Six that this imminent event has been somewhat diffused.

I can get Yonnie and T—

No! The elderly cleric shot back, his thoughts so sharp and fearful that they almost fried a few synapses.

Damali winced.

They are friends to you and your team, but multiple thrones sit vacant. The temptation for a master vampire to claim one is too great. He could even seat his mate. Then, where would that leave us? Now do you understand why you and Carlos weren't informed?

Damali nodded. *I understand, but they already know about the Damned.*

We don't care if they know about the Damned. If they are inclined to assist by eliminating any roaming undead all the better. But Yonnie doesn't need the temptation of an empty council-level throne. Father Patrick's mental voice had become a strained whisper. *Tell Carlos to call me the moment he's lucid. If he is going to petition Adam . . . well, let's just say that they have very different personalities and backgrounds. I'm concerned.*

Yonnie and Tara have a bounty on their heads if they go subterranean because they helped me and Carlos, so I don't think they'd risk trying to go underground on us, Damali said firmly, hoping the old priest would relax.

Every person living has some demon that they fight. Ego, fury, hurt, insecurity, lust—pick one, dear Neteru. Even if they have conquered it, this dark energy could make choices they have to make very difficult. Weaknesses become magnified during this turmoil. Close the portals and that will cease. Destroying Lilith is the first step. Finding the antidote for all those infected but not yet lost is the second step. If we get the book to release all those from the dawn of time, that would be the pinnacle of a successful mission.

Damali remained very still. The elderly priest had mentioned the book earlier and then evaded her question for more information about it when she'd pried. Now it had been mentioned again. She seized upon the opportunity during the seconds he rested and gathered his thoughts. The Book of the Damned. *What is it? Who has it? What does it do?*

We have yet to be sent a sign about how to acquire this—we know who has it, but where it is hidden is unknown. Just like the antidote, this remains a mystery. . . . We were hoping to have more before we contacted you, he said, still skillfully evading her direct questions. *In the past, there was never a cure. Before, a total biblical-level wipeout had been the Almighty's answer . . . and we hope that will not come to pass again. Our information is only twenty-four hours old. You have not been kept in the dark long. Don't lose faith in us at this juncture.*

Again, Damali hesitated, letting the information Father Patrick had just disclosed sink in. She wondered if this explained Carlos's behavior. Everybody on her team, herself included, had been off kilter. Damali closed the door on that part of her thoughts.

How is your team faring, Damali? Father Patrick asked, probing further.

Damali sighed and gave in. *Issues are bubbling up and personal fires have been flaring up faster than I can put 'em out.* She let her breath out hard. *This book, we have to find it. Period. The antidote could even be in there, who knows?*

Like I just said, we know who has it . . . and we know what it contains, we just aren't sure where it is. Father Patrick hesitated and let out an audible breath into the speakerphone.

Talk to me, please, Father. How can we beat this problem if we can't even know what our weapons are?

The Chairman has it, he finally said in a quiet mental voice. *Any of those fallen into the realms through trickery or deceit must be called by name from the angels' voices to release them from bondage below. It will not release the Lilim or any fully turned entity until they are exterminated. But these walking dead, the food of the realms, will be called into the Light and given a second opportunity to make amends. If we had that, we could save any and all who died from this recent outbreak . . . maybe even some of those from before it. But the clock is ticking. If the planet becomes overrun, Hell will commence the Armageddon, not the other way around, as it should be—and our side may not have enough souls left in our coffers to battle what is to come. The Creator might have to scrap the most magnificent experiment—humankind . . . the whole planet. By fire this time.*

"Whoa!" Damali said, breaking eye contact with Marlene and raking her locks. The entire team watched her stalk back and forth. What Father Patrick said was enough to spike her sensory capacity to overload. She didn't need prompting to ask the elderly cleric her follow-up question. Pure frustration riddled her system—she'd held that freakin' book in her own hands when she'd gone into Council Chambers to beat the Chairman's ass down . . . and she'd let him have it back? Damali groaned and briefly shut her eyes. No wonder the old bastard was so ready to cut a deal! Yeah, she'd wrested the embryo from Lilith, but she still felt like she'd failed.

Steadying her nerves, Damali addressed Father Patrick in a subdued mental tone. *Assuming it will be next to impossible to get this book from the Chairman, let's go back to the antidote as plan B. What is it? How do we get it out, worldwide, before any infected person drops? That's what we have to find out.*

I wish we knew, Father Patrick mentally replied, his mind so weary that Damali could barely hear him. His sentence came across as a rasp. *Until we know if it's a prayer, something dispersed in solid or liquid form, and what elements are involved, we can't fathom a delivery system. This is also how the governments got involved. A few of our elite members, who shall remain nameless for the sake of propriety, had top-level conversations with world leaders. This is serious, Damali. I'm not authorized to say more. Just know that extreme human measures are being considered to quell the contagion that none of us are happy with.*

Humans always tend to mess things up, and governments can't be considered rational. Far from it. Damali sighed and rubbed her temples. "Thanks for the heads-up. I'll explain what I know to the team and investigate. Why don't you try to get some rest? You sound bone tired, Father Pat."

"I am, sweetheart. Truly, I am."

CHAPTER FOUR

She'd watched dawn come in as she lay on her sofa, glad that she'd been able to get the family to give in to her need to be alone despite the attack. There was no reason for them to worry about her falling asleep. Fat chance of that after everything had jumped off. Add a serious case of bad nerves to the fact that she had been up almost all night with them, deep in strategy at the dining room table, her not being alert should have been the least of their worries. She needed space to think.

By the time she'd dragged her weary, ragged body home, fending off complete protest from the team, she was simply ready to drop. She'd thought she'd never get out of there, though, when Yonnie allowed his voice to descend to a purposeful octave and calmly asked if she wanted an escort home. Not.

The only reason she didn't make a big production out of telling him to back off was that Tara would have been embarrassed, and this was just some Yonnie, master vampire, bullshit to get under her girlfriend's skin in front of Rider, who apparently had an attitude about Tara's glimpse at both Rider and Carlos. But the team bugging hard about it had frayed her last nerve.

The point everyone seemed to miss was as long as Carlos was handling his business, Yonnie would never step to her, out of respect and because he and Carlos were fam. . . . But if Carlos ever stopped handling his business, well . . . It was the way of the vamp world. That was what had bristled Tara, and the message Yonnie was trying to send—that he had options. Both of them were crazy.

Oh, yeah, there had to be some seriously dark energy afloat. Damali rubbed her eyes and tried to wake up fully. But personal issues, lusts, struggles, whatever, paled in comparison to what they were up against. She had to remain clear about that.

After the conversation with Father Patrick, she didn't have enough energy to try to wrangle with the Neteru Queens. But once she recharged her mental battery, she'd try to make contact with Nzinga to learn more.

Bottom line was, she had to figure out how to locate Lilith and the Chairman. Up till now, she really hadn't been hunting them; she'd just been trying to heal herself and her team. She now wondered how much of that was because of the dark energy that had been released, and it made her question whether or not she'd been wrongly focused on her own immediate concerns, versus her overall mission as a Neteru. Had her plan been logical—retreat and get strong, then get back into the fight?

That's what unnerved her, not knowing if her logic was sound, her strategy tight. She was now also beginning to question her intense desire to live away from the team. Was that just a normal evolution of her growth as a woman and a Neteru, or something motivated by deep, hidden, selfish reasons?

She let her breath out hard and closed her eyes. What she'd seen and had come to learn now made sense. She kept reminding herself not to be judgmental. Father Patrick had said this open portal mess with bad vibes floating around affected everyone differently.

First things first: get Carlos up and sober, then fill him in. Rider and Shabazz had committed to getting him up and pouring coffee into his gullet. Mike and Inez had to be found, and they had to get on a flight back home, and once home, get debriefed. Salt supplies had to be reinforced to do roofs, windows, doors, and the house perimeter—a FedEx shipment was on the way from Stateside clerical Covenant contacts.

They still had to figure out a way to lock in on the Chairman, and for that, Carlos Rivera had to be in his clear and present mind and stop avoiding his role as a pivotal team seer. But now that the team knew what it was up against, sensing for it would be a little easier. Maybe.

The new day's light hovered over her like the comfortable old blanket she'd curled up under on her living room couch. She rubbed her cheek against it.

Slowly sitting up and then standing, Damali allowed the blanket to trail behind her as she walked to the bathroom to splash water on her face and brush her teeth. She didn't bother to turn on the light and draped the blanket around her shoulders like a poncho as she stared into the mirror. She hadn't even taken off her clothes and was still wearing the bright orange T-shirt and faded jeans she'd had on the night before.

Weariness made her limbs heavy. She padded quietly toward the kitchen in her socks. For all the protest about needing her personal space, it had always been her intention to christen her brand-new bed with Carlos. Then the walking dead had showed up at her door. A real groove buster.

A hot mug of tea was in order. By rote, she reached up into her brand-new cabinets, found a box of green tea, and began preparing a mug by drizzling raw honey over the organic tea bag and then flipping on the burner beneath the kettle. All of a sudden she smelled metal and snatched the kettle off the flame.

Oh, yeah, water. Everything was brand-spanking new. Nothing in her new house was old and worn and comfortable or broken in, except Jose's blanket.

Angry hisses and sputters sounded from the sink as Damali turned on the faucet and filled the kettle, then stood by the stove, watching the blue flame tickle the bottom of it.

Too much heat without enough water . . . Leo flame hadn't respected the Scorpio water. Carlos had a point; *she* wasn't big on the solitude of majestic Arizona, either.

Soon steam rose from the small hole in the kettle's spout, letting out a soft whistle. The fusion of heat and water had changed the two elements into something else. It created a sound—a high, whining rush of transformation. She turned off the burner. What was she missing? she thought as she dunked the teabag in and out of the water.

Pulling her blanket closer around her, she walked through the kitchen to the back deck. She needed air, to be outside. Probably as much as Carlos needed his own environment, something familiar, something that gave him some measure of control over whatever was going on in his life. Here, he didn't have that.

Footsteps down the side path made her straighten her body, wipe her face angrily, and spin on the intruder.

"Yo, D," Jose said. "You okay?" He hesitated and looked at her tear-streaked face. "After last night, and a lot of the things you told us while Carlos was passed out cold . . . I was worried." His gaze sought hers and trapped it. "And, if Yonnie happened to fall by to try to mess with your head while you had a lot on your mind, I brought my crossbow to stake his ass in lair in the morning. Hope you don't mind."

She nodded and then laughed self-consciously through the tears. "I move around the corner, and still nobody knocks?" She was glad that he smiled, because the statement wasn't meant as a dig, just a friendly tease. She made a fist and raised it toward the sky. "It's a Navajo-Latino thing, and I wouldn't understand. It's cultural—on the Navajo side, no one owns the land, so it's cool if you just roll up on 'em as long as they're outside. On the Latino side—why use a phone when you can just fall by and see if a sistah is home?"

Jose's smile widened. "Yeah, and a sister got her cultural ways, too. She woulda hollered in my window by now, if I had my own spot—talking about, 'Yo, Jose, wanna go kick some sounds? I got this song in my head! Wake up!' "

"Oh, now, see—you wrong, Jose!"

They both laughed as she ran toward him and gave him a big hug.

"I miss you already," she said, laughing harder as he hugged her tighter. His faded blue plaid shirt and rumpled jeans were a sight for sore eyes.

"You my boo, girl. We should be down at the beach, eating some tacos, Rollerblading, hanging."

"Clubbing!"

He held her away from him with a wide grin. "D, don't tease me like that. This town has one bar with sawdust on the floors, one movie theater, one good diner, one freakin' grocery store, but five ammo shops!"

"And you've gotta drive fifty miles to hit a Wal-Mart to buy some drawers," they said in unison and laughed.

"Brother, I ain't trying to look a gift horse in the mouth or talk about your people's land, but—"

"D, it's a one-horse town. You ain't gotta tell me."

Again they laughed, and she slung her arm over his shoulder like old times.

"Remind me why we came here again?" Damali said, giving Jose a wink.

"Something about some vampire friends of yours," he said, laughing as they made their way back into the house.

"Oh, so now it's on me?" Damali stopped in the kitchen and folded her arms.

"Yep, fearless leader. See, me, I woulda risked the hotel circuit till we could build in Malibu or Beverly Hills or some-freakin'-where other than here."

"Stop lying, Jose," she said, laughing harder. "How were we gonna keep all the kids in the house, straight and safe?"

"Yes, Mommy dearest," he said, bowing his head slightly, then looking up with a mischievous smirk. "But in a minute, they're gonna get one helluva education all cramped in that rickety house of Pop's."

Damali cocked her head to the side. Jose laughed and ran his palm over his hair.

"Your girl made Big Mike some ribs the other night before they announced another Houston trip, and uh—"

"Noooo . . ." Damali covered her mouth.

"Shabazz been in there doing Kung Fu on tables and shit," Jose said, laughing. "Anything wood is fair game for a brother's tension. Lost sections of the dining room in the backyard. So when Mike split, him and Mar was out a few nights ago. Marlene and Shabazz left this morning, too. You been missing a lot of drama while being over here checking on contractors, fixing stuff up, and then when you finally pulled out of the minicompound all hell broke loose." He laughed harder. "I don't know where they are now, truthfully. After you ran it all down and left, we started losing household. Guess everybody needed somewhere to go chill."

She covered her face and laughed out loud. "Oh, my God!"

"Berkfield ain't no punk, either. Rolled right after Shabazz and Marlene got ghost."

"Marjorie and Richard split and left their kids? You have got to be lying!" Damali walked in a circle, the blankets swishing behind her like a royal robe. "Everybody's all right, though? Nobody's seen anything weird and been touched by anybody outside of the house, right? For real, Jose." Her laughter had gone, her expression was tight.

"Naw," he said, giving her a hug. "They cool. Just blowing off steam like we always do before going into another big battle." He chuckled low. "You know that gladiator-type shit . . . good meal, good woman, good night's sleep, then get strapped and go to war."

She immediately relaxed and put her head on his shoulder. Jose's warmth felt so good, just like his hands against her back did. "All right. I'll stop being mother hen."

"Good," he murmured, rubbing her spine. "You're too tense, though I can understand why."

"You always make me feel better when crazy shit is going down," she said, sighing from the knots he was unfurling in her back. "Damn, that feels good."

He breathed out a contented sigh, and the warmth of it

rippled through her hair. "It's all good, D. You ain't hear this from me, but earlier this week, Rider put a rifle on his lap while we was all playing cards and gave J.L. *the eye*. Gave him the don't-try-it-while-her-pop-is-out big-brother thing, feel me? That old equipment shed behind the house got stories we'll all take to our graves, but if J.L. had lost his mind and taken a walk in the moonlight with Miss Kris, and Rider had been roasted enough to try to stop a martial artist on a mission—hey, he mighta whupped Rider's ass. The house is a powder keg, D. I think the only thing that kept J.L. chill was the girl's brother ain't warmed up to the concept yet, and Dan has Bobby's back—so."

"Lawd have mercy." Damali shook her head and left Jose's loose embrace to go turn on the kettle again. "See, that's why a sistah had to be out."

"I can dig it," Jose said with a smirk. "Don't worry about your boy, Carlos, either. Rider had his back. That's why I came by, so you wouldn't worry. Brother is still fell out on the porch swing and sleeping it off, so like I said, it's all good."

The mirth peeled away from her once more. *Oh, no, not yet. They had been back, the old them, now the moment had evaporated like steam.*

While she appreciated Jose's update on Carlos's whereabouts, she really wasn't ready to interject that into the happiness he'd brought through her door. Mention of Carlos meant that she had to think about the thing she was trying not to think about. In a round-about way, Jose had given her a full account of where everybody had been, except he and Juanita . . . Not that that was her business. And then she'd have to think about all sorts of other things, which returned her to the concept of sharing, which she'd successfully banished for five minutes of free thought. So she did what Marlene always did when the subject matter got thick, made tea.

"I've got green, mint, uh, strawberry, echinacea, uh, golden seal, and—"

"Mint's cool, but you got any Joe in the house?"

"Coffee, oh, yeah, sure. I forgot that you and Rider don't

do herbals first thing, uh, not sure where it is, umm . . ." She sounded like a mad hatter, and knew it, but couldn't stop herself as she banged open cabinets and shut them, moving in jerky, confused, starts and stops.

"It's cool, D," Jose said, his voice mellow and amused as he neared her. "It really is cool."

His hands on her shoulders stopped her desperate search for coffee grounds. It stilled her body, but made her mind fly out of her ears and her heart nearly pound out of her chest. A simple nod without turning to face him was all that she could manage, and she understood what he meant by it all being cool—problem was, it wasn't.

"I'm glad you liked the blanket," he said quietly, his body close enough to hers to allow her to feel the heat of it adding to the blanket in its own distinct layer. "I kept it on my bed for years . . . and, uh, wanted to give you something that always comforted me when I was alone."

Oh, shit, she was gonna have a heart attack. No words formed in her mind or her mouth. Her vocal chords were frozen. She could only wrap the blanket closer to her body to both stave off the shiver his statement had produced and to acknowledge how sensual an act giving her the blanket had been. It was a profound gift, something to be cherished, and it had been offered with enough measure of respect, without totally crossing the invisible line. But the gesture was also beginning to print a license for him to do that. All those nights when he'd wanted her . . . wrapped in *this* . . . Didn't he understand that she was also a tactical sensor! His hands on her shoulders and touching the threads, was making the fabric practically come alive around her like a caress. Plus, hombre had a little vamp in him, too. . . . Oh, Lord . . . Everything she was feeling the night before while standing in front of the refrigerator was waking up inside her.

"D, I have a confession to make," he said quietly, "and I hope you won't be mad at me."

She swallowed hard and was barely breathing. His hands trailed down her arms, but he might as well have run them down her back.

"I wouldn't have stopped by if I thought Carlos was here . . . I mean, unannounced like this."

She closed her eyes. "I know," she whispered.

He leaned his chin on her shoulder, his warm breaths coating her neck, making small tingles run down her spine and setting a slow smolder to her throat. He smelled clean, masculine clean, with an Ivory Soap foundation that she'd just begun to notice. She stood there, immobile, separating the scents of him in delicate layers. Mint mouthwash, Ivory Soap, shampoo, male chemical pheromone . . . Until this moment, she hadn't really understood just how sensual a creature Jose was . . . at least not the way he was making her understand it now.

"I don't know how to say it," he murmured and then sighed.

She kept her back straight and her body extremely still, not sure whether she should melt into the invitation and close the sliver of space between them. She struggled with a response. She couldn't say that honesty had always been theirs, because they'd been lying about this very thing to each other, as well as to themselves, for years. The word *trust* came to mind, and she seized upon it.

"We've always been able to trust each other," she finally whispered, "even when we weren't sure of anything else."

He nodded and laid his cheek on her shoulder to replace his chin, and wrapped his arms around her to gather her hands where she clutched the blanket. His fingers twined with hers and he let his breath out hard again. "I love you, D . . ."

Her response was a thick swallow. *Oh, shit . . .*

"Like in a way I can't explain . . . it's that trust thing you said. I want us to stay friends, like the way we were just laughing outside. Do you know what I mean?"

She opened her eyes wide, glad he couldn't see the shocked expression on her face. Friends. *Friends?* Yeah, cool, right, exactly. Friends were a good thing, this was a friend-loving-closeness-hug, not a man-soon-to-be-a-lover-in-about-two-seconds-hug . . . Oh, my God, she would have been too embarrassed. The portals needed to be vacuum sealed, not just closed, if the mess had her acting like this!

"See, I know, from time to time, things between us would kinda get thick, and that was my fault," he said quietly on a soft expulsion of air. "D, I'm sorry I took you there and made you uncomfortable in the house, ya know?"

She nodded quickly. "No, it's cool, Jose, we—"

"No, girl," he said gently. "Let me finish and get this out, once and for all."

Damali pressed her lips closed and stared wide-eyed at the cabinets.

"I just have so much fun with you, we click so good together, when we make music, compose, do the stage it's like . . . like I can't even talk about it. And we know each other so well . . . like we can finish each other's sentences, and, God knows, you're beautiful. . . . But I had to get over it. You didn't feel that way toward me. Carlos was the only brother that made you feel that, and I had to respect that. Had to suck it up. That was my own head-trip, and I was about to lose somebody real important in my life because I couldn't accept the way things were. In fact, he's cool people, too. I was about to create some drama in the house, and half of me was wondering if I was what made you move so you didn't have to deal with that. I'm sorry, if I put you in a position. *That's* what I truthfully came by to tell you, since you were all alone in here and we could really be real."

He lifted his head and turned her around slowly to face him. Her eyes sought the floor, but he put a finger under her chin to lift her head.

"D, if I was the reason you moved out, come home once the compound is built and there's real living space. If not, cool. But if I had anything to do with it, I'm sorry."

She shook her head no, too rattled to immediately say a word. "No, Jose, it wasn't your fault, and there's never been a reason for you to apologize to me about anything. I moved out because it was just time, ya know? I've never been on my own and wanted to see what that felt like."

He smiled and kissed her forehead. "Sometimes it's good, sometimes it's bad. Sometimes it's fun, and sometimes it's lonely as shit. Like everything else, it ain't perfect."

She gave him a platonic hug and shooed away the heat that he still produced in her body. The daggone blanket was cursed. She smiled inwardly. Nah, it was blessed. It was her crazy brain that was twisted.

Jose awkwardly pulled away and turned off the burner on the stove. "Kettle's been singing now for about five minutes."

Damali glanced at it, feeling warmth creep to her cheeks. "My bad?"

"I know," he said with a wry smile. "I didn't hear it, either."

They looked at each other, a silent understanding passing between them.

"It's time to turn the flame down before the kettle burns."

She nodded and slipped around him to find two clean mugs. Oh, shit. She nodded as she walked. "Good idea. Oh, yeah, you wanted coffee. Ummm . . . where did Marj put—"

"You got a pop or some iced tea?"

She stopped, looked at him, and went to the fridge. "I drank out of this," she said quickly and shoved the iced tea back onto the shelf. "But—"

"That's fine," Jose said, leaning against the sink. "I'll share your spit while you share my blanket."

She held the iced tea midair. "You want a glass?"

"Do I need one?"

"No."

He stopped smiling for a second, took the pitcher from her, and turned it up to his mouth. After a long swig, he shoved it back into the refrigerator and wiped his mouth on the back of his shirtsleeve. "We do it like this in the house behind Marlene's back any ole way." Then he burst out laughing.

She was so shocked that it took her a second to laugh

with him. It wasn't the tea confession that had paralyzed her; it was all the double meanings and the sheer sensuality of the way he'd done it, like a quiet striptease. His vamp roots were showing; all that was missing was a little hint of fang. She couldn't tell if he was just messing with her or serious, but the whole thing jacked with her mind. Laughter was a good cover and a good release, just as it had always been between them. She made herself laugh very, very hard.

"I'd better go," Jose said, still chuckling. He kissed her cheek and began walking through the house.

"Tell everybody I said hi."

"Yep," he said, and gave her a wink. "Maybe if I go back to bed, I won't be put in the doghouse."

Damali straightened, every hair on her neck bristled. "Oh, puhlease," she said as upbeat as possible. "Who's gonna put you in the doghouse?"

"'Nita. Just promise me you won't floss that blanket around her, okay? I know y'all have beef, but do that for me to keep the peace, boo? She's still a little salty about the fact that I insisted you have it, since it came off my bed. . . . Women can be so superstitious and territorial, but, uh, it's cool. However, there's a limit to what y'all will and will not tolerate, and a brother being AWOL first light, is one of 'em." He kissed her quick and winked at her again. "I'm out."

She waved, smiled, even laughed a little, and then leaned on the doorframe and watched him jog down the path, but he picked up the pace to a flat-out haul-ass once he hit the road. That annoyed her to no end. He was running for *Juanita* so the heifer wouldn't be pissed. Damali briefly closed her eyes.

She had to let it go. But at this insane moment she didn't want to share him, at least not his laughter, or whatever. Then, she had to get real.

He'd braved being cut off and returned to monk status; he'd brought her his blanket, dashed to her house at dawn to deliver a message . . . five miles down the road, no car to wake up the house.

This was private, between them, another gift to be tucked away in her mental cedar chest, black box. This same man had let fate cut out his heart, but still was a soldier. This same man had ridden like a bat out of Hell on a bike to save her from said same. This man had handed her a pile of ashes when it really mattered most, an act that he knew would probably change his world—but he did it anyway. He'd allowed her team to build a life on his land . . . had *provided* always when it counted most . . . didn't come home drunk. He'd sipped her iced tea, shared spit and shared a blanket, said he loved her, added the caveat about being her friend to keep it smooth, and then walked. Went home to where he was supposed to be, and didn't make a false move. Damn . . . what a man. Juanita had better recognize. That shit Jose just pulled had wet her drawers. If that girl *ever* broke his heart . . . Oh, no, Juanita had better be clear; *Jose was a gift from God.*

With an exhausted sigh, Damali hugged the blanket closer and simply allowed herself to feel just a little bit sad.

She went into the house, glanced around at the open, bright space, and still felt like she was imprisoned. She couldn't run far or fast enough from the feelings that had shaken her. As long as there was evil on the planet, she would never find peace. Peace was a hard commodity to come by, just like privacy and a chance to explore new things like a normal human being was . . . and the right to make a few mistakes along the way.

In this very moment, she hated sharing her entire life with the planet. Jose had made her wonder what it might be like to do something truly selfish, just for a little while.

Damali quickly banished the thought, but it crept back slowly, regardless. Maybe it was the effect of everyone living in close quarters for months? The house down the road had been a real nightmare of too many people under one roof. That had to be part of it. Everything had been so crazy it was laughable. Almost. She walked through her small house, picked up her mug, added fresh hot water to it, and went out onto the back deck to stare at the surrounding mountains. Her head felt like it was about to explode.

Marlene and Shabazz had one bedroom; Mr. and Mrs. Berkfield had the other. The team had quickly constructed two triple-level bunk beds and wedged a cot into one room for the guys. Necessity was the mother, or father, of invention and was all that was available for the formally unpaired men in the house, so that Carlos, J.L., and Jose could be on one side of the room in a bunk, Big Mike, Dan, and Bobby Berkfield could be on the other, with Rider's cot wedged against a wall in the submarine-size enclave. Ridiculous.

A brawl was imminent, if things didn't change. It wasn't much better for the ladies' room. She and Inez had been bunkmates, like an adult summer-camp arrangement, while Juanita and Kristen shared a double bunk bed.

True, that wasn't as intense as the guys' room, but the claws came out after the first week. What was personal space? They might as well have rented out a matchbox, and after a while, everybody gave up protecting their small spot of territory. Sharing, coping, having one's space invaded were constants; missing clothes, toiletries, combs, and brushes were standard. A black hole in the universe opened and swallowed things in the confusion. It was impossible to find anything, forget about going out unwrinkled or a quick change, and one virtually had to take a number and wait in the hall to pee. If you got hot water, you had to say thank you, Jesus. The guys gave up shaving, unless it was on the back porch using a coffee mug, hand mirror, and good judgment.

Sharing was the watchword of each and every day. Damali sipped her tea. What the heck were they being prepared for now? Or was this *it*—the prelude to something even worse, like living in caves of huddled humanity during a planetary wipeout from On High? Anything this intense was always a sign. If they closed the portals, delivered the book, and got the job done, then what? There was always a reason more than the obvious.

But that was just the problem; she didn't feel like sharing, especially if the future looked so grim. Damali sipped her hot tea more deeply and watched the steam from it curl up from the surface with fury. As far back as she could remember she'd had to share *everything*.

While in foster care, she'd had to share clothes—hand-me-downs to be more exact. She'd had to share someone else's parents. Ultimately, when she'd run away, she had to share a sofa in Carlos's mother's home, and Lord knows share a bathroom, share chores, meals, the one telephone in the house, share all. Then the Guardians found her, and she had to share living space to a point beyond ridiculous. Had to share all her hopes and dreams and aspirations with the public through her music, and share her life and fate with the greater good of the world as a Neteru. Had to share her privacy with relentless, hounding media. She wasn't even going to think about the money they all shared. That was the only thing she didn't mind putting into the communal pot.

But there were some things that were still so difficult to share, like Marlene's attention and affection, the only real mother she'd ever known, was once all hers . . . after Christine became Raven. But now Marlene was to be shared by new, younger Guardians—and whatever was left was split between Shabazz and worry for Kamal. That was okay, she supposed. However, a sigh still brushed past her lips as she blew on her tea to cool it. At least Kristen still had her mom. For all her kooky, overzealous ways, Marjorie Berkfield was a good mom to have.

Her best girlfriend, Inez, was shared with a baby—but she'd never lost her friend in all that. Inez was always available to laugh and talk with, even if she'd never before told Inez about her crazy life. That was not what they shared; it was the love. A pure girlfriend-to-the-bone love that was very distinct from Marlene's mother-love, which never competed with the baby's needs—they both loved Inez's tiny boo.

Yet it was so odd that, with the little one safely stashed in Houston at Inez's mom's new place, and even living under the same roof with her best cut-buddy on the planet—who now knew all, and knew why she'd never been told about her secret life before, she felt further away from Inez than she ever had. Inez was now shared with *her* Big Mike, and although she was happy for both of them, she missed Mike's hugs, his doting concern, and most assuredly his laughter that now seemed reserved for Inez. Mike had been her big teddy bear. Now, she had to give him up to 'Nez.

Truthfully, all her brothers had been shared away. . . . J.L. was now Krissy's, Dan and Bobby were best buds; Shabazz and Berkfield were ironically getting tight as the two most-married men in the house with live-in wives. Marlene and Marjorie had that to share between them. Inez and Big Mike had the new bloom of love. Rider had a pain so deep that he nursed it in a bottle of Jack Daniel's . . . so gone were the days of the two-by-two details and solo talks they'd shared. And then there was Jose.

She tucked the thought closer to her as the wind caught the end of her blanket and made her hold it more firmly. She did *not* feel like sharing him, with of all people, Carlos's old girlfriend. She missed Jose enough to bring tears.

Morose thoughts continued to fill her head as she quietly sipped her tea and looked out toward the vast canyon walls. Why couldn't Carlos understand that she'd needed the space to think all this out? She'd shared her mind with Carlos, her body with him, even her heartbeat and her soul. All she was asking for was a little time to make the mental transition to sharing the rest of her life with him. First, before she did that on a permanent basis, she'd wanted to see what it was like to not have to share every fiber of her being with someone. She had no concept of what it might be like to keep a little of self in reserve. Up till now she'd been a love-to-the-bone, give-it-up-to-the-bone, max-it-out kinda sister.

There had to be a way to find herself within all the layers of the shared one. Now the Covenant was telling her for real to share the world, and her man was drunk as a skunk, and she couldn't even share the burden with him.

It brought tears to her eyes to realize just how angry she was at him for being messed up at a time like this, even though, she knew it was irrational to feel that way. She just couldn't help it.

Sometimes there were so many people and priorities pulling on her, demanding a part of her that she felt schizophrenic or like she had multiple personality disorder. She didn't want to feel stressed like that when she became Mrs. Carlos Rivera. So, today, and for as many days as it took to reintegrate into a sense of balance, she wasn't sharing her living quarters. At least she could demand to keep her body to herself for a little while.

"Shoot," she said quietly toward the canyon. "I even shared my damned Isis long blade with a brother and lost it, for all the good that got me—giving up throat. Was I crazy?"

Damali shut her eyes, becoming peevish at the memory of having the old Neterus strip her of the only thing that seemed to truly be hers. The dagger being returned was a consolation prize, to her mind. But the memory of the long blade made hot tears rise to wet her lashes.

She'd even had to share her child with another female's womb . . . then subjugate her natural instinct for the good of the world to protect it, and cut what had once been hers out of Lilith's foul body.

Damali hurled her mug of tea over the deck rail. "Don't you ask me to share another fucking thing!" she shouted and then began to sob. Oh, yeah, whatever had begun to seep into the earth's atmosphere was strong.

CHAPTER FIVE

He felt like shit. Somebody had mercy and had thrown a blanket over him on the outside porch swing. Stiffness riddled his body and connected to the pounding in his temples. He couldn't immediately open his eyes and face the blast of Arizona sun. But the fact that it was hard to breathe made him struggle to sit up.

Carlos eased open one eye and peered at a blurry image before him. Faded Navajo hues went in and out of focus. Rider was sitting on the steps, his head down and face hidden beneath a weathered, brown ten-gallon cowboy hat. An Indian blanket was wrapped around him, but didn't fully cover the rifle on his lap. Rider's chest rose and fell slowly with the steady rhythm of slumber.

As soon as Carlos stirred, Rider's index finger twitched against the gun trigger. He lifted his head slowly and stared at Carlos.

"Not bad for a tired old man."

"Not bad at all," Carlos said, his voice coming out like a frog's croak.

"I had your back," Rider said, and then reached behind the post he was leaning against to retrieve a bottle of Jack Daniel's. He opened it with one hand, screwing the cap off with two fingers while pushing the bottle between his thighs.

Carlos shielded his eyes from the sun with his hand. "What time is it?"

"Morning," Rider said bluntly. "And too damned early for me to be drinking, so I've heard." He shook his head and smiled, and offered the bottle to Carlos. "Ain't for me. It's for the snake that bit ya."

Carlos wanted to nod, but couldn't. The thought of moving his head brought tears to his eyes. He leaned forward by raising only his shoulders off the swing, and extended his arm to receive the bottle, wincing from the slightest exertion.

Just the smell of alcohol made him want to wretch, but he leaned over the side of the swing and took a shaky sip of it anyway. The moment the liquor hit his lips, it burned, and the hard swallow sent an acidic scorch over his tongue and down his throat to smolder like liquid fire in the pit of his stomach. Two seconds later it was back up again, along with everything he'd ingested the night before.

He held on to the wicker, shuddering, heaving, his eyes closed, upchucking his guts, sweating, while Rider calmly struck a match and lit the end of a cigarette. Smoke curdled the smell of vomit under his face and set off a new wave of nausea until all he could do was dry heave.

"Marlene's method of cleansing takes too long," Rider said, once Carlos had flopped back onto the swing. "I'll get it before the flies do, sometime later today."

Carlos lay on his back, breathing hard in short bursts, willing away the nausea. He didn't know whether to thank Rider or to attempt to jump up and kick his ass. "Thanks, man," he finally said between pants, opting for the more reasonable choice.

"Like I said, I had your back." Rider stood slowly, took another drag on his cigarette, and shook his head as he looked down at the porch.

"Damali call you?" Carlos asked with his eyes still closed.

"Nah. Could smell you coming from half a mile away. Burnt ash and booze. Figured you and me had a lot in common."

Carlos attempted a slight nod, but didn't open his eyes.

"I used to show up at this very house like that," Rider said in a wistful tone, moving downwind from the putrid mess Carlos had delivered on the porch.

Carlos winced and pushed himself to sit up. "I've gotta get this up before Marlene freaks."

"She ain't here, so no rush," Rider said coolly.

His mind wasn't making synaptic connections, and it was hard to judge time. Scratching his head didn't help jumpstart his brain. All he could imagine was that it had to be late, if Mar wasn't around. "Well, if Mar won't bug, Marjorie sure will."

"She ain't here, either," Rider said calmly, sitting on the rail on one haunch and flicking ashes over it. "I'm babysitting today."

"Huh?" Carlos groaned, and finally swung his legs over the edge of the wicker swing, avoiding the throw-up by his feet.

"Well . . . it's like this," Rider said in a weary tone, inhaling slowly and making the red embers at the end of the cigarette glow. "Last night, after the group powwow, which I'll fill you in on in a moment, Miss Inez, as you recall, had left her usual kitchen magic under aluminum foil before she'd gone out of town again, made all these vegan dishes that Marlene has been insisting on. Actually, they were pretty good reheated. But then the girl messed up and made a rack of ribs with a side of potato salad to go with the greens and cornbread, especially for Mike—which is what sent Mike on a mission to Houston with her in the first place. Now what'd she do that for, I ask?"

Carlos laughed, even though he had to hold his skull with both hands to do so. "Oh, shit. Chain reaction."

Rider flicked his near-dead cigarette butt over the rail with two fingers. "Kaboom. How long did it take Mike to be out and hop a flight to Houston with Inez?"

Carlos smiled even through the pain.

"I know you're still in hurtin' from a night out with the fellas, but I want to elaborate on the chain-reaction theory. Now, as you remember, dude cleaned off the last bone, dropped it in his plate, girlfriend reached for it to take it back into the kitchen—next thing you know, Mike stood up,

grabbed his Hummer keys, and asked Inez to walk him to his
vehicle. Ain't seen 'em since. But I don't think even a werewolf would mess with him last night."

"No doubt," Carlos said, and leaned back against the furniture to keep the porch from spinning.

"Next thing you know, after our late-running convo last
night, Shabazz was saying, 'Mar, can I talk to you for a
minute?' You know how smooth he rolls—made it seem like
they needed to convene about the situation at hand, and those
two were out the back door. Not sure if Marlene zapped
them into another dimension or what, but they ain't home."

Carlos didn't say a word and just stared at Rider and then
closed his eyes again.

"Berkfields broke camp, too. Dude stood up, got a gun
and his keys, and said, 'Marj, let's go.' Didn't think the man
had it in him." Rider laughed.

"She went, just like that?" Carlos was incredulous, and it
made him open his eyes to squint at Rider.

"You missed it," Rider said chuckling. "Her face got all
flushed, and she hovered around the children, giving them
instructions on what to do, her cell phone number, and then
looked at me with these puppy dog eyes, and I knew I was
the babysitter. So, I holstered up and told her I'd slow down
on the Jack and things would be fine." Rider sighed. "But not
before I laid a hand on J.L.'s shoulder. That's when Berkfield
nodded and walked out the door." He smiled at Carlos.
"Some things don't need to be said. They just boil down to a
man-to-man understanding."

Carlos knew exactly what Rider meant. "Listen, the thing
last night with my boy . . ."

"I understand," Rider said. He looked down at the vomit.
"No blood in it, so I reckon you're fine."

"No, man, that's not what I'm talking about."

"You staggered your ass up these steps with my help,
starting at twenty-five feet out in the front yard, and fell
down so hard on the swing that somebody shoulda yelled
timber. I've been there. Gets cold outside at night in the

desert, so I threw a blanket over you. Every now and then I'd put my eye on ya, only because you were tossing and turning so much, like a man with a lot on his mind—and I didn't get concerned until I saw a little fang crest . . . but, hey, it's daylight so I didn't dust you in your sleep. The fact that you actually did go to sleep at night helped me put things into perspective."

Rider pulled out another cigarette and allowed it to dangle from his lips as he searched for his matches again. "Me, Dan, J.L., and the kids had a great night of poker."

Carlos didn't respond for a moment. Several things were competing for dominance in his cloudy mind. He noticed, too, that Rider hadn't mentioned Juanita or Jose's whereabouts. The one thing he knew for sure was that what was said openly was as important as what wasn't said at all. He also hadn't mentioned Damali. Big, obvious oversight. Major.

"You need to stop smoking, man. Not like I can tell you what to do, but that's like slow suicide, and I don't wanna see you go out like that."

"Appreciate the sentiment," Rider said, allowing a slow release of smoke to filter out of his nose. "Guess we're all prone to relapse." He stared at the end of the cigarette. "Haven't done this in almost thirty years, but a lot of things are working my nerves."

Carlos let his breath out hard and shut his eyes again. "I hear you."

"Do you?" Rider said coolly.

"Yeah, I do."

"Let me explain something very slowly, then," Rider said, easing off the porch rail and stretching his back. He glanced at the rifle that was leaning against a post. "Me and the old guard have approximately one more month to finish training you, right about when your house will be finished, and then you'll be a full-fledged Neteru. What you do with this second chance is your business. I'm a very simple man, with very simple requirements to live. I understand vices and make no judgments about what other folks do. I've accepted

my fate. I don't ask for a lot; I'm very philosophical in that
way. At my age, I avoid unnecessary stress; I don't battle
over bullshit. But every man has his limit."

Carlos stood with effort and went to find a mop. Nothing
more needed to be said to Rider, except maybe thank you.

Rider looked at him hard when he returned to the porch.
"Did you or did you not hear me say we had a powwow,
once? A meeting, twice?"

Carlos just stared at Rider for a moment. "Everything's
fuzzy, man."

"Then, you need to clear up your head, pronto. Damali
was here, after a demon attack."

Carlos dropped the mop.

"Father Patrick said call on a seer-lock. Airwaves are
compromised."

Carlos sat down slowly.

"Your homeboy, Yonnie, watched the front yard, while
Tara stayed on the porch to protect you . . . in case whatever
tried to smoke Damali came for you—but let me add that the
Neteru apex you're beginning to trail sent a little red through
her eyes. So, I sat out here with *both of them*," Rider said,
his voice tightening and escalating with every word, "to
keep you from being turned into a Third, and then subsequently getting your heart ripped out by your best man, if
she couldn't help herself!"

Carlos squinted as much from the volume of Rider's
voice as from the scenario he painted. What Rider had endured was too insane. "Man, I'm so—"

"Don't fucking say it!" Rider shouted, pointing at Carlos.
"Damali was in there locking with Mar to see about the fate
of the world. I'm out here *babysitting* you while watching
my woman, who has already gone off with another vamp
bastard, try to sip air and be cool in both his and my presence! We got kids in the house, and some crazy bullshit on
our asses. Maybe a compromised were-human out in the
woods nearby, a Zen master that knows this and is ready to

turn the house out if Marlene breathes wrong—while my ace, Big Mike, who can body slam anything, is out in Houston eating barbecue and getting laid!"

"Rider, man, lower your voice. I hear you," Carlos said, holding his head.

"Lower my voice? Lower my voice!" Rider hollered, walking in a circle with his arms opened wide. "What the *fuck* is going on, I ask somebody! Our primo sensor, smooth operator, the one who knows all this demon realm shit like the back of his hand, is dead damned drunk—and so pitifully so—that a master vampire can give Damali a nod with *full fangs* in his mouth and ask her if she wants a lift home?"

"What?" Carlos tried to stand, but had to sit back down.

"Damali is gonna have to fill you in, or Father Pat—somebody—because right now, I lack the patience!"

Rider punched a porch post and walked back and forth. Carlos held both sides of his skull and tried to stop the reverberating gong Rider's bellows created.

"But, I'ma tell you this, captain. The girl was angry. Had a right to be. Don't take that shit out on Yonnie, you deal with it—because Yonnie did what any male of any species would do, all right. He saw an opportunity. Damali was spittin' nails, she was so furious. There was something lurking out there—she got one of them—her dead foster father and—"

"What?" Carlos whispered, allowing his hands to drop away from his skull.

"I take it you know the import of that?"

Speechless, Carlos couldn't even nod.

"Yeah. That's why Yonnie offered her a master vamp transport lift home with the caveat that, if she wanted, he'd hang around till dawn as her personal bodyguard. He was gonna do the invitation by mind lock, seeing as how we were all on the porch, by the time she was ready to leave . . . and Tara was there. But, Damali said no, so he had to just put it out there and see if she'd take the bait. Now you can evaluate that however you'd like."

Rider stared at his hands, using them as invisible scales in the air. "One way, a man could say, my friend is honorable. I'd do no less. On the other hand, one could say, I played myself. Girlfriend is old enough to take a nick and still do daylight. She killed a predator, but her emotions were raw and vulnerable last night, and I was out cold."

Both men stared at each other hard.

"You better get real clear this morning," Rider said in a mercifully quiet voice. "You've got a family, a post to man, and responsibilities. There were kids in the house, what if one of them was yours?" He sighed wearily, but his tone held no apology in it. "Me, yeah, I'm probably an alcoholic, I'll accept the title. But I'm a very functional one. *So,* know this. I'm never away from my post when I'm supposed to be there. There is no old buddy from my old days in the streets that can come into this family unit and pull me outta here and get me to the point where I imperil my own."

Rider leaned against the post and looked at the mess on the porch floor. "Except Tara. Yeah, I screwed around and got more than nicked. But I even let her go, my heart, so I wouldn't come back in here one night and not be myself—you got that?"

"Rider, man, listen . . . I—"

"I don't want that sonofabitch on this property. Period. I do not ever want to have to babysit your ass for the bottle or any other vice, not if you're gonna take equal partnership to lead this household. Period. If one Neteru goes off shift, the other one goes on—and when y'all can find time to do what you've gotta do, somebody's fucking radar better be turned on, because, if you haven't noticed, the Levels are consolidating power, heat in the system is ramping up."

"I know, man, but—"

"No, you don't know jack! My old friends had bad habits, too, dude. Mike ain't on our shit list, because he informed us where he was going, when he was going, and when his flight touches down this afternoon, *he'll be lucid.* Your ass, most likely, ain't gonna dry out for another twenty-four hours. I've got a cell phone number to everybody else that rolled outta here this morning. Even if their cell phone vibrates so hard it gets up and walks across a hotel nightstand, I can raise a *lucid* Guardian within an hour, the moment they catch their breath and say their last 'I love you, baby'—you hear me? Your days of being absent without leave all night and coming back fucked up and needing to regen for twelve hours of daylight *are over.*"

Carlos let his breath out hard and leaned on his forearms.

Rider lit another cigarette. "Stupid as it sounds," he said, dragging hard on the butt and exhaling rage with the smoke, "I almost kinda liked it better when you were all vamp. Was easier. We knew what to expect, and the one thing we could always count on was *nothing* would roll up on Damali and possibly take her out. You were on the case. Wouldn't even let us do anything that could put her in harm's way. You were the fortress, man."

"I liked it better that way, too, hombre," Carlos muttered. "You just don't know."

"Yeah, well, pull your shit together and stop bellyaching," Rider said, his glare focused on the walkway and he drew in another hard drag that hissed. "I liked it better when I was twenty-five years younger. Liked it better when I could take one of Tara's Fourth-gen nicks . . . Oh, *yeah,* there were things I liked *so much* better than this current state of affairs I find myself in—like babysitting a new male Neteru who has yet to get his head screwed on straight. I bet Shabazz liked it better, too, when Kamal was in Bahia, but he ain't. Guaranteed Berkfield liked it *way* better when he was just a cop, and wasn't policing demons away from his daughter or watching her about to get her bones jumped by our team's computer whiz kid. But shit happens. Things change. You find yourself in new circumstances, and gotta cope. Grow up and take a number. Everybody on this team has something they liked or wanted way better than this."

Rider flicked away the half-smoked butt and looked at Carlos without blinking. "By rights, I should be the one who was lying passed out on that swing. If you had any sense, you would have been the one over there at Damali's new place, no matter what she'd said, talked your way into her door—like the master you used to be, and made the best of the new circumstance. You've got opportunity and gifts you're not even using, brother. The thing that's kicking my ass is, of all the people on the team, if you would get the spirit of this change together, you could have it all like it used to be. . . . You've got the money, the girl is still crazy about you—don't ask me why. All the newbies hang on to your every word. Had Dan reaching for reasons why you were out cold." Rider pulled his fingers through his hair and hocked again.

"There's a lot of things that are real different, man, that are hard to explain." Carlos scanned the horizon. There was no way to capture it all on the porch.

"My simplistic trailer-park-roots advice is this. Don't allow time to pass and wind up living on that swing, because your boy bested you at your own game, or a Guardian brother just happened to be in the right place at the right time . . . or we go do a job in some foreign land and she rolls up on one of the one-hundred-and-forty-four-thousand Guardian options out there and makes a decision because they had their heads on straight and you were off the job. The quicker you let go of what was old and figure out how to work with what's new, the better.

"I'm going to go do some target practice, something useful and productive that'll keep my skills sharp and keep me out of the doghouse, to release some of my old tensions," Rider said with sarcasm. "I had your back, last night. Still got it, but the Yonnie thing worked my last nerve. I need to go shoot something."

Carlos looked up slowly. A combination of emotions tore through him. Rider was pissing him off, but truth resonated within every angry word. Guilt lacerated him. Rage shook him. Worry made him weary. Damali's state of mind and what he'd missed while out sent dread and a spike of adrenaline through his every cell. Then the layers and degrees of all of those things, plus so much more, began to peel and blister. Humiliation was in the mix; he just couldn't separate it out from the rest.

Rider nodded toward the mess on the porch and began walking down the steps. "You need to clean up your own shit before the young bucks and the women see it, dude. Stop wallowing in your own crap. Find out what the new mission is from somebody that has patience, I'm not the one today. Call the priest, whatever. Then go down the road and fall on your sword like every man has to do when he fucks up real bad. It's simple."

Carlos stood watching Rider's back as he trudged down the path, kicking up dust before rounding the house. What was there to say? He sent his line of vision on the horizon and squinted and then stared in the direction of Damali's new house.

Was it any wonder that she was lukewarm about getting married and wasn't ready to tie the knot legally, on hallowed ground? He'd felt it before, but knew it now. Rider hadn't lied. Could he blame her? Damali had waited all her life *for this?*

Carlos glanced over his shoulder at the puke on the porch and frowned. For all he knew she, by rights, might be blaming him about her losing the baby. Or, maybe it was the way they just weren't the same when together . . . like that last time together in Philly could still be in her head—he was angry, she was angry, and he'd never touched her like that in his life . . . nothing had been right since that.

The insane part was, he didn't even know where to begin to make that up to her. Or maybe it was simply the Light being too done with him. After Lopez, he could understand why Heaven would be fed up enough to make Damali turn away from him for good.

"I don't know," Carlos whispered, closing his eyes to the too-bright sun. Maybe it was all of it, or none of it. For the first time in his life, he wasn't sure what to do, and she wouldn't even really talk to him . . . kept everything to surface bullshit. At the same time, he was just as guilty, because there was no way he could honestly talk to her about this.

He just shook his head, which made him wince. Damali had actually gone down to square off with the Chairman like he should have. . . . She ran the team better than he probably ever would. She knew the Neteru code cold. She had met with her queens and they'd offered her swift guidance, when his kings had simply marked him and left him to figure life out on his own.

Plus, she'd shape-shifted so smoothly that it gave him chills when she went from black adder to panther, and had held Hell in check until she hit multiple targets with authority. Damali was moving up in skill and rank, while he was on the bottom rung of becoming whatever he was supposed to be. Rank busted. What was he supposed to do with that? More important question: What would she wanna do with that? With him?

No doubt about it, she was evolving into something more spectacular than she'd already been and was in full control, total command, just like he used to be. He was proud of her, but the joy was bittersweet . . . just like she'd crooned to all the masters in Sydney, it was a bittersweet transition, from time to time.

Even up in Gabrielle's establishment, Damali had to show him how to get back on his horse and ride . . . and the way she'd bent light up his spine and had him close to pure ether. . . . There were no words for it. Girlfriend was *bad*. She had to be simply tolerating his ass these days.

That was unforgivable; not her actions, but his. No wonder she didn't feel like it, all their love notwithstanding. Familial love was something real different from Eros, any fool knew that. So when she says, "I love you, baby," what does she really mean? he wondered. Which kind? General, like

family, or specific, like you're my man? But that was a stupid
mental question, because what had he put down with authority lately?

Skills all fucked up, head jacked, powers shaky . . . Shit,
he couldn't stand his damned self, why would his woman?
So, no, it was better that they didn't try to mind lock. Maybe
they both had enough sense to know that they might find out
some real deep shit that neither of them was ready to address.

Carlos hung his head. Every part of his body felt like he'd
been beat down. He missed it all, and couldn't lie to himself
or the Light about that any longer. He missed everything, the
old nights, to be more precise . . . damn . . . when a throne
gave him absolute power and control over everything in his
world. A time when he could walk through walls, bulk to
beat down any predator, step to any challenge . . . with strategy like a razor, game to the bone. Variables, not a
problem—he could work four corners of a room with unpar-
alleled mastery, because he was a *master*. He could blow
Damali's mind and show her some shit she had never seen
before, and leave an echo print on her soft skin that would
make her holla just from the heat of his breath against it.
Those nights were gone. He had to suck it up and deal with
his new reality, or new sentence.

He thought for sure after he'd been shown some new shit
by the old boyz in Ethiopia, and then on the road, things
would go back to the way they were. But how did he begin to
deal with the fact that now he was always two steps behind
her, instead of leading the charge?

Damali had taken to the Light like a fish to water; he'd
been dragged into it kicking and screaming and was currently drowning in it. The Light had blessed her with radiant
beauty and unstoppable power; it had stripped his ass bare
and bled him out, as far as he was concerned. Fair exchange.
His baby had rolled on Level Six, pure gangsta. He'd seen
her do that cold-blooded shit with his own eyes, which had
left him both proud of her, but fucked up behind it. The com-

bination was unsettling. Somehow that was different from what she'd done in McGuire's castle, because at the end of the night, then, he was still Councilman Rivera . . . he owned all the territories in the world, and had worn her beautiful ass out lovely in the desert.

"Ain't that always the way," Carlos absently muttered as he began cleaning up the porch, tying everything he'd been thinking about into a tidy military-style bundle to clear away.

Yet, a jumbled, tangled pile of thinking lay at his feet. He might as well have dumped his dresser drawers and tried to quickly shove everything back into them. Same process. Once everything was out, one had to deal with every individual item, carefully lift, handle, and fold each piece, quite a process if the furniture was overstuffed from the get-go. His black box was. He hated cleaning out his box as much as he hated his turn doing team laundry and cleaning up the aftermath of a night out with Yonnie. It was sloppy.

Carlos glimpsed the mop with sudden disdain. The mundane had claimed him. He had been given the gift of life, but from all indicators, he was still trapped in another world, one of mediocrity, filled with senseless struggles that caused nothing but heartbreak. Yeah, he was still serving time, more like marking it than living it. Cool. He'd figured it would go that way—maybe he'd traded a living hell for a dead one. He'd amassed enough debt for either side to make said point.

"*Es decepcionante.*" Very disappointing, indeed. Carlos glanced through the screen, hoping nobody would come outside to see him at the messy task of cleaning away what he'd upchucked. What he had now were spotty powers that worked when they felt like it, and a family to care for when he couldn't half take care of himself.

And what about the vamp females that would inevitably come out of the shadows when he reached his apex for real? What then? He was *supposed* to be this millennium's male Neteru, but wasn't even sure he could take down one vicious vamp female and dust it if it rolled up on him in the midnight hour; but he knew Damali could. He'd seen her nearly smoke four vamp bitches with their masters present. So now Damali was his bodyguard?

It wasn't supposed to be like this. He couldn't even look at her, right through here, and abruptly trained his line of sight on the horizon, remembering the freedom of wingless flight. Mist. Smooth exit. Except that wasn't an option this morning.

To his mind, there was just a certain way things should be done. The complex problems really had simple solutions, but the whole issue of souls and their metric weights added variables that frankly seemed to cause more confusion. The angels knew everybody in Hell was double-dealing, so why didn't they just come down, go *prang,* and fix this shit with the quickness? He knew the Light had awesome veto power, but the way they used it just strung his brain out.

That was something he definitely had to ask Father Pat one day. He had questions like, why all the riddles, intrigue, mayhem, and choice drama? Lucifer had aces and nonsense up his sleeve, so the other side, to his thinking, should just do the damned thing and straighten out the madness. Zap that bastard, too, while they were at it, and be done.

He'd had this partial conversation about the use of power when the Covenant had first rolled up on him in a parking lot at Nuit's building. What now felt like a long time ago seemed to be a simpler time, too. Just whack one slimy mofo and save his woman angst. But even then the Covenant couldn't negotiate directly with him to cut a deal. They had to take it higher up, and wait for a long decision. Whereas the side that shall remain nameless seemed to work on a different timetable. Instant gratification.

Like, in the old nights, he could have solved Rider's problem with one feral elevation nick, and made him a master so his woman would *never* stray again. Rider was drinking and smoking himself to death anyway—there were viable options . . . if one wanted to get technical. It wasn't his first choice, but he was sure if he was in a position to make a tender offer to a man slowly losing his mind over something like that, hey, the thing would be simple. He knew Rider well enough to know that if the shoe were on the other foot, hombre would be down to do whatever needed to be done. That's what he liked about Rider—the man was practical, a realist, said what others were too chicken shit to say. He respected that.

They could have discussed it over Jack Daniel's, shook on it, and the deal would have been done. It wasn't about allowing a respected amigo to suffer. Rider was grown; one allowed a grown man to choose his own way out. At least that's how it was done where he was from . . . East L.A., by way of Mexico, and a small pit stop along the way. But topside or sub, you didn't leave your tight homeboy to twist and have his heart butchered slowly by memory Harpies or his guts pulled out by shit too hard to digest. A favor was in order, for a real good friend caught between a rock and a hard place. *De nada.* Same night. Right on the spot when he and Rider stood up from their bar stools.

How different was what he proposed from watching a fellow soldier blown half to bits, still alive, guts lying everywhere . . . no chance of recovery, and begging for a bullet in the temple to stop the pain? Done quietly on the battlefield every day with honor.

Carlos shrugged and glanced up. No answer. His solutions spiraled darker as he continued to think about it all and mop off the porch.

To keep the peace, since they were family now, and a strong family was a necessity in any realm, he would have given Yonnie enough playmates to take the sting out of the loss . . . he'd get over Tara with the replacements he could have made for his main man. Then, by rights, he woulda backed Kamal up to an appropriate distance so Kamal could get his head straight and go home, and Marlene could relax enough that Shabazz could stand down without losing face. Respect for the family's Aikido master and their philosopher extraordinaire coulda stayed chill. *That* was power.

There was a way to do everything, and a way not to.

That's how he saw it. Regardless of the Light, all of this was sloppy. "I ain't trying to offend," he said quietly, talking to the porch floor. "I just don't understand.".

'Cause he mighta been able to share a little suave with Dan, so the young buck could go pull a superfine babe older than Krissy, get laid on the regular by a double-D-cup blonde, and stop wigging every time Berkfield's underage daughter was near J.L. See, that was the thing to do to deescalate a potential nuclear situation. It didn't have to be like this.

He would have just taken Bobby out into the night, too, while his momma wasn't looking, and gotten him sho' 'nuff straight. Marj was worried about homeschooling her boy. . . . Sheeit, he woulda schooled the boy right, and all would have been very copacetic. She could tell Krissy whatever, and let her daughter eventually grow into her own.

Carlos smiled. J.L. just would have had to deal until then, like he did. He loved the brother, but J.L. wouldn't die from having his nose wide open, would just feel like he was gonna, but hey. He'd waited for Damali, and had lived . . . well, kinda sorta. Survived was more accurate. Still. Her daddy was in da house, and Berkfield was a good man that he owed, so even in his old life, he wasn't gonna fuck with certain protocols. Peace.

That's right. Besides, he mighta been able to have a little convo with Juanita to make her go on and be with Jose, no past haunting thoughts allowed. He'd wipe the slate clean. Jose deserved that level of man-woman lock without her side glances toward an old flame, and in that very brief platonic discussion he coulda made Juanita think hombre walked on water. Sheeit, and for his brother, 'Nita would have been the alpha and the omega. Problem solved. No more drama.

Yeah. If he was back on his old block, back on a throne, he woulda given Jose a double dose of some mad-crazy shit, 'cause he owed his line brother his life for watching his back . . . woulda given him all he wished he could have given Lopez to make up for the fallen. That woulda been a fair exchange, even in his old world.

Coulda then put them all in an off-da-meter lair with every convenience, but built like Fort Knox. Wouldn't have turned nobody but Rider, all Guardian souls would have been intact, minimal losses. Everybody happy. There were a lot of things he used to be able to do without breaking a vein. The Light would have lost the only weary soul in the trans-actions, Rider's, one that's quickly slipping from their grasp any ol' way, if they didn't give the man a break and some im-mediate relief.

"He's only human," Carlos said, his voice tight from anger, going down the steps to retrieve a garden hose. Who knows, since it would have been done for love, maybe the Light coulda worked a deal for Rider, too? Shoulda. Maybe they wouldn't have been too salty with him for doing it, since it woulda been a mercy nick? Moot point. He no longer owned the equipment to do anything like that.

Regardless, in his old nighttime splendor and under his protective seal, within his heavily fortified lairs, they would have all lived like the royalty they were, and not been fugi-tives livin' on the run. Carlos sprayed off the mop and then shot water across the porch, lost in darkening thoughts.

What good was money when you couldn't spend it to the max? Screw the police inquiries about where he might have gotten phat-paid, and fuck the feds, whoever, his shit would have been all vamp. Untraceable. Situation smooth.

That would have chilled out Marj, therefore Berkfield—cool people who deserved some respite from worry, like everybody else. Fam. He woulda taken care of his peeps, all of them. That's what he'd tried to do before he'd been turned. It was still in his DNA. Serve and protect, but he pre-ferred to do the shit with style.

Carlos laughed quietly. "Yeah, but don't worry, I would have also given a healthy tithe on the down low to you, Fa-ther Pat—wild as that sounds. I would have been discreet for both of us to stay politically correct."

He had to get out of his own head before he lost his mind like Rider. Because, if he'd had it his way, after all that, then he woulda stepped to the Chairman mano-a-mano in Hell, like it should have been done . . . handled his business for both himself and Damali—snatched a bone out of that old bastard's ass, then come home to his woman, righteous, and laid down V-point so hard she woulda walked away with twins. Carlos smiled. One day. Maybe one night.

Then all would be right in the world, and nothin' would have dared to slither up into his domain topside to make any of the teams ever have to go to war again. Shit, after that, he mighta even been so bold to have taken the Chairman's throne, fair exchange, almost, given the blues the sono-fabitch had levied on him . . . but there would never be enough to repay what he'd done to Damali.

However, the shit woulda been cool, until he said it wasn't. *That* was power. Being able to protect his family with unquestioned authority and to make their world sweet. Paradise. No static. Plush environs. To know what they wanted before they even had to ask. Ultimate provider. Stone-cold soldier that nobody fucked with, thus no one dared fuck with his people. *That* was how a man was supposed to handle his bizness.

He, as the man, was supposed to have that burden solely on his shoulders; his family was supposed to live, laugh, relax, be taken care of, all needs met. Bam. Consider it done. Every man's secret dream was to be able to do that.

Carlos dropped the hose and stared at his palms. "Is that so wrong?" he whispered.

His woman wasn't supposed to have to do shit, unless she wanted to . . . and he was supposed to hook her up so lovely that she didn't wanna necessarily do jack but chill. His baby could just sing and leave her blade at home. Talk about a dream come true . . .

She wasn't supposed to have to go to Hell and back and be worried about being attacked all the time . . . too scared even to think about carrying their next child, too stressed to sleep at night, too nervous to make love to make another one. Wasn't supposed to be buggin' about being his wife or tying the knot legal . . . talking crazy shit about living by herself to have space to think. Think about *what*, after all they'd been through? If he was on the job, there'd be no decision. Be no arguments. The word *no* about everything lately would be banished.

The shine had gone out of her gorgeous eyes under the strain. No wonder her silver never lit; the girl was exhausted. Beyond fatigued. He'd allow that to happen to her on his watch, was off the job, so she had to pick up the damned slack. Isn't that how his mother grew old fast, dealing with his father's pitiful bullshit? God, don't let that happen to him.

Carlos took his time walking up the steps. Coffee was calling his name.

Naw, this was not supposed to be the way it was. Damali deserved the world, and at one point, he'd been able to give her that. His state of affairs had become a travesty, and yet his woman tried her best to make it all seem like it was okay. It wasn't. He knew it; she knew it. That's what she had to think about, most likely. But that she'd made the attempt only made him love her more . . . and made him equally more determined than ever to fix this bull fast.

"This ain't me by a long shot." Carlos sighed heavily and looked at his hands, then snapped hard once. "Power used to jump off with a pop, just like that," he whispered, enraged as he stared at the flimsy screen door. "So, if I'm the male Neteru, where's the serious juice that comes with the new title? I got a woman and a family to take care of. Y'all listening? How am I gonna take care of my kids when we have 'em?"

By any man's standards, especially his, if the truth be told, his old throne was something hellacious to be reckoned with by comparison to what he was dealing with now. It was about resources and the broad definition thereof. Always had been, he'd told Father Pat that from night one. Rider said talk to the old priest—about what? It might not be what the

Covenant wanted to hear, but he was being honest in the silent morning hour.

Facts mentally dissected in the cold light of day weren't always pretty. He had his reasons for doubt, issues that had not been addressed, a legitimate argument, and nobody was giving up answers that made sense, to his mind. All of it tumbled in on him like a ton of loose pyramid bricks.

To him, his soul was tethered by steel cable to his understanding of manhood. Period. It felt like C4 had been rigged to that definition, then exploded, and his soul had caught the shrapnel, took the impact as the blast whipped up the tie line; it had snapped and was strangling him.

He knew he'd been tripping since Philly, but couldn't help it or stop himself as his tortured soul began working on his embattled mind, unraveling it as what was left of his soul clawed to survive, until his body had gotten involved and simply malfunctioned. All aspects of the dilemma were unacceptable to him. The Light needed to get with that.

This new life had disintegrated everything he believed a man should be. At this juncture, he wasn't sure if he cared if the Light took his thoughts the wrong way. So what that they had issues, he did, too. Yeah, he'd work for them from either side, as he did before—if it ever came down to that, again. He knew the deal in spades by now, aces wild. His woman and her family needed the table slanted to the good just to grant them peace. No problem. But not being able to do that for them the way he felt it efficiently needed to be done was torture. Was it wrong for a man to dream? Was ambition with good intent a sin? Not hardly. Not where he was from.

Carlos opened the door the old-fashioned way, walked into the house, and let the screen door slam shut behind him.

CHAPTER SIX

The moment it dawned on her that she was a sitting duck for a family-inspired home invasion, Damali dashed away from the front screen, hit the bathroom, and was in and out of the shower in less than five minutes. Jose's fall-by was just a precursor. She could feel it, and needed a few hours to sort out the tangle of thoughts in her brain.

"Oooohhhh, nooooo," she said loudly while ripping through her bureau drawers to find her underwear, red camisole T, and her earrings. She was out.

Damali flung open the long walk-in bedroom closet, snatched her black leather pants down and yanked on a pair of boots. Her baby Isis blade went on her hip, and her black sunglasses got hooked to the cleavage section of her T-shirt. "No, no, no, no, no, no, no, no no," she repeated as she hurriedly stuffed money and I.D. into her pants pockets.

They must think she was born yesterday. She knew how family could be, and how this was all gonna go. Now that there'd been a demon sighting and all this other madness in the equation, freedom was gone. She hadn't even really had her own place for twenty-four hours!

Before they'd all been alerted that anything in the universe had gone awry, it was bad enough. She knew the family's initial strategy; the first weekend, everybody was being cool to allow Carlos operating room. Then, once they figured brotherman was tightened up, they'd start falling by one by one with rental requests. Not that she could blame them, but that was not the point. They knew, just like she did, that there was no way in the world she could be so cold as to deny a family member sanctuary, a hot shower, chill time on her deck, access to her music room, whatever. How could she tell the people she loved, people who had taken bullets for her and had almost died many times in battles too crazy to mention, No, you can't use my place to get your head right? Yeah, right, like she wouldn't share hot water with them after all they'd been through together. But that *still* was not the point!

She could hear it in her mind, playing out like a horror movie. "Yo, D, uh, you gonna be home all afternoon?" Or, better yet, "Yo, baby girl, uh, the shower situation is kinda tight over at the house, and I was wondering . . ." Now it was gonna be, "Hey, D, we were thinking, two-by-two detail is in order over here. So, uh, me and my lady are just gonna crash here with you to be sure you can get forty-winks, then when you wake up, we'll go to bed—cool?" She *knew* her brothers.

"No! Hell no!" Damali said, stomping in the dust as she made her way to her Hummer. Her brothers would be in there trying to use her house as a bachelor pad, regardless of demon sightings. Probably even more so because now that meant there was imminent danger, and that did something crazy to all their libidos, like Jose admitted. Crazy-azz gladiator yang.

It was plain as day. A setup. Marlene and Marjorie would be over there next, *suggesting* that maybe the females in the group should move in with her temporarily until the compound was built, that way the fellas could spread out and chill out, and it would be one big slumber party until they moved out to the next location to find their targets.

She could hear them now: "D, baby, the women in the group are all new, have to finish being trained in sharp-shooting, Aikido, blah, blah, blah, and Krissy is sooo young to be over there in all that mayhem. Tara could even come by some nights to teach the girls the ways of vampires so they'd have a jump on them in a real-life situation. Plus, the female psyche needs a level of calm for true intuition to kick in." Damali yanked open the car door. "No!"

A Jeep engine sent a panic attack through her. She jumped into her Hummer and started the engine, looking in the rearview mirror. Too late. Inez was back, had spotted her, and was waving at her. "Shit!" She slapped the steering wheel, but then smiled brightly and waved at Inez. They had pulled out the big guns—old-school guilt. Now how was she gonna tell her best girl no?

Inez's Jeep pulled up next to Damali's Hummer. Music was blasting from the stereo and Inez leaned across her seat to yell out her window to Damali.

"Hey, girl!" Inez said laughing. "Where you going?"

"I, uh, was just gonna pop into town, see if I could pick up a bottle of wine, or something." Damali lifted her ponytail off her neck to allow the air to cool her skin. "Did anybody at the house fill you in on what's been going on?"

"No, girl. Carlos was in some meditative trance, Rider was out there with Mike, blowing shit up in the yard, everybody else told me to go ask you, since the old heads were on an errand. So, here I am!" Inez turned off her engine and jumped down out of her Jeep. "I'll ride shotgun," she said without waiting for Damali to respond. "But, I'ma tell you now, Carlos don't need no more alcohol in his system. Brother was tore up!"

"The wine is for me," Damali said flatly.

"Then, girl, why ain't you say so?" Inez said, oblivious to her mood. "Let's go."

She knew Inez well enough not to immediately launch into a discussion of pure terror right off the bat. Her girlfriend would freak, go hysterical, so she had to deliver the news calmly. Besides, she remembered what it was like coming off the natural high of a fantastic getaway with the man she loved. Damali sighed; a wave of sad memory washed through her.

Damali gripped the steering wheel so tightly that her knuckles were beginning to lose color. Inez immediately reached for her radio, turned it on, and then clicked it over to accept a CD.

"Chile, you can't get nothing out here but country western. I swear!" Inez fished in her oversize Louis Vuitton purse, found her CD case, and began flipping through selections. "Girl, we need some riding music." Inez laughed and pushed a CD into Damali's dashboard. Her head began bopping the moment the equipment ate the disc. "Awwww, yeah, get back, get back, you don't know me like that!"

Damali floored the gas petal, but didn't say a word. Her jaws were locked so tight she thought she'd chip a tooth. Inez's effervescent mood was turning hers darker. She said a mental prayer, *Please, God, don't let this chile start telling me nothing I don't need to hear.*

"Girl, I'm so glad I caught you before you rolled," Inez said, slapping Damali's arm and giggling. "I have the *scoop* for you."

Damali glanced up at the ceiling. Oh, so God had a sense of humor this morning. Fine. "Girl, what's been going on? How was your trip to Houston?" Damali let her breath out slowly and put a lilt in her voice. It wasn't Inez's fault, but she wasn't feeling the drama right now.

"Listen," Inez said, looking around as though there could possibly be anyone else in the car. "I understand why you couldn't ever let me know how you was livin', or introduce me to none of your brothers . . . but *girl.*"

"TMI," Damali said laughing. "Too much information before you even get started, okay. Don't tell me nothing about—"

"Oh, Damali, I have to tell somebody or I'm gonna bust. He is soooo nice," Inez said and swooned in her seat.

"Yeah, Mike is cool people, girl. A gem, for real."

Inez nodded emphatically. "He's real deep, ya know. Real old school, laid-back, and a gentleman."

Damali couldn't disagree and that much she could talk to Inez about, so she relaxed. "Yeah . . . a big old teddy bear with a soft heart. Once he takes to you, that's it. You're his family." Damali's words came out gently as the wind whipped through the vehicle. The beauty of the colors around them sent her mind a million miles away. Why was she running from these people? "But, don't let that big teddy-bear vibe fool you," Damali added with a laugh to jettison the despair. "Mike is the last person you want on your ass if you cross him."

Inez laughed and kept bop-time with the music. "Brother is scary strong, girl!"

"But gentle—just don't be no vamp or he'll blow your ass up." Damali laughed and shook her head.

Inez gaped at her, hanging on every word with the pride of ownership emblazoned on her face. Damali smiled wider, yeah, it was all good. She'd let Inez vent and would then fill her in. The mood she'd been in was beginning to lighten and she was suddenly glad Inez had come along for the ride. Where was she going, really, other than away from her own home that had just been built? Crazy.

"I saw him sucker punch a werewolf, once, coming at him full charge. Was like in the cartoons," Damali said with sisterly pride, laughter becoming a tonic throughout her system. "The mug stopped, shook its head, like yada, yada, yada, and Rider got him, single shell. But it was Mike's swinging wild, cinder-block hit that slowed that sucker down."

"Yeah . . ." Inez said with a breathy sigh. "I've been scared of stuff all my life, girl, but when that big tree trunk steps in front of me I know everything is gonna be all right." Inez leaned in closer to Damali. "He likes kids. . . . I showed him my boo and everything, and he carries her picture in his wallet now—can you get to that? Her own daddy don't even do that. This is the craziest life—I mean, I never expected my life to turn out like this, much less meet somebody like him under these circumstances . . . but . . . D . . . Lawd, chile . . ."

Damali started humming to the next cut. This is where the conversation was about to take a dangerous turn. She was one beat away from shouting, *la, la, la, la, la—I can't hear you.* "Yeah, Mike loves kids," Damali said as a diversion. Yup, go back to basics, family, and very generic topics— *please.* "Worked with a lot of kids from the neighborhoods through his church, rec centers, schooling the little knuckleheads, and I don't imagine, even with a nine in their hands, too many were about to start no mess with Big Mike. Like I said, he's the last person you wanna step wrong to and have on your ass."

"Correction, girl," Inez said with a giggle. "If anybody is gonna be on your ass . . . daaaayum!"

"See, now!" Damali said, laughing and turning up the music volume. "I do not need to know that."

"But, D—"

"La, la, la, la, la—I can't hear you!"

"But, oh, my God!"

"No, do *not* tell me no mess—that's my brother!"

"I know, girl, and we was cool for all them months, got to know each other first, 'cause I had to calm down from trippin' so hard about having to put my baby girl somewhere safe and the fact that there *were* actually demons, and shit, and plus, had to learn how to fight, and, but then, D, last night—"

"Stop!" Damali shouted, turning up the car stereo so loud that the button wouldn't click to the next level.

Inez laughed hard and turned it down. "For real, what had happened was—"

"Not listening, glad y'all are in love, TMI, not my business, uh-huh, not my business, it's your birthday, whateva, I ain't listenin', 'cause it's my brutha, shut up, 'cause you my sistah, whoop, whoop—"

"Girl, you crazy!" Inez laughed so hard that her head nearly collided with the dashboard. "Stop!"

"You stop, and I'll stop." Damali wiped her eyes still laughing and tried to focus on the road. "We're going in here, get some licka, and go home. I don't wanna hear no mo', got it?"

"Girl, neva in my life have I seen fourteen—"

"La, la, la, la, la, I am *not* hearing you!"

Inez laughed as she watched Damali literally run from her through the store aisles. Yeah . . . maybe Damali was right. Some of this she couldn't tell another living soul. She was so

happy she was about to burst, and had to keep telling the little butterflies in her belly just to calm down and be cool. But
every time she thought about her man, a new wide smile
flashed across her face.

She leaned against a shelf, almost crushing the snacks,
but damn, a sister was too content. The brother moved real
slow, methodical, they way he stripped off his shirt—she
could still see it in her mind. Dark Hershey's chocolate, that
was the color of his skin . . . with a chest and abdomen cut
so righteous she had actually covered her mouth. She closed
her eyes and smiled, remembering the lopsided grin he gave
her when she'd done that . . . and the way he never lost eye
contact with her as he undid his pants and stripped them off,
causing her to gasp in awe.

Inez wrapped her arms around herself. Damali needed to
hurry up, she had to get home. What was she thinking out
here shopping with her girl, when her six-foot-eight pleasure
giver was back at the house? They was girlz, and all, but
shoot. Especially the way his big ole country hands could
cover her entire behind like he was palming a basketball . . .
legs like tree trunks, and how he had so much rod she had to
sit on his lap or get split, have mercy!

All she could think about was how he was strong enough
to actually stand up . . . *stand up*—and walk with her, talking yang in her ear, asking her what she wanted while holding her heavy ass four feet off the floor . . . neva missing a
stroke—the man could *wurk*. In his arms she felt like the
prettiest, thinnest, tiniest little thing, and she'd never felt like
that in her life . . . told her the sweetest things, made her cry
it felt so good.

She was getting the chills just thinking about those arms
of his, the way the muscles stood up in them she could literally see each strand while he'd held her, and his back . . .
and shoulders, and his butt, Lawd save her. Then, before the
night was over, she'd finally figured out how to make him
holla and lose his mind. It had been a pure victory to take

him there, to make him stop acting like she was made of glass, and stop whispering all low thunder and cut the natural fool. She'd felt like a queen. Mike was *her* man. That's what he'd told her. Called her baby . . . *suga*. Inez shivered.

"D, you wanna hurry up getting that wine, girl?" Inez called out, swallowing hard.

Damali glanced at Inez and hastened her steps away from her girlfriend. No, she was not hearing any of it, and the vibe coming off of Inez had enough static charge in it to make her hair stand up. Damali almost ran into the adjacent aisle trying to mentally blot out the too graphic images of her big brother.

But Inez followed her around the store like a stalker. Every aisle Damali went into, Inez was right on her heels. Her best girl was harder to shake than the press. Each time she tried to tell her some amazing attribute of her brother, Damali held up her hand and made a guttural sound. People in the packaged goods store must have thought she had some type of disability, because her responses to Inez were a series of *up, ot, ut, hupp, hut,* and *nopes* with her hand jerking up every five seconds, which only made Inez laugh and pursue her harder.

"Okay, okay, okay," Inez said, teasing her in a forlorn voice. "But if I can't tell my best girl about the best time I've ever had in my life, then who can I tell?"

"Tell Jesus," Damali said, laughing harder. "Take it to the cross," she said, singing the old spiritual through the aisles.

"Girl, you crazy? This I cannot take to *noooobody,* especially not Him!"

"Then, there you have it. Your secret is safe between *A* and *B,* that would be you and Mike, and I'ma *C* my way out of it."

"You wrong, girl."

"It is not wrong for me to preserve my sanity," Damali fussed, putting two bottles of champagne and a merlot on the counter. She eyed the cashier skeptically, and slid her cash across the counter, not touching his hand. Then she ignored his offended scowl and discreetly waited until he put her cash down and slid it back toward her, hoping Inez didn't notice as she collected her change and rattled on with her complaint.

"Here's the thing, 'Nez. I do not ever want to be sitting across from y'all at dinner in the compound and not be able to look my brother in the eye because I know too much of his business. So, on this one, spare me the details."

"Aw'right, aw'right, aw'right, I get your point." Inez sighed but her smile was still bright. "You happy, though?"

"Yeah, I'm happy," Damali muttered, as the cashier rung up Inez's purchase. "Wait. Let me get that," she added quickly, as Inez was about to place cash in the guy's hand. Nobody needed to touch anybody, especially in this potentially infected town.

"*That* does *not* sound like happy." Inez's hands went to her hips.

Damali watched the cashier load her bottles into a bag. "My happy isn't going to sound like yours, because yours is brand spanking new. What you hear is mellow happy. Been-to-Hell-and-back-and-I'm-okay-with-the-situation happy. There's a difference, which is not to be confused with unhappy."

Inez fell silent for a moment and Damali clasped the verbal respite and hung on to it. She marched out of the store with purpose and looked down the strip of small shops. It wasn't such a bad town. Decent people all just trying to live. The reservation retail operation was sparse, but farther away toward the open tourist areas, there were a reasonable amount of things to do. She prayed the demon had visited only her.

"Y'all had a fight?"

Damali climbed into the Hummer and started the engine.

"He didn't stay last night, did he?"

Damali sighed. "No. And it wasn't a fight, just a disagreement. He hates this place; it's so different from L.A. But we all know why we have to be here, so, sometimes you just have to make the best of the hand you're dealt."

"He'll come around, girl."

"Yeah," Damali said, pulling away from the curb.

"You know, he ain't even trying to get with Juanita no more, if that's what you're worried about."

"I'm not worried about no damned Juanita."

Inez smiled and riffled through her purse for a new CD. "Cool, 'cause her and Jose got that on lock."

"Good." More information that she didn't wanna know. Damali let her breath out hard and checked the rearview mirror as she pulled out.

"You know . . . maybe me and Mike and you and Carlos could go hang out sometime?"

Damali kept her eyes forward on the road and her mouth shut.

"I mean, after you guys patch things up, have some *alone* time, maybe we could fall by, open up some wine—I'll cook, watch some movies, or go find a nightspot? You've got an extra bedroom over there, right?"

She wasn't exactly sure where the new spike of irritation was coming from, but it made her ears and face hot. "Yeah, girl," she finally muttered. "Maybe we can do that."

"You all right?" Inez asked, finally catching on to the tension in Damali's voice.

"No," Damali replied. It was time to spill the beans.

"What happened?" Inez clicked off the music. "Y'all really fell out this time, didn't you?"

"When we get back to the house, I'll fill you in. But I had a little visit from an old demon, but I smoked his ass."

Inez covered her mouth. "Gurl! No! Was Carlos there?"

"No. He was out cold over at the family house."

"Get outta here!" Inez folded her arms and shook her head. "No wonder you're salty. Chile, if I had been by myself when that mess popped outta nowhere on me, I don't know what I would have done."

"That's why, all fun nights notwithstanding," Damali said, keeping her eyes on the road, "you have to learn to protect yourself. One night, Mike might not be there—not because he's doing anything wrong, he just might not physically be there when something crazy happens." Damali let her breath out in a rush. "So, you have to know what to do and can't freak out."

Inez nodded and tossed her braids over her shoulders. "I'm just glad he was there when the mess rolled up on us in Houston. Girl, if it wasn't for him, I'd—"

Damali slammed on the brakes and pulled over to the curb. "What happened in Houston?"

"Chile, don't worry. We were out in the park, had the baby with us, and you know Mike . . . easygoing, but he heard something. Told me and boo to get in the car. So, we did. But I saw him tilt his head, roll his shoulders, and walk toward the trees. I was hollering for him to just get in the car, and he told me to put up the damned windows. Wasn't nothing messing with his woman and her kid while he was around."

Inez fanned her face, excitement glinting in her eyes. "He is such a gentleman, all that . . . something pushed him. I couldn't see it all the way. But he body-slammed whatever it was to the ground and stomped it so bad all it left was a black puddle. Then it was gone." Inez shrugged. "He told me that, in our line of work, things tend to seek us out, but it was handled. After I saw him do that . . . girl, once we got the baby back to Mom's, hugged everybody good-bye and kissed the baby, I had to slip out to the hotel with him. That was some heroic shit, D. I can't explain it, but it turned me on . . . like I've never felt. Does that make sense?"

Damali nodded, nearly hyperventilating. "Did he tell you what it looked like?"

"He didn't want to scare me . . . but you know me. I *had* to know. So I bugged him till he told me. Said it was a revenge demon. Head half blown off, chest and stomach all opened, talking shit about getting me back as it disappeared—just to mess with Mike's mind." Inez closed her eyes and hugged herself. "Girl," she whispered. "That's when he pulled me into his strong arms and told me he'd never let anything happen to me or my baby girl . . . or he would die trying. For the first time in my life, being there with him, I wasn't afraid. After that, forgedaboutit. We made love so hard I thought the front desk would call the police." Inez opened her eyes. "You've been there, right? I'ma marry this man, girl. He's the one."

Tears slowly filled Damali's eyes and her hand slowly went to Inez's face to cup her cheek. Her best girlfriend . . . her dear, honorable brother, Big Mike, and every single person they had touched . . . even Inez's baby, her mom, plus every Guardian that Mike pulled into a big bear hug when he got back—her entire world had been infected.

CHAPTER SEVEN

The Guardians who were still in the house sat down slowly as Damali spoke in gentle, soft tones. J.L., Krissy, Dan, and Bobby stared at her, unblinking. Big Mike folded his arms and drew in shuddering breaths, then pulled Inez into an embrace as silent tears streamed down her face. Rider kept his chin up and his gaze fastened to the window as he dragged on a cigarette. Jose stared at his fist—he had given a welcome-home pound to Mike—then glanced at Juanita, who simply appeared numb. Carlos leaned his head back on the doorframe and closed his eyes.

"Marlene and Shabazz, Marjorie and Berkfield, are the only ones, besides me and Carlos, who aren't infected," Damali said quietly. "But, there's no way they won't be, eventually." Her gaze drifted out of the window, as she spoke. "I've already mentally alerted Mar, and she's breaking it to Marjorie and Richard as we speak." But, in truth, how was she going to split up the team? Human touch was so automatic, such a reflex that sooner or later, when someone is in tears, when food was being served . . .

Father Patrick's voice came through the speaker in heavy, fatigued jags. "All of us have been infected, too, Damali. We're just finding out that the only cleric available to come to your team for assistance is Monk Lin. The rest of us are quarantined."

"Then don't send him here," Carlos said, pushing off from the doorframe. "The man is safe, and—"

"He's the only one among us who has not been fully

compromised. Therefore, his judgment is sound. He is seasoned, his many issues are resolved. There is not much within him for the darkness to dredge from his soul to turn his mind. His code is to serve; his life is one of selfless commitment to humankind. There is nowhere to hide from this, nowhere to run. He will accompany you to wherever you must go."

"What do you suggest, Father? Beyond the obvious," Carlos said calmly, not opening his eyes. "We can't stay here quarantined if we have to move around the world to find the Chairman and Lilith. We're all walking biohazards. Every hotel we check into, restaurant we eat at, plane we fly on, limo we take, we're potentially bumping people in airports, train stations . . . How do we move without spreading this shit?"

"Live your lives as normally as you can and find the antidote . . . close the portals. Every human being may potentially be already infected; it could be dormant and resident everywhere worldwide. That's the issue; we don't know, because they have been moving about as you indicated."

"Then why don't we do this all together, Father, one last time, like old times?" Carlos asked, beginning to pace. "If it doesn't matter now that this shit spread, then, what difference will it make if we're all strapped and go out in a blaze as one?"

"Because," the elderly cleric said, his voice a shaky murmur, "those of us affected earlier are already beginning to show deteriorating signs of change."

Damali and Carlos stared at each other as the mute team passed terror-stricken glances.

"We're sending you an unaffected spiritual warrior . . . who, by the time he reaches you, may have been bumped or touched just handing his plane ticket to someone. It doesn't matter. But for the moment, he's the one that is strongest."

"How much time we talking, Father?" Rider asked, looking at Damali.

"Your team has maybe thirty days until it begins to implode like all the others. We aren't concerned any longer about the spread—that's imminent, whether your team does it, or it happens organically from others. What has to happen is you all must work quickly while you have time and your minds are still functioning correctly. Stay steeped in prayer; if you can find the book, all the better. That way, if any of us must be put down . . . then at least we'll know we'll see each other one day in Heaven."

"My baby girl," Inez said through a hard swallow. "My momma . . ." Her voice trailed off with a thick, stifled sob.

"Oh, God, 'Nez," Mike whispered, holding her tighter and rubbing her back. "I didn't know I was a carrier, I was just trying to—"

"It wasn't your fault, man," Rider said, and stood. "Wasn't nobody's fault."

"Listen to Rider," Father Patrick replied in a gentle voice.

"We'll find the book and the antidote. We'll take Lilith's head off her shoulders, trust me," Damali said, her hardened gaze roving the team. "My people ain't going out like this."

Carlos nodded. "Not on our watch."

As soon as her defeated team waved good-bye, Damali flipped open her cell phone. She had walked out of the house so upset that she hadn't even spoken to Carlos. Motion had jettisoned her through the door. The need for head space to think, develop a strategy, and get in touch with her Neteru Queens had put rigid purpose into every footfall. She had blindly gotten into the car, fired up the engine, and had driven off, heading back to her house. The blackened spot in her yard had been her destination. She had to get more info. Carlos's mind was still murky and polluted with alcohol residue. A mind lock was impossible. Her fingers hit speed dial.

The first time she placed the call, it went right to Carlos's voice mail. She tried again, even though the family house was right down the road, but that was the *last* place she wanted to be. She knew what would happen. Going there was like getting trapped in quicksand. She couldn't stand around consoling people or wringing her hands. This man's system needed to be purged, he had to be clear—they had work to do. On the third attempt, he answered.

"Be ready in twenty minutes and pack a bag. I'll meet you by the side of the road."

"I know this sounds crazy, but I don't feel so good, D, no bullshit. But give me a half hour, and I'll be ready."

"Peace." She flipped her cell phone closed and leaned back against the seat, gripping the wheel.

Carlos stood on the side of the road away from the house, wearing a faded blue shirt, old jeans, scuffed-up Tims, and dark shades, looking like a bewildered hitchhiker. All Damali did was lean over and open the passenger side door. He jumped into her Hummer, dropped his duffel bag at his feet, and closed his eyes.

"We need to be one team, gotta lead this with authority," Damali announced in a sharp tone. "There's too much at stake for you not to be straight. Your system has to be righteous and on fire. So, you're coming with me so we can do this by the book. Mar is gonna be holding down the fort at the house, as soon as she and 'Bazz get back."

"I think I'm gonna throw up," he said, shielding the sun from his eyes beyond his dark glasses.

She surveyed his color. The man was practically gray. Served his dumb ass right. Damali pulled away from the side of the road and drove back to her house. "Did you eat anything today?"

Carlos shook his head no. "Don't mention food."

She was beyond through.

Damali turned off her motor with attitude and jumped out of the car. She rounded it, flung open the passenger-side door, and stepped back, arms folded. "If you're gonna barf, do it in the dirt, not on my leather interior."

Carlos nodded, leaned over, and obliged her.

"I've got mouthwash, toothpaste, hot water, and towels

inside. Some roadie. Damn." She strode ahead of him, swinging open the screen and inside steel door so hard that both slammed.

This was why she wasn't trying to get married. At a time like this, and he was sick from overindulging with his boy? For better or for worse—yeah, she could tolerate vampire status as worse, more so than general-purpose man-stupid. Being a vampire was a condition, like a disease, but this mess didn't make no sense! For richer or poorer—hell, she'd gone out with this fool when he was scuffling in East L.A. and she didn't have a dime, and was happier. Forsaking all others—shit, she'd only been with him. Till death do you part—shoot, she stayed with his behind even after he'd died, and even slept with him, so whateva. He had some nerve challenging her commitment. And this yang wasn't how he needed to be handling his business.

Damali yanked down fresh towels, an unopened toothbrush, and a bottle of mouthwash from the linen closet and thrust it at Carlos as he slowly came down the hall.

"Thanks, baby. I really appreciate this."

She didn't say a word as she watched him meander to the bathroom and begin stripping off his clothes. No, no, no, see, this was another reason why she wasn't even trying to get married. Yeah, when it was all romantic in the castle, it sounded good. But the old dolls were right. Once everyday reality hit, and all the magic was gone, the wife would be the one picking up funky-drunk clothes and whatnot, when there were *serious* matters at hand. Uh-uh. And, yeah, they had money, but maid service wasn't an option. It wasn't like they could just hire some innocent lady to come in daily to sweep up, pick up, dust and polish around weapons, and do toilets with the undercover lifestyle they lived. She hadn't been able to do that in L.A. when they did have a compound.

All this bullshit, when they had really tough situations to attend to? And he had been whining about not liking his fate? She'd give her blade arm to go back to the old compound days of just fighting regular demons, and being able to quell a night-crawler disturbance by the easy swing of a sword.

He didn't like the old mundane arrangement? Everybody had a round of chores—but as a wife, she knew how the thing would go! Just like all of a sudden, Big Mike had been acting like his legs were broken now that Inez was putting plates in front of him and doing his dishes. The new terror at hand would change all that, she bet. Like how Shabazz took liberties with Marlene, and Berkfield was the worst offender of them all. Yeah, everybody just got a wake-up call.

Before this recent serious turn of events, all Jose had to do was look toward the fridge, and Juanita had a beer in hand, dashing in his direction . . . and poor Krissy had been spoiling J.L. rotten. *That's* why she had to get the *hell* out of that house. The dynamic had changed. It was like sex made people stooopid! All bullshit aside, when it came down to a firefight, and it got real, wasn't no gender in the game—so why in the hell should it be all rosy-cozy during so-called normal hours of operation? The only ones who had sense were the brothers who weren't getting any. Maybe the clerics in the cloister had the right idea.

Damali cringed as she heard Carlos upchuck again. For a minute she wished he could still wave his hand, snap his fingers, and change his environment. Cleaning the toilet behind some man was not her role as the Neteru, and the wife gig wasn't all that it was cracked up to be. No, why trade in a perfectly reasonable title to be a babysitter, nursemaid, chambermaid, and cook? There were no words. She'd hand his ass a mop, bucket, sponge, and some Lysol and be done with it.

Damali went outside and leaned against the deck rail. Some first weekend alone. All because she'd held her ground, and was sick of his tight jaws, bad vibes, and attitudes for the past several months, he gone and gotten himself totaled? Right now he was useless.

She'd been very understanding, allowing him to grieve,

go through all the changes necessary, readjust to the group situation. She'd practically kissed his behind to keep the peace. But did that matter? No. He'd allowed Yonnie to take him out and get him wasted like that, with so much pending? Oh, so how was he gonna act when they had a really big fight? The Armageddon was about to kick off any day now; in fact, it might have already started. Carlos had to be razor sharp, and ready to rumble when the going got tough. That was what was panfrying her brain.

What he'd been sulking about had been relatively minor, truth be told. But was this how it was gonna be? What had possessed her to go get that man? She could have handled this as team leader herself. The next time, if there was a next time for her to feel compassion toward a dumb bastard, she'd kick herself first.

"You okay?" she yelled back into the house.

"Yeah," she heard him yell back.

"Whateva," she muttered and stared out at the canyon.

The late afternoon sun had begun to color the horizon burnt orange and deep, pastel rose. Thick cumulus cloud formations soaked in the hues within a shocking blue sky.

"What am I doing out here on Indian reservation lands?" she whispered, briefly closing her eyes. "I should be staking Lilith right now in whatever hole she slid into."

Damali opened her eyes, expecting to see the same landscape before her, but instead, she was looking at herself earlier that morning.

It was disorienting and fascinating as she stared back up to the deck from a bird's-eye vantage point. She saw herself holding a mug of tea, nursing it slowly, Jose's blanket around her shoulders, the fragrant steam curling up from the mug under her nose. The surreal blended with the real as she remained still and watched. Then the steam turned dark and angry, became billowing black smoke that entered her nostrils, violating them, knocking her head back . . . and when her head lowered again to take another sip, her eyes were not her own.

"D, you got a bucket?"

Damali snapped out of the vision and placed her hand over her heart. "Yeah, I got it," she yelled back, and began to run toward the door.

Something definitely wasn't right. These bouts of rage, weird energy, even the feelings she'd had while Jose was with her . . . and his very sensual dance down the line of propriety. No. Something wasn't right. She knew she'd been affected. Maybe Carlos had been, too. She had to lay off the rage at him, become centered as one. Father Patrick tried to warn her, warn them all, but it was such a very subtle change that it was hard to know what was justified and real, and what was not.

When she entered the kitchen, Carlos was there, standing in the archway to the hall with a towel wrapped around his waist. His well-sculpted body was damp, and she watched rivulets of water course down him. What disturbed her was that there was no attraction whatsoever. Even sick with a hangover, the man was fine, and he was hers, and they loved each other, but she was nearly revolted. Instead of continuing to stare at him, she quickly bent and began hunting under the sink for cleaning aids.

"I got it, D. It's pretty nasty. Been cleaning up all day."

"Why don't you go lie down, and let me do it. You sure you're all right?"

"I haven't been able to keep anything down, much less smell food. Maybe I've got the bug on top of everything else we're dealing with . . . I've been out drinking before, but I can't ever remember feeling like this."

"Baby, go lie down. I'll get the bathroom," she said quietly, and gathered up a sponge and disinfectant.

The flu? It was May. Carlos had a constitution of iron. So did the rest of the squad. And his statement didn't make sense. *The flu?* After what they'd just been told? Living in close quarters, if it was something communicable like that, then everybody should have been feeling under the weather. But he'd passed Marlene's inspection . . . hers, too, as far as

any traces of returning vampirism was concerned. No. This
was so much more. The infection. Damali watched him walk
down the hall, and she glanced at the bathroom mirror as he
passed it. He still had a reflection. If the dark energy was affecting him, then the only thing that should be coming back
would be the vamp virus. Strange.

Father Patrick had given him the once-over thoroughly
before being called back to Rome. Imam Asula had seen him
before Mecca requested his presence. Monk Lin had also
done his divination on Carlos before heading back to Tibet,
and Rabbi Zeitloff said things were cool before he took off
for Israel. The ground they were on was hallowed, Yonnie
didn't nick him . . . It was daylight, but Carlos was puking
up his guts. There was only one explanation.

Damali screwed up her face as she went into the bathroom. She made a yucky pile with Carlos's cast-off clothes,
which were destined for a garbage bag, and then the laundry.
She peered into the toilet and at the splatter where some of
the refuse had missed. Green bile confronted her, but that
made sense. If the man hadn't eaten all day, and had been
projectile vomiting all day, then that would be the only thing
left in his system. But it wasn't the sight, it was the smell.

She covered her nose and mouth with her hand and
opened the window. Naw . . . she'd lived with men long
enough, and had seen them come in after a binge, especially
Rider—who didn't lose his lunch like this, and it *never*
smelled so foul.

All of her Neteru attributes kicked in and surrounded the
stimuli. She opened her third eye and looked at the mess.
Within the dark, green slurry were thin threads of blackness,
almost like filaments running through it. She edged closer
and put out her hand, and allowed her palm to hover over the
nastiness. Heat. Serious heat was wafting up from the splatter. She uncovered her nose. The smell almost made her dry
heave. But it wasn't sulfur. It was something worse, almost
metallic . . . like burning metal, aluminum. Gooseflesh rose

to her arms. Mentally, she replayed the sound of his distress. A high-pitched whine was buried in the guttural sounds as he'd vomited . . . "Just like the tea kettle," she whispered.

Damali hurriedly cleaned up the mess and balled up his clothes with the sponge, careful not to touch any of the bodily waste. She ditched it in a white kitchen trash bag, and went into her cabinets, pulling down the stash of real house-cleaning aids that Marlene had left; holy water and purified sea salt, and then went to the front yard.

She flung the bag down on the dirt next to where Carlos had left another splatter of bile. Carefully, she uncorked the bottle and began dousing the site, and then flung salt on top of that. Instantly, black smoke billowed up from the spot on the ground where he'd thrown up; a small gap in the earth groaned open, and sucked into itself, taking the bag of clothes with it.

"Oh, shit!" Damali jumped back and flung purified salt at what had disappeared. The ground shuddered, and then the spot covered over with dead grass again, as though nothing had ever been disturbed. She ran into the house, added anointing oil to her arsenal, and dashed toward the bedroom. He was a Neteru. He was supposed to be immune, not a carrier!

Carlos was resting on his side, under Jose's blanket, shuddering and beginning to convulse.

"D, baby, I'm sorry I'm so sick."

"Carlos, listen to me," she said quickly, brandishing her bottles. "I don't know where Mar is right now, and I'm gonna call her again, okay? This isn't a hangover."

He peered at the sun. "Close the drapes? I feel like shit."

"No, you need the sun," she said, and went to his side. In a flash she had put oil on her fingers and then touched them to his forehead.

Immediately, he flung off the blanket, sweat forming on his brow and then coating his chest and abdomen.

"It's so fuckin' hot in here—I'm flashing hot and cold, can't get comfortable, can't—"

"Shhh . . . be still," she said, dropping salt around the edge of the bed as she walked and quietly prayed. She watched him slowly begin to stop shivering as the room darkened. Daylight was waning and she circled the bed with liberal splashes of holy water, and removed Jose's blanket from him, replacing it with her duvet.

Unsure of what had just transpired, she knew enough to know that Jose's grandfather's blanket held some serious shaman charge. Whatever was going on with that, it was not the thing to have covering Carlos, until they were all sure what they were dealing with and how it would individually manifest. She watched him slip off into a mild slumber as his body relaxed, his temperature normalized, and the shivers abated. She stroked his mussed hair and anointed his forehead again with oil, and then kissed his temple.

Finding the night-light by the wall switch, she clicked it on and stood by the door, watching the sun finally go down and disappear. After what felt like forever, Carlos stirred. It had only been a half hour, but while one is hoping and praying, thirty minutes might as well be thirty years.

"Hey, baby," he said, opening his eyes slowly and rolling over to face her. "You have my word, I'm never going out drinking with my boy like that again. I swear."

"I believe you," she said, her voice devoid of emotion. Panic had made her eerily calm. "What did you drink when you were with Yonnie?"

"I told you last night. Too many vodka martinis and a bottle and a half of Remy to chase it."

Damali remained fixed in her position against the doorframe. "Did he put any color in your glass?"

Carlos sat up slowly. "No. Why?"

"Before we knew what we know, we'd relaxed and were all using cell phones lately, since we'd mistakenly believed there'd been no real threat for months. But we weren't dealing with the fact that the Chairman is still out there, and we know we haven't heard the last from Lilith. So, I'm opening my third eye, and you're going to open yours, right now," she said too calmly. "Then, I'm going to ask you again. Did Yonnie put any color in your drink?"

"Okay, okay, okay," Carlos said with a weary sigh. "He didn't, but for a second, I sorta had a relapse and asked him for a hit." He stared at her intensely. "But my boy had my back, and told me no. That's when he brought me home to you. All right? Satisfied?"

He pushed himself to the edge of the bed with effort when she didn't reply, and stood, seeming indignant.

"I want to ask you another question—because I'm worried."

"Yeah, all right," Carlos grumbled.

"Have you ever considered what just *thinking* about a blood hit could do to a Neteru?" She kept her voice calm, even, and very psychiatric. "You're about to go into the male version of my ripening. That is a very powerful transitional time. If you are unclear, in any way, about what your leanings are, you could do metaphysical damage to your gifts . . . especially with the dark energies that are polluting our topside environment."

Damali pushed away from the wall and entered the room. Yonnie making a pass at her, Jose's quiet way of sending her an open invitation, Tara's near fang drop, every strange behavior within her team family slammed into Damali's brain at once.

She stared at Carlos. Her gaze was unwavering, but her voice was tender. "Baby, I know this whole Arizona thing isn't you. Honestly, it isn't me. All of it has shredded everyone's nerves. I'm not trying to push you away. I just needed space. We have to work on this big problem together. One unit. Really, what we both need, once we conquer this together, are environments suited to us, not this training camp mess that we're dealing with now. We are supposed to be out in the world, but not of it, and unafraid, dealing—not sequestered. But, until we just learned about the new threat, all I was trying to do was make sure the others could fly . . . It's like, I had this sense that something crazy was on the way. It had been giving me nightmares for months. Now I know why. Do you understand?"

He nodded. "I know. Intellectually, I know," he said, tightening the towel around his waist. "Some days, I could be really cool with the new powers, or the lack thereof. I could intellectually deal with you running the show, until I could step up and we could do this thing side by side, as equals. I could deal with being equals." He shook his head and set his jaw hard. "But being less than that around you is fucking me up. I ain't gonna lie. Some days, I'm just so damned mad, and I don't know why."

Carlos looked at her in the dim light, his eyes searching hers. "It's so much responsibility, D. When my brother and my boyz died, then it was just me and you. For some crazy reason, I could deal with that. But, now I'm tight with a big family, and I'm a nervous wreck half the time, worrying about the kids, worrying about Mom Mar, Marj, my brothers . . . like, if any of them go down, I'd wig. And then they all got infected. My worst nightmare came true. I couldn't do shit about it, couldn't just go handle this shit in a cloud of black smoke and save them all from this heartache." He stared at a point on the wall and continued. "Did you see Mike's face when he knew he'd brought the infection home?"

Carlos shook his head. "The man was doing the right thing," he whispered. "He'd beat down a demon, saved his woman and her baby, and made love to her—which is gonna kill her. Then came home the conquering hero and slapped everybody in the house a high five. Tell me how to wrap my brain around that, Damali? All I keep thinking is, if I was still a Council-level vamp, I could be the team's front line of defense, walk back into Hell, and go get this shit right. At least I could go get y'all some decent information. North America was my zone, girl. I'd know what was going down on American soil before the fucking government, believe that. I hate this new shit, D."

She came to him and placed her hand over the brand scar he'd always wear on his chest. "I know. It is a lot of responsibility, a lot of weight to love all those people. But that's part of being a family, baby. Love is risk. The harder you love, the greater the risk, but I wouldn't want to go through life without having experienced that."

His arms enfolded her and her head found his shoulder.

"The thing I love about you so much is, you *would* walk into Hell to make it all right, if you could," she whispered. "But your role has changed, baby. You have to stop looking backward. We have a month, maybe, and time is our enemy. I know you love every single soul on the team, but you can't play God. Neither can I."

"But it's more than that. I feel connected to them beyond words—like they're my skin. And, I find myself hardly able to watch the news, because when somebody is shot, some kid is killed, some part of the world blows up, I live with the sadness for days. I never used to be like that, or care like that, and it feels . . . it feels . . ."

"Like the weight of the world is on your shoulders?"

She smiled. He nodded and closed his eyes.

"Yes. That's *exactly* what it feels like."

"And I bet you get really pissed off when you see injustice and corruption." She kissed his cheek as his head found the crook of her shoulder.

"Oh, baby," he murmured against her neck as his arms enfolded her tighter. "I can't do this . . . be squeaky clean, always making the right choice, always answering the call to arms for some crazy shit in the world that's bigger than all of us."

She rubbed his back. "This shit is scarier than being a vampire?"

"Most definitely," he said with a sigh. "It was go for self. They was ruthless, I was ruthless, what-the-fuck-eva, wasn't no friends in the game. That shit was easy. The only person they could take as a hostage that woulda made me slow my roll was you—and since you can hold your own, hey. But now. Damn."

She nodded and hugged him harder. "You're gonna be all right. We're gonna do this thing."

He lifted his head and stared at her, his eyes glistening in the semidarkness. "That's what I'm afraid of," he said quietly. "You were never ruthless. You never played games to the bone. Never lived some of what I lived. That's as much a part of me as this new thing I am. There's a part of me that misses the adrenaline rush of rolling like that . . . and the power. You never sat on a throne, and you cannot know what it is till you've done it."

She listened to his quiet confession without judgment, applying the balm of healing through silent understanding. "Baby, you'll integrate all of that over time, after we get through this major job we've gotta do. Like I've told you before, you have to take all of that cunning, and all of that master-of-the-game drama you have inside you, and use it for the good. If the Light spared you with this madness developing, then they must have had a higher purpose for you. They don't make mistakes and do things by accident, but they will use an accident that has occurred in the most awesome ways."

"You keep telling me that, and I keep hearing that, but . . . y'all don't really know what goes on inside my head sometimes."

He gave her a sly smile, followed by a deep kiss. "Like, I miss this for instance," he said, kissing her neck and making her chuckle. "And I miss that, for instance," he murmured, fondling her backside. Then he outstretched his arm and snapped, and looked over his shoulder and sighed. "And I damned sure miss being able to change a room to go with my mood." He chuckled sadly. "Right about through here, there should be torches in the joint, you naked and sprawled in the center of my bed, in my lair; then I could get creative. Then I'd let you recover while I took underground limo service and work a deal to shut down the slime creeping out of the realms . . . then I'd come back before dawn, and, you know . . . we'd celebrate." He shook his head. "I don't do Navajo prints, okaaay."

She laughed through the worry, and pushed him away

with a teasing shove. "So, okay, we'll have to do some things the old-fashioned way. Once all this is over, tell the builders to funk your place out the way you want to, and I'll promise to stop by and get naked in the center of your bed. A sister can do that, and sprawl, if that will chill you out."

"Yeah, but damn, ain't nothing like doing this," he said with a snap of his fingers, gazing at her fireplace, "and starting an inferno." He offered her a sheepish smile. "Be honest, D. You loved it, didn't you?"

"I loved *you*," she hedged, not willing to give into the dangerous fantasy.

"You had instant maid service," he said, coming closer to her.

She looked away and began folding the blanket. "I'll live."

"But you liked some of the trappings of—"

"Carlos, baby. Let it rest." Her tone had come out a little more forceful than intended. She made a tight, neat, pile of her duvet and put it on the chair across the room. "That was then, this is now. Don't forget about the dark energies that are a real threat. Focus on that and any solutions you can come up with. That's the priority. Me and you need to lock, develop a quick strategy, and then roll it out to the team within the next day or so. Even if we don't turn, as Neterus, we're not immune to the effects. We've gotta be careful."

When he didn't answer, she looked at him hard to be sure he was clear. "Your mind is a weapon, and you'd been dwelling on the old powers so much that it gave you the blood hunger for a minute while you were in transition. The result was that when you drank alcohol, hanging out with a vamp buddy and probably hashing and rehashing the old life, it made you sick as a dog—almost like you'd gone out and fed. You understand how dangerous something like that can be?"

"Yeah, yeah, yeah," he said, losing all mirth in his tone. "I know. My boy said the same thing, but, like I said, we ain't going out like that no more. I've felt like shit all day, but whatever was in my system passed. So, I'm cool. No need to get Marlene to posse up and get everybody in the house bugging me about potentially being infected or my judgment being compromised."

He looked at her; she held his gaze, considering. Tonight, all right. But if he had any more signs of flux, Marlene would be the first person she'd consult. Then she'd call Father Pat.

Several questions continued to nag her as she stared at him, though. One was, if he was going through a Neteru chemical flux and smelled as fabulous as he did last night, how did Yonnie countenance that with Tara present— especially with dark energies swirling that should have made Yonnie act off da hook? Even though they were boys, a male master vampire would go nuts and into instant battle bulk from just a whiff of male Neteru pheromone. Conversely, if Carlos was fluxing to vamp, she should have picked up that vamp tracer the second he was in her presence. Scratch waiting. As soon as Marlene came back, they needed to talk.

Then there was also the issue of her libido being on low tide when it came to him—even while he had a near apex going on. If there was dark energy afoot, and lusting for Carlos was definitely one of her weaknesses, then she should have been all over the man. What was wrong with her? Every overture he made toward her didn't even make her stir . . . except for when she thought back on their old nights together. Yet, earlier that same day, when Jose had neared her, he'd made her so hot she was ready to jump out of her skin.

Carlos cocked his head to the side. "I thought we were supposed to be opening our third eyes to each other tonight?"

Damali glanced away. "I just did it when I asked you about the blood hit. I respect your privacy, and wasn't trying to probe beyond that, uninvited."

"D, maybe it's me, but you've seemed a little distant, lately . . . like, no matter what I do, I can't break in." His eyes held hers captive. "You're talking about being honest, hiding nothing from each other so we can do what we've gotta do as a team to address this new threat, and not looking backward—but I know a black mental box when I feel one. Talk to me."

She swallowed hard and sent her gaze on the floor. She hadn't been able to see the flicker of silver in his eyes, much less the gorgeous solid ray they cast when he was thoroughly turned on. More than that, his skin didn't ignite under her palm any longer. The hardest question to ask herself was, why not? How badly was he infected? How badly was she?

"It's stress, baby, given the circumstances," she said, hoping that her quick diagnosis was accurate. "That's what's creating the box. I haven't been able to focus on my music, either. All the moving, running around, coming up with long stories to soothe insurance companies, negotiations to get the new compound built on safe lands, I mean, all of it was just probably catching up to me—then we just got whacked over the heads by this new, horrible, mad-crazy shit . . . Carlos, that's the only reason I can't focus to open up that private cell right now."

"Yeah, okay," he said quietly, glancing around the room for his duffel bag. "I hear you, D. Stress. That's why we didn't mind lock anymore *before* we found out about this new drama, or your voice didn't shatter glass when I was with you, like it used to—okay. I know what's in the box *now;* we heard it late last night and this morning with the teams. New threat; that I can deal with as a reason. But before, what was that? Even now, truth be told, if that's all that's in there, I thought you said we'd tackle it as one?"

She wrapped her arms around her waist.

He began walking in a circle, looking on the floor for what wasn't in the room. "*Stress.* I got you."

"It affects women differently than men," she said defensively. "I was stressed before, too—since Philly."

"Yeah, so I've been told," he said coolly. "All I'ma say is this, though—stress is being dead, in Hell, and having six levels of bullshit chasing you, without daylight as an option."

He looked at her hard, then stared out the window. "Get a

total mind lock on with me now, then—since we're a so-called equal partner team."

Damali closed her eyes, her body tensed. She couldn't do it. There was something inexplicable revolting her. "Baby—"

"Do it now, or I'm walking!"

They stared at each other.

She shook her head as tears filled her eyes. No. She was not allowing him into her head with something she didn't understand within him. "I'll get your clothes. They're in the living room."

"And, as I recall," he said, not budging, "with all that chasing you, an Isis blade raised, and a whole house of Guardians in hot pursuit of your whereabouts, a sister didn't allow stress about real estate and insurance companies and a new CD to cool her off. Maybe I'm not remembering things right?" He brushed past her and paced toward the living room in search of his bag. "Yeah, D," he yelled over his shoulder. "We're *both* under serious *stress*."

CHAPTER EIGHT

The path beside the country road was so dark you could barely see your hand in front of your face, unless, of course, you had Neteru night vision. But the way Damali was acting had cut him to the bone. He would have walked that path blind as a matter of pride, and there was also this thing called principle.

From the distance, he could see the lights on in the family house, and as he walked it amazed him how short the human memory was. Everything was immediate, temporal, in the present tense. Just like people could watch the news broadcasts and be horrified today, but forget about a major incident by the next afternoon's headlines. He could never figure that out; his brain simply didn't function like that. He remembered all, and knowledge was always power.

But the past didn't seem to matter to Damali unless an argument cropped up, and then the woman could rethread history all the way back to the dawn of time. He would have laughed at his situation if he weren't so angry. True, there were more important matters to think about, but at the moment, he just didn't have it in him.

His focus would become laser as soon as he took a walk and cooled off. If any OD jumped out of the bushes, he'd squash it, the way he felt right now. Besides, as far as contagion, things couldn't get any worse than they already were. They needed a solid plan, a way to bait the Chairman and Lilith out of hiding. He and Damali were the only ones who could do that, if she could get her head together enough to work as a team. But that was the problem, she wasn't used to doing that—she was only used to giving orders, and like he'd told her before, he wasn't some flunky lieutenant of hers. Not by a long shot.

Damali was downright *wrong,* the way he saw it. She'd obviously forgotten about how he stood by her side when she was sick. Oh, like restarting a sister's heart and begging for her life in prayer—*as a vampire,* standing in a damned cold shower, willing her to live wasn't nuthin'? *That,* compared to a night out with his boy?

She was off the hook about silly shit. His timing might have been bad, but his intent wasn't. Had he known about all this infection madness, did she actually believe he would have gone out and gotten plastered? Then to have to be read the Riot Act by a damned alcoholic for a night out with his boy, simply because no matter what the circumstances, Rider would have a problem with Yonnie, even if they were going to a church for Bible study!

But, if he brought up the obvious past that he and Damali had shared, and spoken on the fact that she'd fluxed and lapsed while she was learning how to be a Neteru, she'd no doubt start arguing about how she was sick because of him in the first place. Then it would only be a matter of time before she threw up the whole issue of losing her Isis long blade because of him. Yeah, all right, so she stayed by his side when he'd turned vamp. Okay, they were even. So what was her beef?

Though all of that was true, she'd willingly gone there with him. Women always had some tricked-up logic.

Not to mention, after *all* that they'd been through together, it now boiled down to her having second thoughts? *At a time like this?* Why?

Before, it seemed like when there was a crisis and heavy drama to contend with, the two of them were on fire. But the moment things got sort of normal, then girlfriend's mind started working overtime about woulda, coulda, shoulda. *He* was the one who should be having second thoughts! This was her family, her world, her environment, not his. This was her plan, her path, her mission, not his. However, *for her,* he was willing to try to deal with it. . . . Yet now she's all distant and acting funny when they needed to come together and beat a new threat as one?

Crazy part was, his boy Yonnie was all messed up because his woman couldn't let go of the past. No matter what Yonnie had done in the present, like saving Tara's ass, giving her a necessary throat feed, and even being cool with her man wasn't nothing? If Yonnie temporarily made a seduction attempt, he understood why. Pain was pain, and his boy was bleeding bad. Up on that porch, seeing Tara near Rider probably was what had made the brother drop fang. Rider still had Tara's mind on lock, and the past was making his boy miserable. Actually, it was making both men miserable, and where was the female justice and logic in that? he wanted to know.

He couldn't even begin to fathom what Shabazz was going through, even though Kamal had been chill enough not to fall by with theatrics. Still, 'Bazz's pride had been whittled down to sawdust when Kamal rolled up on them in Philly, shape-shifted, and blew Marlene's mind. The subject was so hot, so ready to blow, that even the newbies knew to stay clear of 'Bazz in the house. A woman could make even the coolest brother wig. So, again, he wanted to know, where was the justice? At least Marlene seemed to have enough sense to recognize that the past could be a dangerous thing, or a good thing, depending on when a particular skeleton leaped from a closet.

They had more important things to deal with than this! Why couldn't she give up a lock!

Marlene had maturity; that had to be it. While on the other hand, his woman seemed to have no memory of even the recent past, and Damali could only focus on ridiculous shit. Yeah, he'd gone out drinking. So! Yeah, he sorta missed the old life. And? He wasn't no choirboy when she'd met him, and she needed to get over it. Fact was, all of them had to be flexible and change, like Rider said. But change was a two-way street. So, what did she want from him?

Carlos stood in the driveway looking at the family house. He didn't want to go in, but where else was there to go? If he took his Jeep and began driving into town, that joint practically rolled the pavement up near midnight. If he drove farther into the tourist areas, the whole American-family-on-vacation groove would truly work his nerves, especially knowing half the tourists were probably already contagious. But it was time to get his hat and be out for a coupla hours.

Adjusting his duffel bag on his shoulder, he walked toward his Jeep. The plan was simple: drive till he ran out of gas, refill at a truck stop, and push forward to L.A. Talk to Yonnie; figure out something to stem this tide of demon food fleeing over the portal walls. Get a hotel room, get on the mental phone, tap Gabrielle's head, and start looking for solid leads from his old world, as well as get some permanent real estate to set up a new base of personal operations.

Within twenty-four hours, he'd wire transfer some money and throw down his American Express card and get some real custom-tailored rags from Rodeo Drive so he could operate, since time was of the essence. Next stop from there, go visit the Lamborghini dealer, and find his boys from the old neighborhood to custom-kit that bitch out—transportation was a must. Build an arsenal in the new joint, and order some electronics, an HD-TV; stock his bar; call his boy, Yonnie; order furniture to his liking; maybe even pick up a rottweiler puppy. Whatever. All of this could be accomplished in one night and one day, and he'd be good to go.

Then, he'd contact so-called home and let the squad know where to reach him if things got hectic. They could inform Damali, if they had a mind to. Fuck it. He would do this Neteru thing his way.

• • •

She watched him from the shadows, deciding how to approach him. Summoning up her nerve, Juanita sipped in a shaky breath and willed her legs to walk forward. There had never been a time since the church in Philly when she'd had the opportunity to be alone with him and away from anyone else so they could just talk. It was now or never. The memories simply wouldn't fade. He was still her *papi* . . . even while loving Jose, and her *papi* was still just as fine as ever and getting dogged by a woman who clearly didn't know what she had. Damali was crazy; but she wasn't. If girlfriend wasn't treating Carlos right, she would.

The look on his face drew her from beyond the shadows. For a moment, all she could do was stare at him, remembering what his hands felt like, the sound of his deep whispers in her ear, the way his full mouth tasted . . . those intense brown eyes with black lashes that lowered slowly when he laughed, or wanted to make love. She let her gaze pore over his face in memory before fully stepping into view, taking in every inch of his bronze skin, down his throat to his hard chest and fantastic six-pack that was visible even under his shirt. She'd always loved the slight cleft in his chin and the way he walked, almost more of a lope than taking steps . . . had always loved him from the start . . . woulda given her life, cared for his momma, woulda had his babies, whatever he'd wanted, if he'd never let her go. And if he ever breathed her name like he had before . . . *'Nita* . . . consequences be damned, she'd go to him whether he had fangs or not.

A curvaceous female form stepped out from behind the house and approached him slowly, making him jerk his attention toward her. Oh, man, just the person he *didn't* want to see.

"Hey, Carlos," Juanita said shyly, half waving and coming nearer.

"Hey, 'Nita," he grumbled and hoisted his bag into his Jeep.

"I was just taking out the trash and heard someone in the front yard." She looked up at him, coming closer than he wanted. "Guess I'm still a little jumpy when I hear stuff, you know? I'm pretty freaked out, but I'm trying not to panic. I know you got this covered, right? It's gonna be okay, right, Carlos? You could always make things work out. I have to keep believing that."

He nodded. "You'll get used to being freaked out and then just dealing. But, yeah, baby, I got dis. Don't worry." He tempered his next response, fighting with the urge to argue with anyone in earshot, because in truth, Juanita didn't have anything to do with his foul mood. "Look," he said more gently, "none of this is normal. You've been through a lot, and having your senses on point ain't a bad thing—*that* is the *only* thing about all of this that's normal. So keep being jumpy, right through here."

She nodded and leaned against his Jeep. Her sad smile and big brown eyes made him remember just how pretty she was and how gentle her heart could be. Guilt stabbed him as he stared at her. It was obvious that they both quietly remembered what they'd shared, but were unwilling to speak on it. It was better that way.

"You going over to D's after you get some more clothes?" she asked softly.

"No," he said, not wanting to discuss Damali with anyone. "I need a break. Might drive up to L.A. for a few days. I've got some contacts up there. Sitting on some Indian reservation worrying ourselves to death ain't accomplishing shit."

She looked at him, her eyes containing a request to possibly come along, but her smile seemed to hold the question in check. "Oh," she murmured. "Under different circumstances, I'd ask you if you wanted somebody to ride shotgun."

He smiled. "Under different circumstances, I'd ask you to go with me."

They both glanced back at the house.

"Thanks, again." He hesitated. "No. Let me say this right," he murmured, gathering her hands within his and staring into her eyes. "Thank you, Juanita, for always having my back, for stepping in to guard my mother and grandmother . . . even when you didn't know that's what you were doing. I don't know what to say, but I really appreciated that. You were always there . . . no matter what I was doing, what crazy life I was leading, you know?"

"I loved you," she said in a patient tone just above a whisper. "Would have gone to Hell and back for you, too, baby."

He dropped her hands slowly before he forgot the present. "You did, time and time again—especially when I was building my street business. But you weren't supposed to be in that, you deserved better. I ain't gonna let nothing happen to you here, either."

"Is that why you left me, Carlos?" she asked, stepping closer and looking up at him. "I need to know that, now more than ever before."

He nodded and looked away toward the house, unable to continue to stare into her deep, brown eyes. "That is the *only* reason we broke up when we did." He returned his gaze to her and something within him, reflex memory, made him trace her cheek. "You deserved better than I could give you, then. I had all the money in the world, but it was dirty money, drugs had funded what I owned, and the life was mad-crazy. . . . You wanted children, a clean life, stability. That was something I didn't have to give."

"Then," she said softly, covering his hand against her cheek and closing her eyes. "You didn't have that to give me, then."

"Or now," he said, gently slipping his hand from beneath hers to jam into his jeans pocket. "My brother, Jose, got that for you now. He's a good man. Once we squash this current bullshit, you two have a life and a future."

"What's so different about this life and the old one?" she whispered, looking up at him in the moonlight. "It was dangerous then. It's dangerous now. There were predators then. There are predators now. We were worried about family then. We're worried about family now. I don't see the difference."

Carlos closed his eyes and let out a patient breath. Women had some tricked-up logic, and it was beginning to twist his. Juanita was stirring him in ways that he shouldn't remember . . . and the fact that she'd always accepted him—the good, the bad, and the ugly, and still had his back, was beginning to corrupt his judgment.

"The difference," he said, opening his eyes and staring at her hard, "is that this time, whatever dangers we all face, it's for a worthy cause." His comment sounded like something Shabazz would have said; in fact, he was sure the older brother had told him that, too. But it worked under pressure, and Juanita would have to accept what he'd just said. If he made the move that his body was suggesting, all hell would surely break loose in the house before dawn.

"I suppose you're right," she finally said.

Carlos almost let out his breath hard in relief. "You and Jose go way back, too. You met him first. You loved him hard. Remember that, 'Nita. Like I said, he's a good man and deserves your all. Lord knows, I can't give that to you the way he can."

She nodded and stepped back, a sad smile still resonant on her face in the darkness. "He and I were together when we were just kids." She chuckled sadly and pushed her hair behind her ear. "We were running from demons, then. He brought me here, long after Rider had left . . . and we shared that wonderful summer. Then, the shaman said they needed to make us forget about the demons so we would have peace, but they made us forgot it all—because if we didn't, I wouldn't have met you, he wouldn't have rejoined Rider to hook up with the team. It all came back slowly over time as we walked over our old haunts, like ghosts of the past. I guess I was just her placeholder." Again, Juanita pushed the hair behind her ear that kept spilling forward.

He watched the way she did that, remembering. Her hair was so soft, like dark, silken threads. Her gaze searched his face, and he could feel her absorbing every detail of his mouth before she swallowed hard.

"You were never her placeholder," Carlos said quietly. "You were . . ."

"The one who was there when you needed a woman to

love you more than her next breath. The one who was supposed to have your babies, if that's what you wanted—and
you didn't. Not from me. I was supposed to whisper in your
ear in bed at night . . . reminding you to do the right thing
without making you angry. I held her place, because she
wasn't supposed to do that for you, then. She had to remain
a virgin. And not just sexually. You wanted her to stay pure
and separate from that part of your life. But not me."

"Oh, baby . . . listen . . ." Carlos said softly as tears rose
to her eyes. He wanted to hug her so badly that his arms
ached. "Com'ere. It wasn't like that."

"I'm infected," she whispered, hugging herself. "Dirty."

"I'm immune," he said quietly.

Slowly Juanita filled his arms with quiet defeat.

By instinct, he stroked her hair as she laid her head
against his chest, and he could feel her holding back an intense sob as she breathed in stilted shudders.

"I held her place in your family, Carlos. She was supposed
to be rising in her career as a singer and out slaying demons. I
wasn't supposed to be anything special. But you needed someone there to look after your momma and grandmom so you
could go out into the world and become all that you are now."

He nuzzled her hair, remembering how good it smelled,
what it felt like on his face when it spilled forward to wash him
in silk. The debt burden on his shoulders increased by another
soul weight and made him kiss her temple. "You *are* special . . .
your heart is one of a kind." He let her go slowly because there
was more than her soft sighs that he also had to remember. He
watched her draw away slowly and lean against his Jeep again,
hugging herself to replace the loss of their embrace.

"Jose is a lucky man. Not many get to go back to a
woman like you and pick up where he left off." He raked his
hair to give his hands something legitimate to do.

"I know . . . but, after time and distance, and things happening . . . sometimes the heat can change."

Her statement was too profound, and his strange curiosity
about the inner workings of the female mind drew him.

"I hear you," he said, "but, after y'all work through the changes, you can get that back, right?"

"I don't know," she said, pure honesty threading through her voice as she hugged herself tighter. "Sometimes, it's like we'd never been apart, and then there's this wall of private experience that we've had in between, and we can't share that with each other, so . . . it creates a . . . I don't know what it creates, but something always gets lost in that in-between. Am I making sense?"

She was making more sense than she could ever know. He nodded and sighed.

"Then, I guess you have to work on creating something new." He glanced back at the house and then at her. "If we hooked up again, we'd have that black box, too. Comprende?"

Juanita looked at him, an old blaze smoldering and consuming her eyes deep within her irises. "Yeah. I know. But . . . I remember too much sometimes. . . ." Her husky voice trailed off as she stood straighter and pushed off the Jeep. "What am I supposed to do with that?" Her gaze trapped his mouth, and then sought his eyes. "Or, let me ask you . . . What do you do with that?"

Carlos swallowed hard and found the tree line. "I tuck it away in a black box in my head, 'cause I love my brother, and ain't trying to hurt nobody ever again in life." He folded his arms. Shit. He shoulda said because he loved Damali . . . why hadn't that come out of his mouth, too?

"You're right. Guess I was just tripping down memory lane because my man came in this morning with *the wall,* and I knew where he'd been."

Now she had more than his full attention. His line of vision snapped away from the tree line and captured her eyes. "Talk to me, 'Nita. For real."

She shook her head. "It's my trip, not yours. Go to L.A., be safe, and when you get settled, let everybody know you're all right, cool?"

She came in close to him and planted a soft kiss on his

cheek, and then brushed it away with a featherlight touch of her fingertips. "I'm crazy, Carlos, to think I might be in love with two men at the same time. You're right. He's the one, now, I guess, and always has been. Forgive me for trippin' out here tonight."

He could only stare at her. Women could do that? Be in love with two men at the same time . . . beyond sex, heart deep, like that? Part of him was oddly jealous. It was an ego blow to know that someone else had taken his place so thoroughly, so completely, to be equated with the singular love that she'd always had for him alone. Now, he had to share that—even though it was the right thing to do and made sense.

He battled with his irrational feeling as he moved away from her. His emotions were all jumbled, but they were what they were. True, he'd wanted her to be happy with somebody new . . . but not totally to the point where it eclipsed him. The whole conflict was also doing weird things to his libido. Right now, looking at her, remembering, thinking too hard, he was almost ready to ask her to go with him to L.A.

"Your eyes are glowing silver," she finally said with a smirk when he'd offered no comment. "I suppose it's time for me to go in the house."

"Yeah, baby. Go back in the house. I'll watch you to be sure you get in safely."

She didn't move for a moment. "Remember that night you called me out of the house and I came to you?"

Again, he didn't answer her, shame halting his words. How could he forget calling her past his mother and grand-mother's prayer barriers for what might have been his first real throat feeding? He didn't want to ever have to remember that or ever think about that.

"My soul knew what you were then, and it didn't matter," she said in a breathy whisper. "At that moment, I wanted you so badly that I would have been with you no matter what the final consequences."

She allowed her words to fall between them in an open offer. He knew what she was saying, just like she did. The ball was in his court.

"Go in the house, Juanita," he whispered, but not as firmly as he should have.

"Your eyes haven't glowed for anybody in a long time," she said as she brushed past him, allowing the body contact to linger before they parted. "I'm flattered that I was the one who brought the silver back. I didn't mind being her place-holder. *Ever.* Thank you for that."

"*De nada,*" he murmured, and watched her leisurely stroll down the path and up the steps, her round backside sashaying as she sauntered away.

The screen door slammed behind Juanita and snapped him out of the trancelike sensation. Carlos opened his Jeep door with care and slid into the seat and started the engine. Instant images slammed into his brain in jagged still frames as he backed out of his space and pulled onto the road. A Navajo blanket covered his woman. Male hands ran down her arms and made her shiver. A mouth nearly caressed her throat. Her eyes closed. He could feel the desire thick and hot within her. She laughed from way down in her soul—someone had made her laugh and had filled her with sudden joy, even with every-thing going on. He could taste iced tea in his mouth. Her eyes opened wide with surprise and also disappointment. Her ache to be touched by this intruder was palpable. He could feel her body sway to the invitation. The male smelled like Ivory Soap.

Carlos gripped the steering wheel. If he'd known all that, then fair exchange was no robbery—he should have told Juanita to get into his car. She had every right to be salty, if all that had gone down right under both of their noses. He'd been blind, but women always had superior second sight. He owed Juanita for that, now, too. Once again, girlfriend had had his back . . . like Damali should have, but didn't.

Yeah, he knew the blanket that rested on Damali's bed; it was the blanket that had made him sick, it was so hot . . . the bed that she couldn't get into with him . . . the blanket that she slept beneath each night . . . fibers that were alive with another male's energy. Juanita didn't have to say a word. He knew the Ivory Soap and the scent that went with it, and the brown eyes that drank Damali in. Juanita's touch had transmitted that knowing to him . . . as did her sad agony for having to still compete—when Juanita shouldn't have had to compete for anything or anyone at this point. Just like he shouldn't, and Yonnie shouldn't.

This was beyond fucked-up.

She took her time going out onto the back deck, sensing her environment, fully alert to possible danger. But she would not live like a prisoner behind locked windows and bolted doors. The dark side would not be allowed to take her freedom; otherwise she might as well be dead.

When she got outside, she flipped on the floodlights, needing illumination. The darkness had become suffocating around her. She carefully set down a bag of Red Sea salt close to her. By rote, she began to work her body, hoping that would bring clarity to her mind.

Her daily routine of exercise had been destroyed over the past months, and she wanted to regain all that had been disrupted in her life. Tonight she needed clear vision. There was only one way to achieve that: Suspend all personal problems and then home in on a solution. She hadn't even been able to focus enough to raise an audience with the Neteru Queens.

Anything close to normalcy, in her abnormal world, was a soothing dream that they all clung to. Just like the holiday seasons were always celebrated the same way; no store-purchased gifts, only one handmade or self-made item given from the heart to each member of the house. The rest of the giving was for the community, spreading love and cheer, and offering helping hands to less fortunate people they'd heard about or seen on the news. For them, that was normal. She and the Guardians had their own rituals and ways to give thanks. Like Shabazz had always said, it was imperative to

keep a routine, stay focused on one's blessing, lest one's
spiritual, mental, and physical muscle give way to flab.

Her mind was muddled, her spirit was sagging, and it
wasn't about letting the body go to pot, too. The trinity
worked as a unit. Personal gratification, personal problems,
all that needed to be sublimated for something greater than
herself.

Damali propped her feet up on a deck chair, her boot toes
slightly bent. Her face repeatedly neared the wood planks,
her left arm behind her back, her full weight on her blade
arm—then she slowly stroked the muscles, made the burn
work sinew in her upper body, torso, shoulder, stomach, and
back. She needed her blade arm strong and readied at all
times, whether Madame Isis was still with her or not. She
needed Carlos, whether he was with her or not.

"Twenty-two, twenty-three, twenty-four, clear the mind!"
she shouted, keeping time with the one-arm, military push-
ups. At fifty, she switched arms, blew stinging perspiration
away from her nose with a puff of breath, and began again.

Her body was in tip-top condition, so this sagging libido
thing had to be a function of her mind. But why? Minor
spats be damned. He was right. She shouldn't have been
feeling this way. But her gut was rarely wrong. Lack of trust
had been a shadow around her every time Carlos came near.
Without that, she couldn't relax. If she couldn't fully relax in
his arms . . . But that made absolutely no sense. What about
him was not to trust? Even if it was some temporary infection . . . they were supposedly both immune.

She'd trusted the man when he'd become a vamp. Had
trusted him with her throat and her very life. Had entrusted
her family's safety with him. Now this?

"Thirty-four, thirty-five—aw, shit!" Her left arm was
slightly weaker than the right, and she could feel the muscle
in it trembling as she tried to reach the fifty push-up mark.

Was it that she didn't trust herself? She jettisoned the
thought as she unfurled her right arm from behind her back

and began again from the number one, this time using both arms to lift her body.

Damali splayed her fingers against the wood and looked straight ahead through the deck rail into the darkness. She lowered her body in slow movements to burn the energy in agonizing increments and then rose without taking her eyes off the mark. Facts aligned in her inner sight. The man's clothes had torched and smoldered. The earth had swallowed them whole, along with his bodily fluids. He'd fevered and convulsed under a prayer blanket. He'd presented fangs, and daylight had kicked his ass. His recovery was full, as soon as the sun set. Marlene needed to know that, as soon as she got home. Where was Marlene—Shabazz, Marjorie, and Richard! No one had answered the calls all day! Another hour and she'd mount a search party. Marlene had received her transmission. But no answer?

Carlos's Neteru pheromone spike didn't freak out a master vampire the way it should have? If Carlos was somehow turning, even that shouldn't have backed her up and cooled her passion for him. If he'd gotten temporarily infected, that shouldn't have done it; it didn't affect her like that with Jose—it had the opposite effect, in fact. What was it?

"Fifty." Damali stopped, breathing in long and deep through her nose and exhaling through her mouth. She pushed up, jumped to her feet, and then stripped off her pants and boots. Standing on the deck in her T-shirt and underwear, she went to the deck rail and balanced her thighs on it just below her pelvis. Time to work the abs.

She laced her fingers behind her head and bent over the rail until she could see her knees on the other side of it. Then she raised herself in backward sit-ups, shooting for the goal of one hundred.

Each time she lifted her body, she kept her eyes on her focus point—a cactus twenty feet away. At the thirty-eighth sit-up, she noticed that it seemed to move, but focused physical exertion sometimes created mirages. She stopped briefly, mentally swept the terrain, and resumed. However, she began to lose count and to forget about the slow smolder raging in her abdominal muscles. The cactus seemed framed by a glow not created by the floodlights spilling from the porch.

An iridescent, bluish tinge soon conquered the yellow, artificial light surrounding the desert plant. The thick, prickly body seemed to grow narrower and slimmer each time her line of vision went away from it to stare at her knees and then returned to it. The bulbous knots on either side of the cactus soon became curved, ornate silver, and she stopped at the ninetieth sit-up to stare at it in awe.

Sweat poured down her face, blurring her vision, stinging her eyes, dripping off her nose, but she could not unclasp her hands behind her head. Seven jewels glinted in the distance. The body of the cactus teased her as it split into multiple blades becoming one.

"My Isis," she whispered, but still couldn't move. Tears of joy and frustration rose to her eyes, yet anticipation kept her frozen. A coyote howled in the distance, Native American flute music filtered into that from an unknown source. She saw a female hand yank the sword from the dirt and grasp it. From somewhere within, she knew it was her hand. An owl screeched. Then, in an instant, she saw the unidentified hand swing the blade at a dark form walking toward what had once been the cactus. She flinched as the blade sang in the wind, adding chants to the sound of the flutes, and then connected. The strike echoed the unmistakable sound of tissue being severed—then came a thud. The form dropped, and a head rolled toward her, spinning so fast in the yard dust that she couldn't see it until the creature looked at her with glassy, dead eyes.

She screamed and turned away, jumping off and backing away from the rail so quickly that she knocked over the deck chair that had been behind her. Carlos's face disappeared. The Isis was again a cactus. A car was entering her driveway. She grabbed her pants and yanked them on, forgetting about her boots. Terror shot through her system and sent her running through the house. She'd beheaded her own man. Oh my God!

Breathless, she ran out onto the front porch and down the steps in her bare feet, expecting the vehicle to be Carlos's. When the sheriff got out of his squad car with an elder from the tribal council, her gaze raked them for an explanation.

"Chief Quiet Eagle, Sheriff Lightfoot, what's wrong?"

The elderly man shook his head and deferred to the sheriff, a man in his mid-fifties. He adjusted his tan trooper hat, and mopped his brow.

"Ms. Richards, we need to talk to you. There's been an accident."

She looked so young and pretty standing in the middle of the road. His speedometer was cresting seventy-five miles per hour and climbing when he spotted her wearing a blue calico dress that floated in the wind. The scent of lavender filled the cab of the Jeep. She was almost sheer, luminous . . . "Tara? Oh, shit!"

His foot slammed the brakes, and she became a doe, her golden eyes caught in the headlights, her body frozen, so huge and immobile as his Jeep swerved and the deer went through the windshield.

Blood was everywhere—his, the doe's, maybe Tara's, he didn't know. He could smell gasoline and smoke. Not a good combination. A heavy body was on him, pinning him down. His car was listing to one side and without looking he knew he'd been thrown into a ditch.

The first thought that entered his mind was *Yonnie will freak*. Rider would, too. Using all his strength, he pushed at the tawny furred body and used his shoulder to lean against the door. Half falling, half sliding, Carlos hit the ground with a thud. His hands were bloodied from the deer's remains, and he rounded the hood of his Jeep to see if she'd come around.

"Tara, girl, aw . . . man . . . I'm sorry, I couldn't stop." He touched the creature's forehead just above its glassy eyes, and watched the blood trickle from the doe's nose and mouth. "Come on, chica. You all vamp—wake up, baby. Call Yonnie to feed you. C'mon," he said, his voice becoming more strident as he talked to the dead animal on his hood.

Then he stopped. Wait a minute . . . a female vampire couldn't be taken out by vehicular homicide. He checked the animal's chest. Nothing had punctured the doe's heart.

Carlos stepped back and wiped the blood from his hands on his jeans. This was *just* a deer. "Damn!" He blotted his bloody nose on his forearm and then kicked his tires, but laughed with relief.

"Tara," he yelled out again into the nothingness around him. "Girl, don't roll up on a brother like that. You could have . . ."

His voice trailed off. Tara hadn't responded. The insistent echo of gasoline and blood dripping from his Jeep sounded one in the same. The smell permeated his nose and made him tilt his head to the side. He closed his eyes, breathed in deeply, and swallowed more of his own blood. Salty fluid covered his tongue, but he hocked and spit, trying to forget what it tasted like. A slight tremor ran through him, and he turned away from the deer and then shoved his hands in his pockets as they began to shake. "Oh, shit, not now," he whispered, and began to limp away from the toxic site.

A deep, gurgling rumble came up from his stomach. Hunger ate at him, making him breathe hard. The sound of the drips became louder, all-consuming. Sweat began to form along his brow and crept down the center of his back. The animal on his hood twitched. In a lightning response he turned to stare at it. A pool of dark liquid had formed on the ground and was spreading toward his feet. His knees locked as he willed himself not to bend to touch it or taste it. But the beautiful crimson edged toward him in a sultry, hypnotic beckoning.

Panting, Carlos shook his head no and backed farther away—but his eyes remained on the dead creature's jugular.

Reflex made him run his tongue over his teeth. When he nicked his tongue, he closed his eyes. Four inches of feeding-length fang had invaded his mouth.

A wretched sob tore through him as he walked still farther from the smoking vehicle. The night darkness was so clear that it might as well have been high noon. He could hear every skitter on the plains; the coyotes had stopped howling. He held his head with both hands as the pain from his accident faded, his legs felt stronger, and he heard his body mend on its own.

"Noooo!" he yelled, his voice tearing into the night and stilling all creatures within it. Another sob filled his chest, seizing his heart, stopping it briefly, before it began beating again. "Why?" Carlos whispered to the moon, casting his gaze heavenward. She knew. Damali had to have felt this coming. The vibes in the house had been weird, too—but before the *infection*. Everyone was acting out, prone to excesses and fixated on the carnal before the contagion ever hit. A vampire was in their midst, and their senses had to be evolving and locked on it, but daylight had been his cover.

The moonlight offered no answers, but the wind kicked up to bring the blood scent closer to torture his spirit. He had to focus and think: Marlene would never leave newbies; neither would Shabazz; nor would Marj and Berkfield leave their kids like that. Not at a time like this. They'd all left the house before any infected team member had touched them. Just like Big Mike would never, *ever* leave his post, no matter how seductive the booty—not with untrained kids in the house, and the way Rider was drinking, then back on nicotine? Maybe they'd all been infected much earlier than they'd realized?

The Covenant brothers had all skied-up and just left the compound to go back to Rome, and Mecca, Tibet, and Israel, with a new Neteru that had a month of training before the big spike to go—because they'd admitted to being infected earlier. That had to be it. Plus, Kamal had left his men in Bahia, chasing an old flame from who knows how long ago, and laying for Shabazz to mess up just once? *Never,* unless something really strange was affecting them all beyond the dark poison leaking from the portals. They'd been told that was what was wrong, but he could feel something else was more wrong than that.

How could the contagion have been so insidious that none of the seers picked it up in advance or none of the brothers had caught a vibe and stepped to him if he was fluxing back hard? Tara was AWOL since she'd guarded him on the porch, as though she didn't trust herself around him? Yonnie was acting strange, too, a master vampire caught up in a love-jones—unheard-of. Juanita being drawn to him just now, to that degree, making her ridiculously bold? And Jose making an outright run at Damali, and *Damali* almost going there? Uh-uh. Something more profound than dark portal energies had to be spiking all these turns . . .

Jesus help him . . . help them . . . They didn't know about him, but they had to be feeling whatever bizarre energy was causing this hard flux. Every Guardian had to be caught up in it, sensing it down deep mixed with this new portal problem, too. Nobody had been right since Philly, which was a little more than six months ago.

Carlos tried to steady himself and force unadulterated logic to the forefront of his mind. For the first time since he'd come back, he hadn't been able to connect with Father Patrick. When the team had a meeting with the elderly cleric calling from the Vatican, he'd been passed out cold—more than drunk, almost as though heavily drugged, and excluded from the communication . . . like he was a pure vampire. Damali refused a mind lock repeatedly, something a full-fledged Neteru instinctively was supposed to do against a vamp. . . . But he'd been one before, and she'd never refused him then. Why now, even if he was temporarily fluxing?

Maybe she didn't trust herself, because something inside her knew that they'd both been contaminated? But if everyone on the team had become infected over the last six months, why hadn't they manifested the horrible final stages within thirty days, like every other human was supposed to experience? There had to be more to this problem than any of them knew—*What was it?*

A basic vamp turn should have registered, regardless, unless they were all already so compromised that they couldn't pick it up. It was the only explanation that made sense.

Carlos wandered off the road and into the sparse brush, then finally dropped to his knees, unable to continue to fight the urge to return to the fallen deer and feed. It was only a matter of time; he had to stop lying to himself. The acid burn was in his stomach; blood was in his nose. Normal food didn't stay with him. Five more minutes, and he'd have to give in to the deer. But why would Tara do something like that to him? They were family! Was she trying to seduce him? Was it the near apex that would make her do something that crazy?

"I did *everything* I was supposed to do," he said through a bitter sob, his face turned toward the sky. "I served my time, didn't I?" How could the Light do him like this?

He was about to stand, but a force compelled him to remain paralyzed on his knees. He couldn't get up, and he struggled with the unseen as though someone or something had placed powerful, invisible hands on his shoulders. The touch burned worse than the blood hunger, and he cried out in agony as it spread throughout his body. His voice created sound waves that began to shimmer around him, and soon he was covered in a moving globe of bluish white light.

"Be still," a booming voice said.

The light around him was blinding.

"You have a debt to pay," another voice said.

"You have purpose, as you are," a third voice said.

Carlos shielded his eyes with one hand, but still could not break free of the force to stand.

"You are the only one who can enter the darkness to retrieve *the book*."

"What book!" Carlos shouted, not ready to give up any information while unsure of who or what he was dealing with.

"The Light seeks the unholy *Book of the Damned*," a thunderous voice replied.

"Your destiny is incomplete," another said, and then the globe retreated from Carlos.

He was on his feet in an instant. The blood hunger had abated, and he glanced around, terrified and confused.

"One-half of your pairing is to protect the innocent," a voice said.

Carlos spun around, unable to get a bead on the direction the voice was coming from.

"She guards the living," two more voices murmured in unison.

"You guard the dead, and are to deliver us the lost—those who were stolen."

"I don't understand," Carlos whispered, his voice catching in his throat.

"All seats at the table are vacant. The Chairman has fled his lair. We shall find him. But only one from his line can retrieve *The Book of the Damned*."

"The Chairman's book?" Carlos said slowly, and remained very, very still. He knew the objective, but that the Light was commissioning him to go after it *down there* was unfathomable. Maybe they thought it was topside. He posed the critical question to them to be sure he was clear. "The one he keeps stashed in his Council Chambers . . . under the crest at the *blood table?*"

"Yes," three voices said flatly.

Carlos watched a blue light appear in the distance and then become three entities. The light that emanated from them was so bright that he couldn't make out their faces or what they wore; they just seemed like three talking spheres of light. The moment the moonlight glinted off their shields he knew what they were: Warrior angels, ring six—and they'd come out at night?

"There's only one way to get that," Carlos said, his voice shaky as he replayed their request in his mind. "If it's not topside, somebody would have to go down to Hell, get into Chambers, and go to the table . . ."

"Precisely," they said as one.

"But, I'm not a . . . I can't just . . . I'm—"

"We cannot tread past the borders of Purgatory without setting off the alarms of the Legions," the entity with the strongest voice said. "It is not an option or a request. The time is now. This is a command from On High. They have gone too far. They have our Covenant cleric in their book of treachery with your name beside it as the one who felled him. We cannot allow them to have both a member of the Covenant and our male Neteru within that book. That sacrilege is too great. The cleric is the one also from your vampire line, a defect that gave him the weakness to succumb to your lure. Though he, like you, had chosen a different path— the Light—your irresponsible use of power sent him into the darkness and tethered you to him as a consequence."

"Lopez?" Carlos whispered, already knowing the answer, and now knowing why the guilt had lacerated his soul so much. Were it not for him, Lopez might have been able to withstand his attraction to the one thing that would make him shed his clerical collar. Carlos hung his head. The debt was definitely heavy. Yeah. The angels had a right to make him go back down into the pit to go get the soul he'd compromised so that universal order would be maintained. He sighed. It was back to the Old Testament, *an eye for an eye* . . .

"He retrieved your ashes," the lead voice thundered. "Return the favor for your brother without question, and also redeem yourself."

"But you all allowed me to relapse?" Carlos was incredulous. This wasn't the side of a cliff to find a lair; this was a trip down *to Hell*. "You tested me with a deer! I know I owe him my life. I want this team healed, too, and will go. But if you wanted to send me on a mission like that, then send me strong, not weak. Why would you—"

"Was the man you sent to his demise stronger than you are now when you attacked him with a demonic lure?"

Their voices created an angry cacophony of rapid questions and demanding statements that split the night air and kicked up the winds.

"Was he more than you are now when he risked life and limb to perilously, fearlessly retrieve your ashes?"

"Dig deep into your conscience and answer with truth!"

"He, of mere flesh and bones, did this with a pure heart, and the dark side snatched his soul in wrongful treachery. We want it back. Along with all the others."

"He cannot be damned."

"Your desire for worldly things allowed you to relapse."

"You were not careful in what you had prayed for!"

"Your soul desire for your old existence attracted that energy to you while the portals were opened and darkness was afoot. Your soul mate warned you. The female Neteru *knew*."

"Your Guardian brothers warned you."

"A vampire even warned you—a friend."

"You did not listen, and opened your delicate transition to a choice border that had been breached in Philadelphia."

"Breached again by the infection."

"Until we saw you fight the hunger, we could not be sure whether the darkness had taken root."

"Lust for power, lust—period—has always been your issue."

"The female Neteru's body shuns yours, because your soul has been tainted."

"Her spirit is drawn to the Light within."

"It is dimmer now than when you were dead!"

"But I was *saved*," Carlos argued, feeling rage at the injustice of being relentlessly tested beginning to form within him.

A silvery blade of lightning lit in the sky.

"Yes!"

"From that point of your salvation and rebirth, your debts had been wiped clean!"

"Your seven-year sentence erased!"

"Your burden lifted!"

"You had but to hold the line."

"Seven years had been collapsed to seven months!"

"The Neteru preparers showed you the Arc of the Covenant—but that was not enough!"

"You were given the weapon of Heru!"

"You were marked by Ausar!"

"You were being refined."

"Honed!"

"Patience was lacking!"

"Your faith in our methods was weak!"

"Spiritual armor was nonexistent! Ego ruled—fallen from potential grace like the first angel for the same offense! *This* is how you were infected, and your debt began to spiral once more!"

Carlos stared at the lights in the sky unblinking . . . he'd played *himself* . . . oh, no . . .

"Only you who have been polluted can cross the dark realm's barriers to bring us the names. Each soul that was snatched into darkness by treachery, each soul that was put under torture and duress until it capitulated to the dark side can be freed to stand with the Light at the final hour, if we can call them to us by name, by location. *We need the location,* send—"

"Polluted?" Carlos shouted. "*I* was tricked; *I* was corrupted by larceny, and did my time. I didn't know what you were doing!"

"You did not have to know," the strongest voice in the triumvirate said. "Blind faith is what was required."

"We had shown you *enough* by bringing you back!" another said.

"*That* was a miracle."

"*That* was enough."

Carlos swallowed hard as sweat poured down his temples and causing his tattered T-shirt to cling to his torso. He had really messed up this time. The Light didn't negotiate.

"But you want me to go back down there with a blood-hunger jones and get a book in that condition?" Carlos stammered. "What if—"

"Silence!" the entities shouted together. "Our priest was corrupted at your hand!"

"You will know no peace until you reverse this transgression," the lead entity said flatly. "He must be one with us. You wanted to lead—lead! Your team depends on you. Stand by the female Neteru in copartnership or be banished from her. She cannot be unevenly yoked with the darkness, and will ultimately seek the Light within the soul of her Guardian brother, whose soul is not tainted by power lust. He respects her position. Her body is already beginning to yield toward him. You are unraveling your destiny and hers to be as one. This is your handiwork!"

"We must have the soul of the virgin Covenant priest and that of our male Neteru," two angelic voices said in harmony.

"Neither can be captive within the Dark Realms! Not the priest!" the lead entity shouted. "Your burden in that would have been also mitigated—had you not compounded the problem with a total disregard for the blessings after you were reborn. *That* is what created your new debt, not the cleric's weakness. That had been forgiven. Your continuing power lust and desire for your old darkness after the miracle of salvation was not. Correct that injustice to reestablish your light! Our priest is being tortured."

Carlos remained still. The truth made him shiver. He'd sent a priest . . . a male virgin, *down there* from an errant display of power. He'd given him the fever to want to be a vamp, worked him down to a loss of faith by way of a seduction trance. Carlos shuddered when the bright lights before him blazed brighter, clearly enraged as the images swept through his mind. Instantly he saw Lopez's death.

Lilith had locked in on the man's last thought. Carlos closed his eyes. Instead of a prayer of protection, Lopez had wanted absolute vampiric strength, like his before he'd gone to ash . . . wanted to go after Juanita and save her from it all to be with her, and then leave the church. The pulse ran through Lopez, burned his aura red for a moment; Lilith saw it through the clerical prayer barriers and speared Lopez, hoping it was him . . . then flung Lopez's broken body aside like a rag doll, enraged. Lopez had had so many emotions running through him at the time, there was no telling what level his soul had bottomed out on.

"Yes," the voices said in unison. "The debt is profound. The search delicate. His energy is scattered on almost every level."

"He was a priest," the voices whispered. "Do you know what they do to the men of lost faith down there?"

Carlos wrapped his arms around himself, hung his head, and tried to fight back the tears. Lopez was beyond damned—the poor man was fucked. Just like the Guardian team was. He knew he had to work quickly. The thought of Padre being down there all by himself on whatever levels he landed upon made him want to tear his hair out. But to go down there in a weakened condition was suicidal, and they knew it. He looked up slowly, wondering if that was the trade they'd decided upon to right this wrong?

"You possess a dangerous new gift by accident of the dark side's unrelenting larceny."

Carlos remained silent, his gaze intense. Something else was going on that he didn't understand. He would definitely go get his man Lopez and would go after the Chairman and Lilith, but their urgency seemed to contain more than that. So, he waited.

One of the angels stepped forward, and all around him in a three-dimensional panorama, the final battle with the Chairman and Lilith replayed itself. Carlos stood as a spectator, his eyes wide, and his jaw becoming slack as he watched Damali raise her short Isis and gore Lilith. Then, what had been eclipsed from his mind was revealed.

Dark, sputtering, living smoke exited Lilith's body, rushed toward him, filled his mouth and nose, strangling him.

"The essence of Level Seven entered the strongest dark male as a carrier. *This* is what began the contagion and allowed it to remain topside! Lilith opened the portals, but through you, ensured her doors would not be closed when her husband began to search for her."

"She flees him, and must keep him preoccupied in his realm's chaos to buy her escape—hoping to rush the Armageddon through the contagion."

"If the Armageddon is rushed, she might be able to form an alliance with the new leader of the darkness to stop her imminent extinction. This is her goal."

"*You* were the carrier of her deceit, her dark energy that has kept open the doors. You became that because your spiritual armor and faith was weak when you attempted to battle a strong entity from Level Seven."

"Why would you attempt a battle with her without being readied by a soul shield of faith? You needed more than exterior weapons."

"We have held the line for your team, the Covenant, and all other Guardian teams since the Philadelphia incident, but they are weakening as more of the Damned find the openings and pollute the gray zone of earth. Each escapee weakens them. Each passed infection to the living weakens them. They are beginning to lose the inner battle. Our teams are in jeopardy, as is humanity."

"This must be corrected."

"We have waited patiently for your spirit to evict pride, ego, and power lust on its own—to no avail. Your prayers have been polluted with requests for the old life."

"The Most High grew weary of your shortsightedness and answered your requests with hopes that you will find the lesson within the tribulation your arrogant petitions have caused, and grasp the truth henceforth."

"Please," Carlos said quickly, going to his knees again. "Tell Him, for real, I didn't know and—"

"The female Neteru was once almost lost to this same arrogance," the lead voice said gently.

"I know, when I was a vamp," Carlos said, his voice becoming strident, "I—"

"No," they said in unison. "It goes back further than that.

You kneel before us in the Light, yet you are still blinded by your own ego. Her father was a man of the cloth and thought he could battle evil alone. Arrogance. Damali senses this repetition of history at the core of her soul, although her human mind cannot translate it. *But she knows* and warned you hence. Her father did not reveal his strategy to able spiritual warriors around him. He deceived his wife, his spiritual partner. They lost their baby to the whims of the world . . . and only through angelic intervention was our Neteru saved."

"Recall that her father succumbed to Fallon Nuit," the lead voice said. "His wife, Damali's mother, eventually fell to her own inner weaknesses, and was also thus temporarily lost—*two pivotal Guardians* that were the spiritual leaders of their team. Only serious petitions and the guiding Light of their child, a Neteru, elevated them. We are on the verge of now losing two Neterus. Your first child has already been lost. History, repetition, but each time the lesson and challenge is more severe. *You* are supposed to be the spiritual head of your household, as a male Neteru, and work in tandem with your partner, as well as your team. But you cannot play God. This is why the Creator took such grave exception to your transgression."

Damali's warning slammed into Carlos's brain. Instantly, he knew what the angels were referring to, the image was so clear. "No, no, no, no, no—I take it back. All of it!"

"It is done. We are but messengers and must work with what we have been given—you, in this state of confusion. The task is daunting, but we serve the Most High. We do all without question. A direct order has been given us. We *never* challenge that."

"Time is short."

Silence surrounded Carlos. He could only stare at the brilliant beam of light that washed over him. This was possibly the most foolish thing he'd ever done in his entire existence.

"Yes," three voices said quietly.

"Therefore *you* must close the portals—since the energy attached to *you*. And you must also deliver the book and ensure that the two evil heads are severed—one male, one female—at the darkest levels, to restore the balance. The energy could not have entered you as a male Neteru, had your choice been crystal clear—but it wasn't. Nothing will challenge you as you reenter the unnamed place. We will use the larceny of the dark side to lever the good."

Carlos brought his hand to his throat. New tears rose to his eyes. He had brought contagion to his team—to the planet—to Damali. "They set me up . . ."

"We know. That was not our doing. Never our intent. But you must acknowledge and repent your collusion in allowing them access through your own lack of faith," the entities said quietly, their voices gentle and floating on the Arizona wind. "But they also put you in a position of strength that they had not bargained for—strength stemming from loving the young cleric who they snatched, like a brother. That is your weapon: You dearly love your earth family. That you still love the female Neteru from the depths of your soul has always been your strongest weapon. It may be the only one left to you . . . after. Remember the basics. Faith, hope, and love—the trinity. You lacked faith. Hoped for the wrong things. Love is your only anchor. Cling to that as you build the missing elements within before your tie to the seventh level of darkness takes even that."

"Level Seven? You've gotta help me. Fortify me! I cannot be connected to that place!" Tears streamed down Carlos's face and his hands left his throat to reach out toward the Light beings before him. "Don't leave me to fight *that* with a third of what I need!"

"We have never left you. But to break their hold, you must do something in equal measure to their dark strength. Bringing us the book will break it. Energy transference is the only way."

Carlos stared at the twinkling stars. The Light had begun to recede from the sky. "Please tell me how, then," he whispered. "I need direction; just tell me what to do."

"We seek not only Padre Lopez's soul, along with countless others, but the essence of yours to protect that as well.

Bring the ultimate darkness into the Light. We cannot go that deeply into the nether realms to do this for you—you must fight for your own soul and the souls of others that have been trapped, like you once were," the lead voice said. "Be vigilant. They seek the return of what they felt has been stolen from them. You. The one that has proven to be their best and yet worst soldier turned general of the Legions. Both sides have equal claim. You are one of our best, and possibly our worst, earthbound warrior of Light. Our faith, hope, and love in what lies deep within you is the only thin line of silver light that allows you to not be beheaded tonight."

"When our female Neteru injured the dreaded one, Lilith was too weak to close the doors of darkness behind her," another said, but his voice began to sound as though it was fading away.

"The Chairman fled," the lead entity said, his voice rising with urgency, "but his book is below. We must burn his energy out of the book to break the hold the darkness has on the stolen souls of millions. . . . The Chairman is the direct spawn of he who remains nameless, and never had a soul to anchor them within the Dark Realms. He never would have succeeded were it not for the pressed pages made from stolen branches and twigs of our Tree of Life and our Tree of Knowledge in the Garden, when he breached Paradise. It is through his book of dark conversion that we reveal all that has been stolen from our side from the beginning of time. The one who remains nameless also seeks him, and has sent out his Legions to hunt him down. They care not that they befoul innocents on their quest. They must be stopped. Bring us the book."

"You have only seen one beast, because he homed to your dark thread and followed that thread to the female Neteru's childhood fear of him. That was the only demon who was able to penetrate the hallowed barriers here—*because of you*. She feared nothing else as strongly. Your interlocking dark energy with her darkest fear was the only thing strong

enough to allow that. But you have not seen all the other per-
versions that have come to the surface, because you have
been sequestered on hallowed ground," the third entity said
as he began to disappear. "Evil has insinuated itself among
everyday humans. Soon, they will not be able to continue to
remain blind. We are in the final days. The book is filling too
quickly, tipping the balance in the wrong direction."

"You want me to go down to Hell, bring you the book,
and then what?" Carlos said with his arms outstretched.
Panic kept his body rigid, but his tone was filled with awe
and respect.

Only one entity remained. "We will send you a sign when
the time is right to go to the chamber. Only then retrieve the
book, and deliver it to us—*but do not sit in the Chairman's
throne*. If you do not heed our warning, you could be lost to us
forever. You must journey far by earthly measures to find what
you have lost—a part of yourself. Integrate that first, and then
collect the book. Your mission is thus, do not question more."

"But what sign!" Carlos yelled, confusion and frustration
adding to his panic.

"She will know. Listen to the signs uncovered by her
Neteru visions. Work in tandem, never alone."

The Angel lowered a sword in Carlos's direction; the
powerful gleam of silvery blue light emanating from it hurt
Carlos's eyes. "Come to terms with your fate," he warned.
"You, like she, are our Neteru. Never forget. Never surrender. Know and choose your side for the battle yet to come.
Their trickery and guile have returned your demon abomination of fangs and all that comes with it. Use the trial wisely
against the darkness . . . always remember the greater good."

And just like that, the last entity was gone, taking the others within a splinter of light that closed in upon itself on the
blue black horizon.

Carlos stood still, listening to the wind howl around him.
"But what about daylight, the blood hunger, all of the crap
that comes with the fangs? How am I gonna live with my
squad, with Damali? Wait!"

A too-bright star began to strobe above him. He knew it was they, but for a moment, there was no answer. Lightning blazoned the sky again in a quick flash, and the answer entered his mind in the same thunderous voice that had previously battered his ears.

You are a fusion of Level Seven; all dark levels within the nether realms fear what you could be. . . . This thing draws terror from even their kind. It walks by day, has control over its hungers and lusts; it is a slave to nothing, except absolute power.

"What is this *thing* that even you as warrior angels are scared to name?" Carlos whispered, staring at the sky where lightning had scorched it.

The response that entered his mind made him back away from the lonely spot in the canyon-side where he stood and begin a flat-out run back to Damali's house. He ran as though he were the wind itself. Tears flew from his eyes as his velocity increased to make the shadowed landscape a blur. No, no no, they had to be wrong. *Please God, no,* not after all he'd been through and showed of his real heart. His body went hot and then cold, nausea riddled him, but he ran, trying to run away from his very self.

He saw her driveway, barreled up her steps, and pounded on the door. Her Hummer wasn't there; he collapsed against her screen, sobbing out loud. It could not be true. No, not in his body, not in his mind—*Por Dios,* protect his spirit. His woman's instinct was correct; her Neteru alarms had been going haywire since the Hell-smoke had possessed him. She was correct to keep her distance, but he needed her to tell him it was going to be all right. If no one else in the universe believed him, she must. "Baby, please come home!" he pleaded between sobs.

He banged futilely, knowing that there was only one place to go, the family house. But that was impossible now, not like this, not until he talked to her. Marlene didn't have a cure; Heaven didn't have a cure. No one could help him— only another Neteru would understand—only his woman, someone who loved him to the bone, no matter what, would go down to the depths with him, and had enough light and faith and hope and love . . .

"Oh, my God," he wailed, scrabbling in vain at her locked door. "I cannot be on the brink of turning into the Antichrist! Help me, D . . . Don't leave me like this!"

CHAPTER NINE

During the drive over to the family house, Damali prayed out loud, and prayed hard. Her panic-laden entreaties ricocheted between the Almighty, any available guardian angel listening, and her Neteru Queen Council. She put out her quiet-hysteria all-points bulletin with tears brimming in her eyes while she clutched the steering wheel.

With portals open and demons running rampant, who knows what could have happened to her man? Was she crazy, not going after him and arguing that he stay until daylight? What had been on her mind! Marlene, AWOL? And that hadn't shaken her to her knees? The rest of the older team members hadn't responded to a significant crisis—and that hadn't jolted her brain to wake up from its self-indulgent haze? Oh, yeah, she was definitely infected. Carlos had to be, too. *Just let him be alive and uninjured.*

Damali jumped out of her vehicle, ran up the front steps, and barreled through the front door. Her heart was pounding so hard that she almost couldn't hear the sheriff and the tribal leader's quick footfalls behind her. Every member of the team was on their feet, and Damali almost fell from relief when she saw that Marlene, Shabazz, Berkfield, and Marjorie had returned.

"Chief Quiet Eagle had a vision," Damali said, out of breath as her gaze swept everyone in the living room of the family house. "He brought his grandson out to our road, and sure enough, the sheriff saw Carlos's Jeep totaled with a doe on the hood."

"We set up orange barriers and flare markers so no other vehicle will plow into the back of the wreckage. But it's pretty much in a ditch off the road anyway, so in the morning, the tow truck can come to flatbed it."

"Am I missing something?" Marlene said, her gaze locked with the sheriff's for a moment and then with Damali's. "Search party? Paramedics!" Marlene swept away from the sofa and went to stand by Damali.

The elderly man, who had been silent until now, shook his head no and began speaking slowly in Navajo so that his grandson could interpret.

"In the morning, like the Jeep wreck," the sheriff said with an apology in his eyes. "There was nobody in the vehicle, and I scanned the area with floodlights from my cruiser. He wasn't there. My grandfather advises—"

"Damn all that," Shabazz said, pounding Mike's and Dan's fists. "Our brother could have been injured, limped away from the crash, and passed out. We don't roll like that."

Rider and Jose looked at the old man and then the Sheriff.

"Wanna give our brother Shabazz the unedited version of what Pop said, Sheriff?" Rider walked over to the breakfront and gathered up ammunition. "I can't speak it, but I can pick up a few key words and phrases, even though I'm rusty, and that ain't all the old man said."

"We ride," Jose said bluntly. *"Tonight."*

The old man began speaking again; this time he withdrew a shaker and a small, leather medicine bag with an eagle feather attached to it, and began gesturing wildly with his hands.

Jose and Rider watched him intently, as did the rest of the group.

"The doe had two puncture wounds in its throat," Jose said in a quiet, defeated tone. "Local nearby ranchers outside the sacred barriers have been losing livestock recently. Carcasses drained, mutilated. People behaving strangely, too."

Knowing glances passed around the team.

"He says we should watch the news and read the papers, not just from this town, but from other cities as well. Crime is up, like people are possessed. Strange types of senseless acts of violence are taking place. There have been bizarre sightings of things that cannot be explained. Not just here, but in many areas, many cities." Jose rubbed his palms down his face and briefly closed his eyes.

The old shaman nodded and folded his arms with satisfaction in his unwavering stare.

Damali closed her eyes. It was spreading.

"Grandfather says there's a bad spirit afoot. Whatever's been making bad things happen in the world is trying to infiltrate sacred lands. He has called a meeting of the elders at the sweat lodge tonight. The elders are reconsidering your building permit, and will refund any monies you have given them." The sheriff looked away as though ashamed.

"That is bullshit!" Dan shouted. "Not to mention illegal! We've already poured the foundation, have construction crews out there, and contractors, not to mention the fees to the architects—"

The old man held up his hand and spoke in a calm, determined tone.

"Grandfather says that the nation is well aware of the expenses, and will reimburse you from the nation's casino funds, but there is not enough money in the world to pay for the devil to lodge here." The sheriff looked around with a pained expression. "The ways of my people are . . . different. Perhaps in the morning, when heads are cooled, we can thoroughly inspect the doe and come to a reasonable compromise." He glanced at his grandfather and the group, and then sighed.

Kristen and Bobby drew in close to their mother. Berkfield's arm went over Marjorie's shoulders. J.L. closed ranks with Dan and Jose, their chins held high and their eyes burning with determined intensity to defend the house, or die trying. Nobody cared who touched whom; they were one team and would go out as one. Jose nodded to Mike, and accepted Mike's handoff of Inez, as Jose's other hand pulled Juanita in closer to his side. Marlene picked up her stick and took a position in front of those who would undoubtedly remain at the house.

Damali looked at Marlene. "When we get back, I need to fill you in more. You and I have to talk."

"For sure," Marlene replied, her intense gaze boring into Damali's.

"Like Jose said," Big Mike repeated, gaining a nod from Berkfield. "We ride."

"Old squad," Shabazz said, motioning to Rider, Big Mike, and Berkfield. "We take our lead tracker, audio sensor, and a healer, along with Damali, our lead seer. I've got your backs as lead tactical sensor. J.L., Jose, you two stay here on monitors and as a nose to be sure nothing untoward blows through this door. Dan, you're on ammo with Jose. Mar and Marjorie will be in here as senior and junior seers to pick up anything before it even shows up on the radar. The rest of y'all chill and stay strapped with a weapon until we get back."

The lights of the family house were like a beacon. All that he cared about, all that he loved was at risk. He wanted this nightmare to be over. *Tonight.* Waiting was out of the question. Damali hadn't answered her door, and he knew where she was—home, with the others. A place that he could no longer go in his condition.

Carlos wiped his face with both hands and walked down the steps into the front yard. He paused as he passed a blackened section of grass that had not been there before. He stood still and sniffed, and a rank metallic smell entered his nose. He rounded the small patch of pure darkness and then stooped to further inspect it. Something magnetic drew his arm away from his body, made his fist open, and invited his fingers near the patch of sullied earth. He immediately knew what it was; the place where he'd vomited, where his clothes had been deposited in a trash bag in the yard . . . where the earth had swallowed his dark essence back down into the pit.

And she'd seen it. Had anointed him. Damali had witnessed all of this and still came back into the house to allow him to lie in her bed, trying to heal him, purge him? He owed her more than an apology.

"Oh . . . baby . . ." he whispered into the night. "You still had my back. I should have never doubted you." He stood and walked around the dark patch, closing his eyes as he considered the enormity of her love. She'd kept his secret, always had, and had tried on her own to bring him back before alerting the team. She *knew* he was turning back and had something else too horrible to name within him. She'd felt it, but never disclosed it. She had also held him in her arms, but simply couldn't get past her inner alarm barriers. Nothing was wrong with her; it was him. Now he understood it all.

Renewed panic entered him as he opened his eyes and glanced back at the lit house in the distance. If all he needed to do to put this to rest and keep the team safe was to deliver the book to angels, then that was a small thing, at least compared to what could result if he didn't.

The pull to the black circle became stronger, almost a lure, and with Damali on his mind, he stepped into the center of it. Instantly the ground gave way, yawned, and sucked him down, burped, and then closed over him.

Rider stood in front of Carlos's wrecked Jeep, sending a UV halogen flashlight beam onto the doe, and then neared the dead animal. He drew in a deep breath, closed his eyes, and shook his head. "Wasn't Rivera," he said, disgusted.

Damali touched the animal's throat, peering at the gaping puncture wounds. She measured the bite marks with her forefinger and thumb. "Too small. This isn't Carlos's jaw range. It's—"

"Female," Rider said, flatly. "Goes with a tracer of lavender that I'll never forget."

"Tara?" Shabazz said, nearing the carcass. He spread out his hands and then pulled them away from the animal as though it had burned him. "Definitely female vamp vibration."

Mike cocked his head to the side. "Incoming," he muttered, and spun in the direction of the bramble a few feet away.

Tara walked out of the darkness. Her shadowed form remained partially hidden until Rider killed the lights. This time, without Yonnie there to immediately observe, she allowed her gaze to appreciate Rider fully.

Old memories died so hard, as did one's soul. Every facet of him took her back to a lost oasis in her mind. He still had that sinewy, lanky build, and gorgeous hazel eyes, even when they flashed in her direction with anger. There was a quiet passion beneath his hard gaze, just as the way the muscle flexed in his jaw told her all she needed to know. He felt it; she felt it. Maybe one night; but not tonight. She breathed in his earthy scent, picking up his adrenaline-laced blood, and watching his nostrils slightly flare to breathe her in, too.

She wanted to whisper to him that it had been a long time, but thought better of it. She allowed her mind to scavenge sensations from memory . . . his rough, guitar-calloused hands, and how wonderful they felt gently caressing her skin. The warmth of his body, the exacting rhythms of his deep breaths when he was in her arms . . . and the impassioned sound of it when it hitched just behind her ear. His hair, his laugh, his wit, his touch . . . his good heart. A thousand years would never replace the loss. She loved him so, but had hurt him so badly that tears rose to her eyes in the dark. Yet, there had been no other way. One more kiss, one more night, and she'd turn him. That couldn't happen. He deserved better, and she loved him enough to set him free.

"I'm sorry that you all had to see that," she said quietly, her eyes on Rider, meaning more than the bleeding deer. "It was my intention to remove the animal before you did, but the trooper and the old man arrived before I could."

For a moment, he just stared at her and then sent his line

of vision toward the dead doe. "Nice to see you again, too, Tara," Rider said in a tight voice. "How've you been since last night? Guess you can tell we've been just peachy."

"Rider, listen," she said gently. "I—"

"What's to listen to, darlin'?" Rider snapped, cutting off her statement. "You had to eat, jacked up our boy in the process, but he's only a human. You got our near-apex male Net stashed in a love lair, or did you have him for a light appetizer, maybe the main course? Or did you save the big game for Yon—"

"I don't know where Carlos is. I didn't send the deer into his windshield, either. It was running from my hunt and froze in Carlos's path. Before I could help him, a bright light sent me back and away. I was temporarily blinded, and I don't know what happened. I needed to feed once the light receded, because I'd been rendered *blind.* I was injured! Do you understand?" she said, her voice as brittle as Rider's. "I didn't call Yonnie to help me—out of respect for this land, and for you."

"This is getting us nowhere," Damali said, giving Rider a look to tell him to chill. Hummer headlights made everyone's faces seem elongated and eerie, but she shook the dread. If lights came from the sky and chased a female vampire away, then it stood to reason that Carlos was still in good graces. She hoped. Damali turned her attention to Tara. "Can you track Carlos now? Are you all right?"

"Thanks, Damali," Tara said in a huff. "Yes. I am fine. I've healed." She scowled at Rider, and then addressed Damali again. "But I could not locate Carlos, even after the light receded. I fed as quickly as possible to regain my sight, and then began to search for him. I was frantic. That's why I left the carcass, hoping he might home back to it, if he was experiencing a relapse. Then the sheriff came before I could dispose of it and I had to conceal myself. When I saw your Hummer approach, I was hoping we could search for him as a team." Tara had let the offer dangle, placing extra emphasis on the word *team.*

Damali nodded. "Let's do that, then." She looked at Tara, then at Rider, before glancing at Shabazz and Mike. "We all have to pull together on this. If one of our team is out there and down, time is of the essence—given what else might be out there." She stared at Rider hard. "Tara just confirmed that Carlos didn't relapse. This was her kill. However, she and another member of our team have superior night radar and range."

"Rider, man, we ain't trying to rub your nose in the situation," Shabazz said carefully, "but Carlos's boy can cover more ground in the air with Tara than we can on foot or even in a vehicle—plus he can pick up a human blood tracer faster."

"Word," Mike said, adjusting his semiautomatic. "But it's up to you, brother. Respect."

All eyes were on Rider. He hocked and spit and walked away toward the Hummer.

"Call the sonofabitch," Rider muttered. "Just keep that bastard out of my face."

His descent was immediate, but not disorienting like it had been in the past. Nothing reached for him or scrabbled at him as the black siphon pulled him deeper. All it took was his thought, *Level Six Chambers,* and he landed on his feet just outside the Vampire Council's Chamber doors. Not even the bats crowded among the stalactites and stalagmites moved. Hooded messengers bowed and closed their red, gleaming eyes, their skeletal bodies trembling beneath tattered black robes as they lowered their massive scythes. The gaseous fumes that swirled up from the Sea of Perpetual Agony didn't even make his eyes water. His nose seemed impervious to the harsh sulfuric blasts. Even the heat emanating from the bubbling red-orange surface felt like a cool breeze. All moans and shrieks and wails ceased.

Somewhat bewildered by the reception and his instant adjustment to the environment, Carlos proceeded down the narrow crag and stood before the doors of the Vampire Council's Chambers. He reached for the golden fanged knocker, expecting the customary entry-check bite, but the demon-headed knocker closed its eyes, retracted fangs, and the door creaked open eerily.

Carlos stood outside the huge black marble double doors, frozen in wonder for a moment. Not even the Chairman had access like that. The knockers always did a vamp black-blood ID check to ensure no imposter was entering for a coup. Down here, illusion and treachery were the order of the night. The doors just opened like that? He felt another potential setup, but no alarms were sounding in his gut.

After struggling with the conundrum for a bit, he soon gathered his courage and walked forward, not waiting for the underworld to change its mind. He knew only one thing for sure, power was respected, but that was always a temporary condition. Therefore, whatever the angels had jolted him with, he couldn't waste time thinking about it for too long. The mission was clear: Get the book and get out.

As he crossed the familiar marble floor, however, the level of disrepair did give him slight pause. Thrones were overturned and broken; there was a huge gaping fissure in the floor. Residue of black blood spatter marred all surfaces, staining everything like it was crude oil goop. Wall torches appeared to have been ripped from their mounts. Rubble and crushed granite was everywhere. It seemed like a veritable war had been fought within the once revered hall. It was obvious that whoever or whatever had been searching for the Chairman had exacted serious pain from any entity that had been foolish enough to remain here to try to take a stand.

Carlos glanced around, the eerie desolation unnerving him as he approached the barren, dust-covered, pentagram-shaped table that sat silent and abandoned. No longer could one hear the constant trickle of blood that used to run through it. All motion had ceased; blood was dried and clotted in the veins and arteries of the marble and had come to a dead halt. Inner lair, granite coffins of the councilmen had been reduced to piles of ash and small stones. Mere pebbles represented the once ornately carved caskets now. No respect for the dead resided here. True, Damali had dusted the remaining council suckers, except the Chairman, but it was also clear that someone or something else had come in there behind her, and it had been very pissed off. Girlfriend didn't do all this damage while she'd been here.

The kingdom of the vampires had obviously been served a death knell. Level Seven was definitely in full effect.

Carlos peered down at the crest at the center of the table, wondering. The eyes of the demon head opened slowly and stared back at him. Fear flickered in its red glowing eyes as it submissively retracted one battle-length fang and one broken fang, then shuddered. Carlos glanced back at the Chairman's throne. With all the devastation, what if the book had already been stolen? They hadn't considered *that?* Why would it be left here? Clearly, unless the Chairman had some serious special power over that artifact, the one who will remain nameless would have already seized the prize and have it in his possession—and there was *no way* he was going down *there* to retrieve shit.

Carlos wiped at the thin sheen of perspiration forming on his brow. The decision was clear. Report back that the book was gone, and where its probable location was now. Let 'em know the condition of things below, and they could concoct a new plan. That was the ticket. *He was out.*

He began to draw away from the table, wondering if just a mere thought would jettison him to the surface without incident, or if he had to risk calling for one of the trembling messengers. In the few seconds that it took him to draw a rational conclusion, the crest shuddered and yawned open on its own, revealing the vacancy beneath it. Confirmation. Cool. Even the fucking crest was scared shitless. Obviously it didn't want to be ripped open again and violated. He could dig it. Been there.

As Carlos edged away, stepping over toppled, abandoned thrones with care, and avoiding the Chairman's at all cost, memories coalesced within him. Ultimate knowledge lay as rubble at his feet. Carlos hesitated, suddenly remembering his old throne. Everything from his line from the beginning of time resided within it, and had offered infinite knowledge. No. He kept edging away. His orders had been explicit. Never sit in a dark throne again, especially not the Chairman's.

Before he could clear the circumference of the table, something very odd began to happen right before his eyes. The rubble of the Chairman's throne slowly gathered. Carlos was transfixed as stone sealed in upon itself, black marble smoothed, deep crimson velvet rethreaded as though new, dust filtered away, and the Chairman's throne righted itself from the floor and regenerated. His first impulse was to run . . . but a slow trickle of crimson ran down the arms of the throne, pooled at the edges of the demon handgrips, and then dripped to the floor in a long, string of inviting ooze. Then, in a slow, sulfuric burn, Carlos watched his name become etched in the hieroglyphic-like markings at the top of it, replacing the former Chairman's.

Blood scent filled his nose and made him lick his lips. "No," Carlos whispered.

The throne whispered back, its call like a siren's. "Come, and know all." Multiple voices wafted out to him, offering the blood scent as a lure. The slow ooze that had pooled on the floor instantly rippled across the marble to Carlos's feet, covering his Timberlands, circling his ankles. Blood soaked into the hem of his jeans, climbed up his legs, lapped at his thighs, stroked his groin, then wet his T-shirt to travel up his neck and stroke the place along his jugular until it burned like a lover had caressed him there.

Carlos weaved and caught himself against the edge of the table. The scent was intoxicating, but didn't make him nearly as heady as the hint of power the throne begged to share. He'd always secretly wondered what gave the Chairman such absolute reign over the other councilmen. If each of their thrones held the wisdom and collective knowledge of their lines on a given continent, then what the hell did the Chairman's throne hold?

The blood that teased his throat spread under his nose and across his face in delicate tendrils, licking at his nostrils. Carlos held his breath for a moment, fighting the urge to inhale deeply as he staggered away from the table and kept his lips sealed firmly shut against bloody invasion. He shook his head no as he turned to stare at the throne. No . . . he was out. The book wasn't there.

Standing there, soaked with blood, tears forming in his eyes, his body began to shudder with feed desire. He hadn't sipped in any air and was suffocating. He angrily wiped the blood away from his mouth, took in a huge gulp of air, and closed his mouth quickly. But the taste in the scent lingered on his tongue . . . made him close his eyes, slowly part his lips, and a tiny tendril entered his parched mouth where air was allowed to seep in.

Flavors and colors from all the blood consumed from generations of vampires coated his tongue, opened his mouth wider, until the blood ran over his face like a river, pooling in his opened jaw, lowering fangs, and he swallowed.

The throne pulled him blindly as a deep, sensual moan came up from Carlos's abdomen. Blood washed his face; it was impossible to see. The rush of it was so intense that it deafened him, filling his ears, invading every orifice, until he sank against the crimson velvet panting, swallowing, shuddering, crying, laughing, his palms welded to the hand rests.

His body arched as a black electric volt ran through him. It snatched open his third eye, bludgeoning his senses, burning out his cerebral cortex with so much information transmitting so quickly that he sat there like a vegetable, twitching and jerking in the horrible seat. His spine groaned, writhed to the surface beneath his skin, and then snapped, tearing away from tissue anchors and cartilage, making him scream as vertebra became one with the high-back marble throne for a moment, and then reentered his body, regenerating with new circuitry and bits of black matter.

Carlos slumped forward, panting, sweat pouring down his

frame, his clothes burning away while blue-black flames
scorched his skin, but he was unable to move. Then the surface of his skin became suddenly cool. A new torrent of
blood filled his mouth, and he greedily gulped it, regenerating more as he did so.

Pain abated. The room again went still. Strength slowly
crept into his naked limbs. Fear fled his heart. Knowledge
from every throne in the room had a new lord. A sly smiled
graced his face. Information poured into his mind in streaming, endless still frames . . . then with agonizing pleasure.

Every carnal act that had ever been committed on the
planet sent shock waves of ecstasy through him. Depraved
or otherwise, it didn't matter. He could feel the impact of it
all, every touch, every shudder, every moan, every gasp,
every whimper—it all collided and fused into one sensation.
He came so hard his heart stopped. His pulse was measured
in elongated wails each time his body jerked and emitted
thick, black emulsion from his member that wriggled in a
slimy wash of tiny black tadpoles over his stomach, his lap,
and his thighs.

Carlos's fingers gripped the hand rests; his nails grew,
carving into the marble with hooked talons. His eyes were
sealed shut, but as he opened them, a black gleaming ray
covered the floor where his line of vision went, scorching
new sections of marble away.

Battle-bulked to proportions he'd never dreamed possible, Carlos stood abruptly. Dark ejaculate slid from his
body, splatting to the floor in thick, wriggling plops from his
thighs. He stared at it dispassionately as his legs turned into
granite. A scaly, spaded tail swished a razor-bladed tip at
what was moving at his feet, making the knots on his spine
feel tender as he flexed his spine. Then his toes welded together into gleaming, black, cloven hooves. *Interesting.* He
chuckled, his voice booming like thunder and sending small
rocks to the floor from the abraded walls. New, leathery
wings unfolded from his shoulder blades and cast a dark
shadow from their broad span. He spun to face the throne

that had consumed him, fury at the treacherous invasion closing his talons into a fist.

He hurled a punch that exploded against the marble and decimated the throne to bits of stone once more. Breathing hard, he could feel sudden heat flare from his nostrils. He covered his nose with his hand, and it came away with blue flames. "Well . . . I'll just be damned."

Yonnie touched down and stared at Tara in the moonlight. "Something major just happened."

She nodded, glancing off into the distance. "I know."

"We've gotta find our boy before the others do," Yonnie said, worried. "Fuck all that bullshit with Rider. I ain't even thinking about that right now. We need to get back to the group and let 'em know something big is going down."

Tara nodded and disappeared.

CHAPTER TEN

He should have been trailing blood, from the looks of this accident," Damali said, her keen eyes to the ground as their Hummer bumped over the rough, off-road terrain.

"Not picking up anything," Rider said, hanging his head out the window like a hunting dog.

"Hold up, y'all," Mike said. "Tara's voice."

Shabazz brought the Hummer to a stop. "Be cool, man," he said toward Rider. "She's not alone, dig?"

"Yeah, peace, whatever," Rider said, and sat back in the Hummer.

Damali jumped out and Yonnie and Tara materialized. "What's the word?" Damali said, her gaze going from Yonnie to Tara and back.

"No sign of him," Tara said nervously, "but Yonnie picked up a significant power surge."

"Subterranean," Yonnie said, glaring over Damali's shoulder toward Rider. "Ain't felt that since the Chairman went topside."

"What does it mean?" Damali clutched her baby Isis blade tighter.

The rest of the team piled out of the Hummer.

"Everything all right, D?" Shabazz said, looking at Yonnie hard.

Rider cocked back the safety on his weapon. "Any problem, li'l sis?"

"Everybody be cool," Big Mike said. "What happened underground, man?"

Yonnie shook his head, but kept a lethal glare on Rider.

"That's just the thing. I don't know and don't have an underground pass no more to go check it out."

"Where *is* my *fucking* book!" Carlos bellowed, making the table shudder as his fist tore away a section of it.

The crest rolled back, opened again to the vacant space in its vault, and began to smolder as Carlos's glare remained on the emptiness.

"I know it's not here!" he shouted. "Tell me!"

Within seconds white mist began to form within the empty space, and Carlos blew on it, sending plumes of cloudlike smoke away from the opening so he could see the bottom of the vault. But instead of gleaming black marble, blue, snow-covered mountains appeared in a wavering hologram-like form. He stared at the illusion, his eyes narrowing as he received sensations, judged distance, and homed in on a location. The Himalayas. He nodded and waved his hand over the opening, and it sealed. The crest looked at him and bowed its head, shivering.

"Very good," Carlos muttered. "Very, very good."

"Transport!" he bellowed, and wrapped his wings around his naked body.

The doors to the chamber quickly opened, and several hooded messengers rushed through, bumping into each other, stumbling, and falling prostrate on the marble before him.

"Your Excellency," the one closest to his feet said in a shivering croak. "We are humbly at your service."

As his temper receded, Carlos's form began to slowly normalize.

"Mr. Chairman," another said, and then looked up, screamed, and covered his head as a black bolt of energy snuffed him from the floor, leaving ash in the entity's wake.

"Please, we beg you, Your Excellency, have pity on us. Do not take out his foolish mistake on the rest of us, *we know* who you are," the lead messenger groveled. "He was new, insane; please accept our apology on his behalf for ti-tling you beneath your esteemed Level-Seven rank."

Carlos folded his arms, not sure how to respond. He thought

he'd acquired the Chairman's title . . . but clearly that was not the case. He used the end of his spaded tail as a toothpick, cleaning a twelve-inch fang, thinking, then clothed himself as a distraction. The black designer suit and custom-tailored shirt felt good as they slid into place, and all evidence of his brief tryst with the throne did as well. He retracted his wings and tail, then walked around the messengers cowering on the floor, the sound of his black, alligator-skin slip-ons making soft taps against the polished stone. He smiled. Yeah, much more genteel than the clatter of hooves. A brother always had to be smooth.

"I want to check out the response on all the levels as I go up," Carlos said evenly. "Need to be sure respect is in the house across the board."

"Yes, sir," the lead entity whispered. "We assure you it is, though, sir."

"Good."

The messengers hadn't lied. When Carlos's funnel cloud came to a swirling rest at the edge of the were-demon realms of Level Five, all howling ceased. Heads lowered, bodies shuddered, and he stared at an old werewolf senator that came out of hiding, his tail between his legs in dog-pack submission. A were-jaguar senator crept forward from the big cat clan and crouched low, holding his breath.

"Your Excellency," the wolfen clan senator said, keeping his head lowered, "we do hope you will forgive the previous . . . uh . . . disrespect shown to you while you were a vampire. The tensions between Level Five and Level Six are legendary, but had we known you were being groomed for ultimate descent—I assure you, our response would have been much different."

"Woulda, coulda, shoulda," Carlos said in a bored tone as he stared out into the black forest. Thousands of gleaming yellow eyes stared back at him, unblinking, waiting for his word and his determination of their realm's fate. He walked with his hands behind his back, a cunning smile on his face

as he circled the huge werewolf senator and shook his head.
Bones from thousands of years of feedings cracked and
crunched under his feet like gravel.

"Forgiveness. Hmmm . . . Don't have it in me," Carlos
said, removing his hands from behind his back and staring
down at his neatly manicured nails. "Matter of fact, talk of forgiveness down here is considered blasphemy. Am I wrong?"

A collective gasp filtered through the looming, black trees.

The huge beast began to snuffle and whimper. "Sir, yes,
but, really, all I am asking for is—"

"Mercy?" Carlos hollered. Then he laughed. "Motherfucker, *you* are trying my patience."

Wails and sulfuric ash followed Carlos in an angry chimney,
the bright red glow of a total inferno helping to jettison his
transport to Level Four. "I want that entire level smoked, do
you hear me?" Carlos commanded his messenger as they
came to the swamplands of the Amanthras. He absently
brushed the intermittent rain of maggots off his shoulders
and surveyed the bubbling black tars and slithering dampness all around them on Level Four. "If the fire goes out on
Five, and the explosions stop, I'm holding every messenger
on Six accountable."

Again, his courier was prostrate, shaking his head as
hard as his scythe trembled. "Your desire is our every command, sir."

"Good. Then get up off this nasty, slimy shit, and be a
man," Carlos said, pure disgust entering him. He snapped
his fingers and the wetlands dried into desert region. Immediately, huge black serpentine Amanthras rushed forward,
gasping.

"Your Excellency," the presiding member of the Amanthra Congress croaked. "We beseech you—we cannot survive without the liquid slurry of dark dreams and fetid
desires."

Carlos watched without emotion as the body of the huge
serpent begin to decay. Once-gleaming black scales with-

ered and began to peel off the beast, dripping yellow and green acidic blood to the dry ground, as they fell like singed roofing tiles to the hot sand. The gills behind its Volkswagen-size, serpentine head struggled open and then shut in shuddering gasps of agony. Smaller serpents squealed and writhed closer to their leader, until a knot of smoldering demon flesh began to melt in one putrid heap.

"Yo *holmes*," Carlos said smiling at his messenger. "Ain't these the guys that sided with Fallon Nuit against me and my lady?"

"Yeth, thirrrr," the messenger lisped, his eyes glowing red within his faceless hood. "Traitors."

The huge Amanthra banged its head against the hot sand, and Carlos watched the sand heat go from a low blue glow, to red, to white hot.

"Please . . . ," it croaked, a viper fang dropping off and torching on impact as it hit the sand.

"Turn off the water on Levels Three and Four," Carlos ordered. "Send the wetlands to the fucking ghosts gangs—and let's see how they like their new decor on Levels One and Two. Fuck the terror cells, too. No more dry boulders and canyons for those motherfuckers to hide in. Let the succubae and incubi drown in their own bullshit. *Vamanos*."

Long agonized wails of pleas and shouts followed him. The word *nooooooo* still echoed in Carlos's ears as he materialized not far from where his Jeep had been wrecked.

The messenger bowed. "Your instructions will be adhered to with all the resources of our realm, sir."

"Cool," Carlos said, walking away. "Kill the sulfur and take your raggedy ass back from whence it came. Don't come up here unless I call you."

"Sir, your wish is my command. However, do you need protective escort?" The messenger seemed frightened and confused as it stared at Carlos. It began to amass a dark cloud around itself as a precaution in case Carlos's temper flared at the question. "Someone of your stature could be a

direct assassination target by the dreaded Light," the entity
added in an apologetic, shaky voice.

Carlos hesitated, and held up his hand, making his courier
forestall his departure. The two stared at each other. The
courier lowered his gaze and waited for instructions. Carlos
wasn't angry, just concerned. In truth, he'd never considered
that aspect of risk. But then he brushed aside his doubts.

He wasn't worried about the other demon realms, visiting
them had told him all he needed to know. They had been suf-
ficiently punked down. Anyway, the Light had sent him back
down there to get the book. This was their mission, so why
would they smoke him? The book was missing, and like before, he'd come back stronger and with critical information—
plus he'd really fucked up the realms as a show of good
faith. They knew the deal. Power was worthless unless one
used it, and power always demanded that it be used. He
could handle this shit, just like he'd handled everything else
before.

True, he'd taken an accidental tumble in the chair he
wasn't supposed to sit in, and had gotten a little blood in his
mouth, but he also found out the semi-accurate location of
the book. So, it was all good. It had to be. If it was topside,
with all this new power at his disposal, he could get to it in
no time—so what would be the problem?

Carlos yanked on his suit lapels to straighten them and
lifted his chin, smoothing his collarless black silk shirt with
a cool palm. "Naw, man," he finally said. "I always roll solo,
and I don't need no witnesses to the throw down I'm about to
lay on my woman."

The entity smiled as a sulfuric plume swirled at the hem
of its robe. It cut into the earth with its scythe, creating a
ragged fissure that belched black smoke. "As you command,
sir. *Always* as *you* command."

The Chairman looked out over the pristine, deserted beach
that sprawled beyond him like a crystalline white carpet beneath the moon. He'd always loved the Mediterranean and

had forgotten how majestic it was. A clandestine meeting with *her,* here? He'd already been seduced by her voice from the moment she called.

If she would agree to meet him here like this, alone and unarmed, her potential for getting whatever she wished to extract from him was excellent—even if she didn't need to know that.

He'd worn Greek gladiator armor for her, to suit the occasion. Had she any idea of what she did to him just from a call? He smiled and tried to stem the roiling anticipation that waiting for her produced. He just hoped that the diversions he'd thrown in the searchers' paths would keep his father off his trail at least for the night. But when he didn't immediately see her, it began to occur to him that his father's powers could have produced her call.

Panic swiftly set in. Topside pressures and atmospheric distortions had possibly eroded some of his keen perceptions. He should have known. . . .

"It's been a long time, Dante," a low, gentle female voice said.

He watched her melt away from a palm, shimmering like the dark waters of the sea. It had been so long since she'd allowed him to even glimpse her that his mouth went dry.

As she turned to face him, her gleaming silver, heart-shaped Sankofa tattoo at the base of her spine became a beacon. His eyes followed the low ruby cut of her backless gown, drinking in her voluptuous body.

"Eve," he murmured as she slowly approached.

"Dante," she quietly replied. "Thank you for agreeing to meet with me like this."

He nodded. "When you called . . . how could I deny you?" He opened his arms for her, hoping she'd fill them. "I've missed you so."

She stepped forward a bit, but not close enough for him to embrace her. "I was a young girl, and you took advantage of me that way before."

He smiled and slowly lowered his arms, disappointed. "I

was a young man, rash and impetuous, passionate. Yes, I took advantage of you, my love, but that doesn't mean my emotions were fraudulent."

She nodded and sighed sadly, and then flipped her long Egyptian braids over her shoulders. "I know, but—"

"Tell me, my still-gorgeous Neteru, do you ever think of that time we shared in true paradise?"

"I try to focus on the present, Dante. It's best that way."

He neared her and cupped her cheek. When she didn't flinch away, he closed his eyes and sighed. "I've missed you so, Eve. Level-Six banishment wasn't Hell. Being without you was."

Her hand covered his. "Then I suppose we both experienced our own brand of said same."

Her admission lowered his head to her neck and created a shudder that they both quietly shared. But she covered her jugular with her graceful hand.

"We need to talk about my younger sister Neteru."

"After so many years, might a lengthy discussion wait until near dawn?" he asked, breathing the question.

She smiled as his fangs crested and she stroked his dark, curly hair away from his face. "You came to me as Achilles," she murmured.

"You have caught the irony of this choice, yes?"

"It was very, very sweet of you to do that," she said in a soft, breathy whisper.

"You were always my weakness from the moment I laid eyes on you . . . you know that. Invincible to all but you."

She smiled and he traced her mouth with the trembling pass of his thumb.

"At least I can still make you smile, even if I can't bend your will to commit to me. I'll settle for that much right now." He studied her face, his thumb etching a distant memory into it. "When I look at you, I think of our son. How is he?"

"Well," she whispered, her gaze becoming pained. "Still resentful of his banishment sentence, but he seems resigned to serve it without incident."

The Chairman nodded. "He gets that from my side. The ability to endure until opportunity knocks. But I still think it was harsh to imprison a being with such potential and passion for life into a realm practically devoid of sensory—"

"Cain killed his brother." She looked at him hard, stepped back from him, and wrapped her arms around her waist. "Don't ever forget that, Abel may have been Adam's progeny, but he was still my child . . . one who, like Cain, I loved with my complete heart and soul, Dante. Do not minimize what Cain did."

He neared her and delicately collected her into his arms and stroked her hair. "I'm sorry. I know you were always torn. . . . This is why I didn't want to belabor a conversation laden with guilt and pain when there are so many other pleasurable things we could do tonight. Let me make it up to you now."

She shook her head no.

He sighed and loosened his hold on her. "Yes. I forgot. How *is* Adam? Still coruling the male Neteru round table with Ausar and wielding an iron fist, or has he mellowed, like me, with age?" Jealousy swept through him as he stared at Eve. "I'm surprised he was secure enough to even allow this visit. What has changed?"

"He doesn't know I'm here."

Her statement riddled him with desire adrenaline. "You came to me *on your own,* unsanctioned? Again . . . like old times?" He was barely breathing as he stared into her dark, exquisitely beautiful brown eyes. "I promise you," he whispered through fangs, "I've learned so much more over the centuries, your transgression will not be in vain."

"Aset sanctioned it. My queen sisters know I'm here, but what stays at our oval table remains between us."

Her admission stabbed him. For just a fleeting moment he thought that she'd finally come to resume what had been torn asunder. There was no way for him to mask the disappointment. "Then I take it you are here on a mission, rather than for a tryst."

"Dante, please. This involves your realm as much as it does mine."

She had his attention. He wondered how much she truly knew of his Level-Six banishment.

"Lilith burned you," Eve said, placing her hand in the center of his chest. Then her hand went to his jaw as his once-brown eyes began to flicker red then black. "As long as you remained on your throne and the portals were closed, our respective sides kept a margin of order."

He captured her hand, kissed the back of it hard, and walked away. "That is what I always so loved about you, Eve. You were always the epitome of diplomacy. A gorgeous, fair, sensual diplomat that could always understand both sides of the equation and appreciate the delicate nature of things. But that bitch, Lilith—"

"I know," Eve said carefully. "However, our young Neterus were too emotionally traumatized to act quickly enough to behead her. *It was their child.* In Lilith's sloppy departure she left the gates opened from her previous scheme. Initially, the dark Realm's food sources, the Damned, began to escape sporadically. Now all original demons from those realms are currently flooding topside, like lemmings fleeing from something chasing them underground. But no order has yet been given to commence outright war. I came to you to understand why you would destroy your own human soul supply, and would allow your own armies to be turned to ash, if—"

"It wasn't me," he said flatly. He kept his gaze on the ocean. "You might as well know that my throne has been turned to rubble for assisting Lilith. I cannot return subterranean, even if I wanted to. Father's orders." He looked at her hard. "We go back many years, and I trust that you and I have at least some honor between us. For helping the young one I lost all that I owned. This stays between us."

Eve nodded. "Fair exchange.

He nodded. "Then do not rob me of my dignity."

"I won't." Eve allowed her voice to drop to a sensual murmur. Dante didn't need to know that they were fully apprised of his reasons for helping the Neteru team. She moved in closer to him, baiting him with his oldest vice—herself.

"I always loved you," he said quietly.

"I know," she murmured. "I could also never get you out of my mind. It cost me a throne, too, Dante. Aset rules the Council of Queens, not me. That is why I had to inform her."

"They made a very poor choice, then," he whispered, stroking her cheek. "The first Neteru on the planet . . . soft, innocent, trusting, and beautiful beyond comprehension . . . one that trailed ripening like . . ." He closed his eyes briefly. "There's been no other made like you."

She covered his hand and allowed a well-timed sigh to escape her lips as an answer, and watched him swallow hard.

"There's been no other like you, ever, Dante," she whispered, her tone husky enough to lower his fangs to passion length. She hadn't lied in any of her statements, therefore there was no way for him to detect fraud. She'd never forgotten him, or how he'd deceived her. There had been nothing like him ever created. It was all the truth.

"I was a virgin when we met," she added in a wistful tone. "Do you remember?"

"How could I forget?" he whispered, now embracing her fully and allowing his hands to trace her shoulders. "You still remember . . ."

"Vividly," she said, nipping his neck and eliciting a gasp from him. "Where's your lair?"

"The Himalayas," he murmured, beginning to slip her gown off her shoulders. "We could go there tonight, if the Mediterranean doesn't please you."

She briefly captured his Adam's apple between her teeth, then released it, and spoke hotly against his skin. "Show me in my third eye, first. I need to be sure we won't be discovered or that Lilith won't intrude."

"You would allow me to lock with you?" he asked, his

voice now gravelly as he began to move against her while
nuzzling her hair.

"Only if you are honorable and do not attempt to harm me."

"I proved honorable when I assisted the current Neteru,
did I not? Harming you, dear Eve, is the last thing on my
mind. Believe me."

"I don't know," she said, pulling back a bit to string him
along. She theatrically glanced at the sky and then back to
him as though a lightning bolt might strike her. She used
seconds to her advantage. Her hesitation made him pause
and give her a bit of distance for her safety, not wanting anything to spoil the opportunity. But in the brief silence, she
could feel his anxiety crest like his fangs.

Their side knew his actions had nothing to do with
honor, but self-preservation, and a chance to keep what
would have become his father's second heir from taking
over the world so that he could. She was only here because
Damali's call had registered on every ring of Heaven. The
Neteru Council of Queens had dispatched her as the most
efficient assailant to get critical information from the only
source that had it.

"It was a very odd bargain," Eve finally said. "But you
helped our Neteru and kept the Antichrist from the planet for
a few more years. Thank you." She glanced around nervously again. "Maybe if you let me know where to meet you, we
can work something out."

He held her face with both hands and placed a kiss on the
center of her forehead, making it burn. "Meet me there," he
whispered, "and whatever they do to you for the offense will
be worth it in the morning."

"It had better be," she chuckled. "Nzinga will cut my
heart out, if you-know-who doesn't get to me first."

"Then tell Him to send you to me. Shit . . . I'll resurrect
you," he said, becoming bolder as his desire built.

"Can you do that without your throne, and the assistance
of the fallen angel . . . since I'm already dead?" she asked as

innocently as possible, already knowing the answer was no. "Because, then . . ." She allowed the possibility to hang between them.

The Chairman sighed, appraising her beauty and wishing the tedious conversation could wait until another night.

"You are well aware that my father is insane and took issue with his wife's treachery . . . and my assisting your Neteru to injure her. Since the embryo went into the Light, Level Six cannot procreate. Vampiric turns are going to ash, until he is finished with his rage. I may have overstated my capacities at the moment, but for you, dear Eve, I would endure another thousand years of his wrath." He chuckled sadly. "If you visit me, and they find out, at least we'll be together in the realms, hmmm?"

"Oh, Dante," she whispered, her hand going to her mouth, avoiding the twisted offer and decisively changing the subject. "What does that mean for the vampire nations—and you?"

"Nothing," he said as calmly as possible, her concern for him a torch to his libido. "He simply replaced me with his other heir apparent. That's who flushed the pit in the midst of his young, blind fury."

Feeling suddenly trapped, the Chairman stepped away from Eve, walking back and forth as the gravity of the situation and the indignity of it accosted him. He began to talk with his hands as he sputtered in outrage. "Young, stupid, insolent bastard! He thought he could just step into a ruling-level throne and run six realms without grooming and experience!"

The more he paced, the more fury entered his system as Eve stared at him. "I would have shown him *everything* I knew . . . brought him into his season with majesty in due time! But the sonofabitch pulled one of the most treacherous coups I have ever witnessed. Then, he threw it all away by flooding the realms instead of closing the breach and rebuilding layer by layer. His dark energy is scattered, affect-

ing everything, bringing notice!" He parted his hair with his
fingers and stared at Eve for answers. "What is wrong with
our children? What has become of our future? They don't
take a stand. They waffle from the Light and into the darkness, and back. How can either side empire-build on sand?"
He looked down at his Grecian sandal–clad feet and then
bent to collect a fistful of the grainy beach, allowing it to filter away through his fingers.

She came to him and hugged him, and her compassion almost made him sob. "I don't know, Dante," she whispered.
"I don't know. We have the same problem on our side."

"Things should be black or white, shouldn't they?"

He held her back to stare into her eyes.

She almost felt sorry for Dante as she watched him
struggle with the way the world had changed since his time
in it. It was so tempting to ask who this new heir was, and
how to locate him, so that the young Neteru could slaugh-
ter him. But she didn't dare press for more information
than she'd already gleaned through just the merest suggestion of an affair. Any more, and she would have to offer
Dante a night—an unacceptable trade. So she gave him
empathy instead.

"Things were indeed once black and white," she finally
murmured, her tone wistful. "But your father's bargain created a gray zone . . ."

He came to her and leaned his head against her forehead.
"My absolutely insane father . . ."

"Dante . . . listen to me," she said softly.

He kissed the top of her head, stopping her words. "I love
the way you say my name, even under these circumstances. . . . Say it again, on a deeper breath, and allow it to
run all through me." He couldn't even bring himself to smile
as her eyes searched his face. "I can't talk about this sordid
shit in the realms anymore. . . . Send me a pain block
through your voice . . . my name lingering in your mouth as
I capture it." He closed his eyes and attempted a mental
siphon without her permission.

She chuckled. "The answer is no before you even ask. Do not go further into my mind for an immediate beach-front seduction."

He pretended to shudder just to keep her melodic laughter mingling with the pound of the surf. "Just another little mind lock, Eve, after all these years? They surely aren't still guarding you as though you were a teenager. . . . You're a grown woman now, love. . . . They'll never know."

She laughed and pushed him away, seizing his mercurial transition into a good mood as an opportunity. "Who is the new threat? I'd rather have you on your old throne, where order was maintained, than this new problem." She folded her arms over her breasts. "At least you and I understood each other. You were never rash and impetuous." She smiled and gave him a sexy wink. "Well, maybe just once."

"Ah . . . you *do* remember." He clucked his tongue and chuckled low in his throat as his hot gaze raked her. "Flattery will get you everywhere. But to extract that level of information, only a barter in Dananu would be acceptable."

"Propose your requirement," she whispered to him in Dananu.

Just allowing him to see that she remembered all he'd taught her at the base of the Tree of Knowledge compromised him fully, so a flat-out seduction attempt was more than fair, he reasoned. He filled his hands with her hair and took her mouth slowly.

"All night, once again . . . in a garden. Then we can discuss it."

He watched her study his face, then glance up at the stars as though seriously considering his offer. The seconds of hesitation that she drew out made him tremble. But suddenly every light that had been in the sky, save the moon, went out. She giggled and shook her head.

"No can do," she whispered seductively. "They'll do the Armageddon, first, before they cosign that."

He chuckled low in his throat and ran a sharp fang down

her jugular. "I ought to bite you just for teasing me—just take the plunge out of spite."

"And torch on impact," she whispered. Running her hands over his broad shoulders. "I have very old silver in my veins that stirs hot when unwilling . . . Shall we be serious?"

"You're sure you're unwilling?" He nuzzled her hair. "Not even for old time's sake?"

"No," she cooed.

"Why are you so uncooperative, love?"

"It's my job," she said laughing low and sexy.

"Then I guess the new kid on the block is going to have to work this out on her own," he said, kissing Eve's temple as he fought off a shudder when she stroked his neck. "This one is formidable. Might be her Achilles' heel," he added, teasing her to keep her smile radiant.

"I guess we'll just have to see," she whispered, closing the small space between their bodies and allowing her hands to trail down his back. "Since you insist on being so stubborn."

"This is unfair, Eve." His eyes held a combination of amusement and anguish. "Your side is as ruthless as mine."

"How so?" She cocked her head to the side, waiting.

His arms enfolded her again as he openly inhaled her scent. "You come to me trailing Neteru from the Garden, and tell me your husband doesn't know you're with me," he said, his breathing beginning to labor. "Fill my arms, allow me to sample your skin, your mouth, your voice . . . and your touch." He shook his head with his eyes closed. "Ruthless negotiation ploy and damned near effective," he whispered, brushing her mouth. "They wait until a man is completely compromised to strike. Pit father against son, wait until that son is dethroned, and then put the woman of his dreams for millennia in his arms and ask him a question." He nicked her earlobe and let the drop of blood fall to her shoulder just to inhale it. "Then deny that poor bastard as he writhes while insisting that he give up information they want. Evil."

He chuckled as she smiled wider and touched the drop of

blood to her lips to taunt him. "Eve, you are dangerously close to the edge of battle on this beach. I've been through a lot, lately, and am not quite as rational as you may believe." His voice dipped an octave. "Especially with you . . . I might attempt a violation to go out in a blaze."

"All right," she said with a sigh. "I'll stop, but I had to try."

"So did I," he said quietly in a defeated tone. "I thought everything in the universe was negotiable, love of my existence. Don't leave. I've no one to really talk to or rule . . . and have been alone for months."

She came to him and ran her fingers through his hair as she hugged him. "Sometimes there's room for negotiation."

This time when he shuddered, it was no act.

"Stop toying with me, Eve," he whispered. "There is no such thing as resistance around you. I have to go, if you're not willing. Merely talking to you when I'm like this is worse than a battle in Dananu."

She sighed and allowed her hand to fall to his shoulder. "Then at least close the portals and help us hunt down Lilith."

"I cannot close off what her Level-Seven energy opened as long as she's alive. But hunting her down to adequately repay her larceny is on my agenda."

"Thank you," Eve whispered and took his mouth in a long, sensuous kiss. "You'll help us dethrone the new threat we're blind to, as well?"

"Oh, to be sure," he said, taking her mouth again. "I will bring you his head." He deepened the kiss until a groan fought inside his chest. "You can't see him? Interesting."

"No," she said on a breathy exhalation, practically swooning in his arms from the long kiss. "For some reason he's shielded to hunter councils. That is why we are so concerned." She closed her eyes. "Damn . . . you get me every time, Dante."

"You didn't do too bad extracting from me, either," he said, reveling in the skin covering her spine. "You have gotten older and so much stronger." He took her mouth hard, punishing it, then attended to her throat, but didn't break the skin, just made her gasp. "You said you were concerned—how concerned—tell me now?" he asked in a hissing rush of air, pulling her against him hard.

His hands had begun to slowly dissolve her gown.

She opened her eyes and gave him a glare through a soft laugh. "Not that concerned."

"Let's get back to the part about everything being negotiable."

Again the stars disappeared and angry gray clouds passed over the moon.

The Chairman sighed and let Eve go. "They play hardball with no sense of humor," he muttered. He studied Eve for a moment; the complete darkness temporarily fracturing anything rational left within him. "Only Neteru who has my heart, let me propose a tender offer." He waited as she stared at him, more ravishing in the complete darkness. "If I deliver Lilith's head and dethrone this pretender prince to my throne by summarily exterminating his young, arrogant ass . . . would you be inclined to wager another visit on a moonless night and remove the will barrier to me . . . just for *one* night?" He waited, knowing that he should allow her to answer before speaking again, but couldn't help himself. "That's my final offer."

"Let me take the request up with authorities," she said, smiling at him in the completely blackened night.

"That you would even propose it to your council inspires me."

She chuckled deeply and began walking toward the water. "Oh, Dante, don't be silly. This has to be discussed way higher than in council."

Stunned, he held her with a magnetic bolt of dark energy to keep her from leaving. "You would do *that* for me?" he whispered in awe. "Take such a request that high up?" He closed his eyes.

"I have to go," she said, looking at the dark energy current.

"Wait," he said in a rush, wanting to keep her talking and interacting with him for the rest of the night. "I hear the young female Neteru no longer has her blade."

Eve smiled. "That was a very sloppy attempt to make me jealous, Dante. Really. That was beneath you." She shook her head as his gaze slid away with embarrassment. "If she gets into trouble, you know we'll make sure it's restored when necessary." Eve remained serene. "But if you'd rather take your chances with her . . ."

He laughed, contrite. "She tried to strangle me, Eve. Have you ever? In my own chambers!"

Eve laughed with him and covered her mouth with her hand. "Dante, you are from the Old World with a different set of sensibilities. However, if you insist on running after a younger woman . . ."

"You know you're irreplaceable. She was just a fantasy, a diversion because I missed you so." His smile faded as his face became serious. "With you, I could withstand the night for several more millennia." He stepped closer. "With you, no daywalker would be necessary for me to find contentment."

"Ah," Eve breathed. "Then I stand corrected."

"I am dead serious, no longer negotiating."

Her smile faded and her voice became gentler. "Then I really must go."

"Did I tell you that you're beautiful?" He looked up at the now pitch-black sky. "They can eclipse every star and every moon in the galaxy, but I would still be able to see your radiance in the dark. Stay with me tonight."

She shook her head no, and for the first time since he'd spotted her on the beach, fear reflected in her eyes.

"We have a son together, we made life—you and I. We have history and laughter . . . we *made history,* and—"

"Dante, don't," she said, honest tears shimmering. "This conversation is over."

"Why?" he argued, coming closer as a long blade materialized in her hand. "Because you don't trust me or yourself?"

"Both."

He nodded, satisfied in part. He looked at the Isis blade in her hand and then sought her eyes. "It always looked better on you, anyway."

She lowered the blade, closed her eyes, and raised her chin as though consulting Heaven. It did something to him to see her that way, so near to the breaking point that the joints in her knees were about to bend. He replayed the incident in the Garden for her in vivid color, texture, and tone, and she redoubled her grip on the sword. But the fact that she was strong enough now at her age to resist every psychic bombardment he was leveling at her impaled him where he stood.

"Have that conversation, *please,* and see what they'll allow if I deliver," he whispered in Dananu.

She didn't commit, just began moving forward toward the violet pyramid opening at the crest of the next wave, leaving him to remember everything all alone.

CHAPTER ELEVEN

Hours of searching and the result was still the same: no Carlos. The mission had been in vain, and part of her knew that before she'd even jumped into her Hummer. Daylight might shed light on his whereabouts, but he'd obviously vanished into the night. The team had pulled together, everyone's senses keen and sweeping for injury, demons—nothing. Therefore, his disappearance had to be willful. The one thing she was sure of was, if Carlos didn't want to be found, he wouldn't be.

There was no SOS beacon prying its way into her senses. There was no blood trail for her and her trackers to pick up. Memory of the Chairman, and that demon's AWOL status made one dread with every breath. If Lilith resurfaced, God only knew what Carlos had been up against alone. Still, there should have been a trail.

She reentered the living room of the family house and went up to Marlene. Rider and the others could fill in everybody else. She and Mar needed to have a closed-door, one-on-one. She didn't care how it looked, how people might take it; she was so upset right now that all of that was secondary.

Marlene looked up the moment Damali came through the door and stood. No words needed to be exchanged. Marlene nodded and went toward her bedroom. Damali followed, not even greeting the worried housebound team members. Her man was missing, injured, and had possibly relapsed.

"I know," Marlene said in a quiet voice as she shut the door.

Damali walked in a circle, tugging at her locks. "Mar, there's a huge problem out there beyond the one we already know about. I can feel it, but can't put my finger on it. Call me double paranoid, but my gut ain't been right about Carlos since we left Philly."

Marlene stared at her. "This relapse may be a Net-flux, kiddo. Let's not become overly alarmed. We know he had an attitude when he left, and may have just gone somewhere to chill out till daybreak. None of us with second sight are picking up that he's out there injured, or abducted. In fact, who are we to talk? We're all shaky."

"That's just the thing, Mar," Damali said. "Shaky or not, I can't pick up anything on him. No vibration whatsoever. It's like a total absence of light, nothing to track, and even when he was a vamp, I could home in on the brother. Something even deeper than the infection is wrong with him—I know it."

"It may be us," Marlene said slowly, again raking her hair in frustration. "We're all infected. Like the fact that Shabazz and I didn't want to come home, and *didn't* right away, when there was a serious emergency going on . . . and Marjorie and Richard said they were tired of being parents and stayed away from the house as long as Shabazz and I did. Can you imagine?" Marlene shook her head and glanced out the window. "It took everything in us to fight the urge just to leave the family." She closed her eyes. "The pull just to worrying about ourselves for a change, being together without responsibilities . . . our judgment is impaired, baby. Maybe yours is, too."

She didn't want to hurt Marlene's feelings by telling her straight up that she was no longer banking solely on her mother-seer's second sight, but the fact remained that Marlene's judgment had been shattered and stretched thin since Kamal had hit North American soil and the portals had been opened. Damali chose her words carefully, avoiding the too-hot topic that was currently not her main focus, then stopped pacing and leaned against the dresser to look at Marlene squarely.

Marlene opened her eyes and folded her arms over her chest, allowing her gaze to slip away from Damali's toward the window again. "His energy has been different. Angry. Unsettled. Kicking up a lot of dust in the house, creating an undercurrent. But Shabazz and I have talked about that at length. We'd been through the same drama with you, so we weren't particularly concerned. Plus, with the strained living conditions, the loss of his mother and grandmother, all you two kids have been through, and him being a rogue male that had to come in out of the streets to this new Joe-citizen life . . ." Marlene let her breath out hard. "Showing a little teeth every now and then didn't really worry me, even with what we know now . . . until tonight."

"I hear you," Damali said, pushing away from the furniture. "But, Mar, he came by my house this afternoon in a cold-blooded vamp purge. Shivering, daylight sensitive, and when I doused his clothes and vomit in the yard, the ground swallowed it all whole."

"What?" Marlene whispered. "He's supposed to be immune."

The tone of Marlene's voice and the look in her eyes made Damali hesitate. She could feel her blood pressure spiking within her as she again chose her words with care.

"Mar, listen," Damali said slowly. "He upchucked green bile, which, given how much he'd probably thrown up already, and what he drank last night, made sense. But the smell . . ." Damali wrinkled her nose and shook her head, almost tasting the putrid stench on the back of her tongue as she remembered it. "I took everything, even the bathroom sponge, out into the yard, and doused it. Holy water, oil, salt, you name it. If it was in my cabinets, I beat it back with what you'd given me to protect the house. The shit smoked, the ground opened up, and sucked it down, and then the earth closed over like nothing had ever been there."

"Have you been with him since all this happened?" Marlene began to pace. "Not that I'm in your business, girlfriend, but—"

"No," Damali said quickly. "I hear you, and no."

"Good. Maybe you'd better hold up on that until I can divine something more on the situation."

Both women stared at each other for a moment.

"That's not gonna be a problem," Damali said, her tone distant and sad.

"We'll find him," Marlene reassured her.

"That's not what I'm talking about," Damali said, her eyes seeking Marlene's for understanding.

"Oh," Marlene said in a quiet voice. "Since when have things cooled?"

"Since we got back from Philly. A couple of times, yeah . . . but, it wasn't the same."

Marlene held Damali's gaze, but kept her voice tender. "Why, baby?"

"I don't know," Damali said with a sad smile. "I was hoping you could tell me?"

Marlene chuckled softly. "I can tell you a lot of things, and see a lot, too, but *that* I can't divine for you. Your heart knows the answer, so talk to me."

Damali let her breath out in a rush of frustration, blowing a stray lock up from her forehead. "Mar*lene*. . . . I don't know. I've been stressed, with all this stuff that's going on, worrying about how to keep the uninitiated members of the team safe, the moves, everything. I'm battle-weary."

Marlene shook her head to signal she wasn't buying the explanation. "No, girlfriend. I hear you about the stress thing, but—"

"I know, I know," Damali said, holding up both hands. "All right, here's the deal as honestly as I can tell you." She looked away, finding a benign spot on the wall. "I go to hug him, and I tense up. He goes to kiss my neck, and I freeze. There's this deep-down revulsion that I have to get past; then I have to hide that away in my head, black box it, and then talk to myself while he's holding me to remember, this is my friend, *my man,* we've been through thick and thin, he loves me, I love him. I've got so much chatter going on in my head that by the time everything is over, I just feel relieved, then want him up off of me and out of me as soon as possible. It's all I can do not to dash for the shower. Now, I know

I'm wrong, crazy, it makes no kinda sense . . . and Lord knows, I'm—"

"Stop beating yourself up, right this minute," Marlene said in a firm but gentle tone. She walked away from Damali and went to the closet, found her big satchel, and extracted her huge, black book. "When are you gonna learn that you can come to me with anything, chile? I'm female. I've been there. And every time I have been, my gut instinct was *never* wrong."

Again, there was a long pause as their gazes and minds connected.

"I just figured . . ." Damali's voice trailed off as Marlene shook her head. "Maybe I'm reacting to the contagion, or it's affected me in some weird way?"

"I know how you feel about Jose," Marlene said bluntly. "Know how he feels about you, too. No matter. But he's a carrier, and you respond to him. Your body is functioning normally. It's your head or your heart, maybe your spirit link with Carlos. I don't know."

Shame made Damali's face feel warm. "I don't wanna talk about . . . let's just focus on Car—"

"Girl, please," Marlene said in an exasperated tone, dropping her satchel and the *Temt Tchaas* book on the bed. "The man is fine. Jose is crazy about you, always has been. Y'all are tight, thick as thieves. You guys practically grew up in the compound together and share so much in common. You have a pulse, so, chile, an attraction is normal. Been there, too. Recently." Marlene looked away for a moment, but returned her gaze to Damali's. "But, the thing is, you have a line, he has one, too, and you've both elected to honor it. Cool. My lips on that are sealed; ain't my bizness. So, Jose hooked up with Juanita, even though she's a piece of work . . . but has a good heart down deep; and you've hooked up with Carlos, who also has a good heart—down deep."

Marlene stared at Damali intently. "Now, pound for pound, round for round, given the real special connection you and Carlos have, I'm not understanding what's ringing your alarm bells. The man ain't been nowhere, ain't been with nobody but you."

"I know," Damali said quietly.

"He hasn't flagrantly relapsed, yet. Hasn't said or done anything any more or less annoying than the average male, has he?"

Damali shook her head.

"So, I can get with fatigue, general purpose not feeling romantic due to lack of privacy and chaos—oh, yeah, *been there*. But *revulsion*—your word not mine, seems a little extreme. And all of us who have been infected have heightened libido to the point of the ridiculous, not lowered. I could understand if you two couldn't get out of bed to make decisions or address this new threat. *That* would make sense, given how this mess is manifesting in the household. But you're telling me you're revolted by the love of your life? Uh-uh. Something ain't right."

"I know," Damali whispered, tears beginning to form in her eyes. "What's wrong with me, Marlene?"

Marlene flipped open the book and began furiously turning pages. After a while, she sat down and sighed. "There's a lot in the book, honey. You're a huntress, with vampires as your primary target. You've mastered dealing with that entity. Know werewolves and incubi pretty good, too. I'm looking at your living history, and it stops dead here," she said, placing a finger on the page and turning the book for Damali to inspect.

"The Himalayas? C'mon, Mar, what's that got to do with what we're talking about?" Damali leaned in and sniffed. "New information burns."

Marlene peered more closely. "Just came in tonight." She gingerly touched the still-warm print and jerked her attention up to stare at Damali. "Has Eve's signature vibration in it."

Damali flattened her hand on the page and closed her eyes. A mountain came into her mental view and she recognized it from an earlier vision, but this time landmarks surrounded it to add additional guidance. "The Chairman's lair . . . oh, my God . . . she actually met with him on my be-half. My destiny begins there."

Marlene's brow furrowed as she ran her palm over the an-cient text, the slight brush of her hand making the secret al-phabet sway and ripple as though riding on an invisible wave. "Part of it ends there, too." Marlene looked up. "Have you had any visions?"

Damali sat down slowly on the edge of the bed next to Marlene. "Yeah." Slowly and carefully she related how the cactus in her yard had transformed.

"I wonder . . ." Marlene said after Damali had finished, causing the young Neteru to hang on her every word. "Two things. You could be really angry at having lost the Isis long blade in large part because of Carlos, and that could be driv-ing a wedge between you. I'm no psychologist, baby, but be-ing with him did significantly alter your career path. You wouldn't be the first woman to harbor deep-seated resent-ment, even while loving a man, for something like that."

"I don't know," Damali said, studying her clasped hands. "Maybe. I've thought about it. But if I had to do it all over again for the same outcome, him being alive, I would."

"That's just the thing," Marlene said, her voice warm, and her palms covered Damali's. "It had to be done, you made the ultimate sacrifice on his behalf—gambled everything, gave up something that defined you, and he got to be re-deemed, stepped into your space, your family, your team, and has the gall and audacity to have an attitude about things not going exactly his way."

Damali nodded fervently. "Ungrateful bastard."

"Ahh . . . now we're getting somewhere."

Damali smiled for the first time since she'd entered Mar-lene's room. "Okay, I got beef about a lot of things."

"You're glad he's alive, thank God that he is, but . . ."

"Yeah," Damali said, looking at Marlene without blink-ing. "But."

"Then, because he ain't feelin' no *luv,* and doesn't like the step down from the fabulous, he has the nerve to go out with his boy, Yonnie, and possibly get himself back into trouble again while the world is literally falling apart. All you can think of is all the changes you went through to save his sorry ass in the first place, and all he can think of is how much he hates that a woman had to be the one to pull his butt out of the flames. Which leads me to the second thing I was gonna say. Your energies got disconnected and you're no longer in sync, once the big crisis was over and it was back to everyday life. So neither of you was ready and in lockstep when this new serious challenge came down."

"That is it, Marlene!" Damali shouted. "That's it. In a nutshell."

"Whew," Marlene said, blowing out a hard breath. "If every world crisis could be so easily solved."

"But what about the clothes in the yard and this Himalayas stuff?"

"Were you angry when you doused his clothes?"

"Mad as Hell."

Marlene laughed. "Then, that's where you sent them, girl."

Damali's eyes opened wide. "For real?"

"You're full-blown Neteru, kiddo. You sent something back into the pit, put a fury topspin on it, and it's gone."

"Dang."

"Yep." Marlene grunted as she stood. "The Himalayas . . . hey. We go to the Chairman's lair and dust him, once and for all. Carlos doesn't have time to go through another month of training before he spikes, even though Tibet is where some real serious martial and spiritual arts masters reside. If he has to learn Zen principles and integrate his longings for his old life with this new one in the Light, what better place for him to learn in a hurry; he dang sure ain't absorbing what he should out here in Arizona. I knew that the moment we set foot on this land and stared at the house. Brotherman's jaw locked so hard I thought he'd chip teeth."

Damali laughed softly in relief, remembering the day well.

"Your long blade is missing and you saw it there," Marlene said, packing away her book and satchel. "Maybe that's where you guys will sync up, get back to the crazy normal y'all call normal. Who knows? Meanwhile, can you work on saving the world?"

"Road trip." Damali hopped up from the bed with a wide grin.

"When we receive a sign," Marlene said, her grin matching Damali's. "Let's not rush things."

"No, Marlene. Eve going into combat mode, risking a full seduction info siphon from the Chairman *is a sign*. Don't get it twisted. Girlfriend put a lot on the line, had to open old wounds to come away with that. I owe her. We all do."

Damali's expression went stone serious as she stared at Marlene. "We don't have time to waste; we pull out tomorrow—first light, hit L.A. to get a flight over to China. You and Dan make the arrangements; get J.L. to do it online, if you have to. But do it. Call Father Pat, too. Make sure we can get shots and all that, pronto, so we can pass foreign inspection, not that we'll need 'em if we don't succeed in this mission. Tell him to hook us up with a doctor from the Covenant that's already infected, so we don't hurt any innocents. And since we just got booted off Jose's property, if we survive, when we get back, we can figure out a more metropolitan place to live. Sound like a plan?"

"Sounds like a plan. A new location is definitely in order, if we get through this. It might be a good idea to compromise, too. Perhaps find a spot in L.A. that we can all live with, where the Berkfield kids can go to school during the day, even though Marj is doing her best to homeschool them. They're bouncing off the walls, poor babies, as is everyone else. Vamp incidents are at an all-time low, we haven't seen any crazy were-demon activity, and the Chairman is on the run. We can do a good job of throwing down a prayer line, retrofit a mansion, and get the Covenant brothers to add a little somethin' somethin' to the mix."

Damali nodded hard, but Marlene's line of conversation disturbed her. The woman was in denial. Wasn't thinking clearly. Why was she worried about trivial things when in thirty days, there might not be a world? Damali tempered her response.

"Yeah, because Marlene, for real—you can run but you can't hide, and sooner or later, the newbies have to be able to live like regular people, blend in." That was as much as she could offer without bodily shaking sense into Marlene.

"Couldn't agree more," Marlene said, coming to Damali to give her a hug. "Might stem some of that resentment thing, too."

"Ya think?" Damali held Marlene tightly. Oh, God . . . everyone, even her mother-seer, had lost their minds. "I didn't realize how much of that poison was running through my system." She let Marlene take the statement any way she wanted to, but she'd been referring to the contagion, not some stupid man-woman resentment issue.

"A very famous lady, an old star, Jill St. John, said this when she lost her son: resentment is like taking poison, and hoping the other person dies." Marlene held Damali back from her. "That was so profound, it stayed with me. Here this woman had lost her heart, her fourteen-year-old child to a tragedy, and that was her take on the matter. I learned something from those words, so I pass them on for you to consider."

Damali touched Marlene's cheek, her hand cupping it with tender love. She had to stop the infection. She missed the old Marlene so much she could almost wail. "Marlene, you are so deep sometimes. I've been feeling like I was possessed or like something was trying to get inside me and take over my spirit. Resentment *is* poison."

Marlene nodded and released her hold on Damali. She watched her grown daughter walk away from her, but didn't immediately follow behind her. There was something in what Damali had said; also something had slithered within her daughter's touch. The word *possessed* hung in her mind like a dark cloud. Her lips moved reciting a silent prayer as she watched Damali rejoin the despondent group in the living room. Something was wrong; her internal warning bells were going off.

For the first time in a long time, Marlene was very unsure.

All heads jerked up as footsteps came up the path. Before they could land on the front steps, the entire team was on the porch. Carlos glanced up sheepishly, his ragged, blood-stained jeans, torn T-shirt, and dirt-smeared face made them stare.

"Damn, y'all, what a night!" Carlos exclaimed, shaking his head as he mounted the stairs. "I'm driving to L.A. to get the hell out of here for a short break until we could all figure out what to do, and a freakin' deer jumps into the middle of the road, wrecks my Jeep, messes up a brother's transpo, are you feeling me? I am done!"

He smoothed his palm over his hair as the team stared at him without blinking, their expressions blank. "Then," he said quickly, adding to his story, "I'm trying to find my way back home in the dark, and white light holds me, checking to see if I even smelled the deer—like I'm an addict, or some-thing? What'd y'all do, call the spiritual feds on a brother, or something?"

Shoulders relaxed, smiles eased into expressions, Damali slowly came down the steps. "The angels scanned you, huh?" she said with a slow grin. "Did you pass inspection?"

"Would I be standing here, if I didn't?" Carlos folded his arms over his chest. "Now what kinda question is that?" He shook his head and brushed past her. "No, 'hi, baby, glad you're all right?' Damn, girl, you cold. What is up with you, D? What's the 'get back you don't know me like that' about?"

Rider put his semiautomatic lengthwise, barring Carlos farther entry up the steps. Carlos stopped, looked at the gun, and then up at Rider. All right, sensors were on. Everybody that had someone dear to protect might be able to feel the change. Love cut through all dark-side illusions. He needed to find weak links in the chain. "What's up with that, Rider?"

Rider's gaze into Carlos's eyes never wavered. "Where'd

the so-called angels drop you, then? We had a search party covering the ground from the land and the air."

"Tara came?" Carlos said, acting surprised. He'd seen them both, but hadn't allowed them to see him.

"And Yonnie," Rider said evenly. "Neither one of them, working together, could find you—just like we couldn't."

Again the group went still. Carlos looked down at his bloodstained clothes.

"I hope somebody had the presence of mind to check out the deer that was stuck in my windshield? Take a sniff, man. This was all over my seats."

"The deer checked out, Rider," Damali said, trying to mediate the tension.

Rider refused to yield. "That's not what I asked him. I can smell deer blood from here."

Carlos sighed. "What do you want from me, man? They dropped me far enough away that I could barely see the house lights in the distance, then gave me some long speech about duty to the greater good. But you know how they work. They didn't bother to give a brother a lift home."

Big Mike nodded. "Rider, man, it would make sense that they'd shield him from his old friends if they feared a relapse, given Yonnie and Tara are still . . . you know, vamps, and all."

Carlos fought not to smile. "My point, Rider."

"Why don't you get washed up," Marjorie said cautiously, "while there's hot water, and if you give me those clothes—"

Rider shook his head no, and glanced at Shabazz, who had been strangely silent.

"Not back in this house with newbies. No," Rider said flatly. "If the angels thought you might relapse, then—"

"Well where the hell am I gonna go, Rider!" Carlos shouted, and then looked at Shabazz for support.

Rider hocked and spit. "Metal is all in my throat." He glanced at Jose. "Talk to me little brother. You picking that up, too?"

Carlos's gaze narrowed on Jose. He homed in on the

vamp tracer in Jose's DNA and unlocked the code that was embedded within it: *You can never out your own to humans. Ask Yonnie and Tara, who are several generations up. Your Chairman commands it so, with a little extra topspin that would make old Dante piss in his pants.*

When Jose opened his mouth to speak, he fell eerily quiet and shrugged. Seeming satisfied, Carlos returned his attention to Rider. "Jack Daniel's and cigarettes got your senses off, hombre. You need to chill."

"Jack Daniel's ain't got nothin' to do with it. I know what I know. Something ain't right."

"Maybe we're all just a little taxed," Marjorie offered. "Carlos has been—"

"Acting strange," Shabazz muttered. "Say what you want to, and my job is to groom a male Neteru, but I ain't having a potential vamp flux in here with newbies. Call it misplaced paternal instinct, but something is making the hair stand up on my arms. Dig?"

"So, now I have to sleep in the equipment shed like a dog?" Indignant, Carlos stormed down the steps. "Then at least give me a vehicle so I can drive to a motel."

His gaze went to Marlene's and then Damali's. Both women were impassive, and it totally floored him that Damali had remained silent throughout the exchange.

"Rider and Shabazz are right," Damali finally said.

"What!" Carlos was so angry that he could feel his own breath singe the hairs within his nose on each breath.

"If there's any flux happening, innocent or otherwise," Damali said, unsheathing her baby Isis, "then maybe you'd better come home with somebody who can deal with it."

Carlos almost smiled. He gave the team his back to consider, catching Berkfield's pained expression before he turned around.

"If you're injured," Berkfield said, beginning to walk down the steps. "Maybe—"

"No," Carlos yelled. "Don't touch me." He then mellowed his next response. "I'm fine. Y'all have put me out of the house, so, fine. I don't need anything from anybody." He waited, watching Berkfield remain on the step, unmoving. The last thing he needed was for a healer with sacred blood running through his veins to attempt to lay hands on him. He didn't know what the repercussions of that would be, and would make it a point not even to shake Berkfield's hand until he knew.

"Carlos," Juanita said, coming down the steps past the others. "Listen, it's not like that, okay?"

Carlos tilted his head as he watched her come closer. A thousand thoughts ran through his mind and captured it . . . *Oh, Juanita, ya don't want none of this* . . .

She froze in the path, just like the deer had, and then began backing up the steps one at a time. "But, uh," she said, slowly recovering, "we've got kids in the house. Try to understand."

"Yeah, man," J.L. said, placing a possessive arm around Krissy's shoulders. "That's the only reason people are tense. I mean, with the contagion, and all, who knows how bad any of us is gonna get—and you're stronger than any of us, if you flux out, or something. It ain't personal."

Dan nodded and body-shielded Bobby. "Don't take offense. They can't deal with it. That's the only reason, man."

"Oh, fuck all that," Inez said, her eyes narrowing on Carlos. "I don't like how the man looked at Juanita in front of my girl!"

Inez was practically down the steps, and were it not for Big Mike's hand on her shoulder, she would have been. Up to this point, Inez had been skittish, but was spiking a battle surge within him. He hadn't banked on Inez having the leanings of being a seer, not to mention, he forgot that she was Damali's cut-buddy. Inez was also from the 'hood, and had street sense to hone the other gift she obviously had. Right now she seemed ready to go down for her girl over a respect principle. So be it.

"Let her go," Carlos said, his tone even and lethal. "I didn't look at Juanita no kinda way, and if Jose was cool with it—"

"But *I* wasn't," Marlene said in a flat tone. "He stays out of the house until daylight hours."

Damali gave Marlene a knowing glance. "In the morning, we pack and move out. Everybody get some rest. We're going back to L.A."

He couldn't believe his good fortune. Carlos kept his gaze out the window of Damali's Hummer as they made their way down the road. He used an attitude as a shield to keep her from seeing his overwhelming relief. They'd be off this prayer dirt in no time. It was making him sick.

She jumped out of the Hummer without looking at him. She'd fled it so quickly that she'd practically forgotten to turn off the engine.

"Strip," she ordered, using her short blade as a pointer. "Right here in the front yard. Then I'm gonna douse your clothes, and I want you to see what happens to them when I do. Then you'll be able to understand why everybody is just a little bit nervous around you, brother."

"All right," Carlos said, allowing a half smile to tug at his mouth. "You're the boss," he added, slowly hopping down from the Hummer and pulling his shirt over his head. He held out the ripped T with two fingers and dropped it, as though providing her with a slow striptease. He bent to unlace his Tims, but steadily kept his eyes on her as he straightened and stepped out of them, then kicked them near his ruined shirt.

It was something she'd seen him do more times than she could count, but for some reason, tonight, his slow undressing was so sensual that he might as well have been doing a male version of the *Dance of the Seven Veils* in her front yard.

Damali's gaze traveled across his broad shoulders and the sculpted form of his chest, lingering on each bulge of defined abdominal muscle packs. His skin seemed like fired bronze in the moonlight. She couldn't help staring at his hands as they took their time unfastening the top button of his jeans. Reflex made her lick her lips as his hand slid his zipper down. Her mouth went dry, her face flushed hot. A hard shiver made her belly clench as he rolled the denim fabric away from his body as though peeling back an onion-skin. Just looking at him had made her so wet that she feared the emulsion between her thighs would soak through her pants.

She couldn't move as she watched him; didn't want to move. Oh, yeah, he'd blown her mind with sexy vamp drama in the past, but she'd never almost fallen over at his antics from twenty-five feet away. Her skin felt damp and warm, and before she knew it she was breathing out of her mouth in short sips. Maybe Marlene was right, all they needed to do was sync up . . . and man oh man was she ready to sync and squash whatever had been between them. This was the sexi-est shit he'd ever done to her.

Carlos yanked his pants down his thighs slowly, and let them slide the rest of the way to his feet. His intense gaze held her in place as he casually kicked them toward the other clothes that lay in a pile. She was not looking at his face. Her jaw went slack, her heart seemed to stopped for a few seconds, it was beating in arrhythmia for sure . . . It had been a while, but she didn't remember hombre being hung like that!

He walked nearer, an easy smile of satisfaction rooting her to the top porch step. "Can I come in the house now?"

She had every intention of saying something flippant, but the words got caught in her throat.

"Well, you just gonna leave me out here in the raw?"

She shook her head no. "I need to douse you and your clothes," she quietly gasped.

"Why don't you worry about that, later. Obviously, I've missed you. How about if you douse me in the shower, like old times, instead?"

From some reservoir of common sense, she scrambled together a sentence. "We can't just jump in the shower . . . no . . . uh; we have to use protection. I could get pregnant." She wasn't sure why those words were first to come to her mind or out of her mouth.

Carlos shook his head and clicked his tongue, making a little tsking sound. "And here I thought you'd consider making another baby with me tonight."

Forget warning bells—cymbals went off in her head, breaking what felt like a spell.

"Latex or nothing . . . Why are we even shouting this conversation in the yard?" Damali looked around, confusion eating at her brain. Then she felt her mind pry open and nearly snap.

"Latex?" He chuckled low and sensually, his eyes roving over her body like a caress. "You don't trust your Sankofa to do the work for you?"

In all truth, she didn't. Not tonight. There was something very dark, half scary, but way, way too magnetic about him at the moment. But to admit that would fly in the face of everything Neteru within her, not to mention might blaspheme her Queens. She forced a smile to cover up her distress. *Y'all got my back, right?* she mentally whispered. *This brother ain't no joke. I don't know what's wrong with his ass tonight.*

"Since you're packing heat," she said as coolly as possible, "and talking plenty of trash, a double layer of protection is a girl's best friend. A condom or the couch. Your choice."

"What I've got for you tonight," he said, his voice a tone lower than she'd ever heard it before, "will burn right through latex."

His voice had washed her entire body with a wave of want, and then entered it between her legs to coat her insides with new heat.

"Oh, shit . . ." she murmured, having meant the comment to come out as a possible battle-readiness shout for him to back off. She weaved, caught the porch banister, and gripped it for support as another penetrating wave hit her.

"How many times have I asked you to stop playing with me, Damali?"

As he walked toward her she could feel the warmth of his hands on her body, touching every place he'd learned by heart. The black box in her head felt light, the lid on it struggling to remain shut. Images began to surround it, taunting it to open, and her gaze slowly found his. Tears blurred her sight, and short pants escaped her mouth.

"Baby, stop," she whispered.

"Why?" he asked in a subsonic tone.

"Because I'm asking you to," she said in a near squeak.

"You know you want a soldier, raw, *Mamacita*," he said in a voice so low it rumbled through her and produced a pleasure wave that knocked her head back, causing her audible gasp. "Stop trippin'."

Mamacita? He'd never called her *that* before. Something was definitely wrong. She'd felt every sound decibel from his throaty response drop inside her as though he'd let each word fall like a droplet of water . . . or blood. Circles of ecstasy spread through every cell within her, uniting every essence of liquid in her system to its throb. Concentric ripples connected each spreading ring in a million tingles that felled her to her knees where she once stood.

She could barely lift her head. Carlos's footsteps rang out as they landed on the steps one by one. The vibration along the wood planks from each footfall made her cry out with desire. Every time he spoke, his whisper was a forceful caress that elicited a sound from within her that she'd never heard. She tried to lift her head to look at him, had to see what this new mood of his was all about . . . even as a councilman, he'd *never* blown her away like this.

"I don't care about what happened in your kitchen," he said so quietly that her body began to lift from the porch floor without her aid. "You like vamp. Jose's got that in him, baby . . . *but not like this*."

The moment her head dropped back again, she'd braced for a fang strike, even though Carlos was only a few feet from her. Instead of receiving the bite, she found herself sprawled against the porch floor, actual beach waves washing over her, making her scream from the intolerable pleasure.

Water was everywhere, the salty fusion of it reminiscent

of blood. What felt like Caribbean sun was prickling her skin, licking it as erotic waves repeatedly lapped at her body and continued to sweep her closer to her front door. It was so intense a vision, or whatever it was that he'd produced, she was sputtering salt water and trying to stand, when another wave knocked her down. Sand was under her fingernails as she scrabbled to fend off another tidal sensation.

Gasping, she peered at him, confused, panting out sentences in short bursts while trying to wrap her mind around where this power rush was coming from. This wasn't no freaking relapse! "Male Neterus can do that? They taught you that on the island with the old men—back in Ethiopia? Shit, baby, you apexing on me, or something? You definitely gotta use something extra, for real."

Carlos tilted his head to the side as he stared down at her. Power was an awesome thing, to be sure. But she'd actually felt desire for some vamp perpetrator over him? His distant line brother? Was she out of her mind? She wanted a change? Something new? Something forbidden? Done. No, this wasn't a relapse or anything some old men on an island had taught him. Far from it.

"Girl, I know what you like," he whispered low and dangerously, his voice a swift-cutting pleasure blade, slicing at her resistance. "Be honest. At least with yourself. You want a true baby-maker, wild risk-taker, to-the-bone dealer . . . night . . . thrill . . . seeka, make you wanna holla, mad-crazy soldier, hot-desire waker . . . breath to bone shaker, out-of-body quaker, *yeah* . . . empire builder, dream ful-filla, girl stop playin', 'cause that ain't the half of what you want." He closed his eyes and drew in a deep breath until it hissed. "C'mon, let me get this . . . and let me get it right."

His hands slid down his body, creating an unnatural heat within hers. Her skin felt like it was catching fire, leaving acute pleasure in its wake. She couldn't take her eyes off him, or pull away from what felt like an erotic, magnetic current. He drew in air between his teeth, creating another quiet hiss of pleasure just behind her ear from where he stood.

Say no—How? Tell him back off—not possible. Not when he felt the way he did—even standing just beyond her steps, his scent divine, making her know what he really was with each burning phantom touch . . . all vamp. Maybe more.

"And you love it," he whispered, accessing her mind without permission.

"Stop," she whispered. "This isn't the Carlos I know."

"The old Carlos is gone," he murmured sensually, *"Murió en un desgraciado accidente. No quiero desilusionarte, pero . . . estoy deshecho, cansado . . .* baby, *desnúdate,* then *sufrí un desmayo . . . helado.* Tomorrow we can discuss it. *Por lana mañanas tengo la mente más despejada."*

His eyes briefly slid shut, as though he was regaining his composure, and when he inhaled, it sucked the air right out of her lungs, making her feel faint. She struggled to translate what he'd told her, feeling a shred of truth in the vibration resonating within his statement, but couldn't bring her mind to work that hard for her, not when he was speaking to her low and sexy in Español . . . not when he was working her body the way he was.

"Please, Carlos," she gasped, trying to back away on the porch floor. "I can't think when you get like this, and something is definitely wrong."

"¿En qué estás pensando? But *creo que estás equivocado,"* he whispered, his lids now half lowered as he continued to inhale deeply. *"No te muevas. Ya no hay más. No importa."* He placed his hand on the door. "Permission to enter your house, *mi tresora."*

Something fragile snapped inside her and she nodded, defying every instinct that lay coiled within her. He chuckled so low and deep that she felt it across the porch like a depth charge through her womb.

"That's better," he murmured, slowly walking toward her, his motions so fluid she wasn't sure his footfalls had landed against the floor. "Then . . . permission to enter you?"

Her eyes were shut tight. She heard her front door groan and splinter open behind her, and another pleasure assault washed her into her living room. But when she opened her eyes, she was in a place she couldn't recognize. Naked, writhing bodies were all around her. A shadowed figure was in her doorframe. A pool, marble, togas—oh shit, old Rome!

Before she could protest, every sensation resident in the tangle of human flesh gathered and covered her, entering every orifice, until she wept from orgasmic exhaustion. Through sobs of exquisite relief, she sought a pair of eyes she knew. Her line of vision locked with the shadow in the doorway. Breathless, she waited for the familiar glow of silver, something to make her know that he was still with her, that this was just a phenomenal floor show, but no silver light returned to her. Dark, blue-black fire met her stare.

"If you love me, you'll stop right now, Carlos! Do not bring this bullshit into my house! I forbid it." She covered her mouth with one hand and sobbed as he smiled, and another orgasm arrested her complaint.

"I thought you wanted to *really know* what was inside the mind of a master? I just opened the first layer of my black box for you, baby. Can't handle it?" he said in an amused tone. "Before, you said—"

"That was *before*," she said, pushing herself up on all fours so she could eventually stand on wobbly legs. But she never made it that far.

"Cypress, maybe, then?" Carlos murmured, "The Greek isles? The Oracle at Delphi had some moves you wouldn't believe. Three-way? That was a very decadent era . . . and you are *definitely* in my favorite position. She'll love it, too."

"Don't," Damali said firmly. "Let me up."

"That's right. You're an old-fashioned girl. Old school, Old Testament. So maybe we should just go back to the beginning and do the damned thing right."

Her hands sank into rich, fertile dirt, and vines began to climb up the walls, forming Eden.

"Fallon tried it, I didn't like it," she said quickly, before Carlos transformed into something that might lope over her threshold.

"My bad," he whispered. "Careless and unoriginal. Maybe—"

"Just please stop," she said quietly, needing to appeal to whatever rational part of him was left. "Let me up; let's just be who we are. No games."

A deep chuckle thundered up from Carlos's insides. "No, baby," he said slowly, shaking his head as he made her bud throb harder, "you *definitely* aren't ready for that."

She could see him stroke the line of his jaw as though considering her fate, even with the unnaturally dark shadows eclipsing his face and body. Something was definitely wrong; he'd never violated her like this, and his power had never been this strong. Although he'd never laid a physical hand on her, what he'd done mentally was more than enough. Fighting against the new wash of sensations he was beginning to create, she went for his emotional core—given that her long blade was missing, and her baby Isis had probably fallen off the porch.

"Carlos, I will *never* forgive you for this," she said in a distant tone, glancing away from him. "I can't believe you'd act like this or treat me this way."

He paused. Maybe he'd gone too far. New approach.

She watched him slowly run his fingers through his hair, and instantly, the force holding her to the floor lifted.

Part of him said not to do it, but an overriding desire shunted that protest. He had to get inside her, feel her sweet heat all around him. He'd played too long, had blown his own mind, there was no work left for her to do. Fluid had already filled his shaft, turning it to what felt like throbbing granite.

As soon as the thought was completed, she was outside on the porch, naked in his arms, initially struggling against his hold, her skin sweaty and pulsing beneath his grip until her hands grasped at his back to pull him closer. His mouth consumed hers, devouring her moan, breaking down her resistance. Her Sankofa blazed white-hot silver on her spine, almost searing his hands as they ran down her back. *Damn, her will not to conceive was strong.*

"I want you so badly, I feel like I'm losing my mind," she gasped against his neck, biting his earlobe, her hand covering the place where his tattoo lay dormant. "Just don't make me pregnant tonight, we can't, I can't," she panted in stuttering jags. "Make it burn silver, baby," she said nearly weeping, waiting for his dead symbol to engage. Then she bit his jugular and sucked hard.

Down in seconds, they slammed onto the porch floor, her tattoo literally making the wood smolder beneath her, but her urgent movements under him demanded his earlier question be answered. *Permission to enter?* Her body was on fire, becoming dangerous liquid silver in his arms as her passion for him spread through her Neteru bloodstream. Big fucking variable. Time was of the essence. The throne didn't offer clues about a fully matured female Neteru's secret weapon to withstand an unwilling seduction!

His fangs had ripped through his gums on impact with the porch, but her eyes were still shut so tightly, and her thrashing so erratic, that he knew she was oblivious. The duality of heat was fracturing his intent, breaking his mind. The scorch of her body was dangerous, molten protoplasm from the realms above; his now owned Hellfire from the realms below. The games he'd played to send her to into a frenzy had become a trap that could leave him seriously injured. The dilemma was kicking his ass, burning him up from the need to get with her.

"Permission to enter you," he groaned into her ear. "Just tell me I can."

She nodded, her voice caught on a strangled gasp.

She had to *say it*. The Neteru will barrier was impenetrable in a seduction battle. He could feel a force brutally blocking him, even though her nails scored his shoulders to drive him onward. "Just say it, baby . . . tell me." He was

near tears she felt so good; he'd almost forgotten Hellfire
was no match for her silver heat.

She arched for him, making his request a command.

Frustration tore up wood splinters as he gripped her hair
in his hands, held her face, broke the kiss, and stared at her.
"Say it!"

She cried out his name instead. He closed his eyes and almost laughed. The Light was fucking with him real bad right
through here. He kissed her hard and rolled her over to strad-
dle him. He needed to look into her eyes, get a mind lock going. Had to break the black box in her skull and shatter it. He
could barely retract his fangs to speak. His words came out
as a stuttering plea instead of the thundering demand he'd
intended. "Baby, tell me I can come into you *now*."

"Oh, God!"

Ball game. He dumped her on the porch and had to stand
and walk in a circle. The electric arc that zapped off her
skin almost fried him. Totally sobering, erection killing,
pain so intense that he bit his tongue and almost upchucked
his nuts. Okay, so not tonight. Fine. He couldn't even look
at her as he tried to catch her breath to stop her torrent of
passionate words.

"Baby, what's wrong?" she said, panting, reaching toward
him, beginning to stand.

Horrified that the zap had only further turned her on, he
backed away as her aura radiated pure silver. Reality provided a cold slap in his face as Damali got to her feet. They
used to play hard, play rough, but he was always on *their*
side before. Every physical Neteru change she'd just gone
through under him would have driven him mad—before.
There was no way to do this . . . even if she said yes. Oh,
shit . . .

"Jesus, Carlos, please, baby, no more teasing, no more
playing, you have *got to* finish this tonight!"

The name of the sacred made him wince and turn away.
Tears of agony were streaming down her beautiful face.
Near madness had filled her expression, making her look all

the more ravishing in the moonlight as she'd frantically searched his eyes for an answer before he gave her his back.

"Stop walking away from me!" she nearly shrieked. "Don't you want this? You trying to bait me into a shape-shift? What? Panther? Is that what you want? Talk to me! You want me to drag you into the bushes by your damned throat?" She shouted, and wrapped her arms around herself. " 'Cause, tonight, if you don't stop playing with me after that floor show, I might. Don't tempt me. Oh, God, what is wrong with you?"

He held up his hand, three calls of the Names and his skull was splitting. "Shut up! I can't take it," he shouted, pacing as his ears began to internally bleed. "*No mas, por favor.* A minute. To get my head together. All right?"

He had to get away from her. She was turning him on so fucking bad it didn't make sense . . . drag him by his throat, oh, shit—if he hadn't said the Names, but he knew from all experience, she would again, and again, and again. And she was walking toward him, lit up with silver fire. He'd torch on impact from even a hug.

"Back off me, woman! You know we don't play like that!" he bellowed as he could feel her energy about to dip low and go serious feline when she purred.

She shook her head as though coming to from a punch as she stood on the porch in the buff, and then slowly backed away from him into the house and shut the screen door behind her.

Carlos watched her for a moment, totally defeated and too conflicted to immediately argue. Okay, maybe he'd gone too far, which could be disastrous, if he ever wanted her to chill out and be with him again. The conundrum was profound. He'd wanted to fuck her till she lost her mind, but if he took her there she'd burn him alive. If he did her in a lackluster fashion, she might get pregnant, but damn, what would be the point? The Light had this shit rigged so foul it was obscene. Now he really understood the Chairman and the old boys' problem. Why he was such a necessary pawn in their game. Think, think, think. There had to be some way around the barrier . . . and she'd been so turned out she was ready to serve panther? Sheeit.

But as he hesitated, a tiny, fearful cry from within echoed through his conscience. What was he doing? Why was he doing this? None of this had anything to do with the mission he'd been assigned, and getting Damali pregnant was the *last* thing he should have been trying to do, especially if what he'd seen on the Chairman's throne would come out of his body.

He stood on her porch, breathing hard, as he battled the procreation imperative and looked at the woman he loved, and then clung to that very thin silver filament left inside him. No, she was not to be the vessel for something worse than a daywalker. Jealousy and newfound power had had him in its grip. Unbridled rage had made him show off and nearly stop her heart with pleasure shock. He had to get the Jose thing out of his head and be rational.

"C'mon, girl. I was just playing," Carlos said, fighting the eerie sensation of conflict brewing within him. "It's a male Neteru thing, mixed with a little vamp still in my system from old times, that's all. I'm near my real apex. What can I say?" He opened his arms and smiled, loving how her skin was still wet and flushed from releasing till she'd cried.

"Put my clothes back on," she demanded, breathing hard, raking her hair, but her eyes never left his. "No silver, no ass. I musta been out of my mind!"

He smiled as her gaze traveled down his body and lingered. "I want you, too, baby. The old-fashioned way works for me . . . unless you want to go to the point?"

"Too rough already," she said, standing and slapping remnants of sand off her soaked clothes as he robed her in what she'd previously had on. She scowled at his good faith move and glared at him. "I'm not going to V-point with you—and I thought . . . Never mind. This shit was ridiculous."

He smiled in an attempt to play off the pleasurable horror

she'd just experienced. "I'll be gentle next time, girl . . . for real." He gave her a sly glance, his smile widening as he spoke. "But it did feel good, didn't it?"

She still couldn't see if he had fangs, not that she needed any further proof that he owned them. "No. It didn't. You seriously violated my mind. Don't do that to me *ever* again, Carlos. I'm not playing! I feel dirty, like I need a bath."

"All you have to do is say the word—"

"No!" She scanned the floor for her missing blade.

He produced it for her twiddling it outside the screen door.

"Let me in the house and I'll make it up to you, girl. You've got me out here naked, cold, and that's why I was pissed off. You didn't have my back at the family house, and—"

"Where's my holy water. I'm gonna . . ."

Damali's voice trailed off as her motions slowed down. Damn, she really took this the wrong way, and it was not about allowing her to douse him with that foul concoction of Marlene's tonight. It also disturbed him that he was back to needing a verbalized invitation to cross her threshold. That had never been the case, and it released another inner cry from his psyche that he couldn't totally ignore.

Carlos opened his fingers and splayed them against the shut screen, pulling away the last few minutes, closing his fist around it all, and then hurling it into the back of her mind like an erotic bad dream. "Hide," he murmured behind the small black orb that penetrated the base of her skull. Then he dried her clothes, righted all toppled furniture, put the baby Isis back in her hand, snapped his fingers, and released time.

"I'm going to get the stuff I need to douse you and your clothes. Stay on the porch," she ordered over her shoulder. But her tone was calm, as though nothing out of the ordinary had transpired. "I want you to see how your clothes just disappeared in the yard before."

"Okay, baby," he said in a weary voice, covering himself with his hands. "But can you at least bring me a towel?"

She laughed. He finally relaxed and smiled.

After a few moments, Damali appeared at the screen door. She absently threw the towel she was holding at him and half of it landed over his head. He sat appearing contrite as could be on the steps, watching her make a big production out of dousing his clothes. Total amusement filled him as he slowed her down again, his clothes on the ground disappeared, and he replaced them with new ones.

Battling emotions filled his mind as he watched her. A small inner voice kept repeating the word *danger*. It was a muffled cry, almost a sob. Then a stronger voice would override it and tell him to fuck with her. Carlos dropped his head into his hands and peered up slowly as Damali walked in a haze of altered time. Dear, G—

He stood yelling in pain. White-hot poker heat seized his brain and almost set it on fire. He held on to the rail and looked up. He could no longer hear the Name even casually, not just when he was an imminent threat, but no matter what? "Oh, shit."

Carlos covered his face with both hands and breathed into them with shaky breaths. What if he couldn't cross cathedral barriers, or whatever? What other limitations did his little dip down to Level Seven via the Chairman's throne have, he wondered? Why could he even cross here and be on this land, though? It was all too confusing.

"C'mon, y'all. Don't play me like this. I'm on *your* mission. Yeah, I took a tumble, but don't get new. Hey. For real. I'm serious now."

The starry horizon didn't even squint at him, much less produce a sign. "Okay, fine," he muttered, and sat down, then released Damali from the time aberration.

"I don't understand," she said, walking around the wet heap of soiled clothes in the yard. "Nothing happened."

"Nothing happened," Carlos repeated casually, "because, like I told you—*nothing happened*. I didn't relapse and whatever infection had me earlier passed out of my system. We're Neterus, immune." He looked up at the sky, as though arguing with it. "Everybody is making me feel like I've committed a crime, and I haven't done a thing. Y'all are being real unfair," he said, his face still heavenward. "There's a double standard. When you had your moment of trip-out, they were trying to help you, Damali. Everybody did all that they could to keep you on lockdown and safe in the compound, but see how they do a brother?"

When she didn't answer, Carlos gave her with a angry sidelong glance, abandoning his skyward-hurled argument. "It ain't right . . . and what hurts the most is, you're standing here at the bottom of the steps, a bottle of test water in one hand and salt and Ju Ju oil, or whatever, in the other, just looking at me like I'm the Devil himself."

Carlos swallowed hard and stared out into the distance. "Never thought I'd see that expression in your eyes, of all people, Damali . . . after all we've been through together? Bottom line is, you don't trust me. That hurts more than anything else."

He watched her slowly set the bottle of Holy water, anointing oil, and purified sea salt on the bottom step, then let out an unnoticeable breath of relief.

"I'm sorry, baby," she murmured, glancing back at his clothes, confounded. "We just have to be careful because of the newbies and the portal problem."

"I thought the foundation of any relationship was trust?"

She nodded and came up the steps and sat beside him. "I'm sorry, okay?"

He shrugged, and adjusted the waist of the towel sarong that had been shielding his lap. "Whatever."

"Look, why don't we go inside? You get washed up; I'll open some wine. We'll just chill, try to . . . I don't know, sync our vibe back up. All right?"

He shrugged away from her hand as it touched his cheek, and stood. "I don't feel like making love now, all of a sudden."

She stood and reached for him again. "Carlos, I am really sorry I didn't trust you."

He didn't pull away from her hold and allowed her to hug him, begrudgingly hugging her back, half afraid to touch her. "Been that way for months."

"I know. I've been going through changes I didn't even understand, and I guess I've been shutting you out, like you said. Maybe the contagion got me, too?"

"So, I'm welcomed in your home? You ain't scared that I might turn into a monster?" he said, brandishing fake claws with his fingers in the air and giving her a crazed expression to make her laugh.

"No," she said, swatting his chest. "You can fall by here anytime you want. It's me and you, okay? You have permission to enter, whatever all that unnecessary drama was about."

He smiled, but hesitated. Her mind was strong enough to still hold a bit of what had transpired before his memory block, and was clearly still recording impressions. It was as though her silver-coated gray matter was leaking through the dark orb he'd placed there, searching for truth beyond the illusion. He kissed her slowly, not sending anything extra into it that could make her bolt and run, attempting to erase the last vestiges of any sensations from the previous hour. When he lifted his head, he brushed her stray lock back from her forehead and stared at her mind. "Good."

CHAPTER TWELVE

Yonnie and Tara touched down in the alley on Bourbon Street and looked around.

"I wouldn't have brought you to Gabrielle's unless it was an emergency," Yonnie said, his gaze going toward the pedestrians beyond the shadows. "So be cool when we get in there."

"No problem," Tara said, her voice as distant as her gaze. "I don't have any issues with Gabrielle or her profession. She is what she is, just like we are what we are."

Yonnie brought his attention back to Tara, conflict wafting through him as he studied her calm demeanor. "No, I don't suppose you do," he said in a tight voice after a moment, and then began walking. "I was foolish to think you might."

Tara didn't respond. What was there to say? It was better that Yonnie relive his desires at a coven brothel in New Orleans than to insist on sex from her after he fed each night.

"For the record," he snarled as they exited the alley and blended in with the party people in the street, "I never *insisted* on anything."

"All right," she said, no judgment in her tone, simply fatigue. "Let's not argue about what is."

He grabbed her arm. She looked down at his hold with curious disdain.

"You know for a fact that since the Chairman's throne has been vacated, as a master, I can't deliver a bite that isn't fatal. No turns, no passion nicks, nothing, if it's on a human. No elevations on one of our own. So my visits to Gabrielle's place haven't been all you think." He dropped her arm when

240 L. A. BANKS

he realized that frustration was making him squeeze it harder than he'd intended. "You're the only one who can take my bites."

She nodded and touched his face. "I know." Her hand fell away, and she let out a long breath. "That's why, from time to time—"

"From a sense of pity," he said in a low rumble, "or to protect an *innocent human?*" He strode ahead of her muttering. "Either reason is unacceptable. Especially tonight."

Tara watched him alight the front stairs of the old French-quarter dwelling with the grace of the wind. She stared at his strong back and straight posture, as he held his head high. His dark Afro-style hair shone under the night stars and street lamps, glistening like a king's crown. Under any other circumstances, this man would have been a good choice, given the options her world presented. Yonnie was honorable, handsome, had defended their territory well, his only flaw was, he wasn't Jack Rider.

She took the stone stairs behind him, and leaned on the ornately curved brass rail that replaced what should have been wrought iron, waiting for one of Gabrielle's girls to open the door. Witches didn't do iron, Tara reminded herself, as she slipped off the silver shaman necklace that could cause any were-demon working girls offense.

"Thank you," Yonnie muttered and then depressed the bell as Tara put the jewelry into her coat pocket. "At least for appearance's sake, you could fake being with me as a real lover, not simply my semi-estranged wife."

Tara threaded her arm through Yonnie's, and leaned her head on his shoulder. "I need to go talk to him, so I can finally put things to rest the way I should." She stared up at Yonnie as shadows moved behind the wide, lace-covered, leaded-beveled glass panels in the door. "Let me go see Rider—just to talk. This isn't doing any of us any good."

"I forbid it," Yonnie said in a quiet tone as the door tumblers turned.

"I cannot be with him for the same reasons you can't be with a human. The last time . . . I almost killed him. You know that."

Yonnie's eyes shone with quiet, repressed desperation. "Then maybe I should have let you go see him a long time ago. But then you'd still mourn him."

"I'll always mourn him," Tara said with a sigh. "But at least—"

"I'll consider it. Now drop it," Yonnie said as a petite Asian hostess appeared at the door.

The young woman smiled, her upper and lower canines prominent and glistening. She wore a cocky air of confidence and a skimpy silk kimono that was a mere profusion of red and gold swirls amid patches of mink fur. "Is Madame expecting you, sir?"

Yonnie smiled and pulled Tara closer to his side. "Always."

The young woman nodded, offered him a slight bow, and motioned for him and Tara to follow her. The door creaked shut behind them with no aid of hands evident. On the way to the parlor, they passed an elaborate foyer covered in period tapestry, marble flooring, with a brightly burning crystal chandelier.

Tara's gaze took in the sumptuous space. Red velvet was everywhere, cushioning dark cherry mahogany love seats, chaise longues, and Queen Anne chairs all expertly arranged in gallery seating by a fire.

She sat on the edge of the sofa next to Yonnie, her back a little too rigid for the environment, which seemed to make the young female werewolf smile wider.

"Sir, let me be sure to go over our policies of the house, since your lady friend is obviously new to our establishment here," the hostess said in a demure, silky voice that flowed over the faux couple. "Accept my apologies in advance for what I'm about to say. However, we've recently had some unfortunate results from passion nicks delivered by much lower-level vampires than you and your lady . . . which I'm sure you can understand. But as a precaution—"

Yonnie held up his hand and gave the hostess a sly smile, showing just a hint of fang. "I brought my own," he said, motioning to Tara with his chin. "She knows to only do me."

The hostess smiled. "Very good, sir. I will go fetch the Madame to welcome you for the evening, and so that you may select from our varied offerings."

Tara peered around, more intrigued than offended. She watched a tall, voluptuous female with shoulder-length blond hair walk through the wall. But her fangs were a little over the top, just like her melon-size breasts. She also had the unmistakable glow of recognition on her face. Yonnie stood. Tara's gaze went from one to the other as they gently embraced.

"Love, when Madame said you'd be here, I had to briefly leave a client to personally welcome you to the house." The entity smiled at Tara, sweeping up her hand and kissing the back of it, then transforming into a man. The towering Swedish blond male looked at Yonnie. "She's gorgeous. Beautiful, dark, smoky eyes; delectable, cinnamon skin; hair like black velvet; and her body carved from a goddess statue of old. Sir, you have indeed outdone yourself." The entity's gaze raked Tara in a lusty, open invitation. "What *is* your name?" His patient gaze held Tara's as he transformed back into the long-stemmed female beauty he'd once been.

"Her name is Tara," Yonnie said with pride. "Five feet nothing worth of fine, ain't she?"

Tara smiled and looked at the entity. "Incubus or succubus?"

The entity kissed Tara's cheek. "Does it matter, as long as I can take a throat bite?" It glanced at Yonnie. "As soon as I finish up, which shouldn't be long—he's just a warlock, I could join the two of you? You know, we original Lilim are the only ones left that can take a passion nick without dire consequences, unless you prefer we fetch a human for a little bite-to-ash bondage? However, that is becoming an extremely expensive sport these days, and Madame has issues with the practice in her establishments. She feels it's bad for business, long-term . . . you understand, love."

"No, baby. I'm not going there," Yonnie murmured, stroking her flaxen hair, and eyeing Tara from his peripheral vision. So what if he'd lied. The brothels were still somewhat viable, and she hadn't been treating him right. "It's such a waste of natural resources," he added, returning his full attention to the blonde.

She sighed, shook her head, and straightened the thin strap of her short red negligee. "I'm glad you understand, love. The whole business is so sordid. What has become of the realms whereby one has to utilize excess energy to protect oneself from a simple nick? We truly miss our VIP vampire clientele." She breathed out, tracing his jugular with one finger. "You all were simply the best, and all of the girls are so glad there's at least one master still around." She brushed Yonnie's mouth with hers. "That's why when you visit we spoil you so."

He chuckled as his hands trailed down her back. "Yes, I must admit . . . you ladies do know how to show a brother some love."

"Oh, Yolando," she whispered. "I remember sooooo long ago, it seems, when a love bite wouldn't exterminate and the human girls could add a bit of color to our love games. What do they propose, a dental dam?"

"Yeah, I remember those days, too, baby," Yonnie said, chuckling as he swept the entity's cheek with a brief kiss. "But I'm just here tonight for a divination. Then I'm gonna call it an evening."

The entity pouted. "Oh, poo . . . wait till I tell the girls on the third floor. They have been positively *writhing* for one of your extended visits."

"Give Zaire my *best* regards when you tell them," Yonnie said with a wink. "Better get back to the warlock. Curses can be a nasty thing to have to shake in the morning, especially with all this crazy energy floating around."

The entity nodded and waved over her shoulder as she walked through the wall. "Toodles," she called out, momentarily leaving behind her wriggling fingers and a visible red kiss hovering on them before blowing it to land on Yonnie's cheek through the wood.

Yonnie laughed, rubbed his cheek where the sensation landed, and sat down. "T, the folks in here are cool."

"Like I said, no problem," Tara replied, swallowing away any traces of jealousy that tugged at her. But she lifted her feet up from the floor quickly and hissed, alighting on the sofa like a cat, as a thick-bodied black adder slithered toward Yonnie's shoes and went up his leather pant leg.

"Oh, stop, girl," Yonnie crooned, laughing and struggling with his zipper to let the snake out. "I told y'all, I wasn't coming up to the third floor tonight. I'm with my lady."

Tara leaped back and dug her nails into the wall panel above the fireplace, hanging from it like a treed feline that had seen something to arch its back.

In a slow, sultry, serpentine sway, the adder drew itself out of Yonnie's pants, the head and torso of the entity transforming while her gleaming, black-scaled body remained partially submerged and pulsing beneath the leather.

A dark-skinned black beauty sat on Yonnie's lap, hypnotically swaying from side to side, her long microbraids moving like a thousand miniserpents over her muscular back. Her green eyes sparkled like emeralds beneath the chandelier, and she closed her smoky, charcoal-colored lids down to slits, hissing a hot breath of air against Yonnie's neck.

"Baby, pleasssse, tell me you are going to come sssseee Zaire a little later? It'sssss been soooo long," she murmured, every s holding a snakelike sibilance as she fussed with Yonnie, but never left his lap. "I misssss your anaconda . . . how issss he?"

"Baby, right through here, I can't do Amanthras. You know that's my weakness," he said in a playful tone. "As fine as you are, I'd have to bite you for real without an energy barrier, then you'd be ash before morning. C'mon, girl, stop."

The entity on his lap sighed and drew the lower half of her snake form out of his pants and stood. She caressed his cheek and glared at Tara, who remained on the wall, perched upside down and hissing.

"She needs to chill and learn to respect a little diversity," the shapely Amanthra said, covering her naked form with a thin sheath of transparent snakeskin. She put one hand on her hip, and flipped her middle finger toward Tara with the other hand, as Tara came off the wall. Her body continued to sway in slow, predatory motion as she flashed Tara a pair of huge, venom-dripping viper fangs. "Any day, bitch. I can take a bite as good as give one—so back up off the master when in Gabrielle's house."

"Don't you have a client to service?" Tara said, not retracting her fangs.

The Amanthra put up her hand in Tara's face, then looked around it, blew Yonnie a kiss, and slid out the door.

"T, didn't I ask you to be cool?"

"No, you told me to," Tara said, folding her arms and staring at the door.

Yonnie smiled. He liked her anger. He wasn't sure what it was that had set Tara off, but it was very flattering. Did something nice to her skin tone, made those dark Native American eyes of hers glisten and almost glow red. "If you treated me nicer, with a little more regularity," Yonnie murmured, "I'd have no reason to come here."

Tara moved around the polished wood coffee table. "The Madame is on her way. Focus on whatever's in her crystal ball, would be my suggestion."

Yonnie laughed, stood, and opened his arms for Gabrielle to fill them when she swept into the room.

"Yonnie," she said, careful not to spill her goblet of blood on him as she hugged him hard. She then held him away from her to allow her gaze to rake him. "I was with a client. Oh darling, don't be offended. We've lost so many girls to ash recently that I've had to help out with some of the more aggressive VIPs." She spun to greet Tara and gave her an air kiss. "Things are not what they were. People are literally *possessed*. Insane. What happened to the pleasure principle, I ask? It is driving costs skyward!"

Tara gave Gabrielle a gentle hug and held her hand for a bit, but kept glancing at the goblet and the red stain on Gabrielle's mouth. "Gabby, are there many weres in the house tonight? I know your girls are strictly business, but the client guys from Level Five . . ."

"Oh," Gabrielle scoffed and took a dip sip for her goblet. "All in caged rooms for the night with their female selection from the house. No worries. We haven't seen any senators for a long while now, and those in here aren't going to be of too much concern. Our bars and chains will hold. I reassure you, our bouncers all have silver bullets, should any of them get a little too rowdy."

"Good," Yonnie said, nodding, and picking up Tara's concern as he watched Gabrielle practically guzzle blood. "Like I said when I called, baby, there's been some strange shit going on subterranean. I felt a power surge; so did Tara. Our main man is missing, and yet instinct was telling me he was nearby, but I couldn't spot him."

Gabrielle had changed her hair, he noted. It had once been dyed black. Now she was heavier, thicker, more voluptuous. All of it was disconcerting.

For the first time since they'd been in Gabrielle's house, Tara drew close to Yonnie without having to be asked to do so. Gabrielle tightened the belt on her long, floor-length, black silk robe and flipped her auburn tresses over her shoulder. As she walked deeper into the parlor, feathers from her spiked ostrich-plumed mules gently shifted with the disturbance of air that her hem caused.

Reaching up into the Louis XIV breakfront, she lifted down a large crystal ball and beckoned with a gentle sweep of her hand for Yonnie and Tara to join her at the small round Chippendale table in the private back room.

"Baby," Yonnie said carefully. "What's with the blood? How you feelin' lately?"

"Oh, this," Gabrielle replied in a distracted tone. "I don't know. About a month ago, I started picking up some of my clients' bad habits." She chuckled and placed her hands flat on the table, staring into the crystal ball. "Nothing to worry about."

"Have you been having any bouts of rage . . . yearnings to eat human flesh?" Tara sat slowly and placed a gentle hand on Gabrielle's shoulder.

The two women stared at each other, and then Gabrielle glanced up at Yonnie.

"I only have one body in the refrigerator," Gabrielle said, not answering the question and becoming defensive. "He was a serial killer. We took him out of the general population before he hurt any more innocents, and his soul was damned anyway. . . . We keep food supplies on hand for our werewolves. It's just business. Child molesters, murderers, I think we do a better job at ridding the planet than the human prison system. Don't tell me you've gone—"

"Gabby," Yonnie said quietly, as he stood behind her, held her shoulders, and kissed her temple. "I want you to try to lay off the human food. There's a really bad virus, or contagion, spreading up from the portals. That's why we're here." He stroked her hair, took up one of her hands, and sat beside her. "No judgment, and I know you all just clean up the human scum as a public service . . . but, honey, one night you might cross the line and start going after normal civilians. Then Carlos and Damali, or even your sister, Marjorie, won't be able to petition for you in any kinda way. Feel me? And, you do not want to close your eyes to this life and wake up in the realms where you've got a lot of enemies. All right? I can't go subterranean to help you, if that happens . . . and I can't bring you into my family by a turn to give you a way out."

Her eyes shone with quiet desperation. "You think I'm infected?"

"Given the line of work you're in, baby . . ." Yonnie squeezed her hand. "That's why we've gotta find our boy, so we can close this shit up."

Gabrielle's nervous gaze shot to Tara, and then she dropped Yonnie's hand and stared into the crystal ball. "We all knew that since Lilith fled, things had been different. But we assumed after she and her husband patched up their rift, everything would go back to normal."

"So did we," Tara said quietly, her gaze intent as she stared at Yonnie. "We thought the Chairman might even work his way back into his old position, so that things could . . . stabilize."

"He's still not on his throne?" Gabrielle covered her heart with a flat palm. "He still exists, though?"

Yonnie nodded. "I can't locate my boy; Carlos, but I felt a power surge that gave me ridiculous wood," Yonnie muttered. He glanced at Tara and then sent his gaze into the crystal globe. "It happened so hard and so fast . . . I haven't felt like this since I got made. So, I'm hoping that this is a positive development. Like maybe the energy leaks are sealing up and the portals are closing, that's why the power felt like it had concentrated."

Gabrielle nodded and caressed the crystal ball as her eyes slid shut. "My sight has been a little . . . off. But let me see what I can do."

Yonnie and Tara waited, their breathing becoming so shallow it was practically nonexistent. The ball filled with charcoal smoke as Gabrielle coaxed her divination tool to respond. Tara watched Yonnie as his gaze went out the window, the muscle in his jaw working hard.

Every so often, he'd run his tongue over his teeth, and little by little his eyelids lowered by a fraction.

"You got anything yet?" he finally said, standing abruptly to pace to the window.

He stood with his hand at either side of the window frame, his back to the table, taking in slow breaths and releasing them with effort. His desire was palpable even from across the room.

"The portals are wide open," Gabrielle whispered, her gaze riveted to the ball. "I can't see any activity below. . . . It's like everything's vacated."

"Can you pick up Carlos's essence?" Tara's voice had become strident.

"No," Gabrielle murmured, a frown of confusion crossing her face. "There's no trace of him there. I felt it for a fleeting moment, but if he'd transported through Hell, I know his signature well enough to have felt it, even if he went in as a Neteru. Especially that, because I would have immediately seen silver tracer and human aura where it shouldn't have been." Gabrielle looked at Tara. "He would have stood out like a sore thumb."

"Go deeper," Tara said, her breaths becoming stilted as she spoke. "Go into the Vampire Council's Chamber and see if you can get a glimpse of his throne. If he's been reinstated, it should be intact, blood from the table flowing. Maybe that's why, as vampires, we felt the surge . . . and its effects. Check his torture wall, any place that Carlos might have been dragged to and held hostage."

"If you go that deep," Yonnie said in a low rumble without turning around, "then I'ma need a room for the night."

Tara and Gabrielle glanced up from the crystal ball and stared at his back.

"I can arrange that," Gabrielle said quietly, almost standing to go to him.

"But can *she?*" Yonnie asked, referring to Tara. "This is more than an elevation rush I got here."

Tara nodded, and placed a hand over Gabrielle's. "I'll stay with him. Stock the suite bar. He'll torch you or flatline me in this condition."

Yonnie turned away from the window slowly, his eyes glowing red as he appraised Tara, and simply nodded.

"You all right, man?" Jose said quietly as he came onto the porch. He peered at Rider, whose jaw muscle kept working as though he were chewing tobacco. His gaze discreetly slid to the bottle of Jack Daniel's and fresh pack of smokes that sat beside Rider, untouched.

"Yeah," Rider said. His voice was low and he never turned to look at Jose when he'd spoken. "Time for a change, partner."

Jose nodded and came down a step to plop down beside Rider. "Yeah."

They sat that way for a long time, staring out at the stars and saying nothing.

"You taught me a lot of things along the way, man," Jose said in a cautious tone. "I appreciate that."

"It was my job," Rider said flatly.

Jose smiled. "No it wasn't. Not all the things you taught me since I was a kid. But it kept my head right."

Rider nodded and spit over the edge of the step. "Then I suppose I served my purpose."

"Things change, man," Jose said, his tone gentle, probing lightly as he collected each word. "You taught me that. I had to accept things and move on."

"You are gonna make me open this bottle of Jack and pull out a butt, if you keep traveling down this particular road, partner. Not tonight, okay?"

Jose leaned over, reached around Rider's stone posture, and gathered up the booze and cigarettes to place them neatly by his side. "You told me I couldn't die from this shit, and you know what? You were right."

"I lied," Rider said in a flat tone, and began polishing the barrel of his gun.

"Nah, you didn't lie. I lived, made my peace; I see her with who she's supposed to be with, found somebody else. We cool. It's all good."

For the first time since Jose had sat down, Rider offered him a sidelong glance. "Yeah, you do see her every day, don't you?"

"With him, too," Jose said, opening the Jack Daniel's and taking a swig. "First time they went into a hotel room together, was about to put a nine to my skull . . . And hearing that shit down the hall?" Jose shook his head. "Wasn't right for weeks. But, like you told me, I had to suck it up. That's where she was supposed to be. The two of them are a matched pair; they have the same energy, same lifestyle and mission. The sooner you let it go and realize that it wasn't because she didn't care, wasn't like she didn't ever love you . . ." Jose held out the bottle, but Rider held up his hand and closed his eyes as he took in a deep whiff of its fragrance.

"I still got that shit in my nose," Rider said. "Cap it up for me, would ya?"

Jose quickly complied. "My bad."

"One day I'll be able to smell it, be around it, and it won't give me the shakes, but tonight, while I'm trying to go cold turkey, I can't tolerate it."

"You're gonna feel like shit for a while," Jose said, nodding and hiding the bottle behind him. "If you need a coach, you call me. Sheeit, I still need a coach myself."

Rider smiled a half smile. "Once an addict, always an addict."

Jose pounded his fist. "No relapse, brother."

"No relapse, brother." Rider stared at the horizon. "Yeah. Time to shake this and move on. Might even go buy me a brand-new Harley—red seat this time. Maybe flaming-fucking-yellow. Who knows?"

"New people, places, and things," Jose said, standing and collecting the bottle and smokes.

Rider stood and stretched. "You think Mar is serious about going to Tibet? I can see it now, going on another Marlene-inspired, spiritual, monastic quest to no-man's-land."

"Marlene has more reason to go to Tibet than any of us are talking about, man," Jose said quietly. "How's your nose?"

Rider absently pounded Jose's fist and kept his eyes on the horizon. "Were-jag all in it. How's our brother Shabazz holding up under the pressure?"

"Like me and you—fucked up one minute, cool the next. Sometimes when I get too deep into my own drama, I forget I got brothers dealing with the same pain. But, hey, I'm human. At least I am for the next thirty days."

Rider nodded and sighed. "Yeah . . . Tibet might be a good change of scene."

"Mar already called Chief Quiet Eagle. We're leaving the computers and ammo for them to fend off whatever, like we always do when we leave civilians. Can't ship it no way.

Shabazz already made contact in L.A. for whatever ammo we'll need there on a temporary basis. All we gotta do is get our individual gear packed. Everything else gets donated back here for families in need, and we'll argue about the money we outlaid to build, later, Dan said. So, I'd take that as a readiness call to move out. Marlene wants to get back to L.A., find real estate fast on the fly so we'll have something to come back to."

Rider chuckled. "Just like Mar to try to put a positive spin on things and act like this is a normal, run-of-the-mill job."

"Keep hope alive, man," Jose said, but carefully unscrewed the bottle and took another swig of Jack Daniel's. "She's got J.L. sending plans to Covenant-referred contractors by e-mail; we get our travel shots as soon as we get into L.A. Marlene wants the necessary renovations on whatever we buy done by the time we come home. You know Mar—efficient."

Rider leaned his head back and closed his eyes. "The woman is insane. Tibet is yak country!" Rider lifted his head, opened his eyes, and sighed as he stared at Jose, not at all amused to find Jose smiling. "Dude, it's worse than Arizona. This is not how a man is supposed to go to war or live out his possible last thirty days of life. We are not going to a bachelor's paradise of Far-East exploration. There will be no Japanese geishas, no Thai cottages, or Philippine oasis, or even a good brothel in Nepal along the way. This isn't even the red-light district in Communist China, Jose. Are you hearing me?"

Jose laughed. "I think Marlene is one step ahead of you on the changing of people, places, and things. No packaged-goods stores, no—"

"See, you don't understand my angst. I need at least one vice left to cling to so that I know I'm human—a red-blooded American male."

"Like 'Bazz always says, there's a reason for everything. There are no coincidences in the universe."

"Kiss my ass," Rider said, chuckling, although peeved. "I'd prefer to go out in a blaze of glory."

"Assuming we live, Bobby and Dan gotta learn to focus, get the job done, and tough it out from watching a master tough it out . . . just like our male Neteru might have to get some sage advice about kicking his old drinking addiction from a temporarily celibate male in that last crucial month, hombre. That's why we're heading off to Confucius country."

"Why me? Why not the goddamned Covenant!" Rider closed his eyes. "I'm almost fifty. I can't tolerate—"

"Last round it was me, remember? And what did you tell me?" Jose asked, laughing.

Rider snorted and rubbed his palms down his face, shutting his eyes tighter, grimacing.

"Think about this, then," Jose said, teasing him and making him open his eyes with a poke in the ribs. "Bobby is in his teens. Dan is in his twenties. *They* are in *pain*. This contagion ain't helping."

"Well, since you put it that way," Rider said, shaking his head and rubbing the back of his neck.

"You need to talk to our boy, J.L., too. Now if anyone ever needed a Zen master to get through this mission, it's him. Brother can't even concentrate on wiring tubes or designing radar, much less sending a basic e-mail. Every time Krissy flits by and flops in a chair beside him . . ."

"I know, I know, his circuits blow."

"See, that's why you have a purpose," Jose said with a broad smile, and elbowing Rider in the ribs again as he passed him.

Rider flipped Jose the bird and then smiled. "Since you and Mike don't do nights out with the boys anymore, I guess you won't mind if I take Bobby and Dan to go watch the girls dance the poles in L.A. before we head out?"

"With my blessings," Jose said, bowing like a martial arts instructor with the bottle balanced between both palms. "I cannot go watch the girls without severe consequences, but I can help you pick out a Harley once we return home, O enlightened one."

Both men chuckled as Jose stood up straight. But slowly, Rider's expression became serious.

"I'm cutting back on the Jack and giving up the smokes."

"Good," Jose said, looking at Rider's grave expression.

"Let me ask you something, though."

Jose nodded as he continued to stare at Rider, new worry lacing through him and sobering his mood.

"Is my nose off, or did you smell metallic substance when we were all out there?"

Jose hesitated, and took in a deep inhale. He walked over to the rail, hocked and spat. "Yeah, man. Ain't nothing wrong with your snoz."

"Then why didn't you back up my position in the yard?"

Jose paused and stared at Rider confused. "What are you talking about, man?"

Brilliant morning sun chased the last of the shadows that clung to the living room furniture. Carlos stroked Damali's hair as she finally slid into heavy REM, the nightmares only ceasing their torture at dawn. He stared at the coffee table, where two wineglasses stood near a depleted bottle of wine. Her glass was filled; his was not. Damali hadn't even taken a sip in his presence, but had snuggled against him once they'd sat down and was immediately out.

Despite her conscious confusion, her subconscious spirit apparently guided her not to share a drink of anything with him, not even water, while in the house . . . just as it seemed to block his advances by conveniently making her fall fast asleep and light up internally with protective inner silver. He could have attempted to physically violate her while she slept, but her will was strong even in her unnatural slumber, presenting an impenetrable barrier. She hadn't dropped that, even though he'd fucked her brain real good.

Carlos paused. What was he thinking? It sounded so crude even in his mind. He had *never* fucked Damali. He gently extricated himself from her embrace and stood, needing space to really call it what it was.

He hadn't just violated her mind last night; he'd raped it. He wiped his hands over his face and began to pace, not sure what to do. It didn't matter that, at the moment, she'd never know. The fact remained, *he knew*. What had happened to him last night? All he did was accidentally sit in the Chairman's throne—but he'd gone to Hell and had been forced into one of those before, yet never lost his true self. Why was this time so different? Could the contagion have altered his ability to cope? What if . . . ?

Carlos became still for a moment. He'd violated a direct angelic command to not sit in the throne. Was he insane? They had said wait for a sign, and he hadn't. He rubbed his palms down his face. His judgment was all fucked up.

The reality frightened him. It was as though there were two entities constantly warring within him. He could practically feel it beneath the surface of his skin. Every decision was an acute struggle to do the right thing. By day, he felt different. By night, he had something within his psyche that was too terrible to name.

New fear covered him in a sheen of cold sweat. What if, with this contagion in him and whatever else he'd picked up on Level Six, he didn't have a line? Just like he'd pried open Damali's brain and licked her gray matter until it trembled and shrieked and begged for mercy, one night he might brutally pry open her thighs to do the same to the sacred orifice between them. It would most assuredly not be his tongue that battered her. . . . What if he totally flipped dark, kept her on her knees, and sodomized her—some twisted shit like that?

Last night he'd just come into the throne power, didn't know how to wield it, but like all things, he'd be able to in time, and her barriers would come crashing down. Carlos backed away from her shaking his head. No! What? His brain was flipping back and forth between right and wrong even in pure daylight! He needed to purge his system, and do it fast—but how!

He had to get out of there. He was losing touch with any mission he'd clung to, losing touch with who he had been before he fell into the dark throne and came back as something that now, in the cold light of day, truly scared him.

First her mind, then her body, and ultimately that might break her spirit. It was the way of that realm. Pure darkness knew no limits. Level Seven had no delimiters, no boundaries. Such an assault coming from him, a known, trusted source, might be more soul-scarring than from a stranger, an unknown predator that she could fight to the death before ever submitting.

"Give her back her blade," he whispered to himself as he glanced at her, retrieved and covered her with Jose's blanket, then made his way out the back door. He crossed the deck with purpose. He needed the sun, the Light, to explain.

Stopping abruptly as he made his way to stand twenty-five yards away from the house, Carlos lowered his head in shame, bent his knees, and dropped, not caring that small rocks and sand stones cut into his flesh.

"Please forgive me," he said, clasping his hands. "Don't let this thing take hold in me. Preserve my spirit. Get it out of me. I'm clinging to the thin thread of silver lining. I disobeyed, I know, but we're all infected. . . . Don't leave me. Don't let me hurt her or the family."

She woke up with what felt like a horrible hangover. Damali sat up slowly and glanced down at the blanket that covered her. Vaguely, she remembered that Carlos had been there last night. In slow increments the accident and burning his clothes came back to her, but as she gathered the blanket closer to her, guilt stabbed at her. He'd wrapped Jose's blanket around her?

When she attempted to stand, she was forced to hold her head with both hands. She looked at the small coffee table and the remnants of dirty wineglasses and groaned. "No more, never again," she said with a wince. "How much of this crap did I drink?"

She allowed the rhetorical question to follow her to the bathroom, and then into the bedroom. Catching her profile in a mirror, she looked like pure hell in the disheveled clothes that she'd obviously slept in.

Blurred memories of insane, terror-filled dreams flitted

through her brain like snatches of dark confetti, but she couldn't string together anything that made sense. All that remained was the sensation of pure horror and a throbbing headache that culminated at the base of her skull. Did Carlos leave already?

Then she remembered his potential relapse and began walking through the house with urgency. Her gaze tore through every room, half afraid of what she might see. God forbid that anything might have happened to him. If a pile of ash greeted her somewhere, she'd die on the spot of a heart attack.

But when she ran out onto the deck, bright sunlight made her shield her eyes. Relief dropped her shoulders and slowed her frantic pace.

She stood in awe, slowly lowering her hand from her eyes. He was on his knees with a lemon yellow towel wrapped around his waist, consumed in silent prayer near the cactus that had transformed into her long blade in the earlier vision. The way the new day's light played across his bare shoulders and sent a prism of color between him and the desert plant, made her squint.

Immobilized by the spectacle of watching him send his inner thoughts skyward, she added her own fervent message in silent refrain: *Please let him be all right. Watch over him.*

As though sensing her presence, Carlos lifted his head, stood, and turned to face her. When he stepped before the cactus, Damali stopped breathing. He was in the same position as he was in her vision, his brown eyes begging her with a question that she didn't understand. Pained, worried, glassy eyes filled with unshed tears stared back at her. He was shadowed, and outlined in a luminous frame of sunlight.

Suddenly, she flinched, mentally hearing the wind catch her blade, followed by the inevitable thud.

CHAPTER THIRTEEN

Are you okay?" Damali asked as Carlos came up the deck stairs.

He almost couldn't speak as he stared at her sad eyes. "Yeah, I'm fine," he said quietly. "You okay?"

She smiled. "Must have drank too much wine on an empty stomach last night," she said with a weary sigh. "Guess that's what I get for giving you the blues about going out with Yonnie." She chuckled and opened the screen door. "What's that old saying? *Judge not lest ye be judged,* or *People in glass houses shouldn't throw stones.*"

"I like the first one," he said, his voice distant. "The biblical version."

She turned and stared at him in the kitchen.

"*Let he who is without sin cast the first stone,*" Carlos closed his eyes, gathered up her hands and pressed them to his mouth. "Damali, forgive me. . . . I am so sorry, I'll never, ever, betray you like that again. Just don't give up on me."

She slid her hands away from his grasp to wrap her arms around him and pull him in close to her. She found herself stroking his back and beginning to gently sway him in a comforting hug. This was not Carlos. This didn't even sound like him. His ragged breaths were thick like he was trying not to sob. "Baby, what's wrong?"

He shook his head no, and swallowed hard.

"Don't you think *betray* is an awfully strong word?" she said, trying to reach whatever was torturing his mind.

"Oh, baby, I swear I love you."

Now she was worried. She tried not to stiffen, but every female instinct in her whispered, a man breaking down like this just because he got read for going out with his boy, meant . . .

Again, he shook his head no. "It's not like that. I should have never gone out with Yonnie, and then things got crazy."

She sighed and rubbed his back harder. "You relapsed, didn't you? Be honest."

He nodded quickly with his head buried against her shoulder. "It was a sip . . . some of it got in my mouth. It was an accident. It wasn't supposed to go down like that. Girl, I swear to you, I don't want to go back to that life."

"I know, I know," she whispered as he began to sob. "It'll be all right. You came home, your system purged, it's broad daylight and you're still standing, okay?"

"You think . . . I mean, I can get this out of me, right?"

She held him away from her, summoning an inner strength that came from her very DNA. "You have choices. You had a slip, but you didn't fall." She wiped the dampness away from his face. "Unless it becomes a problem, I'll keep this between me and you; you have to have someone you can trust. *Especially* now, with every Guardian's judgment impaired. It's me and you, one unit."

He covered her hand with his and stared at her through wet lashes. "Damali, get this out of me. Baby, I'm scared."

For a moment, she didn't know what to say to him. True terror filled his eyes, and it was the first time in her life that she'd heard Carlos Rivera tell her anything like that.

"I got your back," she said firmly. "No more slips, you feel shaky, you come to me and we'll ride it out together. Cool?"

Again, he nodded quickly, and blew out a long breath. "I was afraid that I might not even be able to pray after . . ." his voice trailed off and he sighed again. "After things went down."

"How bad was it really?" she asked, gently probing for critical information. When he looked away, she touched the side of his face. "Carlos, look at me. Was it from a throat or a cup or a bottle? Talk to me?"

"It wasn't from a throat," he said on a heavy exhale. "I

didn't hurt anyone but myself." He looked away from her after the admission. "Rider was right, so were the others. Smelling the deer blood messed me up, and I was on the edge."

She let her breath out hard and kept her voice firm but her gaze gentle. Her squad was still on-point, contagion notwithstanding. Clearly, so was she. But seeing this broke her heart. This had to be what she'd been visioning, feeling, dreading for months—not just the portal problem. It was time, also, to change the people, places, and things that could lead him to relapse, but she couldn't drop that responsibility at Yonnie and Tara's feet. In an odd way, they were also family.

"Carlos, I'm not preaching, but I want to tell you what I know. All right?"

"Yeah, baby, anything you know that can help me kill this side of my nature. Go 'head."

"First of all, this blood thirst is not in your nature, it was acquired, like a virus. Remember that *always*. It is *alien* to your God-spirit, and you must separate it from the true light within you." She thrust her chin up, her eyes blazing with righteous determination. "You were *chosen* to be a Neteru. A Neteru is not perfect; there is only One Supreme Being that owns perfection. However, a Neteru is the vanguard of justice."

She placed her hand over his heart and splayed her fingers over his scar. "A Neteru must be strong, is not to be sequestered from the world at large, but has to have the inner strength to stay on the path and to walk through the Valley of the Shadow of Death and fear no evil . . . has to be able to dig deep within to summon the courage to do the right thing *always,* to walk where angels fear to tread, and go down into Hell, if necessary to free the innocent—one's own life the last concern."

She watched his eyes fill and his Adam's apple bob in his throat as he swallowed hard.

"I am those things, Damali. I wasn't afraid to go down to Hell to free the innocent," he said thickly. "I *have* walked where angels fear to tread, trust me on that."

For a moment, neither spoke. Damali nodded and patted his chest.

"You've got the scars to prove it. *This* is the man I know. The man who could fight the blood hunger. The man who could look an entire Council table of demons in the eye and outwit them, out-smart them, and come up holding aces. The man I know is strong and powerful, not from the illusions he could cast, but from his inner self." She gathered him into her arms and whispered into his ear on a harsh murmur. "You can beat this, Carlos. I believe in you."

He clutched her like a man drowning. His hands sought her hair. She didn't understand what had just transpired, but her words gave him hope.

"I'm going to call the family house to find out what time our flight leaves this morning and run by there to pick up some clothes for you. In the meantime, you take a shower and pray, and think, and try to put things in perspective."

The warm sensation of water felt good against his skin, like it was peeling away layers of filth and baptizing him in renewal. Even though he hadn't been able to bring himself to fully explain the depth of his fear to Damali, or the profound sorrow for what he'd done, her faith in him stilled some of the inner terror. If the angels would just hear his cry, would just understand how the chair attacked him, how it had happened not of his own will, how the contagion had helped sway him—

"Speak!"

Carlos jumped back from the showerhead, almost slipping on the wet surface beneath his feet, and then rushed out of the glass enclosure. His heart slammed against his breastbone. Terror shot adrenaline through his system as his gaze tore around the spacious, lemon yellow room.

"Speak!"

He was out, going for the door when it sealed shut by a wall of light. Suddenly every window flooded with light that bounced off the bathroom mirror, blinding him. Light poured in from the edges of the doorframe. Then the walls of the bathroom closed in on him.

"You sat in the unmentionable," one voice said.

"You defied a direct order; the consequences are grave!" another said.

"You acted prematurely," another voice argued.

"You know not what you have done," a chorus said.

"I didn't know," Carlos said, not sure where to turn his attention. Voices had slammed him from every direction, making him whirl around in the now-tiny space. The sensation of vertigo made him fall to the tile floor, but he outstretched his arms, trying to make them understand.

"It attacked me," he said, tears running down his face. "I went in, searched, and under the crest, it was gone—then it attacked me!"

"You were not to go there until you had integrated the fragments of your mind," one voice said. "Your spirit is now in peril."

"We know of the attack," another said.

"You've released the realms. The Damned are now upon the earth with the Lilim."

"Armageddon has begun too soon."

"No, no, no," Carlos yelled, scrambling to his feet. "I didn't release—"

"The original demons of darkness feared coming out to search for their once-captive Damned, until each of their levels was made intolerable, even for them."

Carlos opened his mouth, then slowly closed it. He knew exactly what they meant. When he'd gone level-by-level wreaking havoc, those entities were to hit the sealed portal and be trapped, tortured. Now they'd flooded the earth.

"Yes!" one thunderous voice boomed. "That was your mission, but your timing was in error. We commanded you to wait for a sign! You were to send the Damned to the surface, but not the original demons that feed upon them, only once the book was acquired. Our Light would have held the Lilim back; the Damned would have fled blindly, aimlessly away from the horrors of the pit. This would have allowed us to decimate their numbers with swords raised at every gate, their names listed, and we would have been able to swiftly commend the lost to peace!"

"Now they all hide, unnamed, unseen, and await night-fall," a very quiet voice said. "The Damned, with the Lilim, further spreading the contagion among humanity."

"Like in the days of old, when Lilith spewed a hundred demons a day upon the earth and our warriors slew them by the thousands!"

"Now their leader is within you; they await your command. Their exterminator is also within you. *Decide.* Separate yourself from this iniquity."

"How?" Carlos whispered. "Tell me how?"

"The unnamed one's essence was within Lilith's womb, like the original demons she helped give rise to using the seed of human males. Its abomination filled your lungs, began to taint your spirit, and by day it lay dormant, by night it stirred . . . but the throne ignited it to life. *Kill it.*"

Carlos whirred around in a circle. "If it's in me, then how do I get it out of me?"

"This is your task. Bring us the book. The struggle is within."

"It was and remains in the chamber, under the crest, but your eyes were blind to it because you still lusted for that world."

"The contagion weakened me," Carlos said in an urgent tone. "Even as a man, not a Neteru, I was stronger than that!" He stared at the Light unblinking. "Help me make the separation."

For a moment all went still, and then the battering of voices again splintered into echoes throughout the tiled space, increased in tempo. The tone of urgency made his head pound. He was no longer able to separate where one voice began and another ended. His senses on overload, it sounded like one long run-on sentence spoken by many voices without any taking a breath.

"Yes, the contagion is insidious—that is why we said to wait for a sign."

"You saw the illusion of emptiness."

"We will not leave you as long as your will clings to us."

"Your impatience made you disobey our command."

"The book is still there under the wicked crest."

"We sent the vision, even through the darkness, to guide you."

"The Chairman's blood must be spilled by a Neteru's blade to break his illusion."

"You may not be able to do it now. We can only hope."

Voices collided with voices; information was being shouted at Carlos in varying timbres till he wept. He'd messed up, had finally gotten played. The Light was furious; the dark side was laughing at him. His sanity was on the brink of fracture. The voices bounced off the tiles and nearly made his ears bleed. But they would not relent as the voices swirled around him, gathering like a white-light storm.

"Even the one who remains nameless could not see it."

"They are from the same seed, their treachery near equal."

"Their province over certain realms is distinct. *Only the Chairman ever entered the Garden—not his father.* All of our forces are attempting to assist. The Neteru Councils are involved, as well."

"This is why the Chairman's father hunts him. In the end of days, the book will reinforce or deplete soul armies of Light. His father cannot obtain it without a Neteru's blade."

"This has always been the way. A Neteru's hand allowed fruit from the tree to be consumed—branches to create the pages gleaned, thus a Neteru's hand must break the Chairman's hold."

"This is the only reason his father cannot acquire it; we have been in wait for this opportunity since the dawn of time when Dante went into permanent hiding with *the book.*"

"Your destiny was greater than you knew."

"We allowed you to learn Dante's world so that you could walk through it, but not ultimately be of it, and to teach the female Neteru all that we could not."

Carlos felt hot, wet splashes on his shoulders that burned as voices above him wept.

"Do you know your value to us?"

"You and she were our most cherished weapons."

"A tandem secret weapon, brought together as one. The darkness never knew. We were simply awaiting your choice! It is still always your choice—that is what remains fragile."

Carlos stared at the Light. "All this time . . . you wanted me to turn, allowed it? Needed me to be a councilman? Let us both walk—"

"We never left you."

"We prayed that you would make the right choices, and you did. You both did."

"It was not punishment. You both were being honed for greatness."

"The challenges of this millennium are more arduous; the time draws nigh."

"Desperate times called for desperate measures. What we face now required our Neterus to know that which those that went before them have never known. The Light has ultimate knowledge, beyond the dark thrones—this has always been their quest to seek the knowing of The All.

"The Chairman's head must roll."

"He'd been lied to by his father, was told he would release those armies."

"He is not the one chosen to be the unspeakable."

"Lilith knew this, for she came before him."

"The female Neteru only wounded her, but must take her head, as well."

"The Himalayas."

"The Himalayas."

"The Himalayas."

"We called home the Covenant to prepare the twelve paths for certain war."

"We now directly guard the Neterus."

"Do not defile the Neteru."

"To defile her is to defile yourself."

"Our Neteru is also your Neteru."

"You are a Neteru."

"Do not defile yourself with corruption."

"If you defile the Neteru within you, you defile your other half, Damali."

"The Himalayas," a chorus whispered in unison.

"The list is of those weak in spirit that needed reinforcement, angelic assistance, to make the right choice."

"They were attacked first and then consumed."

"We want those stolen in treachery, the multitude returned."

"Only one with the nameless within him, after the Chairman's blood has been spilled, his essence extinguished, can retrieve the book."

"Our command had purpose. Was to be followed with blind faith."

"You were once polluted by the Chairman, thus the only one on our side who could open his crest."

"The Himalayas was a part of the path; the path that would lead to spilling the Chairman's blood. Then you could retrieve the book without more compromise of your inner Light!"

"Time has sped up. Disaster has been set in motion."

"Spill the foul blood."

"Bring us the book."

Carlos grasped his skull with his hands. The Light suddenly receded, and was gone as quickly as it had come. The room expanded back to normal. The shower was still running. White steam cloaked him and clouded the mirror. It was just like what had come up out of the crest's vault. The Himalayas. He didn't fully understand what he'd find there, maybe the Chairman's lair, but knew enough by this point to do as he was told without question. Thoughts tumbled and spun within him. Something frightening also stirred within him as though it had been slowly awakened. Thoughts became fuzzy and suddenly scattered.

Was he supposed to go back down and get the book right

away, or go to the Himalayas with something he couldn't even name within him . . . with the family and Damali un-protected and near him? To his foggy mind, the answer was clear. Get the book first.

He heard a small squeaking sound coming from the mir-ror. He stared at it intently as it began to scrawl a message in the condensation on the glass. It was written in reverse, and he squinted at it, trying to decipher it. Renewed terror threaded through his soul and spread like an inferno. It read very simply, *Get the book.*

Krissy glanced up from her laptop and over to Dan as he sat at the dining room table playing cards with her dad and a few of the male Guardians. She smiled as he studied his hand and rubbed his jaw, considering his next move. Rider was always a hoot and provided comic relief. Their card game antics made her laugh, and she liked seeing Dan happy instead of tense and scowling at J.L.

Truthfully, Dan was a really nice guy. Had big blue eyes, a sweet heart, was smart, cute in a wiry sort of way . . . con-siderate, listened, was a decent fighter, and was crazy about her. The only problem was that after one kiss she knew he'd only be a brother to her. But the last thing she ever wanted to do was hurt him.

He was family, he was Bobby's best friend, plus her mother adored him. Her dad, well, that was another story. Richard Berkfield didn't trust any guy around her and never had. But he was at least reasonable toward Dan, unlike the way he practically snarled when J.L. sat too close to her. Maybe being a cop for all those years gave her dad special insight. Perhaps he felt the chemistry that was hard to ignore and that they'd attempted to keep secret. Just her luck to have a detective for a father.

She glanced away and sighed, studying her laptop as though its keys might provide answers like a Ouija board. However, she could feel J.L.'s intensity from where he sat in the adjacent chair by the window. No, she would not look up at him. Couldn't. His quiet need reached out to her across the room. It always did. That's how things always got started. She squeezed her knees together and briefly shut her eyes. It had started.

Unable to help herself, she glanced up and her gaze was trapped by the silent smolder in his eyes. Those searching, intense brown eyes were impossible to ignore. She loved what the sun did to his skin as it washed him in afternoon gold. She loved the feel of his hair, black silk, and patient hands . . . haiku fire. She loved his agile, toned body, and the way he moved like a cat . . . a being without bones, so fluid, graceful . . . just like he was on the computers, a mastermind, subtle, wise, a man of few words, though those he spoke were profound. And his mind had been the thing that had stolen her heart. He'd taught her so much. He had been the first guy that really heard her, knew what she was talking about, and didn't think she was an airhead or a geek or weird. He believed in her—*her.* She loved him. That's what she couldn't ignore. That's what her father didn't understand.

Their code was also subtle, codesigned without words. J.L. closed his laptop, asked if anyone wanted a beer, and left the room. She waited until he came back, handed out brews, and then she mouthed hollow platitudes about finding the rest of the girls. She went out the back door; he went out the front door.

Her heart raced faster than her legs as she dashed across the wide backyard toward the toolshed, slipped inside, and gently closed the door behind her and waited. The wait for him to wind an oblique path to meet her was the worst. She never knew if he would make it or get waylaid by one of the other Guardians or what.

Krissy peered through the open shed slats, then leaned against the wall and shut her eyes, trying to slow her breathing. Impossible. Sunlight created splintered beams along the dirt floor and dust motes glistened. She impatiently peeked out once again, then watched pollen and dust particles dance in the air like sunlit fairy flecks that had been stirred from her quick entry. If he would just come to the shed . . .

When she heard footfalls, she held her breath. Her face felt hot. Perspiration made her white cotton shirt cling to her skin. Would this time be like all the others—his kiss and touch interrupted by someone approaching? What if this time he said it was wrong, or that they should wait until her birthday, when she turned eighteen in a few weeks? What if it wasn't him?

She whirred around and pressed her face to the wall slats again, and then let her breath out in relief when she saw J.L. glance over his shoulder and reach for the door. She moved toward him the moment he closed it behind him, but he put his finger to his lips and glanced around the toolshed barn, as though being hunted. She froze, listened hard, but couldn't take her eyes off him. Her gaze became a slow glide down his handsome, symmetrical features; it stopped at his mouth, then continued to his Adam's apple; took in his shoulders and the way his T-shirt clung to him with a thin sheen of sweat; then slid down to his narrow, tight waist, to his jeans.

"Kris, I can't do this anymore," he whispered, and then closed his eyes.

Hurt initially stunned her, but the expression on his face told her that she'd misinterpreted what he'd meant.

"Why not?" she whispered, already knowing the answer. Each time had become more intense, closer to the inevitable, harder to stop. Their secret shed visits had become more frequent with less time between each stolen moment, and they were both going crazy from it all.

J.L. opened his eyes. The way he stared at her made her feel like her legs would give out from under her. He offered her a lopsided smile as his gaze went toward a dried-out hay bale, then over to a row of rusted tools on the wall, settling on an ax.

"Because there's about fifty things in here for your dad to kill me with."

She smiled. "He's playing cards."

"The man isn't stupid, and he's armed and extremely dangerous. A cop, remember."

"Ex-cop," she countered, going to J.L. and filling his arms.

"Worse. That means he's not worried about losing his job." J.L. laughed wryly and kissed her forehead.

"I don't care," she murmured as he nuzzled her neck and her hands splayed across his muscular, toned back.

"I care," he breathed out hard against her hair.

"I know you do. . . . That's why I love you."

"I gotta at least wait till you're legal."

"No you don't," she whispered in a rush against his ear. "I want to."

His grip tightened around her back as his mouth found hers, palms stroking more desire into her shoulders as they slid against her damp shirt then found her arms. A soft whimper entered his mouth and he swallowed it, her body producing friction against his. She thought she would faint when his fingers sought her hair, not the ache of her breasts. . . . She'd purposely not worn a bra just for him, and he didn't seem to notice.

This time had to be different. They could all die any day. She refused to die never fully knowing him. His featherlight touches during stolen moments had made her crazy. Having nowhere to ever really be alone had made her bold. Sleeping in an overcrowded room with no privacy to bask in the sweet aftermath of a secret interlude, ever, made her tug at his T-shirt and deepen their kiss. Working side by side with him every day, all day and half the night, learning his ways, his laugh, his humor, his moods, his deepest feelings, down to his very scent made her throw caution to the wind.

Her touch ran down his back, covered his backside, and then traced his hips until she gained the courage to slide them between their bodies. The low sound he made filled her mouth and caused her to tear away from the burning kiss to gasp.

He shook his head, and spoke in halting, pained bursts.

"Just a few more weeks. I love you, Kris, but I won't make it till then if—"

She kissed away his words and began frantically working on his belt. Her shirt yanked up, and his hot face pressed against her breasts with a groan, making her cry out. The long-awaited sensation caused tears to spill as she staggered backward, blind, eyes closed, kissing him harder, trusting, knowing he was walking her toward the prickly hay bale and she didn't care.

In one martial arts pivot, he was under her, moving in a fluid tide, stripping away her shirt and taking the full punishment of the hay to save her skin.

When Damali pulled up to the front of the family house, Dan was standing on the steps with a duffel bag in hand. He smiled broadly, the sun catching in his blond hair and making his boyish face seem even younger.

"Marlene had a hunch you might be needing these," he said with a smirk, holding out a bag of Carlos's clothes to Damali.

Damali chuckled. "I see Marlene hasn't lost her edge."

"Not at all," Dan said, coming down the steps to hug Damali. "You okay, lady?"

"Yeah, I'm fine, just a little weary."

He looked at her, worried. "How's our brother?"

"He's cool," Damali said. "Just been through a lot of changes, but he'll be all right."

Dan nodded and glanced back at the screen as Jose appeared within it.

"You cool, D?" Jose said, coming out onto the porch quickly and keeping his gaze fastened to Damali's.

"Yeah. Like I told Dan, everything's gonna be all right."

But it wasn't all right. She could feel tension crackling all around her. She stepped over the doorsill and the hair on the back of her neck rose.

Everyone was packed. Suitcases and duffel bags waited by the door. Shabazz was at the table playing cards with

Berkfield, Bobby, and Rider. Everything seemed normal, but wasn't. She could feel Jose and Dan stop for a moment behind her, fidget, and then slide into their seats.

"Morning, y'all," she said in a sarcastic tone, addressing their cool reception with testy humor. "Where's Mar?"

Shabazz slammed down a card hard. "Went to meditate in the woods, again, before we leave this afternoon. Where else?"

Damali chewed her bottom lip and forced her voice to become upbeat. "Cool," she said casually. "Marj around?"

"At the store," Berkfield muttered. "Shopping till she drops, since we're changing locations again. Like we need anything else. If we coulda gotten a morning flight out, then she wouldn't be running around like a madwoman." He looked up with a frown.

"Marlene said a lot of flights have been canceling lately," Rider muttered, studying his fan of cards. "All transportation is screwed because people aren't showing up to their jobs. Drama is breaking out everywhere. In my mind, the sooner we can get this show on the road, the better, 'cause the shit is obviously spreading faster than we'd imagined."

"I can't wait to get out of here," Bobby said, throwing down his hand of cards. "Everything's making me jumpy."

Damali nodded and hoisted the duffel bag up higher. "Guess 'Nez is out and about with Mike?" She glanced around, quietly trying to sense for Juanita without asking her whereabouts.

"Mike does the heavy lifting, both the ladies are buying what we need for the road," Shabazz said, glaring up from his hand. "Least that's the story we got."

Static charge was practically lifting Shabazz's locks off his shoulders. Damali nodded again, trying not to be drawn into the attitudes and vibes that permeated the house. "Cool. All right. Well, maybe I'll catch up with Krissy just to be sure we have all . . ." Her voice trailed off as Berkfield's head snapped up at the same time Shabazz's and Dan's did.

Rider was on his feet with Bobby in seconds, one blocking Dan the other Berkfield.

"Where's my daughter?" Berkfield said, looking at Rider hard.

"Relax, dude," Rider said as calmly as possible. "Let's me, you, and old Shabazz here take a fatherly walk."

"Fuck that," Dan shouted before Berkfield could challenge Rider's reply, making the room go still. "Where's J.L.?"

Jose stood slowly, mirroring Shabazz's moves in a patient dance—and then grabbed Dan as he was about to bolt. Damali dropped the duffel bag and looked at her teammates.

"Yo, yo, yo, what's up with all this, guys?" Damali held her hands up. "We're out of here in—"

"Damali, get 'em off of me or I swear I'll—"

"Let him go," Damali said quickly, going to Dan, watching hot tears rise in his eyes as his face flushed. "Baby—"

"I knew it!" Dan shouted, looking at Bobby and then Jose. He rubbed his nose with the back of his hand, and sniffed back tears of frustration as he sputtered his complaint. "You were supposed to have my back, man! You know good and damned well where she is!"

"Then some-fucking-body tell me," Berkfield said, shrugging Rider's grip off his shoulder. "Wanna enlighten her goddamned father? Huh! Somebody?"

Shabazz shook his head and began walking. "Berkfield, me and you, we take a walk, we talk, and we let cool heads prevail. . . . Aw'right? Been there. Very recently."

Berkfield nodded grudgingly and began to walk. "I need some answers."

"It's best this way," Shabazz said quietly, putting his arm over Berkfield's shoulder. "Better on the team than . . . She's young, could get jacked in a—"

Before the other brothers or Damali could react, Dan had cleared the table and was going in the direction of the kitchen, headed for the back door. Instinct kicked in, and every man in the house was on Damali's heels as she tried to catch up with Dan, who was making a mad dash for the shed.

"Daniel!" She screamed, closing the gap across the big backyard, her legs pumping as her stride ate up ground. "Don't do it, Dan! Don't go in there! J.L.!" Mental prayers came out in fits of breath. *Oh, Lord, oh Lord, not on this team, not another one, not today, not this kid! Get dressed y'all. Shit!*

A shotgun blast made her look over her shoulder and lose ten feet of gain. She saw it in slow motion, skidded to grasp the back of Dan's T-shirt that ripped under her hold. J.L. had stumbled out of the shed, tucking his shirttails into his pants, breathing hard. Berkfield was beet red in the face, lowering a sawed-off and being tackled to the ground. Krissy was crying and trying to get her blouse untwisted. Jose body-blocked Krissy from her father's scrutiny while she righted her clothes. Bobby slowed down, conflicted, caught in the withered grass between his father, his sister, and his two best friends. Rider and Shabazz were trying to extricate a weapon from a father who was foaming at the mouth. Dan was about to get his ass kicked by a martial arts pro.

"Stop!" Damali's heart was beating a bruise into her chest.

Nothing Neteru was working. Her legs were lead, time wasn't stopping, the team had snapped its fragile hold on reality. Where was fucking Juanita when another pair of female hands was needed! Damali flung down the ripped fabric, screaming "No!" as Dan hurdled headlong into J.L.'s abdomen and was summarily flipped to land with a thud on his back.

Dan was up in seconds, pure rage blazing in his bloodshot blue eyes. Tears and dirt had created mud on his face. J.L. almost snarled as murder flit through his normally kind brown eyes. Krissy was sobbing and looking at her father as Rider finally got the gun out of his clenched fist.

"I'll kill him!" Berkfield shouted. "In the family house, with me here, I will massacre him! Let me up, goddammit, now!"

Damali dashed between the two warring brothers, her posture centered low, knees bent, as she hopped in a circle to follow their moves. She eye-spotted Jose and Bobby for assistance. She didn't want anybody hurt, and that was likely if they collided again.

"Everybody chill. One family. One—"

"No!" Dan spat, "Fuck it. No such thing! She lied to me!"

Damali's attention swung between both younger Guardians as Krissy cried harder. Not sure what to do, she tried to keep them talking. Dan had totally surprised her. The newbie was faster, stronger, and had more heart than she'd given him credit for, and to see him out there all jacked around was breaking her heart.

She glanced at Krissy's disheveled condition and then at J.L.'s. Oh, shit. This man was definitely *working* before Dan's red alert, and the girl's father was in it now? J.L. was not about to calm down. All right, new plan. She gave Jose the subtle nod and he was on Dan in seconds with Bobby helping to pin him to the exterior shed wall.

"Dan, listen for two seconds. Okay?" She pivoted her attention to J.L. who looked like he was about to break Dan's neck. "J.L., you can kill him if you two mix it up. He's no black belt, brother. You have *got* to calm down!"

"I will kill this motherfucker where he stands now, D—let him go! He's been getting on my nerves since Philly, aw'right!" J.L. spat and rolled his shoulders. "This is bullshit!"

Guttural roars and a daughter's repeated name amid curses were coming from Berkfield twenty feet away as he wrestled on the dusty ground with Rider and Shabazz and tried to get to J.L.

"There's nothing to listen to, D," Dan hollered, new tears filling his eyes as his focus went to Krissy. "Tell him!"

"You need to stop playing games, Kris," Bobby shouted.

"I told you to just be honest with my boy! Why'd you put him in a position like this, huh?"

"I was not playing games," she screamed, going to Damali and crying harder. "I changed my mind, all right! Is that what you wanna hear? I never slept with Dan!"

"So the kisses never mattered? Is that what you're saying? All those nights we talked, and I held you while you cried about being scared didn't mean shit to you, Kris? Is that it?" Veins were standing in Dan's neck as he hollered, "Answer me!"

Pure shock had loosened Jose and Bobby's hold on Dan, and in a hurt fury he tore his body away from the rusty aluminum shed exterior to walk in a hot circle, raking his hair with dirty fingers. "I cannot *believe* you." He made a lunge, but Jose and Bobby had him.

"Aw, Lawd, Dan, don't get into . . ." Damali sighed as Krissy covered her face and wailed. The girl's business was all over the yard; her father was about to have a stroke.

"I'll kill 'em both," Berkfield shouted, sending up plumes of dust as he struggled. "Rider, lemme up! Shabazz, get the fuck off me! They were both on my baby? Oh, shit, where's Mike's cannon!"

Damali couldn't hold Krissy and body block J.L. at the same time. But even with the girl near her, she could feel humiliation rising off Krissy's skin in a thick, pain-filled emulsion. Dan looked like he'd been slapped—better description, gut-punched, but the young fool's pride was putting him at risk for getting his ass beat. *Stand down,* Damali whispered in her mind. *Please, Daniel, oh, man . . .*

"Okay, everybody just stop!" Damali finally shouted, so confused and upset she didn't know what to do. She pointed at Dan. "She made a choice. How she came to that is between you two. Discuss it later—but one thing is for sure, she shouldn't have to do it out here like this."

Dan shrugged out of Bobby and Jose's hold and stormed away in the opposite direction from the house toward Carlos's unfinished property.

"Do I still need to body-block you, J.L.? You got your head together, man?" Damali asked, hands on hips.

J.L. raked his sweaty hair and grudgingly nodded. He walked in a distracted circle for a moment, and then looked up for the first time at Berkfield. Rage slowly ebbed and awareness set in as Rider kicked the gun farther away while Shabazz held Berkfield down in a shoulder lock. A visible *Oh shit* flickered in J.L.'s eyes. Terror replaced awareness as he tried to summon speech.

"Yeah," Damali said. "Go get your car keys, take a nice, long half-hour ride in the country. Call home on cell before you put your keys in the door, and let Shabazz and Rider have a conversation with a man who is losing his mind, first." She nodded to Bobby. "Go take a walk with Dan at Carlos's and make sure he doesn't do anything rash, and that he's home by the time we have to leave for our flight." She shot a glance at Jose, her nerves too frayed to put things in politically correct terms. "Go find 'Nita's ass and take Krissy over to my house so she can have a good cry and get washed up; give her some of my clean clothes, and let her talk to somebody female—off-site, nowhere near her mom or pop. I'll be in this yard until Berkfield calms down."

When she received grudging nods, Damali sighed, finally hugged Krissy, and whispered in her ear. "It ain't your fault, been there. Just be cool. We'll talk later, but . . . oh, chile, we'll talk later."

Krissy's head was bobbing up and down on Damali's shoulder as new tears began to fall, when Berkfield began yelling again. It took everything within Damali not to go over and slap him. But at the same time, she could dig it. Then again, after seeing what this did to the family, her own past transgressions began to rip a hole in her soul. All she could do was hand Krissy off to the most rational, kindest, most compassionate one on the team, Jose.

"Go 'head, now, hon," Damali said, as she'd heard Marlene tell her so many times before. "I'll talk to your dad.

He's not himself, but he loves you." She sighed as Berkfield started a new wave of hollering.

"Krissy, I forbid you to leave this house, young lady! Where the hell are you going! Jose, your ass is mine if you take my daughter off this lot! Bring her back here!"

Damali ran her hands over her face as her gaze locked with Rider's and Shabazz's. Rider nodded. It was a gesture mixed with a silent *been there on your behalf, kiddo,* and *yeah, yeah, yeah, we'll talk him off the ledge.* Shabazz's eyes were cool as he strained to hold Berkfield and echoed the same silent response. Damali began walking, but something was mentally messing with her so bad that she stopped, turned, and stared out into the dense brush beyond the shed. When Kamal walked out of the thicket and rounded the shed, Damali covered her heart with her hand.

"I heard gunfire report," he said as Shabazz stood slowly and released Berkfield. "Felt you all hyped from five miles away. Ain't been able to lock with Mar. You cool? She cool? Talk to me."

Berkfield was on his feet, but seemed torn and no longer in angry pursuit of Krissy. Rider glanced at the shotgun on the ground and got between it and Shabazz.

"Everything's cool, partner. You cool?" Rider said in an even tone.

"Kamal, the timing . . ." Damali held her head, shut her eyes, and turned her face to the sun. "We cool. Glad you're healed and not coming out of the bushes in Jag. Thanks for the help in Philly, brother. Aw, Lawd. Rider, grab your brother!"

Rider and Berkfield had been flipped and dropped hard in two seconds. Shabazz was liquid motion and charging so fast that for a moment Damali wasn't sure if she could stop him, but she ran headlong toward him, anyway.

"I didn't come to fight, mon!" Kamal shouted, but took a stance, anyway. "The teams are fracturing all over the world! Hear me out!"

Shabazz slowed to a jog but squared off.

Where was Big Mike when they needed him! Damali glanced at Kamal. "Talk fast, man. A lot of weird shit has been happening."

Rider and Berkfield came up moments later, huffing and joining the circle.

"Major dark energy is topside now," Kamal said. "Teams are turning on themselves. The were-human ranks are feeling the charge first. Just like the psychics, anybody with special sensitivities." He glanced around. "You ain't exempt, mon. You need to listen."

"I know about the contagion and I don't have to do shit," Shabazz said in a low rumble, "but stay black and die! We're a Neteru squad, man, so you know we got the word first. All right, so you stepped to the lups in Philly, much obliged. But for putting your tongue down my woman's throat, full team in effect, was way the fuck outta order—so kiss my pure human ass." He looked at Rider, Berkfield, and Damali. "Step aside and get out my way."

"You ever go through a full-moon blast, motherfucker?" Kamal said in a low, quiet growl. "Ever have that kinda adrenaline hit your system with a Level-Seven charge giving it topspin—after being away from your woman for over twenty years behind bullshit? Then you suddenly realize, all the bullshit is gone—she can't have babies, so the only thing keeping you away from her is no longer a problem?" Kamal spit, his glare on Shabazz narrow. "You lucky that's all I did that night!"

Shabazz lunged; Kamal lunged, a shotgun blast report gave Damali, Rider, and Berkfield just enough time to catch fabric and stop a collision.

"Are you insane?" Marlene said, incredulous as she walked down the back steps and stared at Kamal. "Are you out of your damned mind? Tell me you didn't walk into this yard and challenge Shabazz in his own house?"

"No!" Kamal said, his eyes wounded before he tore his line of vision from her.

"You need to let me talk to him, Shabazz," Marlene said quietly.

"I'm not letting you do shit!"

Damali's, Berkfield's, and Rider's heads pivoted and everybody held their breath.

"You're not *letting* me?" Marlene said, cocking her head to the side as her voice became unnaturally quiet.

"Kamal is dropping some serious science, yo, about the other teams that we might need when we get over to Tibet. We don't know what we'll face if our contact squad is compromised," Damali said quickly, trying to avoid another sonic boom. "Let's just all get the info we need, chill out, let bygones—"

"We need her help," Kamal said, not addressing Shabazz's outburst, but seeming to own enough wisdom not to allow Marlene to get cranked up to the next notch of rage, even if it might serve his purpose. He let his breath out hard.

"My men and I went into battle with lupine-demons in Brazil. We didn't do it to code, we shifted for it . . . then we couldn't shake the power of it. My men ain't been right since. We *have to* eat red meat, and you know what we ate before— the temptation is . . . beyond . . . Listen!" he shouted, talking with his hands and searching Damali's eyes with a furtive gaze before finally staring at Marlene. "Drum won't eat store-bought. He's taking down deer, anything in the wild. Ahmed . . . full moon hit and he broke down and sired—all right!" Kamal looked at Shabazz. "No matter what you think, I'm here, not tracking Mar to cause a problem, but because I need her magic, whatever she got in dat black bag of hers to get my team's head right. We can all feel something really big coming, real bad, and we cannot be borderline."

He was still waiting on clothes so he wouldn't freak Damali out with another instant materialization, trying to chill, sitting on the back deck in a towel, when he heard a pair of female footsteps approach. He knew who it was right away and didn't move. Ah, man, and he was trying so hard to just be cool and mind his business. Now what?

The rational part of his brain told him to just get up, go in the house, and lock himself in a room somewhere. He didn't need drama or to be tempted to find himself in another compromising position. Whatever was in him was prone to do whatever, and until he could get that under control, shit like this he didn't need. But the near miss with Damali from the night before was producing a surreal erection as he heard a shy voice call his name. He sighed.

The new and very dangerous part of him smiled.

Carlos leaned forward in the deck chair and folded his hands between his knees, resting on his forearms and simply glanced up. See, he wasn't looking for trouble; trouble had conveniently found him.

"Hey, Juanita," he said in a low murmur. "Want some breakfast?"

She hesitated on the steps and then came across the deck to sit beside him. "Can we talk?"

"Yeah," he said, giving her a sideways glance, amused at how she'd begun to slowly strip the towel away from his body with her eyes. But he didn't move. The internal battle was crazy. Walk into my parlor said the spider to the fly. . . . Umph, umph, umph . . . the woman was fine, he'd give her that.

He watched Juanita play with her long brown hair; nervous energy permeated her entire aura. So did extreme desire, but he let it ride on the wind for a moment. He inhaled the scent of it, let it hit the back of his tongue, and toyed with it in his mouth as he decided what to do with her. Why was she here, what did she want beyond the obvious?

"Last night," she said quietly, her eyes riveted to his. "You did it again."

"Did what?" Carlos tilted his head and stared down as her hand rested lightly on his exposed thigh.

"Called me from the house, like before . . . and I felt . . . I couldn't help coming to you, and then they spiritually closed ranks and I felt the connection snap." Confusion and desire made the words slip from her lips in small breathy whispers. "I saw it in your eyes, disappointment. Like before, but this was so much worse . . . I don't want you to be angry at me, or think that I don't feel the same, but, if it's just for a moment, and not gonna last . . . If Jose ever found out, he'd never take me back after that, and—"

His hand moved to the nape of her neck of its own volition and gathered her silky brown hair into a slowly tightening fist. Her words halted abruptly. Anticipation stopped her breathing and made her bottom lip quiver.

"Always cherish life moment by moment," he whispered, and pulled her into a hard kiss, then released her hair and offered a half smile.

She sat back in the plastic deck chair, hyperventilating with her eyes closed. But the conquest would be so easy that it annoyed him more than anything else. He had his mind set on penetrating liquid silver, although relieving temporary tension did have its merits.

"If you stay here, you know what's gonna happen, right?" He shook his head and stared out across the canyons, estimating time and Damali's whereabouts.

Juanita nodded, her trembling fingers caressing her mouth where his kiss had bruised it before she reached out to touch his. She peered at him beneath half-shut lids.

"Tell me something that would inspire the risk?" he murmured, inhaling deeply as he nuzzled her shoulder, but didn't turn to give her access to fully embrace him. Her shudder and hard swallow was beginning to warm him to the possibilities, but given the time, and the more important issues on his agenda . . .

"Carlos," she whispered, sliding from the chair to pool at his feet. "That time, I thought I would die if you didn't . . . and last night, I . . ." Her hands covered his then slowly traveled up his forearms and shoulders, until they found his hair. "I remember. Can't forget." She kissed his forehead through a breathy whisper and centered her body between his thighs. She rested her forehead on his, her small sips of air gaining in depth and force as she spoke. "So much has happened. I know so much more about how and why we did break up. I thought I was sure, resolved. But when you called me, it brought it all back."

He hadn't moved, hadn't looked up, was just absorbing impressions. He could feel the pulse in her jugular racing, begging to be scored, her heart banging against her breastbone. The delicate skin that protected the crucial vein in her throat literally contracted as he thought about it. He could taste the inside of her sweet mouth go dry. Fascinating. Gooseflesh covered her skin even though it was almost ninety degrees outside. The ache at the tips of her breasts had become united with the pulse of agony between her thighs.

Her skin was now damp all over, her hands tracing his shoulders, timidly, but gaining aggression. Thoughts jumped in spiraling arcs through her synapses, telling her hands to leave his shoulders and find his thighs to make him respond, but not sure what his stoic behavior meant. He heard hope quietly gasp inside her womb, wondering if he was so conflicted that he couldn't move, or so thoroughly devastated by desire like she was that he didn't move because he was afraid of what might happen next. It was all very interesting.

Although disappointed that there was no need to play the permission to enter game with her, since that was a given, there was, however, a slight thrill involved with beating time without ruining his reputation.

Her hands found his thighs as her breathing escalated. He obliged the indulgence by lifting her chin with one finger to stare into her eyes.

"We don't have a lot of time, 'Nita," he murmured. "And when this is all over, we're gonna have to be cool, play it off, no drama. Understand?"

He was pleasantly surprised when she made the first bold move and captured his mouth and began fumbling with his towel, so he figured the least he could do was pull her to

him, let his tongue duel with hers for a bit, and run his
hands down her back. She did have a gorgeous throat, so a
lick just to taste where he might deliver the nick was in order. . . . But he hadn't expected her to cum and start crying
just from that. Cool. But he was definitely gonna have to
step to his line brother for not handling his business correct.
Gave vampires a bad rep, having a woman so strung out that
a little tongue down the jugular would take her over the
edge so fast. What the hell was she gonna do when he
dropped her on her back—flatline? But she did have a nice
ass. . . .

He smiled and ran his hands through her hair as the shudders abated, glancing at the canyon. He didn't know the terrain, but just might hafta serve her proper, for old times'
sake, especially when her mind was screaming conception.

"I'm sorry, I just . . ."

"Shush, don't worry, I'll get mine—and will make sure
you do several more times, like the old days."

She looked up at him, her hair tussled, tears glittering in
her big brown eyes. "All day?"

He nodded as she covered her mouth to stem a sob. "Till
we have to leave for L.A." Something insidious slithered
within him. Damali was always making him turn on his silver, never wanted to get pregnant again anytime soon, and
didn't trust him to be able to care for her and a child. *This*
would *kill* her arrogant Neteru spirit. "You wanna make a
baby with me?" he suddenly murmured, not quite sure why.

"I don't know if my heart can take it," she whispered as
she closed her eyes and more tears fell. "If that's what you
want, *just say it, Carlos.*"

He traced the cord in her neck and studied it with care
and ran his tongue over his incisors. "Don't worry, if you die
in my arms, I'll rectify that. Let's get out of here and get you
pregnant." He sighed. "I'ma need a little more time for all of
that. Cool?"

She greedily took his mouth, and since she was gonna be

a vessel for him, he reasoned, the only gentlemanly thing to do was send a pleasure pulse into her while swallowing her scream. He enjoyed watching her break a nail while gripping the chair arms so tightly, but kept his tongue in her mouth to keep her from saying anything that was gonna blow the groove . . . *Don't say it.* He held her up when she swayed, threatening to pass out. See, this was why Damali needed to stop jerking him around. Normal human females weren't that much fun and this one would be a rag too beat to hell to carry if he dropped a full payload on her. Fuckin' decision, decisions . . .

And why was 'Nita wasting her time thinking about stripping off a T-shirt, when he could do it with a snap. But he liked to watch her work at obtaining what she really wanted. When she yanked at the towel hard to make it finally come away from him, broke from the kiss, and bent her head, he nodded.

Aw'right, *that's* what he was talking about. He covered her breasts with his hands, radiating a mind-bending sensation that began at the stinging brown tips to waft across the entire surface of the heavy lobes and converge on her bud, and instantly knew that was not the thing to do.

This was not D. She was not able to give as good as she got. Juanita threw her head back, sucked in a deep breath, and released a groan filled with words that almost made him stand up and slap her.

"¡Madre de Dios! Por favor, Carlos, take me now, right here, I don't care!"

Carlos winced. Brief clarity assaulted him. Here? What was he doing? Juanita? Shit. He had to separate her sobs from . . . who the hell was hiccup-crying in a Jeep? Damn!

"Pull your thing together, baby. Somebody is coming, you need to be cool," he said as calmly as possible and sat back in the chair smoothing his hair.

"I can't," she said shuddering through another sob. "Let's go inside, I don't care if she comes home. You and I were to-gether first. I'll have your baby, do whatever. Just—"

"Listen to me," he said, holding her by her arms tightly. "You were with Jose first, and if you want this whole house arrangement to stay very cool, check it—that's who's coming up the steps dragging a teenager, looking for you. Feel me?"

He stood up, snapped, and a pair of jeans replaced the towel. He watched her fall on her butt and cross herself, and simply yanked her up, stole the scream from the air, tidied her up, kissed her hard, and erased her mind. Of all days and times. Shit!

"*Ola,*" Carlos said, half laughing. "Man, your timing is deep. We was just talking about you."

"Yo, guys," Jose said very slowly as he looked from Carlos to Juanita and bristled. "Some really fucked-up drama went down at the house." He looked at Juanita hard, his gaze surveying her openly for any signs of wrongdoing. "Kris needs a shoulder, a place to clean up and get her head together. D asked if you would walk point on that, 'Nita, but I'm just gonna ask you once—*you* cool?" Jose waited, his eyes never leaving hers.

Juanita nodded and wrapped her arms around herself. "Yeah. Why?"

Jose stared at Carlos, who just shrugged.

Carlos ignored him and turned his focus to Krissy. "You all right, baby?"

She sniffed, nodded, and barreled into Carlos's arms. Carlos just stared down at the top of her blond hair, placed a kiss on it, and shook his head and tried not to smile. He half felt sorry for her as he absorbed recent events from her mind. Still a virgin. Pity.

"Uh, 'Nita, baby," Carlos said in a low, sexy tone. "Why don't you get this child away from me in my present condition and find her some clean clothes in Damali's room. Talk to her. Tell her how a woman has to be clear in her decisions, so all parties at least understand the basic rules of engagement and territorial lines, or she can leave a lot of fucked-up men in her wake. Not good for house politics, but Dan will survive. Not sure that J.L. will, if he pulls another foolish stunt like that with her daddy packing heat, though." Carlos yawned, pet Krissy on the head, and released her.

"You think he'll be okay?" Krissy sniffed. "And Dad . . ."

Juanita was so rigid she might as well have been a mannequin. Carlos chuckled. The teenager didn't even see it. But Jose was about to get a bone snatched out of his ass if he didn't chill. What was the beef? This was old territory they'd both covered. Shit happens.

"What did you say?" Jose whispered.

Carlos shrugged. "Man, I said a lot of shit. What part of what I said you takin' issue with?"

"In your present condition . . . with my woman standing there holding her breath like she's about to have a fucking heart attack," Jose said through his teeth.

Carlos sighed as Krissy and Juanita slowly drew together and hugged. The image gave him brief pause and he laughed. Nah . . . that would be over the top, excessive, first thing in the morning. "Aw, man, go 'head wit dat shit. I just need some breakfast."

CHAPTER FOURTEEN

Marlene stood with Kamal in the small clearing two hundred yards from the family house, blocked by dense brush. Her third eye continually swept the terrain for any signs of Shabazz.

"We have maybe ten minutes, tops, to have this conversation, Kamal." She glanced around like a fugitive. "I don't want anybody to get hurt. Never did."

"I know," he said quietly. "Neither do I, but it's inevitable."

Marlene closed her eyes and wrapped her arms around herself. "Half of me is ready to tell you that you shouldn't have come. But how can I stand here, by rights, and deny you and your team my assistance after all you did for ours in Bahia and Philly?"

"While I do need your help, Marlene, both you and I know that's not the only reason I'm here."

She didn't answer as he stepped closer and placed his warm hands on her shoulders.

"I've missed you, girl. . . . What has it been in the flesh? Twenty, thirty years? I've lost count of the moons. But this last one, I thought I'd lose my mind."

"Kamal, please," she whispered as his body molded against hers. It was such an immediately magnetic sensation that her hands gently landed on his shoulders. "You know I can't do this. Astral plane is one thing, but this is . . . No."

"What I know," he murmured thickly against her temple, "is that the only reason we separated was because I wasn't supposed to give you my seed. Now that your season for that is almost passed . . ." He drew inhaled deeply. "I see no reason."

"I have a team of newbies," she said quickly. "There's a dark force worse than we've ever dealt with infecting the planet, and I have to ready them—just like you have to go back to Bahia and solidify your men."

"I noticed that you didn't say, because you loved your man so much we couldn't be together. You spoke of duty, respect for your role as Guardian, commitment, but you never even said his name."

Rendered mute by the charge, she stood there looking at the strong African features of his dark, ebony face. His sculpted, muscular body held her for ransom as his tactical energy sent a sensual current over the surface of her skin. No shirt on, jeans slung low on his narrow hips, his smile a brilliant white flash against a flawless complexion. She had to get her mind right and put an end to this now.

"That's not fair," she finally whispered, as his third eye engaged hers in a memory dance. "You know I love Shabazz."

"I'm not trying to be fair," he whispered in reply. "This time I'm trying to win back what was once mine."

He lowered his mouth to hers, testing for acceptance. Her parted lips, the slow slide of hands to rest on his hips, and deep sigh emboldened him. His second sight captured hers and stroked it with an erotic memory that dampened her valley. With his were-human capacity, he instantly sensed it, spiking his arousal and increasing the kinetic connection between his skin and hers. He deepened the kiss and found the dip in her spine with a burning palm.

"You have to stop," she gasped, pulling out of the kiss. "I'm only human."

"I'm not," he replied, filling his hands with her fleshy bottom and pulling her against him, moving to the throb that haunted them. "A man has to use every advantage he's got."

"He'll feel the charge before I even get back to the house.

Don't. He deserves better than that from both of us," she said on another heavy breath against his shoulder, while fighting to keep her eyes open.

"You telling me or yourself?" Kamal murmured, kissing her neck.

"He deserves—"

"To hell with what he deserves, Marlene," Kamal said through his teeth just behind her ear. "I'm marking my territory like I should have years ago."

Before she could answer, his mouth covered hers. His hands emitted a charge that fused with her aura, made her gasp and hold him tighter. Witnessing her intense arousal put tears of want in his eyes as they began to flicker golden-copper.

"Lawd, woman, I've missed you so much," he whispered hotly against her temple, then nipped her ear, her neck, his nails beginning to shred the light Egyptian cotton dress that sheathed her. "If not forever, then at least once more before we both die or are too old to enjoy it."

Her hands trembled as they slid over the dense muscles that surrounded his shoulder blades. She couldn't catch her breath as the memory of his spine imprinted into her palms. When her fingers reached the low, tight valley of his lower back, she shuddered with recall and bit her lip to keep from crying out.

"Baby, stop," she said in a tight whisper. "I'm going to have to douse the charge as it is, before I go home. I can't—"

Kamal's mouth halted her words and his tongue fought with them in her mouth. The low purr inside his chest began to block her reason, just as his hands circling her behind sent acute pleasure all through her.

"Don't douse the charge," he groaned, rhythmically pulling her hips against his pelvis. "Feed it."

Friction from cotton against denim added to the harmony of the chirr of the crickets. Heavy inhales and exhales created a barrier to reason. Searing touches united auras as mouths sought sanctuary in fevered kisses then battled for surrender. Quiet power added a blind in the bush.

"Oh, shit, I can't take it, woman," Kamal finally whispered harshly against her neck. "I can't wait for the next moon, or a group decision. I can't wait until you talk to him, and then allow time for him to grieve. I can't. Don't ask that of me."

She understood completely. Kamal's body was soaked in a blue-charged sheen of sweat. Every droplet of perspiration held a tactical sensor's current. His locks had lifted a quarter-inch off his shoulders, and his eyes glowed solid copper. He'd already nicked her tongue with his upper and lower canines that were threatening to rip through his gums. His release was mandatory, just as hers was imminent. Something way beyond conflict tore at her, dividing her between both men.

Love, loyalty, honor, respect, friendship, peace, laughter, trust—all of that hung in a fragile balance between the man panting in her arms and the one she'd left fuming on the back porch. A compromise was the only way. Men saw things in absolutes. Women saw things in shades of gray. One man needed her in far more than just an immediate sense. Soon the other man would, too. She couldn't betray either, for in doing so she would also be betraying herself . . . betraying the truth that she needed and loved them both for different reasons.

Kamal's suffering had become her own as he continued to bathe her neck in ardent attention. His embrace had become a vise as his pelvis stroked against hers, igniting penetration memory until they could both feel it.

The impact of mental entry arched her back and elicited a unified moan. Instantly his hands scrabbled at the fabric of her dress, raising it over her buttocks, then yanked at her underwear, needing sensation of flesh against them.

Heat filled his hands and almost made him sob. His words came out between breaths laced with a low growl. "Come to me under the moon, baby. Like old times. In the raw, in nature, in the bush. Take me there, girl, before I go crazy."

She knew it was wrong, but it was the only way to make this work for the three of them. A slight violet current ran through her hands as she splayed them on his back and totally opened her third eye to him. She sent the image full force as her hands captured the rise of his clenching buttocks. She increased the intensity as she felt his thick thighs flex, his knees bend, and his arms brace her to hit the ground.

Falling almost in slow motion, she pulled back her hands and he released so hard that his canines ripped through. Panic swept her. If Big Mike was in the house, he would have definitely heard it—and there'd be no keeping it from Shabazz. The low rumble of staggering male were-human completion created a Doppler effect in the bush.

Pleasure waves washed over her before she could think of what to do. It coated her skin, practically entered her pores, as he lay blanketing her heaving, clutching her waist, and accidentally sent her over the edge hard.

Her breathing ragged, she petted his back, knowing he'd be furious once he stopped climaxing. She didn't even flinch or get upset when he raised himself to his hands and knees above her, canines fully distended and eyes blazing copper.

"I wanted you in the flesh, and you know that, woman!" He glowered down at her and then his damp jeans with disgust.

"I'm married," she said in a soft, calm tone without apology.

"You had no right to mind-fuck me, Marlene," he said, hurt glittering in his eyes. His voice dropped to a subdued level. "Foreplay, yes, but . . ."

He quickly sat back on his haunches and then summarily stood, enraged. She watched him begin to pace as she got up slowly, brushed off her dress, and picked up her satchel from the ground. Although they both knew this was best, she also knew a thing or two about wounded male pride.

Marlene sighed and gave him temporary space to calm down. She understood where he was; even though the force of his release had been damned spectacular, that wasn't the point. He'd wanted to control the dance, wreck her will, and be physically inside her to layer his imprint over Shabazz's to tactically eclipse it. He wanted any sensory impression from any other competing male erased. Totally primal, but logical, if she looked at it from his perspective. She wasn't angry that his goal had been to make her sweat, weep, scream his name until she became hoarse. Then, in his male mind, her decision would have been clear.

"You know that wouldn't have been possible, or right," she murmured gently as he stalked back and forth, raking his fingers through his dreadlocks.

"And I suppose now I'm to be grateful that you did what you did?"

She swallowed a smile and took out a small cheesecloth pouch filled with herbs and magnetic stones, and began removing his energy charge from her skin. "I think you enjoyed yourself just a teeny bit, though. Hmmm?" She began walking toward him, amused.

"That's not the point, woman!" he shouted, snapping his arm out and pointing at her hard. "You know me better than that, Marlene. I have more control than that, and you—"

Her kiss stopped his argument as her hands slid down his chest. "Of *course* I do," she said quietly. "I've been gone a half hour when I was supposed to be gone ten minutes." Her eyes held his with a compassionate plea. "If I even begin to think back . . ." Her voice trailed off, her third eye widened, so he could see how she truly felt. "As hot as I am for you right now, no good will come of things. I have to go."

She sighed and looked away from him, sending her gaze toward the house. "If I had let you love me hard and long and in the flesh till I hollered, we'd both get shot." She pulled away and rolled the bag over his abdomen as he relaxed and

closed his eyes. She knew she'd have to work fast, feeling
his body reigniting from her touch as the truth petted his ego.

"You really wanted to that much?" He winced as his
fangs slowly retracted and her palm glided over his navel.

"What do you think?" she whispered, increasing her
pace as her hands began to tremble against his thighs.
"Don't start," she ordered. "Just let me disconnect the
charge so we can let this isolated incident simmer down between us. All right?"

"You know this isn't isolated," he said in a huff, folding
his arms over his chest as she worked on his calves. "You've
been meeting me on the astral plane for years, girl."

"*That's* different," she said, standing. "What we do in our
dreams is one thing. What goes down like this is another."

"That's why I wanted you physically, this time," he admitted quietly, his eyes searching hers. "I can't even tolerate
your hands doing a dousing."

"It's just the contagion that's making it so bad." She kept
herself from glancing at the new erection he owned. She
didn't have to. She'd felt the hard pulse right through his
clenched stomach.

Marlene let her breath out in a slow stream to steady her
conviction. Until now, the astral-plane visits had mollified
Kamal and quenched her without directly breaking
Shabazz's heart. Things had to stay that way.

"I have a list of herbs for your team, along with a Haitian
ritual you all need to do to help stabilize them in human
form. We don't have an antidote for the contagion yet, but at
least they'll be able to control their shape-shifts. It's a strong
dose, given the dark—"

"Tell me you don't feel it," he murmured, cutting her off.
His eyes appraised her for another chance. "Don't give him
the benefit of all my work out here in the bush."

She opened her mouth and closed it. Kamal's animal
magnetism radiated off him, adding a new layer of perspiration and want to her skin. So did his arrogance. But the truth

was the truth. She wanted to make love to Kamal so badly at the moment she could barely breathe, but most likely Shabazz would get his bones jumped tonight. They both knew it. What could she say? That was also her and Shabazz's ritual whenever they were about to go into battle . . . one last go-hard good time, just in case one of them didn't come back.

How could she astral plane visit Kamal during all of that? Just knowing Kamal was on North American soil had Shabazz's locks standing up, with good cause. No. She also knew Shabazz would work hard to reestablish himself as the king of her hill, given this private conversation, such as it was supposed to be. An astral-plane visit was out.

She offered Kamal a scowl. "You guys follow the cleansing ritual I'm going to prescribe, and repeat it three times a day from the new moon till the next full one."

"Don't ignore me, Mar," he whispered.

"I'm not," she said, now furiously scribbling on a piece of paper she'd extracted from her black satchel. She had to keep her hands occupied and off of him. "I'm ignoring myself," she added without looking up.

"Then visit me astrally tonight," he said in a demanding tone necessary to salvage his pride.

When she didn't immediately respond or commit, his request became quieter and more urgent. "Then spell cast," he said, breathing in sharply through his nose. "Soul bind wit me," he whispered. He looked down at his hands, then glanced away into the distance.

She could feel shame permeating his skin and working on her heart. That he was near begging her to fill his hands with her sensory resonance almost sent her into his arms, but she held her ground. It would pass.

He closed his eyes and shook his head no. "At least leave your charge in my hands," he said on a ragged whisper. "*Anything* that reminds me of your touch."

Her palm flattened against her stomach as a hard jolt of

wanting him entered her navel and contracted her womb. "All right," she whispered, allowing him to come forward and gently caress her. "But if I leave this within your hands, you must *never* put this in Shabazz's face."

"Admit to my competitor that I was so unable to pull what was once mine from him that . . . that I had to beg his woman to leave her energy in my palms so I could satisfy *myself* while she was away?" Kamal's eyes held hers for a moment and then slid closed. "Not likely that I'd admit such humiliation to another living soul, especially to another male."

"Baby . . ."

"Shush," he said, tilting his head with his eyes closed. "It's bad enough already. Your voice just makes it worse."

Another wave of hot want poured over her as his hands lightly crackled and started their sensory dance above her skin's surface. She tried to remain completely still as the imprinting began heating her shoulders and breasts while his fingers lightly brushed over her body, trailing down it, encircling her waist, her hips, and her bottom. She shook her head no as they reached her thighs and tried to part them. Too much. Too erotic, even for her to withstand. He began to lift her dress, the goal in his eyes clear as he opened them, asking without a word to plummet into her flooded valley. *No,* she murmured mentally. That would cause an arc that would put her on her back and start the whole mess all over again.

"Please," he whispered, with his eyes closed.

"I'll send it to you mentally. That's as far as I can go."

He nodded and stopped breathing when she honored his request, making tight fists as his hands flared blue-white hot for a moment. He stepped back, sweating profusely, and shuddered. She had to break the connection and began writing again with shaky hands. She looked up and held the pencil just above the pad, frozen, when he stretched out his arms away from his body as though his hands contained something that would burn him. This was bad. He'd told her a lot of things over the years to try to get her to break down, but

she'd never seen him like this. She tried to focus on her remedy, redoubling the herbal dose in the prescription.

"Come to me tonight," he said flatly.

"I can't. We leave for China in the morning. You know that."

"Then when you get back."

"Maybe, but not tonight. And not until we both get our
heads together to remedy this." She handed him the paper,
but he just looked at it, seeming unable to accept anything
within his palms but her.

"You ain't got nothing for this," he murmured, stepping
closer to her and ignoring the paper, " 'cept one ting."

She thrust the paper into his hand, and he finally accepted
it, but not before crushing a kiss into her palm.

"Follow my written instructions to the letter." She
brushed his cheek with a light kiss, cupping it for a moment.
"I have to go," she said, drawing away after kissing him
quickly again and beginning to walk, refusing to look back.

"Then I guess I'll have to settle for anyting," he said and
loped off.

She had circled her body so many times with charge-
diffuser that she'd made herself near dizzy. Her lips moved
in a steady fervent prayer. *Lawd, don't let Shabazz pick up
nothing.* She could see Shabazz pacing on the porch, Rider
at his flank holding the line, with Berkfield almost body-
blocking Shabazz from going down the steps. Damali remained stoic, knowing, no judgment in her eyes and simply
holding her breath.

Marlene briefly met Damali's gaze. *May you never be in
this position.*

I'm sorry that you were. I love them both, too.

It was the only way.

I know. I respect that.

Marlene pulled out of their connection, glad that she and
Damali were more than mother-seer and daughter-charge,
but soul-to-the-bone friends. She also knew Rider, the

group's lead nose, wouldn't give her away. Their eyes met as she came into the yard. An understanding passed between them. They'd both shared and kept each other's secrets for decades. Berkfield cast an intrigued but worried look between her and Shabazz. Damali went back into the house. She could hear the young Neteru walk through it, let the front screen door close behind her, and leave.

"Everything cool?" Shabazz asked, his tone strained and suspicious.

"Yeah," Marlene said casually, walking up the porch steps. "I gave him what he needed. Now he's going home to get himself together. Everything's cool."

Rider, Berkfield, and Shabazz looked behind her as she entered the house and the screen door slammed shut.

Carlos had barely spoken when she'd returned home. He seemed subdued and deep in thought to the point of morose. She couldn't tell if it was fear of what he might do with the approaching afternoon that would soon give way to night, or if he was still beating his own ass for the temporary backslide.

He'd listened patiently as she'd filled him in, but his lack of commentary on the subject stabbed her. As they all moved out to go to the airport, Jose was so closed that she couldn't even begin to figure out what had set him off. With all the mayhem going on, she didn't have time to excavate that particular ruin. Her senses were practically fried.

Her mother-seer *was down*. She wasn't discussing a mumblin' thing. She just sat quietly, staring out the Jeep window. Although Damali had no idea what conversations had gone on in the woods one-on-one between Marlene and Kamal, she didn't need to. The tension in Marlene said it all. But she'd thought they were gonna have to put a spoon on Shabazz's tongue to keep him from quiet rage convulsions.

It was as though Marlene had hung a mental Do Not Disturb sign, and Damali could understand why. Marjorie was whispering platitudes to her husband, trying to work on her son, offering an olive branch to Dan, letting J.L. know he was loved, all the while attempting, without success, to shield her daughter from the whole of it. Meanwhile, Rider was working on Big Mike, trying to keep him from blaming himself for not being there, and Damali was trying to keep Inez from accidentally tripping over a land mine. The situation was outrageous.

It was a delicate dance, one she'd never wanted to have to do. But in the hours between getting everybody deescalated, gathering the remainder of what they'd take, and heading to an airport, she'd thought she might lose her mind.

Carlos sat aloof, as though watching some giant life experiment happening on a microscope slide. That really annoyed her, but then again, she checked herself, remembering he was from a big family and maybe none of this was that foreign. Or maybe he was still beating himself up over the relapse. The contagion was also a factor. She just didn't know.

But rather than batter him with parables and platitudes, she simply gripped his hand and let her faith in him run through that touch as they sat on the flight to L.A., each consumed in separate thoughts. One thing was certain, the information that Kamal had dropped was chilling. His team was almost over the edge, which made her wonder what condition any of the Guardian teams worldwide would be in.

The temporary change of scenery would be good for them all. Twenty-four hours, and they'd be headed to China to summarily deal with the problem.

The Ritz-Carlton in Marina del Rey would seem like heaven, after being wedged in the small house for months. It was near the water, only a fifteen-minute walk to one of their favorite locales, Venice Beach. The boats would be pretty. Shopping and food and nightlife would be accessible. Maybe they could do what they always did as a team—live life to the max for the moment, and then hunker down to go to war.

Marlene and Shabazz, along with the Berkfields, would be able to easily hunt for a property in Beverly Hills or over in Santa Monica—since they had the balance of the afternoon before them. Perhaps Marlene was right about one thing; act as though there will be a tomorrow, and refuse to allow a defeatist attitude to prevail.

Cool heads and calm nerves were necessary, and if Shabazz could follow his own advice this time, routine was in order. Routine kept order. She prayed that her big brother wouldn't snap under his suspicions and could just accept whatever Marlene had told him. . . . Marlene had left Kamal in the woods, after all. For now, given what they had to deal with, that was enough—she hoped.

The Berkfields also needed something to calm their ruffled feathers. Perhaps the delayed flight was divine intervention. This way Marj and Richard could do something normal, constructive, to keep their minds focused on the possibility of tomorrow, like finding a good school to enroll Kris in. Maybe Bobby could consider taking some college courses. She and Carlos could perhaps meander a bit and find places close by that they wouldn't mind living in.

Twenty-four hours was a long time to dwell on disaster. Her orders had been clear. There was nothing in L.A. Her target was in the Himalayas, and for some odd reason, the Neteru Councils weren't allowing her or Carlos just to leave everybody and quickly transport there. Her stones didn't work; neither did his claw of Heru. Everything seemed harder to achieve. The conventional route was the only way.

They all had to find something constructive to do other than sit quietly and sulk and lose their minds. Trying to think on the bright side, she even considered going with Carlos to window-shop for the vehicle of his dreams. Maybe he could finally get his fantasy car and that would lift his spirits. She didn't know what to do, and every prayer for answers that she'd sent up hadn't come back down yet.

Getting back into the real world, being on familiar ground in L.A., would renew each sagging soul, she hoped.

Going to Tibet might mean more than just a battle. Maybe after the Chairman's head rolled, they could stay there for a while to get some spiritual reinforcement through nature, stillness; let the purity of the monks' gentle presence and wisdom restore what had been stripped in battles and compromised by the contagion. Something had to give, Lord. Then they could come home, face whatever, come what may.

She clung to that hope, adding faith and hard love to it as they sat on the short flight, holding it all tightly in her heart the way she firmly clasped Carlos's hand. When he squeezed hers back she fought back tears. *This* was stress.

"Baby, it'll be all right," she whispered, speaking as much to him as reinforcing that promise to herself.

"You wanna go to the beach this afternoon, or go house hunting?" Damali said, trying to shift the somber mood as she and Carlos entered their hotel room.

"We can do both," Carlos said with a slow smile. "I'm just glad to be back in L.A." He blew his breath out hard and flung his duffel bag in the corner. Then, with his back toward her, he quickly began to unpack only the toiletries he'd need overnight.

She refused to stay mired in the team craziness. Folks had gone to the mutual corners for a few hours. It would work out however it had to. Everybody seemed like they'd rather stay busy than focus on whatever issues were drilling a hole in their brains. Best move. That's why she was out.

Rider and Jose had set off to go drool over Harleys. Krissy and Juanita were going to go somewhere and keep talking. Whatever. Big Mike and Inez had disappeared. Dan and Bobby were on a mission to buy laptops and gadgetry, seeming to take comfort in attempting to repair their rift. Shabazz had called ahead to some people who knew some people to have ammo discreetly delivered to the hotel; Marlene and the Berkfields had gone to scope out a new place for the team. J.L. was hanging close with Shabazz, supposedly working on ammo with him, and on how they could wire whatever real estate they found.

But everybody knew the deal. Both J.L. and Shabazz needed to talk to somebody to get their heads right. The appointments for travel shots had been made; a doctor would come to the hotel and administer what was necessary and backdate it. The right paperwork was in process, expertly arranged by Marlene. That meant that for the balance of the day, for once, the team's Neterus were free.

Damali made short work of unpacking only what was necessary. The hotel was a good choice, as it was close to the airport, even though it was more businesslike than the A-list, pampering type of service one could find at The Four Seasons Beverly Hills. At this point, who cared? They'd already shaved off twenty-four hours of living; the infection was resident in them all.

The only thing Damali was concerned with was the fact that she'd wanted the team to be on the periphery of things, not in the heart of it. Right now she could deal with the Old World elegant European design, Italian marble bathroom, and private balcony closed off behind sheers that swathed French doors. She would appreciate all of it, just like she appreciated life with new eyes. Having a ticking time bomb within her and each member of her team had a way of putting a different perspective on things.

Damali almost sighed as she flopped down on the comfortable goose-down featherbed, glimpsing Carlos from the corner of her eye. The other problem was, he didn't glimpse back at her. He hadn't even made a passing reference to anything else they could do that day. Didn't the brother realize they were about to go to war?

She refused to allow herself to slide into a foul mood. She had to remember he was going through withdrawal after a relapse, so his normal responses might not necessarily be all that normal.

He watched with relish as she raced up and down the beach. Damali was like an excited puppy that had been cooped up ~~~e house too long. She made him smile as she'd come running to him, dance around a bit, tease him, and then run off to inspect something new she hadn't seen today in the outdoor human carnival.

If she could just stay that way, laughing and full of exuberant life, his old prayers would be answered. He watched the waves chase her and the sand ooze between her bare toes as she scooted away before the ocean could wet her rolled-up jeans.

"You hungry yet?" she said, laughing, tugging on his arm to let him know that, regardless of his answer, she was.

Carlos smiled. "Not really, but we can go find something, if you are."

He watched her smile fade and become quickly replaced by a worried one.

"Okay, later. Me neither. You wanna go drive up to the fancy-car dealer?"

Her eyes held such expectation and hope that he didn't want to disappoint her. But he didn't have it in him. The fly car was no longer important. A Jeep, something reinforced that could take a vamp crash-landing, would be more practical. "Why don't we go scope out some apartments or some properties?" he said to deflect the trip to the showroom floor.

"Yeah! I'll get a paper; we can cruise by some spots. What do you like?" she asked. "What's your style, brother?"

He chuckled, but was worried. None of her behavior seemed normal. She was running around like no contagion existed, like the portals had never opened, and as though there wasn't a problem in the world. Serious denial.

"Beachfront is cool," he finally said, watching every person on the beach touch someone else in some way or another. Just taking change from a hot dog vendor was potentially deadly. Then his attention went to all the children. Damali didn't see that? "But I'm more partial to looking down on the water," he added.

She nodded and her brilliant smile became wider. "Aw'right. I hear you. Something with a cliff vibe," she said, sounding like an around-the-way realtor.

He forced himself to smile, and then laugh a little. "Yeah,

baby. Some habits are hard to break." Then his mild chuckle died away in increments. "But maybe I can compromise and take a look at the beachfronts." He reminded himself that it was time to change the old people, places, and things, and he'd do that if they ever got back from Tibet.

The cost of every place they stopped and gawked at was sky high, but she was on a mission. She hated the way his eyes remained so sad, a flicker of remorse always casting a shadow within them. Carlos had always possessed such joie de vivre, and something had stolen that from him. Even when he'd turned, he always had a passion for everything he did. Now something she couldn't identify seemed to be quietly killing him inside.

Her hand caressed his cheek as he peered at the third property without enthusiasm. "We don't have to make a decision today, baby," she said in a patient tone. "We can figure it out when we get back from Tibet."

"Yeah, maybe then I'll have more of an image of what I want in my mind." He sighed and watched the waves. "I just feel wrung out, and need to lie down. Just chill for a little while. Cool?"

She nodded and threaded her arm through his and led him back toward their Hummer. "You wanna go back to the room?"

"Yeah," he said, mopping his brow.

New worry slithered within her. Daylight was clearly kicking his ass. It was balmy and nice outside, no intense L.A. heat yet, but he was sweating like he'd run a marathon under the sun.

He looked at her for a moment and held her hand as they walked back to the car, sensing. This mindless afternoon was crazy. They were wasting time. He opened his mental radar quietly as she bee-bopped along as though without a care in the world; he almost stopped walking as he picked it up clearly. Her spirit was dying. It was as though all her frenetic activity was sending out a last gasp to cling to the goodness in life. He couldn't make out what part of this thing that arrested her soul was from the contagion, or perhaps coming from him. Maybe both. What he was sure about was the fact that, if they were linked at the soul level ... and his had been compromised to the max ... hers was fighting despair, defeat, anything that his might foist upon hers to allow the dark side to take it over and win.

They drove back to the hotel without talking. Damali peered at Carlos from the corner of her eye. He was so deep in thought that she didn't want to intrude, and they'd just been through enough drama that she wouldn't insult him with an outright trespass.

Damali squinted at the sun. Maybe he was bugging because it was near that transition time. She'd have his back, though. Wouldn't let him relapse. She let the music on the radio fill in the blanks. Maybe once they did this portal shutdown, things would be better. She kept that goal before her as they valet parked and entered the Ritz-Carlton lobby.

As soon as Carlos was indoors, she noted, he seemed to normalize. His face began to lose the flush it once had, his skin cooled, and his expression became less pained. He even seemed to be breathing easier. But she was very careful to offer no comment as they rode the elevator to their room, went inside, and closed the door.

By rote, she went to the balcony and closed the sheers to discreetly block out some of the sun. "There must be a thousand or more sailboats and yachts out there," she said brightly, forcing her tone to sound upbeat. "Once everybody gets back, rests, showered, and whatnot, maybe we can all eat dinner together somewhere?"

"Yeah. That could work," he said quietly, stretching out on the bed. "I just need to catch up on some sleep, but you need to eat. Why don't you go on down to the restaurant or something, and I'll be all right in a coupla hours after a nap."

"I'm cool," she said, looking at him as he sprawled on the bed. "I can order up some room service."

Carlos slowly shook his head and closed his eyes. "D, for real, right now the smell of food is gonna turn my stomach."

He could feel her hesitate and then tentatively cross the room. He felt her slip onto the bed beside him. The feeling of having to puke up his guts had begun the moment he'd had her best interest at heart. When she cuddled up next to him, curling her body to spoon his and lie with him, the room started spinning. She had to get away from him, or he was gonna hurl.

The minute his brain and conscience began the battle, his guts felt like they were being torn into two separate sides of his abdomen. He'd started to feel like that during the late afternoon as they'd walked together on the beach, her laughter and hopes and dreams pummeling his memory, eviscerating anything foul from his mind, slaughtering evil within. By the time they'd started looking at real estate and talking about the future, he could barely breathe.

Carlos squeezed his eyes shut tighter. It felt like a carving knife was gorging out his gray matter at the temple.

Damali's gentle palm slid down his shoulders, and sought refuge under his elbow to rest calmly on his stomach. "We'll beat this thing together," she murmured.

He gripped her hand and nodded without speaking for a moment. "D, the best thing for you to do right now is go eat, leave me be for a little while, and get the last rays of the sun. All right? Will you do that for me?"

She kissed the nape of his neck, hugged him hard, and then slipped away. He didn't open his eyes until he heard the door firmly click behind her.

His face felt like it was burning up, as did the rest of his body. A liter bottle of expensive spring water, compliments of the hotel, beckoned him from the bathroom. His throat was so raw that he could barely swallow, and as he licked his lips, he could feel where they'd become blistered and chapped.

The sensation drew his hand to his mouth, and he quickly got to his feet and went to the mirror above the dresser, stopping in horror to stare. He needed water, but couldn't make it to the bathroom to get it. He was too thirsty. . . . He needed blood—not water.

Dark circles had begun to form under his eyes and his lips were cracked, a whitish film of dead skin beginning to peel on them. *She hadn't seen that?* As he stared at himself in frozen horror, he watched his red T-shirt begin to writhe and move, and he snatched it up over his head to expose his torso.

Long, straggling welts had formed across his stomach, raising his skin as though something unspeakable was trying to claw its way out of him. He watched, paralyzed, as the marks receded and disappeared. He couldn't move, had no idea what had awakened the beast within him, or how to get it out of him. Just as suddenly as the welts had appeared, staggering lust swept through him and stole his breath.

Stumbling backward, he fell against the bed. Every piece of fabric touching his body felt like it was on fire, scorching his skin. He ripped at his clothes blindly, tearing at the multiple sources of pain until he sat naked, panting, his eyes sealed shut. Images of being with Damali cascaded through his mind.

"No," he whispered through his teeth. "While you're in me, you don't get to sleep with her."

Intense pain gripped his scrotum, but when he tried to call out, his voice was silenced. A brutal force slammed him down on the bed and then dragged him up toward the headboard, smashing his skull against it. He could feel his limbs bound by a force too strong to break, and as he lifted his head and struggled against it, he watched his stomach writhe as though something alive were within it.

A dark dribble of fluid oozed from the tip of his erect member. It seeped down his shaft, creating a puddle in his pubic hair, and then began to send tiny, pulsing tendrils to cover his exposed groin in a dark, siphoning sheath. Agony collided with pleasure until tears stung his eyes. His jaw was

sealed shut; the scream became lodged in his throat. Excruciating pleasure made his eyes close to half-mast. Helpless,
he could only watch the sheath pulse and suck against him as
it flicked at the bulbous vein that was now standing beneath
the head it lapped at, and sent the wet siphoning sound to
pierce his ears to intensify the wanton desire.

The heat of near orgasm clutched his abdomen and made
his hips pump furiously at the air, and then the black liquid dissipated, the force holding him down retreated in a loud snap.

Carlos sat up fast and held his shaft where it still burned
and throbbed, his hand replacing the dark violation. The
head was so tender and sensitive that, if he could have, he
would have bent to suck it himself. Unable to resist the natural urge to release the built-up agony, his hand moved
against the hot, slicked surface in spasmodic jerks, a gasp
blocking a moan, the sound of wetness quickening his movements, until he came so hard that no sound escaped his lips.

Panting, he looked down at himself. Humiliation coated
him and laughed at him from within. The only small measure of satisfaction he was able to hold around his dignity
was that at least what he'd ejaculated appeared normal. But
when he looked up he froze, almost more horrified by what
he saw now than by what had just possessed him.

Damali stood quietly on the inside of the hotel room
door, stunned. Her eyes said it all. Her hand was over her
heart and she didn't move.

He wanted to die. Couldn't look this woman in the face.
Carlos was on his feet in an instant, and he rushed into the
bathroom and locked the door without even glimpsing at
her. He turned on the shower and jumped in.

Now was as good a time as any for the floor to swallow
him up whole and make him disappear.

CHAPTER FIFTEEN

Damali crossed the hotel room slowly, sipping air in very tiny breaths. What would she say to him, if anything, when this man came out of the bathroom? She picked up his clothes as calmly as she could. He didn't want her? He preferred *that* to being with her? Okay, she would try to keep an open mind. They'd done a lot of stuff together, but it cut her to the core to know that he would now rather be alone than with her. She took in a deep breath and let it out as calmly as possible.

Shaken, she found a plastic hotel laundry bag in the closet and quietly shoved everything but Carlos's shoes into it with trembling hands. She didn't understand this withdrawal thing, especially as he was having vamp fluxes, and there was *nobody* to ask about this. She reminded herself that she was no prude; they'd explored a lot of things together. It was his body; he didn't have to share his sexuality with her. It wasn't a betrayal if he wanted to get his shit off all alone. That was cool. She shouldn't have been shocked. No reason to be upset. She'd walked back into the room unannounced, too early. He'd asked for time to himself. *Right, right, be cool, girl.* This wasn't a betrayal or anything to wig about. This was . . . this was . . . Aw, hell, she didn't know what this was. But it wasn't Carlos.

Damali moved like someone had punched her, in stiff, dazed motions to get her ID and some money, a credit card, oh . . . the room key she'd forgotten. . . . She was supposed to be getting something to eat. Not likely now. How was the door open, though? It had locked behind her.

She crossed the room, picking her way along what felt like a vast expanse, pulled the Do Not Disturb sign off the inside knob, and stared at it. Then she quietly slipped out of the room, hung the privacy marker on the door, and walked down the hall. The elevator was taking too long. Her panties were wet. The image of him on the brink swelled within her mind. Her physical reaction was incongruent with the emotions that seized her heart. The stair exit called out to her. She needed fresh air.

She found herself running, not really looking at where she was going—just bolting.

Images slammed against her brain in stop-start patches of lit bursts framed in darkness. Carlos was on her back deck, half nude, wrapped only in a towel. Blackness. He lifted his head and smiled. Blackness. Sweat trickled down the center of Damali's back as she stopped in the stairwell, retched, but nothing came up.

She panted with her eyes closed, trying to battle the next incoming image. "No!" she said between her teeth as she fought to close her third eye.

But she could feel a dark orb of pressure at the base of her skull defying her internal command. She opened her eyes to resume her escape from the building. Blackness.

Juanita was in a chair next to Carlos. Blackness. His hands were in Juanita's hair.

Damali squeezed her eyes shut as the force of the image made her hold on to the metal stair rail. The kiss was electric. She could feel it in her mouth, along with Carlos's intent to sire. Juanita's arousal became her own. Blackness. Juanita was on her knees between her man's legs.

"Stop!" Damali shouted, creating an echo in the abandoned stairwell. She clutched her hair with both hands, puffing and blowing out breaths like a woman giving birth, desperately trying to shake the connection. Blackness. When Juanita went down on him, Damali covered her mouth and began walking in a circle on a landing. This time no blackness gave her a second to recover and brace for the next image.

Her man's hands were in Juanita's hair, guiding her furtive bobbing. His eyes were closed, head back, the look on his face . . . She would slay that bitch! Where was her baby Isis? Damali's hand went for her hip. No blade. Marlene had stripped it and put it with Carlos's claw of Heru, along with her stones—gave it to the Covenant to ship while they traveled past layers of international security—now she knew why! Sure, Marlene might not have actually seen it; Damali knew that in her gut as she honed her inner vision to a laser. But Mar knew to remove their weapons. It was more like her mother-seer had Divine insight than witness.

"Oh, God in Heaven," Damali whispered through her teeth. "I've been here before with this man. But in *my* house? My house!" Her voice fractured as it escalated until what was supposed to be a prayer was a shouting match with On High. "No!" she screamed. "I don't have to tolerate this shit!" Blackness.

Carlos's hands covered Juanita's breasts. Damali stood still as the ache he created within Juanita spilled from her skin to Damali's. Then suddenly, audio kicked in, also kicking her ass. She listened, numb, to Juanita tell him she didn't care whose house it was. Blackness. Carlos had asked Juanita if she wanted to make a baby together? Was he crazy! The question had been asked in a low, sensual, vampirically alluring, mind-bending tone.

"I will cut your dick off!" Damali shouted and started to cry. The sex was bad enough—but to want a child with anyone but her? They were supposed to get married! Hell, they were married, in a way. He'd called her his wife, for chrissakes!

"No honor! Where's my fucking blade!" Blackness.

Jose's face. Her Guardian brother's emotions shot through her like a cattle prod jolt, standing the hairs up on her arms. Blackness. Krissy and Juanita were hugging.

Blackness. Carlos's eyes were considering the possibilities of a ménage à trois. Blackness. Quiet. Impossible. No!

Damali started running again. This was so much more agonizing than the were-demon in Brazil. This was . . . was . . . Family. She ran though blinded by tears. Her man had grown bored, didn't want her, and would jeopardize the family house and all the relationships hanging in the balance just to get his shit off? No respect. No forethought, just pure, stupid lust. At a time like this, when the fate of the world hung in the balance—this is what he did?

She could feel it right through her skin like a stab. This was no illusion, no dream, no internal worry without merit. Her self-confidence as a woman, his lover, his soul mate shredded and stripped away as she jumped down what seemed to be endless flights of steps. She'd been gifted, or cursed, with second sight long enough to know the real Mc-Coy when she saw it. *This had happened!*

A thousand thoughts and options spun in her mind, creating a Russian roulette of murderous intent. Poor Jose! He'd walked in on that? Oh, my God; *in her house?* On the team? Krissy might get pulled shortly, too? No kid could go up against an entity packing council-vamp capacity! Carlos as mere mortal was fucking bad enough!

Damali could see it in her mind. Berkfield would shoot up the joint, leaving bodies everywhere—the man would flip, lose it, and die trying to protect his daughter's honor.

"No need, Dad," Damali said, exhaling and inhaling hard as she bolted toward fresh air. "Before all that takes place, *I'll slay him*—trust me!"

But as soon as the thought entered her mind, a muddy, sluggish feeling began to slow her motions. She could now see Rider and Jose walking toward her as she entered the hotel lobby. For the life of her, she didn't know why she'd been running and couldn't completely remember why she'd been so upset. All she had was the impression of panic still racing through her.

Damali slowed her gait to a quick walking pace, trying to

rethread her thoughts. The only image that came back to her with clarity was Carlos in their room, looking up at her, mortified, and her shock at what she'd seen. The rest of the impressions were fuzzy and only left a bad aftertaste in her mouth, then even that dissipated. She'd figure it out later, and set her sights on her approaching teammates.

Her goal was simply to get past them. She didn't want to talk to another living soul at the moment. However, the pull to Jose came from deep within her core. She needed to talk to him, connect with him. It was an inexplicable feeling, like ancestral knowledge. It just was.

The closer he got to her, the more she felt sure that they needed to have a conversation alone, although she didn't exactly know what she would say. But as his clean energy wafted toward her, it drew her like a magnet. She could instantly feel healing within it. Tears of relief wet her lashes again and began to sting her eyes, no matter how she fought against them.

Jose caught her arm and Rider took off his shades and stared at her.

"You all right, D?" Jose said, searching her face.

"Hon, you look like something's chasing you," Rider said quietly. "Wanna take a walk with us?" He rubbed his jacket to let her know he was packing.

She shook her head no. Words escaped her. Jose and Rider shared a look. It was that look that was beginning to shatter her composure. Damali wrapped her arms around herself and drew a ragged breath to argue, but no sound came out.

"I got dis'," Jose said firmly, his line of vision holding Rider's hard.

"You sure, hombre?" Rider said with concern.

Damali pulled out of Jose's touch and jogged away from them.

He left Rider standing in the lobby and followed Damali down to the marina. It took several minutes to catch up to her and match her stride, but when he did, he just silently walked by her side.

After a while, renewed calm slowed her pace, allowed her to begin to hear the sounds around her, and feel the comfort Jose provided. Bless him. Always there. But what was there to say to Jose that could be shared without a privacy violation?

"I just needed to get my head together," she finally stammered as they strolled along the marina and then found the edge of the beach.

He nodded. "Been that kinda day. I hear you."

"Yeah."

"Been that kinda year, truth be told," he said, and picked up a stone and chucked it in the water.

"Hey! Don't do that," she warned half serious and half joking. "That might have been my fifth insight stone."

He laughed. "My bad. I forgot." Then he made a playful dash at the water but swerved to avoid it. "Want me to go get it? Pick it out from the, what, several million pieces of rock in the sea? I will, girl, you know I'm crazy like that."

She laughed and stopped walking. "Thank you."

He stopped and looked at her. "Don't know what I did, but you're welcome, D. But I ain't scuba diving in jeans for a rock—not even for you, baby." He laughed but his mirth died away when hers slowly became a sad smile.

She looked down and let out a weary sigh. "I'm so tired. Thanks for always making me laugh. Just being my friend."

"That ain't gonna change. Told you that when I came for coffee the other day."

She nodded, but still didn't look at him. "Yep, you did. I don't want that to ever change. It's the only constant in my life."

She looked up when he didn't respond, and saw something in his eyes that she dared not name.

"Mine, too," he said quietly. "So, I'm blessed."

She told her legs to start walking. This was a good time to do that.

"What happened back there, D?"

She shook her head no. "I'll be all right."

He stepped closer than advisable. "If you ever aren't, you know where to come."

She just looked at him for a moment. "I know. And I will."

They stared at each other for a long time.

"What happened this morning when you left to go get Krissy straight?"

Jose looked at her, shook his head, and sent his gaze toward the water, the muscles beginning to work in his jaw. "I'm cool."

Damali nodded and placed her hand on his arm. "If you ever aren't . . ."

He slowly brought his eyes up to meet hers. "Damali, this thing is way too volatile to just put it out there like that, and you know it. Friend to friend, we need to be clear about that."

"I'm sorry," she murmured, and wrapped her arms around her waist.

"Me, too. Because before you tell me that again, I have to be clear."

She nodded and swallowed hard as his hand cupped her cheek.

"I have to know," he whispered, "because if you ever tell me that again, and if I ever see that hurt look in your eyes because of something foul he did, I'll come to you, throwing caution, house rules, lines of demarcation, *everything* out the fucking window. You understand? Don't tell me to do the right thing, if I see you looking like that." He glanced at the water. "Because what I'ma do will be the right thing, and we both know it."

He sealed the gap between them in the very quiet, private place where they stood. Both hands held the side of her face as his mouth lowered to hers. The kiss he delivered was gentle, asking permission to enter, gaining that in slow, dissolving increments as her lips parted, found his tongue and allowed her arms finally to hold him. For that brief moment that the earth stood still, she didn't care who saw or knew. Didn't care if she was making a mistake. She just needed

someone who had never hurt her or frightened her or totally
freaked her out to hold her. A man with no history, but who
had all the history that was necessary when he'd pulled her
into his arms, made her body begin to respond in normal,
human levels of want with no magic at all, except what was
inside his heart. And she was so dangerously close to the
edge of doing something irreversible, if she hadn't already,
that tears streamed down her face and added more salt to
their kiss.

He knew it, she could tell, by the patient shudder that ran
through him. The depth of his knowing came through in the
heat in his hands, the deepening kiss that asked the silent
question—When? They sought an answer with every stroke
down her arms, every hitch in his breath, and tried to tell her a
long story of hunger denied as though reading Braille against
her back. His pulse strummed in her ears, and when his heartbeat synced up to hers she almost cried out and broke the kiss.

She leaned her head on his shoulder and he hugged her hard.

"I know," he said, seeming as though he couldn't take
enough air into his lungs. "You don't have to decide right
this minute, but . . . baby . . ."

"I know, but this is gonna change everything, be really
messed up . . . but I can't go back to my room."

"Come to my room, then."

She looked up at him. "I should have a long time ago in
the compound, Jose. What have I done?"

"Same thing I did." He found her mouth again, but this
time the kiss was less patient, held agony within it. "I'll get
another room, in a different hotel."

She didn't nod, but didn't shake her head no. The heat
seal between them was too thick for her to move, and his
hardness against her thigh said it all. His desire had entered
her pores, along with years of hurt, unnecessary anguish. . . .
It made her close her eyes. "I need to step back for a second."

But he didn't let her go.

"Why do you think I gave you my blanket?"

She nodded. "I knew the minute you handed it to me and Shabazz looked away."

"Then why did you accept it?" he whispered, understanding and confusion competing in his eyes.

"Because I wanted . . ."

"To feel every minute I wanted you in my bed, under it with me, in my arms . . ."

She nodded. "But I knew that was the only way I could really ever experience . . . and I knew—"

An impatient kiss claimed her mouth, scored her neck till tears came to her eyes. Impatient hands flattened against the Sankofa and made it burn till her hands found his shoulders again. A truthful moan collided with hers within the soft tissue of a kiss and drowned it in a hard swallow. A gasp that bordered on a blade cut made a decision necessary.

"I can't."

He nodded. "Knew that going into the first kiss." He closed his eyes and placed his hot forehead against hers and stabilized his breathing by degrees. "You keep the blanket. You let me know. Even if it lies in a cedar chest for ten years, you let me know."

She touched his face and kept her eyes shut tightly. "I wasn't playing with you, Jose. I'm sorry that I just can't, not while . . ."

He captured her hand, kissed the center of it hard. "You don't think I know that? No apologies. I ain't gonna lie, I'm pretty messed up right now, but I'll live." He let his breath out hard and stroked her hair. "But to be able just to know that you were feelin' it, too. That I wasn't all by myself, trippin'." He made her look at him, the quiet passion beneath the surface of him welding her to him. "And if you ever need to open your third eye to come visit me," he whispered, "do it. I don't care who I'm with. Permission to enter and blow my mind like this any time." He smiled. "If I could return the favor, know that I would."

She smoothed his hair back from his forehead and knew she didn't have to nod for him to know that his suggestion wasn't out of the question. "We'd better get back and get our heads right, if we're gonna deal with reality as friends."

He nodded and then dragged his nose across her shoulder, up the side of her neck, and into her hair. It was the way he did it, slow, agonized, his lids sliding shut as she saw him imprint her scent into his memory bank until the day he died. Her knees threatened to give way. The sensation of the olfactory imprinting process connecting to every erogenous zone in him sent a hard shudder through her that she couldn't hide. She felt that create a shiver that linked their spines and made them have to part and literally shake it off, if they were going to be friends. He tilted his head and glanced at the pounding surf.

"Yeah, like that," he murmured and licked his lips with an after tremor. "Salt water. Beach. A gorgeous afternoon. You. Your hair. Your skin. Almond oil and shea butter . . . and you." He closed his eyes for a moment, then began walking away from her. "I won't ever forget."

Carlos landed on his feet, naked, wet, and shivering. Messengers bowed and parted. The cavern went still. He walked forward on a mission, and clothed himself in jeans with one snap. The ground wasn't even hot beneath his feet.

The doors to the great Chamber swung open before he'd even reached them. Carlos crossed the marble floor and glimpsed the newly refurbished inner sanctum, no longer in ruin. His throne shuddered and gurgled with new blood. He ignored it and headed straight for the pentagram-shaped table. He was on a mission. To get the book.

He touched the crest with a flat palm, and then removed his hand. It opened without hesitation, its emptiness glinting torch lights off the bottom.

"Reveal," Carlos said quietly.

The vault obliged and produced the book. He reached down and picked it up, his gaze fastened upon it.

Carlos looked up to the ceiling, watching the newly energized swirl of black smoke that had red eyes. "Topside, same location," he commanded the transport bats, but they suddenly scattered and took cover behind the crags.

Something gurgled within his stomach, sending a pain through his intestines, searing his flesh, making him nearly drop his hold on the precious artifact. His howl elongated with the rip that began in his abdomen. Blood spewed from his body, covering the table, the book, and forced him to stagger backward until the dreaded Chairman's throne broke his fall.

His lungs tore inside his chest and filled with blood, suffocating him. He could hear his ribs snapping and groaning as the unknown pushed against his burn scar over his heart, retreated, and then clawed a huge gash in his stomach.

Blood filled his nose, dribbled out of his mouth, burned his eyes as something black, and winged, and massive, climbed out of the gaping hole, snapping his entrails and ripping his liver, pulling his spleen away from tissue anchors as it birthed from his open wound. Bits of him lay on the floor quivering in a jellied mass as the thing that had exited him spread its blood-wet wings, turned to stare at him with glowing black slits, flicked out a serpent's tongue, and laughed.

It walked around him in a circle, sending the clatter of cloven hoofs to bounce off the walls. An amused expression was on its hideous face, and it politely extracted the book from Carlos's grasp, breaking his fingers backward.

"Thank you," it murmured. "I believe this belongs to me." It sighed, petted the book, and returned a lethal gaze to Carlos. "You don't have the guts to use it properly. Such a waste, when the two of us could have been a united force to be reckoned with."

Paralyzed, Carlos watched, dying, as the thing came for him, grasped him by a broken, protruding rib bone, and flung him out of the throne. Then it sat down, put the book in its lap, crossed its thick, muscular, granite legs, and gripped the hand rests.

Shivering on the floor, Carlos stared at it, semiconscious, and watched the demon throw its head back, groan
and shudder, and then open its eyes, sated. Humanlike
skin crept over its charred body. The wings retracted, as
did its fangs and talons. Its feet normalized, and it
sheathed itself in a black designer suit as the transformation process rippled up its hulking frame. But it saved its
face for last.

It leaned forward, studying Carlos like he was a bug under a microscope, and laughed a deep, thunderous chuckle
of victory as he took on Carlos's face. It summarily sent a
bolt of black lightning across the room to scorch him. But
rather than exterminate him, Carlos felt his body reconstruct
and become amazingly whole again.

"Get off the floor, punk," it said, shaking its head.

Carlos slowly rose, touching his face as he gaped at the
image of himself in the dark throne.

"This is what you could have been," it said in a disgusted
tone. It blew out a long breath. "Woulda, coulda, shoulda, I
suppose."

Carlos couldn't answer. Stupefied by what he was seeing,
he stood in the middle of the floor and only stared.

"Check it out, hombre. You know, we're one and the
same. I'm the other side of who you are . . . the side *even
you* don't want to fuck with." It laughed and stood and strode
over to Carlos, taunting him with the book raised above his
head. "But you had to keep talking to angels. Had to keep
praying. Had to keep making me *fucking sick* inside you." It
shook its head. "Wouldn't even get me laid with the baddest
sister on the planet—now you know I don't take no bullshit,
right?" It bitch-slapped Carlos when he didn't answer and
walked away from him laughing, then whirled on Carlos and
pointed at him. "You brought this shit on yourself, man. We
could have coexisted, if you'da acted right. But your dumb
ass was about to really mess things up for both of us."

"Fuck you," Carlos finally yelled.

"Thanks, already did. Was so good, you even nutted on

yourself, too, which *really* tripped her out. I thought you'd already turned her into a freak, but—"

Carlos lunged at the entity, instant fury replacing common sense and fear. The entity grabbed him by the throat and lifted him off his feet.

"See, that's what I so *love* about, you, man. You got heart. You're *almost* as crazy as I am."

It body-slammed Carlos to the marble floor and folded its arms over its chest as the book hovered inches within his grasp. "We would have made an excellent team, but you kept fucking with the Light. Now you'll have to go your way, and I'll have to go mine."

Carlos glared at the entity, the pain that wracked his body and mind only stoking his hatred for it. As soon as a silver laser cut across the room, the entity jumped back and laughed.

"Whoa, hombre! Not down here. You gonna make me smoke a motherfucker."

Carlos scrabbled to his feet. "I'm not leaving without the book!"

A sucker punch traveled at the speed of thought, connected with Carlos's jaw, shattering it, and leaving him fifty feet away, sprawled on the floor. What felt like razor-sharp claws held both sides of Carlos's head, even though the entity was far across the room. He could feel the bones in his skull separating as the black-glowing eyes in his body double flickered.

"To kill you would not be strategic," the entity said. "You have work to do. I need a Neteru to take off the Chairman's head. That bitch you live with is more seasoned than you, and can deliver. Your punk ass, however, can lead her to him." It flicked out its long, black tongue and blew a kiss at Carlos across the room.

The kiss turned to dark vapor and wafted toward Carlos's opened mind, burning as it touched exposed gray matter and making him yell.

"Forget," the entity whispered. "Shame we couldn't have come to a meeting in the middle." Then it snapped its fingers.

• • •

Carlos stood in the shower with his hands splayed against the tiles. His head hung beneath the pummel of water, and it felt as though the water was slamming into his skull, each drop a sledgehammer.

Oddly, he felt lighter, cleaner, more at peace as he stepped out of the harsh spray and grabbed a towel. He was so thirsty, too, and he opened and downed the liter bottle of water that sat on the sink in one endless guzzle. He was hungry. A burger was calling his name.

Wiping his mouth with the back of his forearm, he went into the bedroom and began to hunt for clothes. When did Damali go? He was seriously hungry, ready to bust a grub, and girlfriend was AWOL. Plus, it was almost sunset and she needed to let him know where she was.

Carlos glanced at the windows and the position of the lowering sun as he pulled on a pair of clean jeans and a T-shirt. Didn't she know he worried about her? Then he smiled and relaxed. What was he worried about? Everything was gonna be all right.

She'd walked along the beach and had found a quiet place of meditation, where she'd hidden within her own thoughts for hours until the sun dipped down beyond the horizon. She watched the waves, hoping their timeless constancy would unravel the mysteries of the universe . . . the mysteries of this erratically behaving man she loved. Damali stood and gave up her search, walking to her vehicle, her spirit in pure chaos.

Tonight she wouldn't say a mumblin' word when she saw him. She'd be on her most effervescent behavior as they all ate dinner together. She'd put on the best performance of her life. She'd act like everything was all right and smile.

But she still had hot tears in her eyes that wouldn't recede like the tide. The mission is first, she told herself, and looked up at the sky.

Tears, a distant female voice whispered in her mind.

Damali froze. She knew that angel's voice anywhere. "Mom?"

Tell no one, child.

Damali nodded as her own tears fell. "I know, Mom. This was horrible. I can't stop crying. I just hate that you saw it."

The angels weep, the voice murmured. *We hear you. Find the tears.*

"They're inside of me," Damali whispered, and kept her gaze to the sunset. "Believe that."

No, the trinity, child, the voice whispered gently. *The tears of angels at the roof of the world . . . those that never touched the ground when the Lamb was slaughtered. Find the temple that holds those tears yet still. Ignite that heavenly compassion with the energy of the Creator. Then remember the blood . . . and cure the world.*

"The antidote?" Damali almost shouted. "Mom?"

Yes. Angelic tears have dried to salt and never hit the ground. The Creator's hand parted that sea, Red, and is in the salt. Salt is in the blood and walks beside you, but living. The Father, the Son, and the Spirit; Red Sea salt, for the Father, the living blood for the Son, and then spiritual tears for the sacrifice. In that order, as it was done.

"That's why the salt was killing them. . . . The Covenant needs—"

Tell no one, not even your mate or mother-seer. You have two of the missing elements at hand. The last element could be at risk, and only your mind is strong enough to hold the secret.

Damali ran her fingers through her locks. "The Red Sea salt is no problem, we have that." She nodded, instantly knowing. "Berkfield has the blood in his veins."

Yes. Be swift.

"The roof of the world is where?"

The Himalayas. Tibet is called the Roof of the World. Seek those who have sheltered these tears for centuries in the greatest temple of all. Only once in history have the angels wept so hard that their tears left Heaven to nearly reach the ground—when the Lamb was slaughtered.

"Mom," Damali whispered with renewed panic. "The Chairman is in the Himalayas. He's got a lair there!"

Yes. Dante knows to seek this missing element. The Chairman would offer a trade for it—you or Eve or both for the world antidote . . . and Heaven might have to indeed comply for the good of the whole. The Light might sacrifice a Neteru in the flesh and one in the spirit for all of humankind, and how would we angels argue such a decision, since the Creator has already sacrificed His Son?

"They would do that," Damali stated, but with a question in the flat response.

I don't know. But you're my daughter. I'm not as evolved as the Most High, and I don't care about the current raging debate about your possible compromise . . . or your soul mate's potential compromise. My love for my child is stronger than warrior angels' admonishments, even at my lower ring. I will always give you insight, living or dead. This is why Dante established his lair in the Himalayas. It was not coincidence.

Damali could hear her mother's voice becoming farther away, as the last thing she said became strident with conflict. "Mom," she whispered. "I love you. Thank you. Just tell me which temple, and I'm there with the quickness. Don't leave, yet."

I have told you all I can without being seriously reprimanded. It is the greatest temple of all. Heal yourselves, Neterus, then the team, first; then heal the world. In that order. Anoint each forehead with the antidote, that minds become clear and spirits unclouded. You, him, then the team, first. The trinity, always. Ohhhh . . . sugar . . . Mommy misses you so . . .

"I don't want to get you in trouble, Mom," Damali said, her voice catching in her throat. "I won't fail. I promise. I won't let what you told me go to waste. I love you, I love you, I miss you and Dad so. Don't get yourself involved anymore. Not even for me, hear, or risk—"

But you are my daughter. You are my daughter. You are my blessed daughter, my gift. My life. I saw them take your baby. I was there through it all. I wept. This is why I challenge the warrior ranks and have secretly brought this to you, out of pure mother's love. They cannot argue with that, or stop it, even in Heaven. Enough has happened, and you held the line. I trust you, even if the other angels are wary. Know that I hold my first grandchild's light in my arms. They didn't get it. I will love you till the end of time. I will give you an edge, but do not forsake this information. This is why you tell no one. Not even Carlos, until you are both synced up. Just go and find it to heal the world. Ohhhh . . . child of mine . . . I love you. I must go.

Damali sat down hard on the beach as her mother's voice trailed off and disappeared. It was all too much, and she did what was human—just put her face in her hands and wailed.

Yonnie instantly lifted his head from the bed, sending dozens of silken pillows to the floor. Tara sat up quickly and touched his arm.

"Get dressed," Yonnie said. "Carlos is outside."

"In New Orleans?" Tara said, moving quickly to dress and follow Yonnie out of the suite Gabrielle had provided.

"*Que pasa,* mutha*fucker!*" Yonnie said laughing as he stopped, appraised Carlos in the new suit, then walked up to him for their familiar embrace. "I'll just be *damned.* Look at you, man!"

Carlos smirked and pushed off the gleaming black finish of his new Lamborghini and accepted Yonnie's embrace. "You're in a real good mood, man. You musta finally got straight."

Yonnie shrugged. "Hey . . . what can I say? You feel that surge that bubbled up to the surface? Has topspin on it like—"

"A *real* motherfucker," Carlos said laughing, and cutting Yonnie off. He pounded Yonnie's fist. But he noticed that Tara hung back, her eyes cautious. "I hear you."

"Hey, baby, what's the matter?" Carlos said, his tone warm and oozing with sensuality.

Yonnie discreetly stepped back from Carlos and stopped

laughing. He glanced at Tara. "I know you are *not* trying to get new with our boy? What's your problem?"

"Does Damali know you're here, in *that?*" Tara asked, her tone cool, civil, and so distant that ice could form around her words. She appraised the car with open disdain.

"Excuse me?" Carlos said, tilting his head to one side, and then returning a hard glare to Yonnie. "You don't have this bitch in order?"

Stunned, Yonnie stepped back further, his eyes holding confusion and hurt. "Yo, man. C'mon. It's Tara. You know she's always got beef about some principle, but—"

"Then you clearly don't have her ass in order," Carlos said, shaking his head. "I figured after the surge and you laid serious pipe, you'd have this bitch eating out of your hand, glad to get a wrist vein."

Carlos narrowed his gaze on Yonnie's jugular when he didn't answer, just bristled. "She throat marked you, and you allow her to dis you in fronta me like that?" He glanced at Tara hard and quickly studied her throat. "Man, you let her have you so out of control that you gave her a permanent mate bite, and she's not humble? And you're *my* lieutenant?" He sighed and opened the car door, allowing his palm to slide across the exquisite bloodred leather interior. "Can't blame you, though. You weren't schooled right from the jump. My bad."

Yonnie backed away farther and pulled Tara close to him. "Apologize to him, baby. He ain't in the mood tonight, okay? Don't take him there."

Carlos looked up with a sly smile. "Let's go for a ride, y'all. The new wheels are off da meter." He chuckled as he saw the couple draw together in fear. "Maybe we can go back to my lair and play, or go eat some *real* New Orleans, for a change, and listen to some live music?"

Neither Yonnie nor Tara spoke.

"Okay, maybe not. Yeah, there's a matter of protocol that I have to address, first. Again, my bad." Carlos laughed and closed his car door.

"She's sorry, man, and didn't mean to offend," Yonnie said, subtly pushing Tara farther behind his back. "Besides, there's this whack shit going down with the portal energy . . . that's probably affecting her. Got a coven divination on it. Seems that something's turned subterranean upside down. Levels Five on up are scrambling to the surface through broken portals, can't survive underground, and are scared to be—"

"Didn't you give her a direct order?" Carlos said, cutting off Yonnie's frantic babbling as he stared at his manicure.

"I'm sorry," Tara whispered in a tight voice strangled with rage.

"I am, too, bitch," Carlos said looking up, his eyes beginning to flicker black. "I didn't like your tone. You took so long to respond to my boy—and you ain't fucking him the way you should be on a regular basis, anyway. I shouldn't have had to send a power surge up here to rectify that shit. Shoulda been *automatic,* just 'cause he said so. Fuck Rider. He's human, and can't do nothing for you, like my boy."

"Yo, man," Yonnie said, his glare beginning to glow red. "That was between me and you, as boyz. As men."

"It is what it is, *man.*" Carlos folded his arms. "Why be a punk, crying in your blood, worrying about—"

"We're *friends,*" Tara shouted. "I cannot believe you are treating us this way. What's wrong with you!"

Yonnie froze. Carlos stepped forward. His voice dropped to a threat level that only vampire hearing could detect.

"Ain't no friends in this game—bitch."

As soon as the words escaped his mouth a vast cavern opened between dimensions, sucking Yonnie and Tara into it. Carlos stepped over the threshold of the yawn in the side of the building, looked back at the motionless pedestrians, and closed it behind him with a snap of his fingers. "Let's go back in time to get this straight."

Tara clung to Yonnie in the middle of the deserted wood clearing.

"*This* is why you have to establish your authority from

the door!" Carlos bellowed, paralyzing Yonnie and yanking Tara from Yonnie's side by her hair as she fought against his hold. "You can't have this bullshit, man. Unless you kick their ass good once, they don't respect you."

"Yo, Carlos, for real, man, stop playing," Yonnie said, trying to break the force around him to no avail. "This is *Tara,* man. Tara!"

"Like that means some shit? I ain't deaf and I know this bitch's name," Carlos said, teasing Yonnie as he gripped Tara's hair harder. "But you never laid down the law with her, never did her right, never put down your territorial marker, so I'll show you how. Then don't you ever act like no punk in my presence again. Understood?"

"Let go of me!" Tara screamed, twisting and hissing, her claws digging into Carlos's hand as her fangs tried to score any flesh on him they could. "You're mad! Completely insane. Get off of me!"

"Let her go, man!" Yonnie hollered, still fighting the paralyzing hold.

Carlos held her jaw, deflecting her missed kicks and punches. "You're beautiful," he murmured, "but too old to be behaving like this."

"Stop," she said, sobbing. "Don't do this."

"Man, for real," Yonnie said, his eyes blazing solid red and full battle-bulk consuming his paralyzed frame. "I will *never* forgive you for this."

"Good," Carlos said, ripping the front of Tara's leather suit away as he stared at Yonnie. "Now you're starting not to sound like a punk." He smiled. "Feel it. Embrace it. Then detach from the emotion so you can do what you've gotta do."

Carlos spun and caught one of Tara's stray punches, and snapped her wrist. Her scream rent the air; Yonnie cringed and growled. With a glance Carlos burned the remainder of her clothes away and ignored her screams, then body-slammed her to the ground and used a black current to open her thighs as he loomed above her. "You have to train them to obey your command like you'd train a dog. Use simple commands to let them know what disobedience can cost. Brother, you've got to say what you mean and mean what you say when—"

Carlos's head jerked up as Yonnie sent a weak current through his black-force hold. The impact was like a hard slap, but didn't faze him. "Your ass must be really salty and really crazy, hombre. But that's a good thing."

"Me and you, motherfucker! Let her go, and we do this to ash!"

"Now, see, this time when you called me a motherfucker, I wasn't feeling no love. It's all about tone, vibe, attitude," Carlos said. "And this ain't even a throat-mate that obeys. You sure you wanna take her place?"

"Do it. Let her go," Yonnie hollered.

"No," Tara yelled, her eyes narrowed on Carlos. "He'll kill you, and it's not worth it. Let him finish, and we'll be gone, Yonnie." She looked at Yonnie, her eyes filled with tears as her voice cracked and became a mere whisper. "Please. Don't provoke him further. Let him finish. We'll both survive."

"This is what I was trying to show you. A lair mate, at Second-gen, elevated by your own bite, should be ready to take the stake, a beat down, what-the-fuck-eva you say her ass should take, even the goddamned sun, to save your ass. She should fear your wrath above anything else. *Now,* girl-friend is clear."

Carlos looked down at Tara, shook his head, and returned his scorching gaze to Yonnie, making his chest sizzle as he spoke. "Your heart should be made of steel. No tail should make you go against your boyz and act stupid. You don't al-low worrying over no dumb bitch to get in the way of real bizness. If this one dies, you go make another one. And the very *last* person you *ever* fuck with *is me.* We straight, *holmes?*" Carlos pointed at Tara in a hard snap and released her. "She's real clear now. *Are you?*"

Tara scrambled to Yonnie's side, her broken wrist immo-bile as she clung to him. "Stand down, Yonnie," she begged when Yonnie's fangs didn't retract and his battle bulk didn't give way. "The wrist is nothing. It'll regenerate after we feed. Don't provoke him. He's crazy, infected, something—I don't know, honey, don't do it."

"See how she's begging you to chill for your own good—that's what I'm talking about. She senses imminent danger, was ready to take the weight, and is very right. I am in a very dangerous mood tonight. Women know these things. Listen to your mate." Carlos began walking in a circle around Yonnie. "She senses the potential end of your existence, if you don't bulk the fuck down *now.* She oughta beg for dick like that, too, man, if we're being honest. But hey, what can I say. I'm on a time frame, and don't have time to show you how to do all that tonight."

Yonnie snarled. Carlos sighed and shook his head as he glimpsed Tara.

"He's still fuzzy about how this all goes," Carlos said, his voice dropping a decibel. "He ain't sure, ain't made up his mind as to what should be instinct, a reflex decision." Carlos snapped his fingers and blew Tara ten feet away to land in a crumpled thud, and then released Yonnie.

Instantly, Yonnie took flight and lunged like a beast that had popped its choker chain. Carlos's massive wings ripped through his suit as he met Yonnie in the air, seized his throat, and slammed him to the ground.

Huge iron shackles formed around Yonnie's wrists as he tried to stand, dazed from the impact. Tara screamed and rushed forward, but was forced to fall back as a huge redwood tree came up from the earth beneath Yonnie's chest, plowing up dirt and stones, scraping the flesh from his torso as massive chains tied him to its trunk and raised him a hundred feet from the ground.

Airborne again, Carlos hovered behind Yonnie, his tail cracking from his elongated spine, stretching away from his body and returning to Yonnie's back in a razor-edged bullwhip that sliced skin from bone each time it connected. The sound of lightning strikes echoed into the night with each torturous whip of Carlos's tail. A long wail of agony followed the sound into the darkness with every pain-filled lash.

Yonnie's claws dug into the tree. Tara screamed out from the ground, circling the base of it with her one undamaged hand reaching upward toward her dying partner.

"No, I beg you," she shrieked trying to climb to greet the assault. "Don't do that to him—he trusted you with that information! Not from the plantation days, do not take him there," she sobbed. Her shrieks became high-pitched sonar as she circled the tree, screeching obscenities. "He'll go mad. You bastard! He trusted you with that pain within him. He trusted you to show you his darkest fear! How could you? I'll take whatever punishment, but don't do that to him!"

"See," Carlos said, delivering another lash. "She said she'd take whatever for you, man. You owe me for teaching your woman this very valuable lesson. No pain, no gain."

"Please stop," Tara sobbed, her words dissolving as she turned her head away. "Even among our own kind, this is . . ."

She crumbled into a heap on the ground and covered her head as Yonnie's wails continued to fill the sky, turning from curses and growls to howls, to pleads, to sobs as his tattered flesh left crushed vertebrae exposed.

"I keep trying to tell you both, *I'm not your kind,* so stop fucking with me!" Winded, Carlos lowered the tree to become a tall post and he glanced down at Tara with disgust. "I should fuck him in the ass, too, for making me have to go there—but he's crying like a little bitch so bad, he's taken all the fun out of it."

Tara jumped up and gently lifted Yonnie's head, trying to cradle it as she stood on her tiptoes to reach him. Carlos snapped and stood back, watching the pair as Yonnie slid to the ground with a thud, and Tara covered his body, baring fangs.

"You've nearly bled him out," she said seething. "He's no longer conscious."

"Then do what you know you're supposed to do, bitch." Carlos began gathering a storm cloud around him. "Tend to your man."

"He'll die!" she screamed, sobbing and jumping up to run behind Carlos's evaporating form.

"Then go kill a human, get a full grub on, and feed the poor bastard."

"You going out with your boy tonight?" Rider said discreetly as he ordered another ginger ale.

Carlos shook his head and took another huge bite from his burger. "No. I'ma put a little distance between us until after we go to Tibet."

"Seems like we're in the same boat, then," Rider said nodding, and rejoining the conversation around him. "Wise choice."

Carlos kept his attention on Damali as their team ate. On the surface, everything seemed normal. The team was laughing, joking, everybody was talking at once down the tables that had been pushed together in the restaurant to accommodate their large party. But Damali's eyes had avoided his all evening. Her smile seemed forced, and although she participated in the dinner conversation, she seemed more quiet than usual. He could tell her thoughts were a million miles away, even though she kept up a good front. He glanced at Marlene, who issued him a look of concern, but it wasn't a judgmental glance; it was something mellow and quiet that said there's trouble in paradise, but it ain't my business. He liked that about Mar. She was cool to the bone. Wise.

He and Damali could talk privately later. His baby had been through a lot, just like he had. Carlos took another bite of his burger, wondering what on earth could have Damali feeling and acting this way.

"You see this shit, Marj?" Berkfield said, sitting up in bed and flipping through all the cable news channels in a blur. "Father Patrick and Kamal told us right. It's like the world has gone crazy. People are definitely possessed. The types of killings . . . a mother cut off her infant's arms? What the hell, Marj! Even if we do close the portals, the insanity that still has to be cleaned up after, you know, hon? The baby is still dead, like how many others?"

Berkfield's palm slid over his balding scalp. "I been a cop for a lot of years, and seen a lot of sick shit, honey. But every day, things are getting worse—like this infection is beyond anything we could ever comprehend. I used to ask myself, where do these animals come from? I don't feel better now that I know. I almost turned into one and shot a Guardian and my own daughter. I'm scared. What if we fail?"

When she remained still without answers, he clicked off the television with an angry snap and searched his wife's face for understanding. "You and I, the kids, and this whole crew have seen entities slither up from Hell, and oddly, I've sorta made my peace with that—because there was a separation, a line between human and demon. But even in broad daylight, I can't make out the difference anymore . . . and that frightens me more than whatever bears fangs."

"I know, I know," Marjorie finally said, beginning to walk in a distressed circle as she fidgeted with her nightgown strap. "Just knowing that there are actually demons is bad enough. . . . Now people are turning into beasts?" She spun and looked at her husband. Panic hitched her voice. "How do we raise children in a world like this? *A mother* did this to her child, Richard. She cut off her *baby's* arms because she claimed she was *depressed?* Dear God. Will we get like that in less than thirty days? Will our children ax murder us? I'm so scared, Richard, I can hardly breathe."

Marjorie stopped pacing and stared at her husband, stricken, as he came to her and held her. Everything was so strange and different in her life, and that he'd also subtly changed was both unnerving, yet also exciting. During the past six months he'd lost his beer belly and his body had hardened under the exercise and rigors of team life. But it was his eyes. They no longer contained the dispassionate malaise of a man who hated his job and was clocking time until his pension kicked in.

No. This Richard Berkfield was different. Despite all the horrors, she'd watched her husband come alive. He now looked forward to each day, felt deeply about the things he saw, and seemed to believe in something greater than himself again. He'd lost the jaded edge and found something beyond the mundane to give him purpose. As she filled his arms and felt his body stir, she remembered his toned, stocky build, broad square shoulders, perpetual tan from walking a beat, and how handsome he'd been when they'd first met . . . all that was back again, except his sandy brown hair, but she could live without that. What she held in her arms was a gift, and she appreciated how handsome he'd become from the inner fire of contributing to something great.

She touched his rugged cheek and gazed into his eyes, marveling at the transformation that she'd almost missed. No matter what was going on in the world or how their lives had changed, she was quietly glad that he had come back to life.

"At first, I thought it was imagination that things were getting worse," she said in a faraway, quiet voice as she buried her face against his shoulder and breathed hard. "On every channel there were horrible acts of cruelty being committed, but I didn't want to believe anything else was wrong. . . . After Philadelphia, I just couldn't take it. The weather was weird, natural disasters were everywhere. Hurricanes, floods, earthquakes . . . and the wars . . . terrorism. Even the church has sickness . . . young boys, to this degree? It wasn't just one priest in one parish." She covered her face and began to quietly weep as her husband kissed her temple hard and just rubbed her back. "I kept saying, things will be all right. Now I know they won't be. We're all losing our minds."

Marlene sat on the bed in her room, staring at multiple newspapers and then looked up at Shabazz. Quiet tension still strangled their relationship, but what she was witnessing went beyond that. "Baby, I know people have been crazy for a long time, but the type of brutality going on now seems . . . I can't even describe it. Father Patrick tried to warn us, we braced ourselves, but even I'm not ready for this." She stared at him. "That's all he was trying to tell us," she added quietly, also saying everything and nothing about the Kamal subject that was still too hot to touch.

Shabazz nodded and kept his gaze out toward the marina, holding the doorframe with outstretched hands. "It's day and night, now. Our Neterus got most of the seriously lethal vampires, and only lower gens are still skulking around, but it feels like something has kicked up a notch in addition to the contagion. The stars say anything to you, baby?" He let the reference go. Some things couldn't be discussed until time had passed.

He turned to look at Marlene when she didn't respond, his eyes filled with pain. "I keep asking the Almighty, why? What's our purpose, now? Are we making any kind of real inroad? Then the contagion was added to this insanity. We'd slay demon after demon, win battles, and then there was always still more . . . like we were all trying to clear a beach of sand using a teaspoon. Then it got to the point where I couldn't read the papers anymore, baby. I could hardly watch the news. It took my mind and my spirit to somewhere so dark that . . ." His voice trailed off and he swallowed hard, and then closed the French doors as though shutting out the world. "Now, if we don't close those portals, we'll be the same horror we used to fight."

Marlene shoved the newspapers off the bed and patted the covers gently, inviting him to lie next to her. She waited until he sat down and then pulled him against her in a gentle hug. "Hold me," she whispered. "Just hang on to me tonight and don't let me fly away."

"Then don't leave me tonight for him . . . even in your dreams," he whispered back thickly.

Her body tensed for a moment and then relaxed. Their eyes met. He knew, and was beyond cool. That was Shabazz; she would have never expected less from him. The master of Zen cool. Was she mad? This was her *man,* her life partner, and she'd almost gone too far.

His eyes had held hurt, worry, and stress had permeated the air around him as he'd neared her. Tears rose to her eyes as she absorbed the doubt-filled expression on his regal, African-featured face. His strength was a mask, just like it was a part of his DNA, but she knew he was quietly bleeding inside.

She loved him so much that her fingers reached out and trembled as they stroked the smooth line of his jaw. A pair of dark brown eyes searched hers, intensely burning with unspoken questions as they looked into hers for answers. She would give him balm and so much more . . . not just because he deserved it, but because she loved him to the depth of her soul. There were things that they'd shared that no one would ever know or be able to understand. He was also her friend.

Warm, dark, walnut-hued skin slid beneath her palm as he hugged her, and her hands traced the steel sinew beneath it that made his every fluid movement graceful. As he lay beside her, he stared at her as her hands worked to remove the heavy burden. She kept her gaze on his toned but weary muscles, watching them as she kneaded his shoulders, his strength-conditioned arms, every defined section of his abdominals clenching as he settled back against the pillows, his thighs and buttocks seemingly cut from sculptured granite. She kissed the wisps of gray that had come into his locks at his temples, and he closed his eyes and wrapped his arms around her.

"I love you," she whispered. "I would never disrespect you like that."

He rubbed her back and pressed her head against his shoulder. Then he kissed her temple. "I won't let you go, either," he murmured. "Not in the end of days."

Carlos sat on the edge of the bed, his attention glued to the television as he endlessly flipped channels. Oddly, the side of his neck tingled where he remembered he'd been given an invisible tattoo.

"Damali, is it me, or does it seem like things are getting real bad, faster than the thirty days Father Pat had talked about?" He looked up at her, and hesitated.

"I don't understand. Demons have always been topside, to some degree, causing chaos," Carlos said quietly, standing. "There was always murder and mayhem, D. In the old days, they might inspire a person to rob somebody. That's wrong, but when the victim handed over the money, the thief rolled. Basic. Or if it got hectic and the victim pulled a weapon, okay, they might get shot—not that I'm saying it's right, but that makes sense, if you're living that kinda crazy, off da hook life. The human side still had some . . . I don't know what you call it. Honor among thieves. Serial killers, rapists, the numbers, man, are staggering, D. How we gonna get this under control fast enough?"

"I don't know," Damali whispered. "We get on the plane, find the Chairman, get him to guide us to Lilith, and close the portals, first, I guess." She twirled a lock around her finger, deep in thought, and glanced out the window, remembering what her mother had said. "The critical question is, even if we find and kill her, how do we get all this stuff to slither back from whence it came? The Damned will either ascend or go to ash if we can deliver the book. But people seem like they're being affected by original demons. . . . We have to somehow get them to go back under, too, once we close the portals."

"You're right," Carlos said quietly. "You can tell that's what's up by the slant on these crimes." He motioned toward the television. "Bank robbery. Should been an in-and-out deal. But to unnecessarily take hostages, mutilate them, cut off their heads and hands, torture . . . baby," he whispered. "That's the Damned. But the outright feedings, those are ODs. This shit has *got* to go back underground. We can't let the human condition go that far. We've gotta fix this thing, me and you, girl."

She stared at Carlos, her stomach clenching. She wanted to trust this man with all her heart, but even her mother had told her to wait and see. She watched true horror glitter in his eyes, as though everything he'd witnessed on television was brand spanking new. And the tone of his voice was so mystified by it all, almost naïve. Fighting evil was their purpose, their mission. This was the end of days, and hell yeah, things were getting worse; they'd been warned. The person who was glued to the news seemed like a person she didn't know. Even his soul felt lighter as she discreetly scanned him; his aura seemed different than it had been since Philadelphia, like a giant weight had been lifted from him. With all that was going on, any change in any of the team members, even within herself, made her nervous.

Yet, to see his righteous indignation gave her hope, even while the thing that had gone down with Jose made normal seem abnormal in their relationship. Especially in the tight confines of a hotel bedroom. There was so much to think about that her mind almost couldn't hold it all.

Just like the horrors on the television, the secret in her mental black box had grown, had a scent, a touch, a taste, a moan and a lingering question . . . what would have happened if she'd made a different choice today?

For the first time in months, she felt the Sankofa tattoo on her back move. She kept her secret to herself as she felt it literally shift position on her skin and face forward, so that the bird was no longer glancing over its shoulder.

"What if we can't find that book in time, D?" Carlos said, his gaze still on the television set.

"I don't know what to say," she murmured, her hand discretely rubbing the stinging sensation on her skin. They had to be tight, operate in total sync, to go after the threat and beat it, but how?

She kept watching him, wondering how he could just act like she hadn't walked in on anything deep a few hours earlier. Denial was one thing, shame another, but this man didn't seem like he even had recollection. He was completely relaxed around her, but she was a wreck around him. What she'd witnessed created a wall, made syncing up as one next to impossible.

Although she wanted to probe him deeper than a discreet surface scan, to do it meant she'd have to let him into her psyche. That immediately changed her mind about entertaining a mental synthesis lock with him. If there was something eating away at his brain, she needed to know how to guard hers before casually dipping into his.

She definitely wasn't ready for him to go poking around within her consciousness.

Chapter Sixteen

Sleep was fitful, and the hours leading up to, and during, the long flight to China were uneventful.

From her perspective, she and Carlos seemed to be cloaked in a surreal, platonic dishonesty that shrouded their relationship. Carlos either knew what she had been alluding to every time she vaguely attempted to find out what was going on with him, or he didn't. She didn't bother to clarify. There seemed to be no point in that. His responses to her were civil, absurdly warm and brotherly in affection, but there wasn't the spark that had once ignited them as a couple. She didn't bother to attempt to stoke those dead embers. He didn't ask any questions; she didn't ask any questions. He'd stayed on his side of the bed; she'd stayed on her side of the bed. She and Jose kept careful distance, just like Krissy and Dan seemed to. Marlene had prepared her for a lot of things, but not this.

Damali kept her gaze dispassionately fixed on the clouds. They'd literally be flying into the future, or the next day, as the case may be, since Tibet was, oddly, thirteen hours ahead of U.S. time. That number stuck in her mind, whittling at it, as she made her peace with another one of Marlene's wild travel routes.

They'd had choices and all of them seemed unacceptable, now, as she sat on the interminable flight. They could have flown into Indore, India, a thirty-four-hour travesty of time, with stops in Frankfurt, Germany, changing planes in Bombay. Then they would have had to endure a ninety-four-mile bumpy drive to Nepal, where it would take days to cross by minivan into what was now called the Tibetan Autonomous Region by the Chinese government—a place that was hardly autonomous, under martial law, and where the culture of the native inhabitants had been suppressed with sheer butchery and terror.

Or, they could do it the so-called easier way, by taking the sixteen-and-a-half-hour-flight to Beijing, and from there take another five and a half hours to get to Tibet's capital city, Lhasa. She just wondered why she and her team always had to do things the hard way. Obviously, there was no such phenomenon called easy. But easy was relative, as was hard. Flying into Beijing was nothing compared to what they had to do once they got to the Himalayas.

To her mind, it all seemed crazy, no matter what Monk Lin had said about the spiritual prowess of the region. If demon madness had come to the surface, there, they were screwed. At least she knew her way around an urban firefight. But in some mountain—nah. Not her environment, and a sister wasn't down with snow.

The only saving grace was that in the one-day wait to get a flight and health checks, the team's elders had found, of all things, an old Beverly Hills mansion to convert. Marlene had slapped a ridiculous deposit down on faith, and walked. It had to be divine intervention, because that helped to keep everyone talking about safe subjects, like retrofitting the new location into what they'd need to survive in the future . . . which oddly kept everyone half believing there might be one.

All she hoped was that when they returned from this odyssey, things would be as close to normal as their lives would ever be. Damali stifled a sigh. She could deal with rickety, diesel-leaking buses that smoked, flatbed lorries to carry her team as far as there were passable roads into the mountains, and even going by yak mounts or horseback up into the Himalayas to find Nirvana, if need be, to stop this insanity from spreading.

She counted every blessing presented that could make the mission easier. First, she knew she should be thankful that it wasn't winter over there, when temperatures plummeted to minus ten degrees, or the rainy monsoon season of summer when the permafrost ground couldn't absorb the torrents, and whole villages were known to be swept away in floods and mudslides.

But they would still have to deal with exploration at severe altitudes of eleven thousand feet or more above sea level, which would offer nasty results on the human body, everything from shortness of breath, lightheadedness, and chest pains, to nausea. She didn't even want to think about feeling ill while trying to divine the mysteries of the universe to find the antidote *and* kicking ass. But she couldn't worry about it, because failure was not an acceptable outcome. *Puhlease!*

Carlos just kept his gaze fixed on the sky. He hadn't bothered to question the intimate details of Marlene's route decisions for this journey. Everything that he could remember from his experiences with Damali's family told him that the reason would be revealed in due time. So, he'd made his peace with this crazy adventure. Actually, he'd embraced it, because something way down in his gut rang out as truth as he sleepily stared out the window. The bottom line was, they had to close the portals.

He'd never been to China in his life; had never imagined that he'd go there under these conditions. One thing was for sure, a change of venue, even if it was to go to war, couldn't hurt. The hotel room felt like a prison cell, especially with Damali barely speaking to him, and when she did it was always a curt snap. Carlos glimpsed her from the corner of his eye as she slept beside him. It was as though everything he said, everything he did, got on her nerves, but he wasn't sure why.

Were it not for the guys on the team, he would have lost it and said something to her that couldn't be taken back, and where would that leave them? Maybe once the team returned

Stateside and settled into a new compound, things would be right again. Probably once he had his own spot and she had hers, they'd chill, the vibe would even out, and everything would be cool again. But he felt strangely unsettled, beyond prebattle jitters . . . like there were things that had gone down that he just couldn't remember.

Bored with the long flight and ready to just get the mission started and over with, Carlos stood and went to sit near Rider, who was always good for a card game. He had to keep moving, do something to pass the time, other than sleep—which, oddly, offered no peace. Fleeting nightmares made peace in slumber next to impossible. Weird images always accosted his mind and dragged it down to places he didn't want to remember. But they'd all told him that would pass with time. Whatever.

Carlos plopped down next to Rider and smiled, brandishing a well-worn deck of cards. He was glad the flight wasn't packed so people could stretch out. It was funny how he'd come to appreciate the smallest of good fortune.

"Hey," Carlos said, beginning to fan the deck as he sat. "You up for a little mental diversion?"

Rider stretched and yawned. "Yeah, dude. After the last series of flights, I'm not particularly sleeping too good in the air."

They both smiled.

"I feel you," Carlos said, keeping his voice low enough so he wouldn't wake the others. "Guess old habits die hard."

"Yeah," Rider said, accepting cards from Carlos as he dealt them onto the seat tray, "this whole extravaganza gives a new meaning to cold turkey." Rider arranged his cards. "It's gonna be cold as shit when we go up into the mountains, and if you ask me, we're turkeys for seeking some lair when we don't even know exactly what we're looking for."

"Word," Carlos muttered, turning over the first card to start their game. "I got a few issues with this plan, brother. Like, before, we knew what we're dealing with, or at least what we were looking for. I ain't got a clue of what our target's lair looks like topside. I know it's gotta be rigged with every possible booby trap known—and our team will be way out of our element on the mountainside. Feel me?"

Rider nodded and threw out a card on the tray. "Something about all this just isn't sitting right with me, either." He looked up at Carlos. "Like . . . I'm worried about Tara."

Carlos didn't throw out another card, but held off his move, studying Rider's expression. It wasn't like Rider even to mention Tara's name, much less admit that he was concerned about her. In fact, to his recollection, it was the first time he'd really said anything at all about her since Philly.

"She's probably all right," Carlos said after a moment, and then selected a different card and put it down on the tray easy.

Rider folded his fan of cards and sent his gaze out the window. "It's not like her to not send a sign that she's around," Rider said quietly. "Yeah, we broke up. All right. I've come to terms with that. But even still, while in Arizona, she'd send me little messages to let me know she was okay. A hint of lavender on an evening breeze, or she might pop into my head in a dream and be gone. I'd just feel better if I knew that she knew we'll be over here."

Carlos folded his fan of cards and then perused them one by one. "From what I remember of the rules from my old life, she can't do international travel without an underground pass . . . and she can't get one of those. Plus, like Mar and Shabazz said, you tell her too much, and if we start seriously kicking ass, she could be captured and tortured for info. It's better this way, man. When we get back then just, you know, let her know you're cool."

"I know," Rider said quietly, returning to his cards. "I wasn't expecting that kind of visit from her. She's got a new life, a new situation, and I don't expect your boy would let her come to me, if she wanted to. All I wanted to know is, if she's all right."

Carlos nodded, but didn't look up at Rider. The request was implicit. "I'll see if I can make contact with her when we get back. Aw'right?"

"Appreciated," Rider said quietly. "Not trying to kick up any dust or start no shit . . . or put you in a position with your boy. Just wanna know that she's still alive, not being abused, or something crazy." Rider suddenly looked up at Carlos. "The last time I saw her, it wasn't on good terms." His voice became distant as pain entered his eyes. "It shouldn't be that way after all we've been through together. No matter what, we're still friends. She's a good woman, and I was sorta . . ."

Rider let his breath out hard as Carlos lowered his eyes to his cards. "My reaction was kinda fucked up when I saw her last. Life ain't promised; shouldn't let the last time you see somebody you care about go like that. You never know if you're gonna get an opportunity to rectify things. Does that make sense?"

"Yeah," Carlos said, resuming the game that they had both clearly lost interest in playing. He knew exactly what Rider meant, and he glanced at Damali and then back at his hand.

As the cards fell onto the tray, each man selecting what he'd hold on to and release, chaotic feelings ate at Carlos's insides. He'd tried to contact Yonnie, but had received no response. That was not like his boy. All he'd wanted to do was to tell Yonnie the same thing Rider apparently wanted to tell Tara, namely that they'd be away for a while and for them not to worry.

He hadn't called Yonnie to go hang out. Hadn't been trying to reach him to break out of the family prison situation, like before—especially not the night leading up to a significant mission. If Yonnie had responded, he wasn't gonna divulge where they were headed. But he could only figure that his boy didn't trust him after the near relapse. However, the lack of faith annoyed him no end. It was just a friendly courtesy call. A *Yo, man, here's the deal. The family will be out for a few,* type of transmission.

All right, so the last time he and his boy had been out had almost been disastrous. Yeah, yeah, yeah, he'd gotten wasted. Yonnie had been pissed off about it all, and had finally brought him home—so Damali could be pissed off. That was a real friend, somebody who cared enough about you to just say no and not be a party to your downfall.

He'd paid his debt by suffering like a dawg the next day and having Rider get in his face. He'd even had a damned deer total his Jeep and land in his windshield after a stupid argument. Why was everybody was so hype around him, and Damali still so jawed-up? It was crazy. Like Rider said, if they were possibly going into the biggest battle of their lives, why was everybody, especially Damali, focused on dumb shit?

Moreover, why was she walking around looking like she didn't trust him? He didn't get it.

Carlos took comfort in the logic he'd woven around the dangling loose ends in his mind. Tara was probably lying low, too, not wanting to be a weak link in the chain, not wanting to run into Rider and have old feelings surface—especially when those feelings could kill Rider, one way or another. A bite from her would turn or kill him, and if she slept with Rider without biting him, Yonnie might rip out his heart. Tara was more of a friend to Rider than he may ever know.

Carlos held on to that card in his mind and selected one in his hand to throw onto the growing pile on the tray.

The team exited the plane and entered the frenetic, ultramodern mayhem of Beijing Airport. A current of alertness bound them as one unit as they made their way through the arduous customs process and produced identification papers to allow them to change flights and board their destination carrier to Lhasa. But the whole team shared stricken glances as they stared at the crush of humanity in just the airport alone. If infection broke out here in China, the problem would be measured in billions.

"Ms. Richards," a customs agent said in a quiet, civil tone. "Would you please have your group follow me?"

Nervous glances passed around the team, but they complied without argument. This was China, not the United States, and it wasn't about slowing down the mission by offending any authorities that may have routine security queries about Americans traveling abroad. They were well used to that by now.

Damali and Carlos shared a glance that quietly communicated the same thing the whole team was thinking: It just would have been nice if they could have flown in under Covenant resources, then again, nobody on the team was ready to go through that again. A low-key commercial flight was fine.

They filed down a long winding corridor and used their music celeb status to help them ignore curious glances from airport travelers and security staff. Looking straight ahead, the team proceeded behind the efficient little man and found themselves being escorted into a small, well-lit room with a row of uncomfortable-looking metal folding chairs. Their bags had all been put in the room, and the team's gaze inspected the luggage as though their eyes were lasers. The same question was on everyone's mind: Okay, who packed a weapon? Who got nervous and stashed some mess that could cause the Chinese police to rip through bags, delay departure, and create a problem?

"Someone in authority will be with you shortly. Please have a seat, and we do apologize for the temporary inconvenience," the man in uniform said, and then bowed slightly, walked out of the inspection room, and closed the door behind him.

Discreet shrugs rippled through the group as they each silently answered the pervasive question. No one was owning up to having stashed something lethal, and Damali could only hope that it wasn't an accidental oversight—like a fifteen-inch Bowie knife, a grenade, or leftover rounds of hallowed earth–packed hollow points.

No one sat, even though seating had been offered. The

customs agent seemed mild mannered enough, calm, courteous, but that was also the way of the Chinese, and didn't mean they were out of possible trouble.

Soon a delegation of military uniformed officers entered the room, along with Monk Lin and two men in civilian clothes. The team bristled and their gazes locked on the officers. Were it not for Monk Lin, they would have immediately asked to be taken to the U.S. Embassy.

"I am General Quai Lou," a man who looked to be in his mid-sixties said, formally addressing the group. "Welcome to China."

Damali returned his slight bow, but kept her gaze on him for a moment before lowering her eyes. Her internal beacon snapped on as she stood up straight, her gaze holding the man with slight gray at his temples and whose form was becoming thick in the middle from age. She turned to Monk Lin and offered him a bow. Instantly she heard his message in her mind. *Do not make these men lose face.*

"General," Damali said in her most courteous voice, "we appreciate the opportunity to travel in your beautiful country."

He nodded, appearing satisfied, but also still seemed somewhat wary. Damali's team didn't breathe. Carlos had not moved a muscle, except to bow slightly. The military guards had not bothered to crease their army green, red-trimmed uniforms by risking motion. They remained erect, eyes forward.

"Your papers are in order," the general said, but kept glancing nervously at Monk Lin. "We hope that your journey will be fruitful."

There was something in his eyes that reminded Damali of fear, but that didn't make sense, unless they had begun to experience the contagion at alarming levels here, too. A simple trip to Tibet by an eclectic group of artists shouldn't have kicked off any particular worry. The Chinese government had hands-down control on the populace, and over the years, Tibetan monks had been slaughtered to the point of near extinction.

Damali glimpsed Marlene. The muscle in Shabazz's jaw was pulsing. Yeah, what was the deal? Over a million people mowed down in the streets of Tibet, hundreds of thousands jailed and sent to labor camps for merely being Buddhist monks. Now a Chinese general was standing in front of her and her team with a Tibetan monk by his side, and *he* had worry in his eyes? Oh, yeah, these boys had seen something over here and her team immediately sensed it as well. All right. Show time. Right from the door.

Monk Lin glanced at the general, and finally received a nod to step forward. "General Quai Lou is from a special division," he said in a quiet, controlled tone, his gaze raking the group. "It seems that his division of the military has growing concerns over past decisions, and would like to solicit your assistance."

The monk's gaze was placid as it continued to focus on the Guardians, but then in an unexpected, mercurial turn, became filled with unspoken rage. The general's eyes blazed with concealed hatred, but his voice remained calm. The juxtaposition was somewhat disorienting. But all members of the U.S. team stood silent and patient, waiting for a sign and not wanting to add more tension to the quiet power struggle that was obviously taking place.

"You are going to Tibet?" the general asked.

"Yes," Damali said slowly, but the question was crazy, because that's what their papers said! They knew, so what was up with that? You didn't just roll into a lockdown country unescorted and without having your itinerary mapped out.

Although her attention was on the general, she kept her peripheral vision on Monk Lin, allowing his eyes to inform her of how to do this dance. Common sense and experience in heavy life and/or death negotiations also informed her moves—nothing was direct. Every move to stall and to draw out the goal, or to take one's time to properly position words, was also cultural and had a reason.

"We are on a pilgrimage," she finally said, not willing to expose her motives until she knew what his were, if then.

"We just want to get some cultural flavor, and take in the sights and sounds from different regions to help progress our music, to make it more world inclusive."

General Quai Lou bowed again and offered the team a pleasant, unreadable smile. "Then you should find some of the old mythology of Tibet quiet flavorful," he said with a smug undertone to his voice as he glanced at Monk Lin. "Although we do not ascribe to such rhetoric, and we have adopted science as our truth in China, I'm sure that as Monk Lin guides your journey, he'll relate this legend to you: The ogress, Sinmo, and the monkey, Avalokiteshvara, were the only creatures living in the high mountains of Tibet at the dawn of time. In her loneliness," he added with an amused smirk, "she sired heirs from this union."

"The general is very aware of this *fact*," Monk Lin said in a brittle tone that was normally not his style. "However, one point of clarification—the monkey was a high deity, not some base creature of the earth, and the deity was seduced by the *du*, a demoness of the rocks, whereupon it fell from its state of grace. Let us be vigilant to tell the traditions with care and accuracy. The monkey, then trapped in its earthly form, made a gift to his offspring—the regional grains, in hopes, we are sure, that they would take to these food choices, and not succumb to the blood thirst of their mother."

Damali stared at the monk for a moment, and then returned a too-pleasant smile to the general. Okay, they had Lilim over here, knew it, and at least a branch of the Chinese army was on to why she and the team were here. But the information he relayed was useful; they needed to know what kind of mess they could confront up in the mountains.

The general smiled, but it was strained as he continued. He spoke in a patronizing tone and glanced at Monk Lin. "This she-devil is said to have sired six offspring from this liaison, and was implacable, causing havoc, until the first king of Tibet's wise second wife, Queen Wengcheng, *of China*," he added with emphasis, "found the geomantic cen-

ter of the region and built a palace on top of this purported
female beast. Thus, Jokhang was constructed. Twelve outly-
ing temples built to hold down the supposedly supine
ogress's thighs, knees, etcetera, in three successive rings of
four temples. You will find the architecture of the region
quite interesting during your stay, we are sure."

Damali held the general's gaze without blinking. Her
mind was rapid-fire processing what her mother had said.
The tears were in a temple. Find the most impressive one,
the greatest one of all. To her thinking, Jokhang was as good
a place to start as any—it had been mentioned, was built to
hold back any drama coming up from a vortex, demon con-
tainment. Yeah . . . all right. She heard the man.

Monk Lin nodded discreetly. "This was done in cooperation with the king's *first* wife, who financed this effort," he
added with care. "She was from *Nepal*," he said with a tight
smile, verbally sparring with the general, "where our esteemed Dalai Lama of modern times fled, when things became tense during the Cultural Revolution in the region. We
have many Sanskrit scrolls that were later translated into the
native language of Tibet about such matters before those trying times."

Monk Lin's serene stare cut Quai Lou and then mellowed
as he glanced from the general back to Damali. "In Princess
Bhrikuti's honor, the main gate is facing west, toward Nepal,
but west is *west*," he said with quiet urgency in his tone. He
looked at the team hard as he paused, transmitting the silent
message that the western hemisphere was a key. "The four
cardinal points are guarded by Four Guardian Kings, and the
Wheel of Rebirth is also there." He held Carlos's gaze for a
moment longer than the others. "You must experience rebirth while here."

"As *legend* has it," the general said in a tight voice, breaking the monk's hold on Carlos's gaze and losing some of his
calm demeanor as he snapped the response.

"What is legend to some is true faith of others," Monk
Lin said in a casual tone. "To offend the holy scrolls by call-

ing their contents legend would be like challenging your biblical texts," he added, but kept his gaze on Damali, as though addressing her and not the general.

The teams' eyes went from Monk Lin to the general.

"We will be sure to be appropriately reverent while in the Tibetan Autonomous Region," Marlene said to break the tension.

"Yes, that would be most wise and most appreciated by those that still *respect* local traditions," Monk Lin said in a flat tone, keeping his eyes on Marlene. "For some believe that when the sacred palace of Jokhang was shelled in recent years and it was literally turned into a pigsty, housing livestock; and when its inner sanctum was filled with blood and animal innards, it could no longer hold the ogress as she'd been imprisoned since the *seventh* century."

An epiphany stabbed into Damali's temple so quickly that she almost visibly winced. *That* was also why the Chairman was here; he was hunting Lilith down as much as they were. Lilith had to be the ogress Monk Lin mentioned, possibly given a different name in this different culture. She wouldn't be so foolish as to go back to the caves near the Red Sea, her original haunt. No, girlfriend would most likely go to a very out-of-the-way location, where she had family—had sired before and wasn't slaughtered. Now, with the new atheist government in full effect, she wouldn't have to worry about humans figuring out how to contain her like they did before.

Damali nodded as she continued to silently watch Monk Lin's tense body language. Up in the mountains, it would be treacherous going and hard for a human hunter team to track her down . . . And knowing Lilith, no doubt girlfriend was also seeking the missing antidote element. Plus, she undoubtedly had more to fear from her husband than the Devil's son, since the attempted coup began with her machinations, and keeping demons topside was her thing— they were her kids; Dante had nothing to gain, really, by keeping her Lilim alive. He was a pure vamp and hated any other breed of dark entity. This was her old turf, so she had to know or sense that the antidote resided here.

"Interesting history," Damali finally said in a noncommittal tone.

With that, Monk Lin bowed again but remained quiet. Damali glanced at the general, who'd retreated behind an iron wall of nonemotion. Okay, the exchange was too deep. They'd all been briefed about the tense political situation over here, and Monk Lin had even been bold enough to allude to the way the Dalai Lama had been forced into exile in India by the Chinese government and how an army had desecrated the holiest of temples, when merely talking politics could land a local Tibetan in prison for twenty years. Now what? How clued in was the general, or was this just Monk Lin's attempt to say what he had to say in concealed terms? If the general didn't know, this was risky; if he did know, it was still risky. Monk Lin gave her a look that didn't invite a scan, and there was no way she'd violate a holy man if he said no. His eyes also seemed to warn for her not to go into the general's head like that, either. Why?

To cloak the discussion in sightseeing and architecture, with a military general present, plus two guys in suits who had not been introduced, gave her the chills—and Lin was quietly telling her to stand down from a scan? Maybe they were infected and it wasn't safe for her mind. As soon as the thought crossed her mind, the monk's eyes told her all: *Don't go into any human brain without knowing if it holds the contagion. The chance of contamination is great, child. Your own mind would then be temporarily compromised, even though you're immune and would purge, but you would lose precious days on the mission.* Damali almost sighed aloud. One of her best tools would have to be shelved over here. Not good. The monk imperceptibly nodded. Damn.

Yet the message about she-devils and sacred numbers and geomantic positions had not been lost on a soul in the room;

neither had the general's obvious concerns. He'd allowed the
monk's flagrant response, had not stopped the monk from
speaking, and didn't so much as bristle when the shelling of
the palace had been mentioned. The fact that the Chinese authorities were even allowing a monk in full crimson Tibetan
robes to be their guide was out of the ordinary. Very, very
weird. The general had to know something; she could feel
his test brewing through her skin.

The mission began to take shape within Damali's mind
between all the seemingly calm surface pleasantries. Monk
Lin's quiet statements had filtered through her heightened
audio-sensing capacity, registering the tension in his voice
through the layers of her extrasensory awareness, confirm-
ing her epiphany: Lilith had spawned here once, just like she
had over in the caves near the Red Sea. Modern-day empire
builders had released her into the world again. Temples had
been desecrated in a land closed off from outside intervention. The ranks of monks, those who would keep prayer
vigil, had been thinned, and innocent human blood, along
with animal sacrifices, had soaked the land, as well as the
holiest of temples, to offer an open portal to whatever had
once been beneath it. If Lilith would come here to breed
once, she might return here to heal . . . and the Chairman
would surely hunt for her essence here in his quest for re-
venge against the one who'd betrayed him most. Oh, yeah,
now it *all* made sense.

Carlos watched the transaction go down from a remote
place in his mind. Power demanded to be used, and instinct
told him that the only reason Monk Lin hadn't been carted
away to a Chinese jail was because he held some type of
power; he had something the general and the two suits with
him wanted or needed. It was time for him to step up and get
into the stalemated negotiations taking place. This was a
male-dominated region, and the general was not about to
give up authority or any information until he had a male in
charge to address. Carlos glanced at Damali. *Yeah, baby, you
know this is what I do best.*

Go for it. I've seen you work, brother.

Her compliment, and the fact that she was cool about the copartnership necessary to achieve the aim of getting more knowledge, made him smile. "We are all looking forward to the opportunity to learn about the rich and varied history of this region," Carlos finally said with caution, but kept his voice eloquent and his countenance humble as he inserted himself into the conversation. "We have often been called the ugly Americans, by right, as we are often too focused on our own culture, and have not learned about others they way we should. Knowledge of others can only broaden our perspective."

The general's more relaxed smile returned. "We appreciate that you have come to China with an opened mind. Our history is long, with many dichotomies. Let us not focus upon our differences, but rather that which unifies us."

Carlos bowed, the team followed suit. The general and his men bowed, as did Monk Lin and the two unidentified men near him. No one spoke. They all seemed to be waiting for some unknown sign to proceed.

Damali glanced at Carlos and suppressed a smile. *This* was the old master of the game she knew, and he wore it well. Her man was kicking more bullshit than the day was long, and she loved watching every minute of the transaction. She was also pretty sure that being a female didn't help in such a male-dominated culture, so she kicked a smooth move of her own, and made it appear that this was actually Carlos's group rather than hers—maybe to some degree it was becoming that. In an odd way, she was all right with the change at the moment. Her own reaction gave her brief pause; she was sharing her command without struggle, something she hadn't done before. Not willingly, anyway.

She shrugged off the new personal epiphany; there wasn't time to explore it now. Later she would consider it. For now she'd focus on whatever worked, just as long as they could get out of this holding cell that was being passed off as an inquiry room.

"General Quai Lou," Damali said as demurely as possible. "Mr. Rivera has wisely chosen this fine country for us to explore, and we are honored that you have allowed his group to tour and learn about the infinite wonders within it. Thank you."

She could not glimpse Marlene, whose eyes had widened, or look at any other member of the team. Their stunned expressions might make her crack a smile, ruin her facade, and ultimately make the general possibly lose face—which would mean they could lose more than just some time and luggage. Losing their freedom and being detained, or possibly worse, kept anything beyond serene, humble submission at bay. It was about playing the politics like poker.

Seeming much improved in temperament, the general motioned for the military men to take the team's luggage. "You will be escorted to Lhasa, and Monk Lin will be your guide from there," he said addressing Carlos. "Do stay with him during your travels, as it is best for foreigners to be properly escorted in areas that have experienced moments of unease."

Carlos bowed again. "We accept your wise advice with full cooperation."

The general bowed, but lingered, dismissing his retinue with quick movements of his hand and did not speak again until the door was completely closed behind them.

New concerns rippled through the group as they waited for the general to make his next move. It was obvious to everyone that potential VIP status of a touring band notwithstanding, most musicians probably never received a military welcome or escort. The question was, what made the Warriors of Light so special?

"Please also allow me to introduce you to professors Dim Huang and Nam Lee," the general said, his smile strained. "In the newness of our exchange, it was a vast oversight. Forgive me."

The team watched as the two seemingly startled men

bowed politely but didn't immediately speak. Damali wasn't buying the general's smooth act. It wasn't an oversight. Clearly he didn't want lower-ranking officers to be in on whatever he'd cooked up or was about to present. She watched Monk Lin nod at them, his gaze warm and supportive, as the first, younger professor moved forward nervously to address the group.

"Your work with *energies* is renowned," Professor Huang said to Carlos, but shared his gaze with Damali to include her. "Our scientists once worked with Dr. Zeitloff," he said with halting words, "and there are others that escaped the unfortunate accidents that befell the advanced team."

"You worked with Zeitloff?" Carlos said, surveying both scientists, and then the general.

Damali shot Carlos a look. Okay, *now* they were getting somewhere.

"Yes," Monk Lin confirmed. "These two are part of a larger organization that the world governments are now aware of."

The older of the two professors stepped forward, bowed gracefully, and spoke in a low, eloquent tone. "Let me be direct," Professor Nam Lee said. "The energies that Dr. Zeitloff's group discovered have been disturbed, just as Monk Lin alluded to earlier." His gaze temporarily captured the monk's before returning to the Guardian team. "We have always known world struggle. We have always endured despotic leaders filled with negative energies and imperialistic desires," he added with a gentle smile as his eyes slid away from the general's hot glare. "All countries have known them during lengthy histories," he then corrected, and waited until the general relaxed. "I am not, of course, speaking of China."

Damali nodded. "Yes, the world had seen its share of this. We understand."

"Good," the general said tensely. "We are not concerned about China, as our leaders are above such corruption, but there are other nations with leaders that possess weak minds."

Carlos nodded. "Yes, and China cannot be impacted by negative energies that may have escaped."

"Mr. Rivera, you understand our position very well," the general said, releasing a long, slow breath. He gave the professors a sidelong glance. "Every nation has nuclear capability. Every nation also has a black market, where weapons of mass destruction can be easily obtained. . . . Human error or human treachery are only averted by people of conscience, no matter how rigorous any nation's checks and balances are."

The general removed his hard-brim cap and dabbed at the building perspiration on his forehead. Damali and Carlos glanced at each other. The team remained motionless behind them as Monk Lin's voice dropped to a near whisper.

"Possession is rampant," Monk Lin said. "Madness abounds. The contagion is happening to humans at every level of society in every country, even here. The professors noticed the dark energies, and continued the work of Dr. Zeitloff after his demise. They tracked down this team through Rabbi Zeitloff in Israel, when the Covenant members met for a very quiet world summit on the issue." Monk Lin paused to allow Damali and Carlos time to absorb the fact that the Covenant had not spilled all the beans to various governments, therefore he was restating the obvious and the team needed to act surprised, accordingly.

Monk Lin continued only after his intense eye contact generated a nod of understanding from the team's leaders. "This is why they had to leave you in Arizona. They'd been called away for the Last Days Summit in Jerusalem. There was a truce, a pact, formed among the world leaders, and the major governments agreed that, in order to keep things from going to the next level, it was in each military's best interest to have these energies sealed away."

"Are you saying you're hiring us to do a world hit on negative energy?" Rider said in a feigned incredulous voice, playing along to further draw necessary information out. "Oh, shit . . ."

The general nodded and didn't bristle from the affront as murmurs rippled through the team. "We have all formed a very quiet coalition and coinvested in the most state-of-the-art weaponry to assist you in your mission. Your accomplishments as demon hunters are now legendary, and the Covenant gave expert testimony that held the presidents and the religious world leaders of many nations rapt as they spoke. You will have worldwide, top-secret clearances while you hunt the darkness, and no local police or media interference in any country. Shortly, our professors will take you into a room and show you the items at your disposal. If you need something that is not present, you have but to tell our top engineers and they will design what you require."

Damali and Carlos stared at each other for a moment, and then at their hang-jawed team. Oh, yeah. This was very bad, if it had come to this.

"You mean to tell us, like some Double-O Seven gadgetry and—"

"Yes, Rider," Monk Lin said with an admonishing glare. "England's best, Germany's best, France's best; the very best from the United States, China, Japan—"

"Every part of the world with nuclear capacity is involved; and many that are troubled by splinter cells and terrorism, such as Eastern Europe, Russia, much of Africa, South America, the Middle East; all are concerned that no one nation should have a lapse in presidential judgment and begin the end of time. Your team was identified as the most effective to these ends." The general removed his cap from beneath his arm and placed it back on his head with crisp precision. "This is not subject to debate. Were you on U.S. soil when the summit concluded, you would have been approached by agents from your own government's Area Fifty-one."

"You all know about Area Fifty-one?" Damali said in disbelief. "The whole alien thing is not—"

"Of course we all know about Area Fifty-one," the general snapped, losing patience. "It is no secret that we all monitor each other's activities. Until recently, until Dr. Zeitloff's work, we thought our only concern was the potential of extraterrestrial species and that fueled space exploration." He began to pace with his hands behind his back. "That is another matter. We are not so concerned about that now."

"Until now," Monk Lin said, his voice as smooth as a silk noose, "many in positions of authority discounted the spiritual dimensions and felt there was only science. Then Jewish scientists like Dr. Zeitloff worked with others and broke the Bible code. They found that the code was mathematic, based on complex algorithms and hard science. Before that, they did not believe other realms and dimensions existed, and did not believe that these unseen realms could have any influence upon life as we know it. It is all numeric, math as the basis of truth, and creates unending fractals that spire in equations that unlock hidden doors—or close them. Many scientists, from Leonardo da Vinci and throughout the ages, have been trying to quantify the mystical, that which mere religious men have always known to be true." He smiled and bowed toward the general. "But they are becoming wiser, now that they have witnessed the unspeakable."

"Sir?" Damali said quietly, needing to know exactly what had manifested over here, and wondering if it had morphed in any way from what they'd seen in the States. "The unspeakable?"

"In a lab," Professor Huang said, his nervous gaze darting between Damali and the general. "One of our top cabinet ministers fell ill. The military thought he'd been poisoned. His family called for the support of monks. Because of his rank—"

"Spirits walked out of the man's chest right before my eyes," the general said in a tense whisper. "Initially we thought it was human foul play that had turned his eyes black and his behavior schizophrenic. Drugs. Poison. Some new biological weapon. That is why he was quarantined to hospitalization in the lab compound, rather than a regular facility with civilians, until we knew what this was."

The general wiped a new sheen of sweat off his brow, his

voice and gaze distant as he spoke. "But we witnessed a dark force exit his body, split his chest open like a can of mackerel! His body died . . . but whatever was in him destroyed his room, shattered windows, and fled. A rain of machine-gun fire didn't stop it. Many men were killed. Only a few of us survived the lab attack. We caught it on surveillance monitors in his highly guarded room. Then we watched his body decay and turn to ash right in front of us. We kept this sensitive information veiled from the media, and have buried the man according to the dignity of his office. But it gave us impetus to agree to join the summit, and our Russian counterparts said they have also seen this type of inexplicable phenomenon. Murmurs are everywhere. We all have presidents and important cabinet ministers being kept under religious vigil. These professors have developed weapons, but . . ."

"Why Tibet?" Carlos said, holding the room for ransom with his simple question. "I know why us, but why this region?" He looked at Monk Lin to offer the most coherent and honest answer in the room.

"Tibet is called the Roof of the World, where Heaven meets earth, and has an interesting history," Monk Lin said in a calm tone. "When Genghis Khan's Mongolian hordes terrorized and conquered all of central Asia, he came to Tibet, note, in the *thirteenth* century to a place founded in the *seventh* century, and stopped at our gates."

Monk Lin looked at everyone in the room with a long, sweeping gaze. "*He stopped.* He could not rape, pillage, burn, or raze Tibet—which had a strong cooperative relationship between the *Bonpo* shamans and Buddhist monks. Rather than continue his rampage, Khan came to an epiphany and formed an agreement between himself, who was known as the Great Khan, the emperor of China, and the monks of Sakya monastery in southwest Tibet." He closed his eyes and bowed in the four cardinal directions to some unseen force, and then continued. "A trinity of alliances."

"The Lamas of Sakya were appointed as spiritual guides even to a man such as Genghis Khan, who clearly understood the use of force, and energies, but who also apparently had the wisdom to not go beyond certain realms without spiritual mediation. The title, Dalai Lama, actually comes from Mongol origins, meaning ocean." Monk Lin smiled at Damali and Carlos. "Oceans bear salt, much like tears," he added with weighted subtlety. "We have already had our experiences with the power of water and the sea. It is time for you to elevate your learning with an old Bonpo master, his title is the Naksong—which means *had been in darkness, what is in shadow,* or forest. The Naksong masters are in touch with the energies of nature; they purify the impure, are herbal healers, but most important, they cure the true roots of evil."

"Carlos said we know why us," Damali said, quietly. "I don't think we do." She looked around the room, her gaze briefly touching each person as she spoke. Something else was going on; it was the way Monk Lin stared at Carlos. "The general clearly has more manpower than we'll ever have." She looked over toward the professors. "These gentlemen have more technology than anything J.L. and Krissy can rig up on their own—no offense guys." Damali ran her hands through her hair. "And a very old Naksong with serious monks flanking him are probably more psychically and spiritually grounded than anybody on our team." She glanced around. "I'm not trying to put down anybody's abilities in our ranks. But hey, let's be real, there's not a monk among us."

"That ain't no lie," Shabazz finally muttered.

Rider pounded his fist. "But we will take you fellas up on the new weaponry. Momma ain't raised no fool."

"It's the bloodlines, isn't it?" Marlene asked in a calm tone. "It's something in the DNA."

Monk Lin nodded and glanced at the two nervous professors and the general.

"We are told that your team has a predominance of people on it that have walked from Asiatic tribes over the Iberian Peninsula and down to North America," Professor Huang said, his eyes filled with hope. "All scientists currently agree that the Native American has roots in Asiatic DNA. Native American DNA is linked to the peoples of Mexico, Central America, and South America. Any U.S.-born African-Americans that share biological lineage links with Native Americans are also able to tap into the energies traditionally taught in the Bonpo belief system."

Jose glanced at his more seasoned teammates. "Me, Juanita, J.L., Carlos, Damali, Mar, Shabazz, all have Native American in us. Maybe Inez, too." He looked at Big Mike. "Yo, man, what about you?"

"Got some Blackfoot and Cherokee in there, my grandma said, not sure how it runs in the family, but it's in there from around plantation days." Big Mike nodded. "That makes at least eight of us from the squad, if Inez don't have it, with two members of the team in the shadow lands, Tara and Yonnie."

"Ten," Damali said flatly, "which mathematically condenses down into one—one team." She nodded. "We got it."

"With three, members, uh . . ." the younger professor said, seeming unsure of how to word his assessment, "that have actually died, at one point. Were in the shadow lands."

"Make it four," Damali said calmly. "I went there for a moment myself. Four is the number of balance, harmony, and represents the four elements of the universe." She smiled when the professors and the general backed up. "But we're all cool now. Those you see here do daylight and don't have the hunger, but we know how hard it can be and how to fight it." She slapped Carlos five. "Guess we just signed on for this mission, huh, bro?" she added, keeping up with the ruse of her and the team being surprised. "Now does Arizona, and being under the protection of the Thunderbird totem for a few, make sense to you?"

Carlos smiled. Yeah, he got it loud and clear, and could have kicked himself for not going with the flow before. He should have known there was always an underlying reason for anything Damali and Marlene concocted.

"Y'all math is off," Carlos said, feeling pride expand his chest as he suddenly, for the first time since Philadelphia, felt truly useful to the team. "Four of us have taken a walk on the dark side or in shadow country, which makes the cardinal points. But don't discount Inez; her people are from South America, and from the south in the States—gotta have some Asiatic strain in her, which is the Native American Indian strain. That brings the total to nine, add the four shadow selves, and we come back to lucky thirteen. Do the math, baby. Add in the Berkfields, Dan, and Rider, we've got them anchoring the four topside, natural elements—earth, air, fire, water; plus two metals—gold and silver, yin and yang energy through Krissy and Bobby, male and female children inseparably linked by blood."

"Sho' you right," Damali said, folding her arms and looking at Carlos with satisfaction and pride. "My bad. Knew you'd figure out why we were here, once we got here. It always works like that." She was so proud of him at the moment that she could have hugged him on the spot, but held back because it just wasn't appropriate. Later.

Carlos's pleased gaze slid away with a sly smile just in time for her to glimpse a slight flicker of silver in his irises, and it did something to her to watch him slowly return to his old self.

Monk Lin bowed toward Damali and then Carlos. "Carlos is correct. The prayer flags you will see on the monasteries will have yellow to represent the earth; green, the water; red for fire; white, for the clouds; and blue for the sky." He smiled at Rider. "And there will be always be a *thangka* of the sacred white yak. No matter that your definition of the elements may slightly vary, your numerology is insightful. All serve a divine purpose."

Carlos bowed toward Damali, and she responded in kind.

"Neteru," Carlos said with a smile. "Lead on, my sister."

"Neteru," Damali said with a smile. "Lead on, my brother."

THE DAMNED

365

"Agreement has been reached. Respect dawns. Let the accord be unbroken." Monk Lin's smile drew to a placid, determined line on his face. "The Naksong works cooperatively with the Lama of the Nyingmapa sect, where I am also from. It is the oldest form of Tibetan Buddhism. I will take you there to this master, where you will learn what you must."

"We will convene in the next room," the general said, motioning for the professors to lead the way. "There, you will be taught how each weapon works, and this will be sent along with your military escort."

Monk Lin looked at the professors and the general, offering them a curious gaze. "Once we debark in Lhasa, your escorts will not be needed, although your support of ammunition will be deeply appreciated. While, the Naksong is old and blind, he will not countenance a military presence while he teaches. He has even forbidden me to give the team their more conventional items until he announces they are ready."

He glanced at Carlos and Damali, clearly referring to Carlos's claw of Heru and Damali's baby Isis without actually mentioning the weapons. When they nodded quietly, Monk Lin bowed, straightened himself, and folded his arms. His stance told all in the room, he would not be moved.

"Monk Lin," the general warned, but there was no longer acid surety in his tone. "Do not be difficult."

"General," Monk Lin said with a cool smile of sudden victory as they all watched the general stand down, "whatever these gentlemen have developed, I am sure will be helpful. But without the teachings of the Naksong, you might as well turn them on yourselves."

CHAPTER SEVENTEEN

It was finally official. Their cover was blown, the Covenant had sanctioned it, and they'd been made by some world scientific organization. No, correction: more than their cover was blown; *her mind was blown.* If the Covenant gave them up like this, the situation was beyond grim.

"D, you don't have to even say it," Carlos muttered as they stepped into an all-white room and stared at row upon row of technology laid out before them.

"Night-vision goggles, standard," Professor Huang said proudly. But his shoulders sagged as the Guardians all glanced at one another, appearing unimpressed.

"Might help in a tight spot," Rider said, folding his arms. "But, in a heavy firefight, they obstruct your peripheral vision, and the added weight on your head keeps you from sensing with whatever you've been gifted with." He glanced at Shabazz and Marlene, who nodded. "Maybe we'll take a couple of those for the newbies who ain't quite up to speed yet." His gaze locked on several large semiautomatic rifles and snub-nosed revolvers that looked like fat, retrofitted Glocks. His smile widened as he studied the hundred-round clips. "I like the peacekeepers, though, gentlemen. Impressive."

Rider tested the weight of the weapons as he continued to inspect them. "Light as a feather, feels good—balanced. Very nice."

Shabazz sauntered over to the table and carefully lifted a thick, short-range bazooka. "Mike, this looks like you, man."

"Be careful with that," Dr. Lee said, removing it from Shabazz's hands and returning it to the table. "Let me clarify the technology," he said, seeming somewhat offended. "The night-vision equipment is not so standard." He walked up to Rider, affixed the lightweight goggles to his face, and simultaneously pressed two buttons on either side of the titanium frames. Immediately the frame sent a blue-white beam around the circumference of Rider's skull, affixing the goggles to his face without a strap.

"Now, tell me what you see," the older professor said with a tone of triumph as he stepped behind Rider.

A wide smile lit Rider's face and then he laughed while the group of Guardians curiously watched him. "Hot damn! I can see behind me, guys. I've got vamp three-sixty, and the goggles feel light as a feather."

"Correct," Dr. Huang said, pointing to elements on the equipment like a male Vanna White. "They are held to your body by electromagnetic energy fields that the human body emits; and through microfilaments, images are quickly downloaded and sent to the front of the goggles in the bottom part of the lens through a laser pulse, to show you what's behind your head. We've blended special lightweight alloys on all the equipment for easy travel, quick-draw ability, and so that the shooter doesn't use unnecessary energy hoisting his or her weapon repeatedly during a battle."

The professor then handed Damali a silver stake. "Put these in the special hip holster we've created. They are silver stakes with a coating of sea-salt crystals and packed with the same element."

Damali held the silver stake up to the light, watching the crystalline surface shimmer. "Whoa . . . If I'd had these when that demon rushed my house, he would have been splatter. Very cool."

Dr. Lee lifted a gun from the table. "Each trigger can be smart-mapped to know its owner or the entire team's fingerprints, should you have to throw a weapon to a comrade—

but if an aggressor should catch your gun in the air, it will not fire, but will instead backfire, sending the shell into the chest of the wrongful shooter."

"Oh, that is mad-crazy," Bobby said, laughing.

"Invaluable in total darkness, these goggles also pick up cold body images and high-pitched sonar transmissions." Dr. Huang flipped down two small stem wires from either side of the silver-hued frames and adjusted them to rest behind Rider's ears. He crossed the room and whispered to Dr. Lee and then looked up. "Please tell me what I said to Dr. Lee, sir."

"You told him that you wanted a glass of water." Rider glanced over to Big Mike. "Brother, is that what it's like, your gift? You can just eavesdrop like that? Shit."

Mike laughed. "I mind my business, and don't speak on everything I hear, though."

"You should be able to hear anything approaching from behind before it materializes," Dr. Lee said. "It must move against the air, or the ground, and disturb natural matter to attack, even if invisible. To keep you from going deaf by a loud blast, the goggles filter out spike distortions. They are designed to shut down any sound above the frequency where normal human hearing can safely detect it. This way, if ammunition rounds go off near you or an entity screeches your eardrums will not explode."

Rider nodded and took off the goggles, thoroughly impressed, but now seeming a little wary of them.

"The best minds in the world have been working on this equipment," the general said, vindicated. "Nothing in here is standard." He smiled and lifted his chin. "The goggles were developed in China, in coordination with Russia. But I must defer to what Japan has brought to the table." He stood back and motioned to a large metal case at the end of the equipment row.

Dr. Huang went to the case and flipped it back, allowing his hands to gently caress the red-velvet interior. Both Damali and Carlos whispered a unified "Wow." The others gathered around the table, murmurs of approval ricocheting through the room. Shabazz tilted his head and allowed his hand to hover just above the intricate gold-inlaid carvings along the slightly bowed, gleaming ebony-hued scabbard.

"Samurai," Shabazz said quietly. "This is a real Sleeping Beauty."

"Indeed," the general replied, motioning for a demonstration.

"When we learned that the Isis long blade had gone missing," Dr. Lee said, "our counterparts in Japan were very concerned. Thus they retrofitted one of their most sacred ancient swords from the dynasties of old," he added, lifting the relic.

Dr. Lee carefully unsheathed the long polished steel blade as Dr. Huang dropped a sheet of paper. With a ringing whoosh, the paper sliced into two clean sections and floated to the floor.

"Damn . . ." Carlos murmured. He looked at Damali. "Baby, that is *all you.*"

The professors smiled. Dr. Lee held the blade out to Damali upon flat palms, bowing slightly as he offered it to her.

"Thank you," she said, bowing and accepting it. She gripped the handle and took a fighter's stance. Warmth and familiarity coated her insides. Emotion caught in her throat as the team backed up and allowed her to test the blade with varying degrees of hard swings and short pivots. She closed her eyes and listened to the blade create music with the air. "Oh, God, it feels so good to have one of these on me again," she murmured as she swung with her eyes closed and then tossed the blade to her left hand, caught it, and held it with both palms, firmly gripping it over her head. "Oh, yeah, this is it."

Carlos watched her, immobilized by her raw beauty. The sight of Damali working out with her blade tugged at his libido. She had always been poetry in motion, but there was something about watching girlfriend work with her long blade.

"May I show you some of the special features of this weapon?" Dr. Huang asked with an undercurrent of excitement in his tone. He stepped forward once Damali became still and opened her eyes, and pointed to the ruby-jeweled eyes of two dueling dragons on the sword's handle. "Press here," he said, "and watch."

Instantly a blue-white light arced down the cutting edge of the sword and rimmed it in an eerie glow.

"UV laser," Dr. Lee said. "While you are an excellent swordsman, Ms. Richards, this Samurai relic is still not as lethal against dark entities as the legendary Isis. Therefore, the Japanese team enhanced it to cut on both the blade side and the dull side, using silver refracted ultraviolet light coaxed along the edge with electromagnetic points."

Damali touched the ruby dragon eyes, and the light disappeared. "Oh, this is *too* cool."

Dr. Huang walked around the table, displaying a series of jagged-edged Bowie knives, small daggers that could be retrofitted for boot or sleeve extraction, and demonstrated how each had the same light-rimming technology that Damali's new sword did. He motioned toward larger blades, showing the team everything from battle-axes to broadswords. "Old-fashioned, but if you are in hand-to-hand combat, a simple stab with a regular blade will not give you much time to react. However, with this improvement, no matter where you cut, the attacking entity should either burn or be wounded enough to give you time to escape."

Carlos nodded and picked up a jagged-edged Bowie. "This is sweet," he said, almost talking to himself. "A nick from one of these, without the enhancement, is just a love bite." He winked at Jose. "But with a little somethin' somethin' on it . . ."

"Right," Jose said with a smile, and caught the blade Carlos tossed.

"Here are small handheld, cold-body-tracking units," Dr. Huang said, picking up small monitors with tiny screens the size of flip-case cell phones. "These can fit on your waistbands, and can be set to quiet vibrate or sound alarm when an entity is present. These are also useful two-way communications devices to keep you linked to your team. Unfortunately, in extreme temperatures, the technology experiences glitches. We've tried to modify them slightly to be as resistant to the elements as possible, with small warming strips on the back that can be peeled away. However, after a while, this affects the unit and renders it unstable."

"For urban transport, we have modified Jeep and Humvee vehicles that you can inspect later, as well as motorcycles."

"Aw, man," Jose said slapping five with Rider. "Tell me you've got a crotch rocket for a brother!"

Dr. Huang nodded with a sly smile. "All motorcycles and vehicles have supercharged turbo engines and have been mounted with cold-body scanners, artillery, colloidal silver exhaust-expulsion systems—in case you are being chased—along with three-hundred-and-sixty-degree front-window panel-imaging systems, satellite-mapping systems, chassis and hood sensors on the cars, and have been coated with a special silver alloy to make gripping the exterior difficult for an entity attacker. The driving, however, still requires expert human skill."

"Unfortunately," Monk Lin said, calmly, "some of the regions we will be traveling to will be passable only by yak and horseback."

"True," Rider said, unfazed. "But with some of the serious ammo these guys just unveiled, this will be like the wild, Wild West days, and I couldn't care if I was on the back of a damned donkey. One of those equalizers in the holster makes it not so necessary to have a fast getaway car. Feel me?"

Shabazz nodded and pounded Rider's fist. "My old girl, Sleeping Beauty, is gonna be jealous when I put one of these next to her on my hip."

The team laughed and fanned out around the table, going toward the weaponry that most fit their personal styles and skills.

"Can we get to the part about the shit that blows up?" Big

Mike said with a wide grin, peering at the table as though it had forbidden sweet potato pies cooling on it.

"Ah . . . explosives," Dr. Lee said, gingerly lifting silver-hued cylindrical objects and setting them down slowly. "Silver and hallowed-earth shrapnel delivery systems within the grenades. We call this one the double helix," he said with pride, lifting a small, pyramid-shaped silver unit that fit in the palm of his hand. "It can either screw onto the tip of a larger shell, like a warhead, and be launched from the hand-held bazookas, or, when hand-tossed, the outer skin flips down to radiate the area with UV light to temporarily blind the attackers and to begin their burn process. While the enemy is disoriented for a few seconds and you take cover, it then detonates with the silver and earth shrapnel."

The professor then walked over to a section that had what appeared to be small, handheld spray units of mace. "This is a lethal projectile with sacred oil, garlic, Holy water, and battery acid—just in case you're dealing with human helpers or contagion victims. If it's an entity, the other elements will stop it, but if it's a human abducting you . . . Need I say more?"

"That's some wicked shit," Berkfield said, picking up a modified mace unit. "Make sure my wife and daughter definitely have one of these."

"And perhaps these also," Dr. Lee said, selecting what appeared to be a thick silver cuff bracelet with intricate Tibetan designs from the table and offering it to Marjorie.

"This is beautiful," she said in awe, turning the fine jewelry around on her wrist and gently fondling the raised snow lions with topaz stone eyes on it with one finger. She pushed at the little creature and let out a small squeal of delight when it shifted on the band and became warm, then held out her arm and let out another squeal as her body became bathed in blue light. "Ooooh! Look! This is wild!"

"The bracelet lights the aura energy field around your body, saturating it with ultraviolet light. If anything is at your throat, or attempting to hold you to deliver a bite any-where else, it must come through that light path as though through body armor." Dr. Lee folded his arms and nodded toward the table. "We have versions of this that adequately pass for male jewelry as well."

"All the guns presented have been retrofitted with cold-body sensors, just like the goggles," Dr. Huang said, his tone becoming more excited as he circled the table. "Just point the blue light and fire, and the shell emitted will fol-low the trail of a fleeing entity, even around a bend or zigzag retreat, until it meets its target. We have used the same technology within a chip on each shell, borrowed from the technology of heat-seeking missiles. But, as with all things, there is a caution. It will go to the surface of any-thing reading colder than the entity it was aimed toward—so be careful using these in the mountains, where the temperatures of rock and ice formations could provide a shield to an attacker."

"Yes," Marlene said, folding her arms, "and where an av-alanche could be kicked off from the blast from any of this heavy artillery."

"Wise observation," Monk Lin said coolly. "This is why the Naksong will teach you how to fight without some of these new toys." He lifted his chin. "In an urban environ-ment, yes. Some of the equipment presented has usefulness. However, let me remind you that in the final hours, if you are stripped of weapons and must battle through night blindness, you must utilize the foundations of your unique skills."

"Sho' you right," Carlos said, his tone reverent. "But, along the way, let us show a spirit of compromise, Monk Lin." He smiled as Monk Lin cut him a glare. "It's cool, man. We hear you. But, in the art of war, it's always better to be overprepared."

This time there was no waiting and endlessly shuffling through slow, snaking lines. The team boarded the private charter, their biggest concern being that, if there was turbulence, with all the ammo packed in the cargo bay, they were what amounted to a flying bomb.

"You know," Damali whispered to Carlos, "since they've loaded us down like this, and have given us all this VIP treatment, don't ya think they seem a little . . . uh—"

"Over the top?"

Carlos smiled, but she could tell it was strained.

"We weren't strapped like this in Brazil or Australia, and I don't necessarily like being a gun for hire by multiple governments. It was better when we were doing this undercover and on the down-low."

Carlos nodded and kept his comments stated in quiet even tones as he watched the military retinue. "I hear you," he said. "These boys need to stay on the plane, or else any locals that have a problem with the Chinese government ain't gonna be feeling us either, when we touch down."

Damali nodded. "Time for détente," she said with a wink.

"We pull Neteru rank, and tell them we've got a vibe, and their energy will distract the target."

Carlos nodded. "I think we're back in sync, baby."

She nodded but sent her gaze out the window. If he remembered that they were out of sync, she wondered, what else was coming back to him as they neared their destination? "We'll let the angels work this one out," she whispered, watching the bright blue sky.

Carlos sat very still. The angels? He rubbed his hands over his face, trying to remember something that was in his skull. He could feel it trying to push its way out, but it kept getting stuck somewhere.

"It is a shame we are headed south," Monk Lin said with a sigh, glancing at Carlos and Damali. "If we had approached from Kathmandu or Nepal, the sight of the Himalayas is majestic."

Carlos held the monk's gaze. The word *Himalayas* was setting off all sorts of warning bells within him. "Can you ask the pilot to circle them?"

Monk Lin stared at Carlos. "Yes. But why?"

Carlos again wiped his palms down his face. Damali was staring, as was everyone else. "I don't know," he said, suddenly becoming frustrated. "I just want an aerial view of the region."

Monk Lin stood slowly, and walked forward, and then whispered to one of the seated officers. Damali watched him convey the request from a distant place in her mind.

"Baby, what is it?" She touched Carlos's arm, but his gaze was fixated to an unseen point beyond the window. She prayed he hadn't been able to go into her mind to capture the secret her mother told her not to divulge.

Carlos shook his head as the plane slowly turned and increased in altitude.

"I'm not trying to be funny," Rider said in a tense voice, "but you know I'm not up for any midair theatrics over mountain ranges. Been there."

"Yeah, man," Shabazz agreed. "Listen, people lost up on Everest in plane crashes, and shit, have had to eat dead passengers just to survive. Let's not go there on no cannibalism tip because this plane hits a bad current or some force smokes our asses in the air. Let's stick to the itinerary."

Marjorie squeezed Berkfield's hand tighter, and nervous energy permeated the plane's cabin as individuals linked up with the persons closest to them.

"Then, y'all need to pray, I guess," Marlene said calmly. "Because if one of our Neterus gets a vibe, we follow it."

While Marlene's comment had stilled any open mutiny, it didn't stop the jitters that everyone felt inside.

Damali tried to share her observation of Carlos's mood with the gorgeous scene unfolding beneath them, while also fighting the temptation to jump out of her skin. She didn't like the detour any more than the rest of the group did, but her gut also told her that this was something he needed to see. Maybe, from some innate place within, this was also part of his quest to find himself, she reasoned, and then tried to relax.

Yet as she peered down she was immediately convinced that this sight was also something she needed to see. It was

as though the heavens were playing with watercolors from
the sky. The angels had poured down liquid hue to splash the
ground. Jewel-green patches loomed beneath them, and then
the landscape became spotted with gorgeous smears of burnt
yellow grasses and barren red-rock plains. The Brahmaputra
River flowed with four other rivers into the mythical
Ganges; then it edged the mountains and towns—indigo pip-
ing toward majestic places where earth had folded upon itself to issue formations of land that jutted up—until they
turned brilliant blue, reflecting white layers of pinkish
cotton-candy sky. Thick white mist buffeted the plane and
opened to spectacular peaks before the plane turned again
and began a descent toward Lhasa.

Oh, yes, this was the Roof of the World, and like many
sights before, she was glad that Carlos's impromptu detour
had led her to witness it. She squeezed his hand and murmured a quiet thank-you. He didn't hear her, but squeezed
her hand back, seeming spellbound.

The collective sigh of relief was released by the team in
loud, ornery puffs of breath, as Guardians folded their arms,
made signs of the cross over their chests, and generally
balked at having their nerves rattled this close to touchdown.
But Damali didn't say a word as she watched the hair stand
up on Carlos's arms. She'd felt the divine, too. The team
simply needed to chill.

As soon as he saw the mountains, a link chain on his
memory had opened. Initially, it revealed only one sketchy
portion of a message; the Himalayas. Slowly, bit by bit,
snatches of knowing returned to take up residence in his
soul. The angels knew that the Chairman would be here. It
all made so much sense, especially with the weaponry that
had been given to them. Armies around the world knew that
something worse than they'd ever encountered was here—
somewhere; humankind was gearing up for war.

The imperative was clear, bring them the head. Not a
problem, on his list of things to do before he died, just like

turning Lilith to pure ash was on his must-see itinerary. But
there was something else . . . something important, something profound teasing the edges of his mind as he stared
out the window and held fast to Damali's hand. When they
were alone, he'd talk to her and maybe she could coax it out
of his brain.

It took a bit of finesse, but they were finally able to convince
the officers to call their general and then to stay on the plane.
The team took only what they needed immediately. Goggles
and bracelets that could be easily stashed in the long duffels
went with them. Small firearms, grenades, tracking devices,
silver stakes, the sword like Marlene's walking stick, anything that could fit into a suitcase or be carried openly without causing alarm also got dragged along. The only thing
they did lean on heavily was their newly acquired VIP status,
and they left the drama of having to check out on the ground
and pass clearances and metal detectors to average civilians.

   A large minivan was waiting to collect them, and the
team gladly climbed into it, happy, once again, to be on solid
ground. But the altitude weighed on their chests like anvils,
and Monk Lin advised nonalcoholic drinks, plenty of water,
and a moderate pace.

   "Once we check into the apartments that have been made
available to you near the Barkhor, we will have lunch at this
plaza, and you can orient yourselves to the only place in Tibet
not currently overrun by Chinese immigrants. The Barkhor is
the intermediary circumambulation around the Jokhang—it
is the heart of Lhasa. Here we will fetch trekking supplies
and mountain-climbing gear, then drop our supplies off in
the nearby apartments, and return to tour Jokhang." He
smiled as he stood and faced the team. "Everything here is
done with patience and your bodies must adjust to the new
environment before we go deeper into the mountains."

   There was no argument as they watched the collision of
cultures pass them by through the smudged minivan win-

dows while it bumped along the road from the airport to the center of Lhasa. She wasn't sure what she expected to see, but this rural land still had everything from what appeared to be smugglers to street vendors, brothels to monasteries. All were competing for existence in a city that had glittering chrome high-rise modernity on one corner, and, on the next, small, hand-built stone structures with inward leaning walls and pagoda-style rooves with dragons and prayer flags whipping in the wind.

Yak-drawn wagons begrudgingly moved aside for diesel-smoking vehicles. Small donkeys swatted their tails, annoyed at young boys and old men that whacked their behinds with sticks to make them continue walking. Women wore thick, multistriped shawls and colorful woolen skirts beneath long-haired sheep shearling jackets with yak-hair hats jauntily cocked on their heads. They also wore their long black braids covered in bright strands of wool string, adding carved bone, animal horn, amber, and coral ornaments into their intricate hair designs. The men had on wildly varying combinations of thick hide jackets and thick woolen pants, to U.S.-inspired jeans with yak caps turned around backward, reminiscent of the Kangols from 'round the way done Tibetan style. They even sported gold teeth and had felt derby hats. Some dressed to the nines in elaborate, brocade *chupa* robes and billowing tucked pantaloon silks, edged in tiger and snow-leopard hides.

Turquoise and silver were everywhere and glinted off reddened cheeks. The city was a veritable rabbit warren of streets in a maze that could make one dizzy, altitude notwithstanding. Whitewashed brick and gold-painted rooves glinted under the sun next to shell-destroyed buildings, and those simply fallen into disrepair. Streets that seemed to go straight up in the sky rivaled San Francisco's Lombard Street, and the steps up made one wonder as elderly people casually walked uphill without stopping to catch a breath.

"The people," Damali whispered, placing her hand on the window. "They look Navajo, or like . . ."

"Any U.S. tribe I've ever seen," Jose said, gaping from

the window. "The cloths are so similar, like that lady's blanket," he murmured, trying not to point.

"I see Mexico City," Carlos said, his tone quiet and reverent. "Guatemala, Peru . . ."

"This is why we go to the Barkhor, first," Monk Lin said, pleasure threading through his voice. "You had to see and be reminded how the fabric of the world is one."

By the time they'd quickly unloaded and returned to the Barkhor, the entire team was moving slowly. Aches and pains from oxygen-deprived cells made them wince as though they had arthritis.

"The people here have more red blood cells than you and have evolved, physically, to cope with the elements," Monk Lin said as he led them into the teeming, open-air mall.

Carlos slowed to let the others pass them and placed his hand on Damali's shoulder. "That's why this is good feeding ground," he said quietly in her ear. "It's isolated. Communications are slim, despite the towers sending news and music into the streets. Cell phones are relatively new, and I bet in the winter, even satellite transmissions are shaky. This place is perfect if you needed to hide, eat well, and heal."

She reached up and touched his face with the tips of her fingers, feeling his warmth seep into them as she only nodded and kept walking. Something beyond the altitude was making her chest tight. The fragrances from the square slammed against her senses: incense and raw meat for sale, pungent spices. Sounds and colors clattered against each other: monks sitting on the ground saying mantras before alms bowls; crimson robes creating neon signs. Blue mountains turned brass by the sun, brushed in gold dust near the dragon-covered rooftops, where the wind whipped prayer flags into flickers of color.

Concealed but noticeable government eyes were everywhere. Controlled mayhem was in full effect. Pilgrims waited in long lines to get into the Jokhang Temple. Some worshipers simply laid flat on the ground, performing devo-

tion prostration. Images of their apartments swirled in her
mind—stairs, small, narrow halls within white-painted
stone, old monastic quarters . . . Damali jerked her head up
before she nearly passed out. *Damn, Carlos smelled so good.*

"This is why we stop and have *momo,* steamed dumplings
filled with vegetables, *then-thuk,* noodles; *dresi,* sweet rice;
soja, butter tea, and *chu,* cheesecake, before we press on,"
Monk Lin said, catching Damali's elbow.

It seemed as though, no matter how crowded the establishments, everywhere they went, all Monk Lin had to do was go
into the back, speak quietly with the owners, and accommo-
dations were quickly made. Today, that was a very good
thing, because her entire team looked ill—well, everyone did
except Carlos. His senses seemed to be on full alert, his gaze
roving, and his color good, whereas everyone else was soaked
with perspiration from the minor exertion, looked gray and
washed out, and their senses were anything but keen.

Yet, as they listened to Monk Lin describe the balance of
the day's itinerary, the warmth that Carlos's body exuded
next to hers was distracting to the point of the ridiculous.
Everyone was laboring to breathe; she was laboring not to.
Every now and then a whiff of his chemistry made her stomach do flip-flops, which ignited a very untimely inner burn.

"As with all things, timing is everything," Monk Lin said.

Damali almost dropped her tea as she picked up on the
last strands of his conversation.

"Buddha's Enlightenment Day is celebrated here, at this
time of year, and we believe your timing in Tibet is auspi-
cious for success."

Damali smiled weakly and set down her cup of tea. Close
call. She had to return her focus to the mission. The high altitude was obviously causing her brain cells to freeze.

CHAPTER EIGHTEEN

A crush of humanity made up of pilgrims and tourists created a cacophony of voices in different dialects as the team waited to enter the Jokhang Temple. This was the only place where they'd been denied preferential status, as the monks who kept the lines orderly seemed to feel that waiting was part of the enlightenment process. But as they waited, the team shared the same concern: In a place like this, and how many others in the world, how did one not touch another living soul? The spread of contagion by touch was imminent. Fighting it on an individual basis was futile. They had to get to the root source, not go about some insane, government-inspired extermination and quarantine strategy. They needed the antidote. The portals had to be sealed.

During the wait to access the most illustrious temple in the region, the open air allowed the team to recover partially and digest their leisurely consumed meal. Perhaps there was some wisdom in the monks' approach. Damali looked down at the polished stones beneath her boots, awed that millions of feet and prostrated bodies performing the sacred act of *chak* devotion—flattening one's entire body on the earth one-hundred and eight times as a rosary bead was pushed and a mantra spoken—had made the stones gleam. There was something to be said for the crush of humanity and the fierceness of spiritual devotion. That, too, was not to be discounted here.

Spirit of the divine most assuredly presided in this sacred place. How anyone could be bold enough to shell this temple and to fill it with desecration would be akin to razing the Vatican. Real bad karma. Enough, also, to make the angels weep. Just thinking about such unholy abuse made her shudder as they neared the courtyard entrance flanked by two willow trees and also hosting a third one that was planted and still living from the time the temple had been built. Another trinity. Trees, perhaps representing what had been in the original Garden. As they passed, she assessed all this like a detective.

Damali looked at the stump planted by Queen Wengcheng that had taken a mortar shell but survived. It told her much about the spirit of the people that still lived here. Tough, but also very beautiful. She clung to that for hope.

Awed as they entered the six-columned portico, it suddenly dawned on her that a woman built this. Yes, a woman knew where to construct this palace. A woman had hooked it up spiritually, architecturally, and the first wife had paid for all this—back in a time when women were treated like less than dirt. Oh, yeah, girlfriend had to be onto Lilith's shenanigans, and men had respected that. Hmmm . . . Okay, dual energy was in full effect, male and female cooperation. Damali took note.

As more awareness came to her, Damali put both hands on her hips and smiled. "Bet a lot of Egypt has some untold designers and architects, too," she whispered, receiving a knowing smile from Marlene. Now she could move forward. A huge part of the worry about where she and Marlene had ultimately decided to locate the team vanished. It was in their DNA, the ability to home to a safe spot to put down roots, no matter how temporary.

"It is in the Aya," Monk Lin murmured, coming near her. "In the bones, we say."

The construction also gave Damali ideas as they walked through the main gate, the Zhung-go, a structure outfitted with a finely carved door and murals of the future Buddha on the left and the past Buddha on the right; soon she became very aware that this part of the stop was primarily for her benefit. Wrathful deities painted in bright hues to protect the hallowed Entrance Hall looked at them with unmoving, fierce eyes. She could tell that the male members of the team were interested, but looking around somewhat detached, while the females in her group were rapt. Jokhang's series of walled spaces were set up like a giant maze.

Guides pointed out that the Inner Jokhang had three stories forming a great square around a huge hall known as Kyilkhor Thil. The inner roundabout was called the Nangkhor, which was to be walked clockwise for enlightenment as prayer wheels were spun. But the Outer Jokhang, referred to as the western extension, housed lesser chapels, kitchens, storerooms, and residences. Detailed murals covered every wall, and on the northern side was once one of the residences of the Dalai Lamas.

Okay, she got it. The new compound design was locked into her brain and Monk Lin smiled briefly, bowed, and ushered them through the balance of the tour with haste. She'd never seen him brimming with such excitement, and it was as though he'd also shared her discovery.

"Monk Lin, we've come a very long way to get a floor plan," Damali said, teasing him in a discreet whisper.

"It is also a battle tactic, what you keep within layers of flanking—circles within circles. It is a map."

The two nodded as they scanned the team. Carlos remained unusually quiet.

"This didn't do it for him," Damali whispered.

Monk Lin only nodded. "Perhaps the Potala will."

"What we need isn't here," she said, quietly disappointed. "But this is the greatest temple of them all."

"I am aware that what we seek on the surface is not here, but this may not be the greatest temple," Monk Lin said slyly. "Ask the Naksong."

He was exhausted and tired of sightseeing. He wanted to get the show on the road. This was not why he came here, not part of the mission. He hated all this vibration drama—why couldn't Monk Lin just point him in the right direction, tell him straight no-chaser where the battle was to kick off, and then they could develop a strategy. Carlos shoved his hands into his pockets and followed Damali and Monk Lin. This was ridiculous.

Another long, slow ride across town set his teeth on edge. Every male on the team had the same reaction. They were all beyond words and kept their gazes out the minivan window, surveying rooftops, alleys, looking at where a predator could exit after dark, and plotting escape routes.

What the females on the team obviously saw as rich history, great places to hunt for bargains and culture, they saw as ambush territory and danger. When was Damali just going to accept that men and women saw the world from two very distinct points of view?

But as they pulled up to the impressive thirteen-story, massive structure bearing what seemed to be a thousand steps built into the side of a mountain, even he was forced to nod with sudden appreciation.

Rising out of the mountainside was a monolithic building of red brick that towered over a lower section of white expansion as though the red encircled the white. Oh, yeah, now a structure like this made sense. Steeply sloping stone stairs gave access to or escape to the layer upon layer of building levels. *This* was a cliff-side fortress, what he'd been trying to tell D.

"One thousand rooms," Monk Lin said. "The White Palace was the seat of the government and the winter residence of the Dalai Lama. The Red Palace was the spiritual center, which houses many smaller chapels . . . often only a human skull or thighbone remains present. Thousands of butter lamps were lit here. This is where we will also find the golden *chorten,* eight in all, containing the ashes of past Dalai Lamas V, and then VII–XIII."

"Wait," Carlos said as the exited the van into Zhol Square. "You have the ashes for the fifth Dalai Lama, plus Lamas seven through thirteen—but what happened to the guy who was number six?"

Monk Lin simply smiled and waved the group forward, his red robes billowing in the wind as they crossed the massive, white stone square that led to a jewel green field of grass that again broke to accommodate what seemed to be a thousand hand-laid stones a city block long in radius. "Between the Red and White Palaces, valuable *thangkas,* huge murals on fabric, were kept in the yellow Thangkas Room—a building off on its own, but containing majesty."

Okay, so the monk was back to riddles and didn't answer him.

"Yes I have," Monk Lin said with a twinkle in his eyes. "You just didn't hear me."

Groans of discontent filtered through their slow-moving team as they climbed the steps. Berkfield was complaining of chest pain. Rider was fussing about not being able to breathe. Mike seemed like he was about to pass out from the exertion. Shabazz was sweating so hard that everything he wore was wet. Bobby had bent over to puke, but simply dry-heaved. Dan and J.L. had stopped with Jose to assist Marjorie, Juanita, and Inez, but wound up getting helped up the steps instead. Marlene stopped every few feet and leaned on her stick. Damali kept her eyes forward like an eagle with something in her sight line.

Yeah, he felt it, too. Something was here. Carlos glanced at Monk Lin and Damali every so often as they passed exquisite red lacquered doors and entered a world that seemed like it went back in time.

Lush gardens manicured to perfection to appear naturally occurring but beyond naturally neat separated buildings within buildings. Red was everywhere, and the color tugged at his distant memory . . . the color offered power, was erotic . . . blood. Gold dust, gold leaf, thrones . . . thrones . . . What was the deal with thrones? Dragons and thrones; doors, three times the height of a man; golden knockers with dragonheads.

When they reached the top floor, Monk Lin placed his hand over Carlos's chest. "Breathe deeply and slowly," he said quietly. "We are about to enter the Room of Eternal Life, where the Dalai Lamas studied spiritual scriptures."

Carlos nodded, yet wasn't sure why. But as he entered the room, crests and seals covered a wall of books. He closed his eyes. Books . . . there was a book. A throne and a book, a book and a throne. He opened his eyes quickly. "What's in the cellars?"

The team drew near.

"The Cave of Scorpions . . . justice, in those times, was meted out harshly," Monk Lin explained calmly.

"They had a cave where they shackled prisoners to a wall and let scorpions sting them to death? Shit," Rider whispered and looked around. "I suppose the old cultures didn't mess around if you didn't pay your taxes."

Again, Carlos closed his eyes. He could see it. Had been there—shackled to a wall, thousands of pests coming out of a cavern, covering the floor, scrambling over his body in the Chairman's Chamber. "I need air," he said, and began walking.

The red was too much, the gold was too much, the dragons were too much, the huge palace felt like a giant box around him—he had to get outside and into the sun. He could hear the others behind him, half walking, half running, bumping past other tourists and pilgrims trying to keep up with him. Damali's footfalls rang out from the group's. He had to get out of this place. Something horrible had happened. He'd been somewhere—thrones—where?

Sunlight poured over him, but he kept going. His brisk pace went to a jog, and then a flat-out run. His footfalls landed on a small footbridge toward an island in the center of one of the gardens. A wide, white building with a golden roof was before him, but sudden peace stopped his dash and he stood before the scalloped terrace and again closed his eyes.

"You have found the oasis of peace just outside the Potala," Monk Lin said in a mercifully quiet tone. "It was built by the sixth Dalai Lama as his personal retreat. The Lukhang is a temple dedicated to the king of the Naga, water spirits."

"The sixth Dalai Lama?" Carlos said, still panting from the run. He didn't express it to the monk, but the place had sexual energy flowing off it like crazy. Water was definitely his thing, and if it was dedicated to water spirits, hey . . .

Monk Lin offered him a droll smile and turned his back to Carlos, holding up his hand for the others in their team not to approach yet. He waited until the group stopped jogging toward them, but stood back, seeming a bit confused.

"Dalai Lama VI was the only Lama to refuse to take the vows of celibacy, but he was an effective ruler, nonetheless." Monk Lin kept his back to Carlos. "One can understand why his ashes were, shall we say, not venerated with the others. . . . This was his pleasure palace, built behind the Potala, much to the chagrin of the monastic orders of the day."

Monk Lin allowed a smile as he turned and saw Carlos's stunned expression. He dropped his voice to an even quieter murmur. "He and his mistress ruled here. He was an artist. I believe a musician. She was a battle strategist and very good with governmental concepts. Together, they accomplished much." Monk Lin covered his mouth for a moment with two fingers, recovered from a suppressed chuckle, and let his breath out slowly. "Your condition is not unique, nor is your pairing with the female Neteru. Your pairing is the reverse of the couple that built this place, gain insight from that. Do not remain at odds with each other." He looked away as another quiet smile accosted him. "This was a sacred place . . . but, uh, our Dalai Lama couldn't keep his hands off her. The orders turned a blind eye."

Carlos folded his arms over his chest, looked away, and laughed. "Yeah, I gathered that. The joint has a serious charge to it."

The Monk glanced at him briefly and turned away again, badly concealing a smile. "My suggestion is that you take a few cleansing breaths, assess what this experience has taught you before we return to the group." The monk offered him a discreet smirk as he glanced down and then sent his gaze toward the blooming trees. "You might need to take a walk to the other side as we tour . . . to save face."

Much improved by the time the group returned to the minivan, Carlos sat in one of the opened sides staring at the ground. He could hear the team talking and laughing, Damali's voice always distinct in his mind above the others. Yet the experience within the Potala had been profound. Something had literally chased him out of the structure. But it wasn't something external, it was something internal. He dug his fingernails into his scalp as he sat, waited, listened to the group get closer and closer. Something was inside his head and couldn't get out. The Potala had images he remembered, but couldn't place, just like sensations rising off the Lukhang had practically knocked his head back.

It had been so strong, just the vibration energy of that location. He'd wanted Damali like he hadn't since . . . Carlos looked up. Since when? He stood up quickly and almost banged his head on the frame of the minivan. He watched Damali laughing and talking as the team approached. Since when, dammit? When was the last time he'd felt a sizzle, much less a jolt? Oh, shit, oh shit, oh shit, what was wrong with him? An ancient building could give him wood and his woman couldn't?

Carlos walked around the van and jumped in next to the driver, panic stricken.

"Okay," Damali said. "I don't know about y'all, but I'm beat and hungry again, and just wanna lie down."

"I second the motion!" Rider shouted over the seat. "And a beer wouldn't hurt."

"For real," Big Mike hollered from the back.

Chaos was in full effect.

Damali laughed as Monk Lin smiled. "Seriously, though.

It's late, gonna be dark in a few, we've been traveling non-stop for a day and a half, have a lot of catching up to do on sleep and our—"

"We have to go to the caves," Carlos said, quietly.

"No, dude! I'm maxed out. No more side trips, detours what-the-hell-ever!" Rider was practically out of his seat, with Jose and J.L. holding his arms.

"Absolutely," Shabazz argued. "We don't do caves with no ammo at sunset, not on zero-freaking-sleep, when there's no clear and present danger. Brother, that's when you catch up, recharge your batteries, and—"

"That's what I need to do. Recharge my battery. Something's draining energy from me, but I don't know what it is." Carlos's tone was flat, calm, and contained no judgment.

Damali leaned forward and touched his shoulder. "You all right?"

"Why didn't you say so," Rider grumbled. "Fine." he said on a hard exhale, pulling his fingers through his hair hard. "To the caves."

The minivan lumbered down Mirik Lam south from Lhasa Fandian and then struggled against a dirt road along the base of a hill that Monk Lin said was called, the Chakpo-Ri, which also faced the Potala in the distance.

"We are at Chogyel Zimuki, also known as Dragla Lugug," Monk Lin said, curiously appraising Carlos as he exited the vehicle. "Go up the steps two stories beyond the gate to the monastic temple. On the second floor is the inner sanctum and the entrance to the prayer cave." He bowed toward Carlos and Damali, signaling that the others might consider staying with the van.

"But, dude, did you say something about Dracula or did I miss something?" Rider said, stroking his chest where his gun holster normally crossed.

No," Monk Lin said with a patient smile. "I said, Dragla Lugug."

"It's almost dark, man," Shabazz said, his tone annoyed

and worried. He glanced at Big Mike and Marlene for confirmation as the team closed ranks around the monk.

"It's something I've gotta do," Carlos said, looking at Damali. "Second sight is down—I could use a good seer and somebody good with a blade."

Shabazz pulled the new sword out of the van and offered it to Damali, but she declined it. He didn't put it back in the vehicle, but held it in readiness, just in case she changed her mind.

"I'm cool," she told Shabazz. Something innate made her know that Carlos needed to again feel like *he* was the weapon. If she took anything with her more lethal than a dagger, it might undermine that. She turned her focus toward him as she patted her bootleg. "I gotchure back. Let's do this."

They entered the spherical cavern and glanced around. Just beyond the grotto-style, two-story monastery, it was as though they'd again stepped into another dimension. A huge center column was inscribed with unreadable etchings, but Damali allowed her fingers to rove over the seventh-century art that told a story she couldn't comprehend in seventy-one intricately carved sculptures.

"This is very cool and very eerie," she whispered as she unsheathed her blade, just to be on the safe side. She kept alert as she quietly searched for anything that could hold angel tears.

But as in the temples they'd visited earlier, nothing was registering. There was also the not-so-small problem of what to do if she found them with Carlos or anyone else there to witness the discovery. She hated keeping secrets from him; it made her sad to have to do that. This was her man, her partner, and they were supposed to be one.

Damali turned her attention toward the only source of illumination, hoping the tiny lights might provide answers. Small butter lamps lit the interior, their smoky essence filtering up to cover the ceiling in soot.

She glanced at Carlos, watching him walk around the miniature prayer altar, and she studied his gaze as he took in the hundreds of religious markings that covered the walls.

"What are you sensing?" she murmured, coming close to him.

"Nothing I should be feeling or picking up from a monastic temple," he said with a half smile. "But I have to remember not to defile the Neteru."

For a moment, she didn't move or speak. A deep, pungent, sensual aroma began to fill the unventilated space around her, making her slightly heady. "Who told you something like that?" she whispered, her breath coming out huskier than was warranted.

"That's just the thing, D," he said quietly, his gaze still raking the walls as she stepped in closer to him. "I can't remember. I just know that I'm not supposed to."

"Who got that crazy mess up in your head," she said, smiling, closing off the space between them. She inhaled deeply and allowed her nose to drag along his shoulder. "Whew, man . . . is that what's been bothering you lately?"

He shook his head and stepped away from her, his eyes on the cave walls. "There's an energy here," he whispered. "Male."

Damali straightened and went on guard. "Friend or foe?" Her eyes darted around the dimly lit enclosure.

"That would depend on your perspective," an elderly voice said from behind the column.

Carlos and Damali whirred around and stood in battle readiness as a small, gnomelike man in a brown robe stepped from behind the column. His face was drawn with wrinkles, his hair white and long, fusing with his mustache and beard to flow down the front of his dark brown habit. His eyes were all white, covered in thick, bluish cataracts. His hands were concealed within the deep folds of his sleeves and he extracted them slowly to press them together and bow.

"I am Zang Ho. You seek the wisdom of the Naksong?"

Damali and Carlos didn't immediately speak, temporarily rendered mute by the surprise.

"Well, well, speak. Be quick. Time is of the essence," the tiny man said with impatience. He swept up to them, seeming oblivious of their size and strength, or the fact that Damali was packing a blade. "I've waited a very long time for you two—and you both are incorrigible." He swept away again and walked around the column with his hands behind his back, and then suddenly rushed up to Carlos, pointed a crooked finger at him and smiled a toothless grin. "Ahhh . . ." he said, inhaling sharply. "The apexing one is here." He spun to face Damali with blind eyes. "The female, too. Humph. Put away the blade," he ordered. "I detest the smell of metal."

Carlos and Damali simply stared at each other for a moment.

"Uh, sir," Damali said, vastly amused by this droll little man who stood all of four feet ten inches tall, if a hair. "Uh-mmm . . . you are the Naksong, we take it?"

He waved at her to dismiss the query. "You are almost ready, but him . . . my, my, my so much work to do and so little time."

"Sir, what do I have to do?" Carlos said as humbly as possible. "I came to learn from a master, because we have a serious mission at hand."

"You were a master!" the old man shouted, becoming indignant. "This is the point," he said, placing a bony finger against his temple. "A general. A master strategist. What is wrong with your mind?" He walked away, swishing his robes against the dirt floor and stirring plumes of dust as he strode around in agitation. "I don't have time for silly questions, young man. Link to her energy!" He folded his arms over his chest and pouted, and then began twirling the end of his long beard between two fingers, waiting.

"We're out of sync," Damali hedged, confused but swallowing a smile. "We're supposed to be looking for some serious demon energy, the Chairman's lair, but, uh, Monk Lin has been taking us sightseeing."

"Integrate yourself," the Naksong said, snapping his fingers. "You must conquer that which is within by using what is within. Then to conquer the external is moot, unless you have achieved that." He walked away. "I am done for the evening."

"Wait, wait, wait, hold up," Damali said, moving to block

the elderly man's exit. "We did *not* fly umpteen hours and get snagged by government forces, get loaded down with artillery, to hear 'integrate yourself,' and go home. Be serious, sir—or at least have a heart."

The old man frowned and turned to address Carlos, tilting his head as he listened for his position in the room. "Feisty. I can see your hesitation."

"Listen," Carlos said, losing patience. "I don't know what you're talking about, and—"

"Then the problem is worse than I thought," the old man fussed, cutting off Carlos's comment. He again began to pace in a circle, muttering to himself, his voice rising and dipping in fits and starts. "In the land of the Arc of the Covenant, did you not receive the tools of the Neteru?" He held up his hand to prevent an answer. "Yes." He began walking again. "In the land of the Thunderbird, did you not receive the mission?" Again he held up his hand as Carlos and Damali glanced at each other. "Yes." He looked up with dead eyes and folded his arms over his bony chest. "But you forgot. Humph! Young people." He began his dizzying circle again. "We are in trouble," he said to the vaulted ceiling. "We are in very, very big trouble if we depend on them." He jerked his head to stare blindly at Carlos and Damali. "Sync up and meet me in the mountains tomorrow. I suppose I will have to teach."

Before Damali or Carlos could open their mouths, he vanished in a puff of white smoke.

"Okay, now that was deep," she said, going to the spot where the little man had been. She stomped on the ground. "Now what do we tell the team?"

"Your visit was fruitful?" Monk Lin asked, rushing up the cave temple stairs before Carlos and Damali descended them.

The group was held in thrall as Carlos and Damali related the bizarre events inside the cave, but Monk Lin whirred around and clapped his hands.

"You have met the Naksong. He has agreed to teach. This

is a divine omen. Tomorrow, we set out at dawn to find the nomads, who will point us to the oracle. She will be able to coax him to us and our lessons begin."

Glances passed around the group as they all got back into the vehicle.

"I just have one question," Rider said flatly, staring out the window. "Why do we always have to do things the hard way, people? Just answer me that, gang, and I won't say another word for the rest of this trip!"

Still mystified, Damali stood before the window in the tight confines of the barren room, watching the setting sun paint the mountains in the distance pink and gold. Where were the tears!

Carlos's arms enfolded her as he looked at the scene over her shoulder, resting his chin on it.

"I'm sorry that I'm such a slow learner," he murmured. "D, I swear, it's like something is in my head that can't get out. Things I should remember by instinct just ain't there anymore."

She covered his hands with hers as he held her, keeping her back toward him as the shared the spectacular view of the Tibetan sky.

"It's not your fault," she said quietly. "Something traumatic happened, and I can feel it just under the surface of your skin. But what troubles me is that I can't pick it up, either. There's a black wall there. Maybe it's just because you went full vamp before, so your Neteru transition is a little slower than . . ."

"I know," he said with a weary sigh. "When we went to the first temple, I felt detached, nothing, as though something was trying to reach me, but couldn't get in."

She turned and stared at him. "A lot of blood was shed there. That temple was desecrated. Maybe you were shielding your mind from that?"

He nodded and moved a stray lock behind her ear. "I don't want to focus on images like that anymore."

"But you can't turn a blind eye to it," she argued gently.

"Close your eyes, try to see what was there at Jokhang. Maybe it will offer a clue?"

He nodded, and slowly obliged her, tuning his mind to the images of the first temple. Soon his breathing deepened and his head dropped against her shoulder. The smell of blood filled his nose, and he tensed.

"Stay with it," she murmured. "I'll be with you in the vision."

Slowly, he forced himself to relax and attempted to re-trace his mental steps through the intricate maze of the sanctuary. He could feel perspiration beginning to seep out of his pores as the pungent scents became nearly intoxicating, covered his face, slid up his nose, and made him weave against her.

Damali dragged her nose across his shoulder. The sensation sent a shudder of desire through him. The images in his head melted into the rooms of the Potala—thrones, books, swirled in his mind. Before long, his breaths were coming out in short pants. He was chained to a wall, scorpions exited the floor and covered his feet, scurried up his legs, and turned into tiny gargoyle-like creatures that grew and became harpies. He tried to jerk his head up, but Damali had a firm grip at the base of his skull.

"Stay with it," she murmured. "I got you. I'm here."

Pain riddled his body, and then suddenly gave way to weightlessness. A dark throne sat alone, smoke pouring over the floor, and then strong desire filled him. His groin felt like it was on fire. Golden fangs opened. A dark book was just beyond his reach. He nuzzled her neck hard, and battled not to score her throat. He could feel his gums about to rip, but as his tongue ran over his teeth, they'd remained smooth, even, flat. A sudden nip against his jugular made him open his eyes and gasp.

"You smell so damned good," she whispered, her eyes at half-mast. "I'm sorry, I couldn't resist." Her hand slid down his chest. "It's been a long time."

He held her upper arms, shook his head hard, chasing the vision, trying to catch it. "There's a book, D."

"Forget the book," she said in a husky tone. "Forget about what happened in the hotel room, okay?"

"What happened in the hotel room, baby?" he said, his voice tight and frantic as he tried to wipe the desire haze from mind. He shook her gently. "Damali. Focus. What happened in the room?"

She rose on her tiptoes and suddenly crushed her mouth against his. "I don't care," she said as she pulled away, and then crushed his mouth again, sending her tongue into it. She swayed in his arms and gripped the back of his hair tightly. "Stop playing."

He stared into her now glassy eyes that glittered with something dangerous. "There's a book—"

She covered his mouth again, her body writhing against his as she yanked back his head, her gaze dedicated to his jugular. The sensation of watching her eyes produced near vertigo, but something inside him cried out for understanding.

"Not while I'm apexing," he said, suddenly pushing her away.

"Are you nuts?" she said, wrapping her arms around herself.

"No. Something's wrong."

"You're damned straight, something's wrong," she said, her tone icy. "What the fuck is wrong with you?"

He blinked twice and stared at her. "What is wrong with you?" he said in a shocked whisper. "D . . . talk to me."

Her arm pulled away from her body as she pointed at him in a hard snap. "Who is she? What is she? You talk to me, dammit." Damali walked away and stood between the two monk cots in the room. "How long have you been dealing with this bitch? Huh!"

Carlos held up his hands. "Keep your voice down. We don't need the family in this. Baby—"

"I remember what happened on my porch," she said, her voice low and seething with rage. Her breaths came out in short bursts; tears rose to her eyes but didn't fall. "You washed me into my living room, opened my fucking nose so wide a tractor trailer could drive through it, and then backed off—left me hanging." She closed her eyes and hugged herself and shuddered hard. "All right. I was wrong about pushing you away . . . about having a temporary lapse and thinking about somebody else for a second. I'm sorry. Okay? Is that what you want to hear? Done. I'm sorry." She wiped her hands down her face and breathed into them, her line of vision again capturing his. "But, baby, don't do me like this." She shook her head as she approached him slowly. "Not tonight."

Information attacked his mind. Her words were connecting to a distant memory, colliding with the present. It was like she was possessed, wanted him more than ever, but he couldn't respond the way she needed him to. The memory contained a red flag of danger. Her body moved too sensually across the floor. Her voice had dropped to an octave that wasn't hers. The competing images of what he knew and what he loved stripped passion away, dulled the ache her sexy advance caused. There was no silvery-gold flicker in her wide brown irises. The inner glow was too dark.

"Back off," he ordered and jumped over a bed to avoid her. "What happened in the hotel room?"

She met him on the other side of the cot in a lightning move. "What did you say?"

He avoided an open hand slap, and grabbed her jaw. Instead of a punch he'd expected her to hurl, she closed her eyes. Her scent filled the room. Ripening Neteru began to enter his nose, but it was off and contained sulfur. That's when he pushed her back and slapped her.

"Damali! Where are you?"

She held the side of her face, looked dazed for a second and then normalized. Her hand rubbed her cheek as she stared at him. "Have you lost your mind?' she whispered in her normal voice. "You hit me?" She spun around and walked to the door. "You hit me in my face because I was trying to kiss you?"

"D, it wasn't like that," he said, coming toward her, but she held up her hand. "That's not what happened!"

"Now I'm crazy?" she said in disbelief. "I'm out. I need air. Follow me and I'll cut your damned throat in the streets."

"D, wait!"

But it was too late; she was out the door.

She walked a hot path—to where, she wasn't sure. The streets were still loaded with pedestrians and tourists. Cyber cafés and restaurants bustled with nightlife. All she wanted to find was a bench to sit down on and weep. The man had hit her, an unpardonable offense. He'd actually slapped the fucking taste out of her mouth. A hundred possibilities ran through her mind. Was he living on the down-low now? Plenty of sisters had to cope with that. Another woman? Relapsing? Detoxing? Whatever. It didn't matter. The man she was with was domestically violent. Unacceptable. She was out. His ass was possessed. Screw the contagion as an excuse. End game.

She stopped on a corner. Where the hell was she gonna go? She was in freaking Tibet and had a mission to accomplish. She turned back toward the building that housed her team. She had to go back, had to get the angel tears, slay the Chairman, and get them all back to the airport in one piece. Had to find . . . her thoughts trailed off as she saw Carlos running down the street.

Her first impulse was to unsheathe her blade and gore him. Too dramatic in a foreign country. She'd get her own room; this bullshit was over. She didn't care what he had to say.

"Listen," she said, one finger in his face as he came near.

"I was out of my mind," he said, then jerked her to him and covered her argument with a deep, sensual kiss. "I've been stressed, you've been stressed. I hate this shit. Let's get out of here. Tibet is giving me the hives." He covered her mouth again before she could respond and set cool fire to her skin.

She tried to pull out of the kiss but felt something close to delirium capture her mind.

"I want this worse than you do," he said into her hairline. "C'mon. Let's find somewhere to be alone." He raked his nose down the side of her throat, sending shivers along her spine.

She closed her eyes, swayed, and dragged her nose across his collarbone. He released a low, quiet moan. The adrenaline spike, along with whatever he was trailing, made her nearly forget she was standing outside on a busy street. It was reflex when she ran her fingers through his hair. She could feel his jaw become packed with sudden steel, just like what was pressing against her thigh.

"Oh, shit, I've missed you," she whispered.

"I know," he crooned, a fang now threatening to break the skin of her throat.

She couldn't take it; he'd pushed her past the point of shame in the streets. She bit him, no hesitation in the strike, and felt his knees buckle. But when she did so, the taste in her mouth was metallic. He lifted his head and smiled, but his eyes were just a shade too dark. No silver flicker behind his irises. His signature scent evaporated. He caught her breath.

"Damn," he murmured. "Perfect vessel."

Before she could respond, he glanced over his shoulder, snapped, and was gone.

She looked up and Carlos caught her. She could have sworn he had on a black designer suit just moment ago, how the hell did he get into a T-shirt and jeans so fast? Then she remembered. Oh, yeah, the bastard had slapped her. She pushed him away, still enraged.

"Do not touch me!" she shouted, not caring that heads turned on the street. "Back off or die."

"D, I was worried," he said in a gentle tone. "I had to. Something sealed the door to our room shut when I tried to follow you, and it took—"

"The angels probably sealed the damned door to keep me from cutting your heart out," she argued, one hand on her hip the other in his face. "Don't you *eva* put your hands on me like that. I don't care who you think you are. I'll have your ass in front of a judge so fucking fast they'll throw the book at you! If you *eva* hit me again, it's—"

"Angels!" he shouted, walking in a circle. "The book! Oh, shit, Damali. I have to get the book!"

CHAPTER NINETEEN

It felt as though her heart was pounding out of her chest as she sprinted beside Carlos through the streets and up the steep incline of steps to the building that housed their team. They banged on doors like the house was on fire as they passed each room, instantly calling a meeting by express method—hollering.

"Yo, yo, yo, heads up!" Carlos yelled, slamming doors with his fist.

Damali put her shoulder to the door of their small room and barreled through it, her gaze sweeping for anything that shouldn't be there. Within moments, the entire team had piled into the room behind her and slammed the door.

"Talk to me, people," Shabazz said.

"Lilith took her body for a second," Carlos said, waving his hands as he spoke.

"He was trailing the beginnings of apex scent," Damali said, walking in a circle, bumping into Carlos, "and he slapped the shit out of me."

"It was Lilith," Carlos said, his voice rising defensively. "I would *never* slap Damali. Something was wrong with the kiss, the vibe wasn't right. That's why I told her to back off while I was apexing. My gut told me to ignore the body—I had to get my head together. I slapped her and her eyes changed!"

"Well, that'll happen if you slap a Neteru, dude," Rider said, but his tone wasn't amused. "Her eyes *will* change, and then the daggers come out. So you'd better hope like hell you slapped Lilith, and not Damali."

"I know what I saw," Carlos argued, jumping up on a bed and staring out the window.

"Let's everybody try to stay calm," Marlene said. "With the contagions, tempers are apt to flare—"

"I *know* what I saw, Mar," Carlos repeated, his voice rising. "This wasn't the damned infection. Even as a vampire, I never slapped Damali—under any conditions, hitting a woman ain't my style. But Lilith, yeah. I'll blow her head off."

"Down in the square," Damali said, her breaths labored as adrenaline rippled through her. "The Chairman came to me, I think."

Everybody stopped moving, and Carlos spun around. "What?"

"He kissed me, and it definitely wasn't you. Metallic taste in my mouth when I bit him."

"What!" Carlos was off the bed and in her face. "You knew it wasn't me and bit that mother—"

"It looked exactly like you, was talking the exact same shit you talk when you want some, and—"

"Okay, okay," Marlene said, coming between the combatants. "They shape-shifted on both of you. We got that part." She looked at Carlos. "You're bait." She motioned toward Damali. "You're the steel trap."

Shabazz nodded. "If he's near true apex, he's a solid lure for Lilith. Damali ain't in phase, so she's gotta take the Chairman's head once he surfaces to go after Lilith or come for Carlos. Male Neteru apex in his zones is gonna draw his old ass out of hiding."

Damali and Carlos parted and went to opposite sides of the room, elbowing past the others. He leaned on one wall and wiped his hands down his face; she leaned on a rickety dresser and did the same.

"All right, I'm bait," Carlos muttered.

"I've got the Chairman's head, no problem. We move out first light," Damali said, regaining her composure. "Just tell me how I'm supposed to lop off Lilith's head when she's inside my body? How am I supposed to do that—and trust me, I want her ass as bad as I want the Chairman's."

"Mar, not trying to add a wrinkle to this loosely constructed plan, but how in the hell did an entity enter a fully matured Neteru like Damali? That's why it was taking me a minute to get with Rivera's defense." Rider raked his fingers through his hair and quickly glanced at both Neterus in the room before his gaze held Marlene's. "I can get with a shapeshift. That's pure vamp illusion shit. But if what Carlos said is true, then Lilith temporarily slid into Damali's body. From all I've heard, that ain't ever supposed to happen."

Damali's hands went to the top of her head as she searched Marlene's eyes for answers. "That's way strong mojo, Mar. Rider's right. Damn, I ain't playing that shit!"

"Lilith is from Level Seven, and she's got strengths beyond the vamp capacity," Marlene said, her eyes scouring the group. "But she needed a host, a carrier, that's already, uh, literally, been inside of Damali's body before. We're all infected by the demon contagion, and Damali's defenses could have been temporarily down, especially with the distraction of her partner going into a full apex." Marlene stared at Carlos. "Talk to me, brother. How you been feeling lately?"

"I'm fine," Carlos said, crossing his arms. "Normal, regular, nothing out of the ordinary."

"Oh, bull*shit!*" Damali said, pushing off the dresser. "You have *not* been fine. You cannot remember things! Your personality runs hot and cold. One minute you don't have enough energy to lift your head off a pillow, the next you're battling insomnia and have all the energy in the world." She shook her head. "Nah. You ain't all right."

"I went out once drinking with Yonnie, and felt bad, but—"

"Noooo . . ." Damali said in a low voice. "That night I doused your clothes—"

"Nothing happened!" Carlos gestured wildly with his hands. "What happened out of the ordinary, D? The clothes didn't even smolder, I was—"

"Like the Devil himself." Damali jerked her attention toward Marlene. "I remember now. He came at me with some shit I ain't *never* seen before, and the Carlos I know would have never come at me like that—had me scared in my own fucking house, crying and shit, then everything got fuzzy."

"*What* are you talking about, Damali?" Carlos stood in the center of the room as the team's gaze bounced from him to Damali and back again.

Damali covered her face, breathed into her hands, and summoned calm. When she lowered her arms, she kept her voice even and controlled. "Outside, just now, you started running and said the angels told you to get the book. When did the angels come? Think back. What book?"

The team parted as Carlos began to pace slowly, his hands balling to fists at his sides. "Yeah. Right. I did. I remember. I was pissed off. Left the house. But . . ."

Juanita walked over to him and placed a hand on his arm. Eyes widened on every face. Damali bristled.

"We talked in the front yard. Remember? You were on your way to L.A."

Damali folded her arms over her chest. "Yeah. What did you and Juanita talk about, Carlos?" Damali's eyes narrowed. "For all we know, her ass could be a carrier—she was out of team sight for a long time before—"

"C'mon, D," Jose said, cutting her off. "I wanna hear what she's gotta say, too. So, let 'Nita tell us what went down in the front yard that ain't nobody know about. I also have a few questions about the vibe I caught when I took Krissy to your house. Cool?"

Damali pounded Jose's fist.

"Aw, shit," Big Mike said, smoothing a palm over his bald head. "C'mon, y'all. We family."

Juanita scowled at Damali and averted her eyes from Jose. "Carlos, you were on your way to L.A. Said . . ."

Her voice trailed off and he nodded. A silent understand-

ing passed between them. Part of the conversation need not
be said. "Then I was driving and—"

"Hol' up!" Damali said, both hands raised. "Skip to, and
then I was driving? Rivera, I ain't—"

"I told one member of the house where I was going!"
Carlos shouted, pointing at Juanita, "because you were giving me the blues. Yeah, I explained that I was out so the
whole house didn't mount up a search party, or try to go after my boy to stake him. Yonnie wasn't in this bullshit. Then
a deer, which I thought was Tara, came out of nowhere.
Smashed my window. I spun out. Started walking. Blue light
came down and covered me! Tara's hunt was on the hood of
my car. She couldn't see me because of the light!"

Carlos was breathing hard as he walked around in a hot
circle. "Next thing I know, voices, thundering voices told me
to get the book and take the Chairman's head. So I went
down to Hell like they told me to do and walked into Chambers! All right? You clear? And it was all fucked up down
there. Everything was trashed. Thrones decimated. The pen-
tagram table leaning. Torches pulled out of the walls. Fucking bats scared to move. But no book!"

"You went to Hell?" Damali yelled.

"To get *The Book of the Damned*," Carlos shouted back.
"Heaven needs it before the big war kicks off to free lost
souls! We all know that. What about this ain't clear?"

Marlene nearly collapsed against Shabazz's side. Marjorie sat down slowly on the bed. Rider's back hit the wall
with a thud. One by one, Guardians attempted to open their
mouths to comment, but no sound came out.

"You went back down there, alone, and opened a seal on
sacred Indian ground to retrieve something like that?"
Damali closed her eyes. "Oh, my God."

"They told me to!" Carlos argued. "You don't negotiate
with angels, you do what the fuck they say when they say
and don't ask questions. It wasn't there, anyway. The Chairman has it! You know that; you had the self-same book in

your hand yourself when you went down there half-cocked on a solo mission, right? And he was the last one that had it. Snatched it back from you on a trade."

"How do you know it was them, real angels, the real Mc-Coy?" Rider said in a quiet voice. "I'm serious, dude? Not like them to send you down there like that without a squad."

For a moment, Carlos didn't answer. Terror seized his words and made him swallow them. "No, man, no. It had to be them. The blue lights. The sky thing they did. Burned out Tara's corneas—that's what you said she told you."

"All right," Damali hedged. "Assuming that it was them that sent you, how do you know whether or not something tagged along when you came back up? Like Marlene said, you could have become an accidental carrier of something worse than the contagion, which makes your bouts of sickness make all the sense in the world to me right now." She put her hands behind her and began pacing where Carlos once had. "You'd just relapsed with Yonnie. Your spirit might have had a fissure."

Marlene nodded and stood away from Shabazz. "Sensitive question in mixed company," she said, looking at Damali and ignoring the others. "You know one way inhabitation can occur, right?"

"Not since we got to Arizona," Damali said.

Carlos sent his hot gaze out the window. The other team members found the floor and places on the wall to inspect. Marlene cocked her head to the side.

"You know what," Marlene said quietly, "you felt this coming, D. That's why y'all haven't been able to . . . Uh, just scratch my other theories."

Damali nodded. "I thought it was me."

"Can we have this conversation with a senior squad only?" Carlos said, his back to the group.

"These are delicate matters," Monk Lin said, his gaze nervously darting around the room. "The Naksong will know what to do."

"Nothing else to discuss," Marlene said gently. "It may have come up through you, but if it's male, like the Chairman, your Neteru toxin will kill it—so it fled. If it's female, like Lilith, it had to go to a vessel that wouldn't struggle with you, wouldn't make you immediately attack it . . . but it can't stay away from you while you're in this near-apex condition. So, people, we have a window." She looked at Damali. "You sleep with me tonight, and I'll salt you down real good, sis. If she tries to come back while you're with me, I've got something for her." Marlene gave Juanita a side-long glance. "You'd better come with me, too, just in case she comes at him that way."

"That ain't necessary," Jose said when both Juanita and Damali bristled. "Me and Rider got Carlos." He folded his arms and looked at Carlos hard. "Don't take me there on this one, hombre."

Rider closed his eyes. "Yeah. Just like old times.

Dawn hadn't even crested the sky in full color yet, but the team was on the move. The silence in the minivan was unbearable as it lumbered along the isolated roads, steadily moving higher into the hills on a steep, laborious incline. The frigid early-morning air was so thin that puffs of steam exited everyone's mouth and frosted the windows. They sat hunched down in their seats, burrowed deep in their thick yak-hair-lined coats, thick woolen pants, and layers of handmade sheep wool sweaters, gloves, and hats as Monk Lin drove.

Every bump they hit, every rut in the road, made them cringe and say a silent prayer that the weapons and explosives loaded into the trunk and roped to the top of the vehicle didn't take a tumble. Theirs was a very fragile line between calm and calamity, and everyone had sense enough to honor that subtle truth.

Rider was the first person to attempt to break the permafrost in the van as he looked out at slowly grazing animals and horseback riders doing stunts in the early-morning sun.

"Kinda looks like those guys are trying out for the rodeo circuit, huh, Jose?"

Jose grunted. Monk Lin peered into the rearview window.

"In the summer, when the nomads push their droves of livestock up in the hills to escape rain and to graze, there are all sorts of games," Monk Lin said in a peaceful tone. "Mongolian horsemen, Tibetans, they come from all over to compete. But these people are generally isolated," he added. "I don't think the contagion has reached them yet, so please be careful not to infect them, if possible."

There was no response in the van from a soul. Rider leaned forward to talk to the monk and to try to restore team unity.

"Uhmmm . . . looks real similar to the tribes in Arizona," Rider said, blatantly trying to bring harmony within the team. He nodded toward a small circle forming and tapped Big Mike on the arm. "Can you make out the drum chords, dude? Music might be bumpin', might be something for us to blend into our sounds, if we live to see another day. Check out the dudes with the long horns."

"Yeah," Mike said and fell silent again.

"Rain dancers," Monk Lin said, trying to help salvage Rider's desperate attempt for peace. "The Bonpo shaman still arranges ceremonies to the elements—much like the old ways on your lands."

"Now, see," Rider said, snapping his fingers. "Common ground. Half a world away and people are the same." He glanced around the van but no one responded. "All right, folks," he said, becoming peevish, "we cannot go see some old master or fight those two very bad elementals we're looking for if everyone has a bad attitude."

Marlene sighed. "I know, Rider, but save it. Maybe the Naksong got something for this?"

After six straight hours of travel, Monk Lin pulled into a small enclave of yak-hair tents. He stretched and yawned and opened the vehicle door.

"I have to add fuel to the van, but it is of no use. To continue up into the mountains, we must go with herder guides and take small wagons . . . you may have to ride horses or yak if I can come to agreement with the nomads."

Damali closed her eyes and leaned back against her seat. She wasn't sure if it was the Juanita issue, the way Jose had reacted, getting slapped—no matter what the reason, or knowing that Lilith may have possibly entered her body; or the bigger problem that Carlos, once again, presented, that was eating away at her nerves. But she wasn't feeling any of this at the moment. She was sick of the entire mission, and they hadn't even begun it.

Carlos allowed his head to hang forward as he stretched his back. Humiliation still tore at him. Why would angels set him up like that? It didn't make sense, and those guys were supposed to play fair. Not to mention, his business was all out in the street, once again, because Damali just had to put it out there like that. He wasn't sure what bothered him more—knowing that Lilith could have possessed her, or that he'd potentially dragged something up like a virus within him. Or was it that the whole team suspected something was going on again with him and 'Nita? Or the fact that Jose had a right this time to want to smoke him? This was too crazy. Everybody was pissy. They couldn't go into battle with distrust and bull between them.

"All right, everybody," Carlos said in a weary tone. He waited until all eyes were on him . . . well, practically all eyes. Damali's gaze was fixed out the window.

"I'm sorry if I messed up. I thought I got a direct order and followed it. I told the Light that I couldn't find the book. Been thinking about this thing all night. Obviously, I don't have fangs and do daylight. I don't have the blood hunger, I'm not sick during the day like I had been, and I'm not going that way anymore. If I flushed both Lilith and the Chairman out of hiding, that's what I'm supposed to do. Last I heard, I'm a hunter. A Neteru. So we *all* need to squash this bullshit and be a team." He glanced at Damali and then at Jose. "We all know what time it is. I haven't cast no stones, so neither of y'all should. That's all I've got to say on the matter."

Juanita glared at Jose when he leaned forward to speak. She held up her hand in his face, and he fell silent. "Do not even go there," she warned. "We've all got skeletons—but I was cool with yours. So turnabout ain't fair play?"

Carlos slapped her five. "I used to say fair exchange ain't no robbery, but I'm reformed."

"Yeah, whatever," Damali muttered.

"You do not want me to out your shit on this bus, girl," Carlos said, jumping out of the van. "I let it go, you let it go. Hear?" He walked away to find Monk Lin.

"Oops," Marlene said, chuckling. "Well. Now that the air is clear, I suggest we all stretch our legs and take a pee break." She got out of the van with Shabazz, who was now smiling.

Soon everyone had exited the van and Damali was forced to as well. Carlos had gotten on her nerves so badly she wanted to scream loud enough to create an avalanche. Instead of that ill-fated option, she trudged behind the team in a foul mood. She tried her best to remain surly, but the curious children that ran close and skittered away behind parents made her smile.

They pointed at her with stubby little fingers and shy smiles, and their big luminous eyes were wide with wonder. Monk Lin had a small gathering of herders around him, offering food and tea, and bowing repeatedly. But they didn't touch him because of his monk status, and kept a respectful distance from the people he'd brought with him, unsure.

"They don't see many foreigners here," Monk Lin told the group as a pretty woman who seemed to be in her forties smiled and giggled behind her hand. "The people here are generous, and believe a monk passing by is a good omen. But it will take much to get her to disclose where the oracle is." He bowed politely and the woman followed suit, peering around him to curiously gaze at the team.

Her smile widened as Monk Lin made the rounds and gave each team member's name, and her expression seemed puzzled as she stared at Rider. She spoke in a soft melodic tone in a language only Monk Lin understood. He chuckled softly and went to each team member one by one, holding their arms, stating their name, and trying to make the woman understand the familial relationships.

Again, she shook her head no, and asked her questions in an excited, amused flurry.

"She doesn't understand," Monk Lin said. "She thinks you are the father and have many wives," he said to Rider.

Rider laughed. "I look *that* old? Gee, thanks."

"No, no, no, it is a great honor she is trying to express. She doesn't understand why you have no wife, so she says you must be the father of all." Monk Lin stepped closer to the group and turned to introduce the small clan that had gathered near the smiling woman. "Mei has seventeen children."

Marlene and Marjorie opened their mouths, and glanced at Damali and the others.

"My, how wonderful," Marjorie said, her eyes wide.

"Girl, you look *good,*" Marlene said, meaning it. She glanced at Damali, Juanita, Inez, and Kristen. "Now, *she's* a warrior—seventeen kids? Puhlease."

Monk Lin relayed the sentiment, and Mei laughed. She pointed at the younger women in the group, a question on her face. Damali opened her hands and shrugged to tell the woman that she didn't have any babies, as did everyone but Inez, who held up one finger. Again, the woman seemed puzzled and she consulted Monk Lin.

The monk smiled. "This may help clarify why Mei is having difficulty with your family structure. Let me introduce her husbands."

The men in the group gave each other very curious glances. Now it was their turn to scratch their heads and smile silently like Mei once had.

"Each of these men are brothers," Monk Lin announced

casually. "There were five in the family, no women in the hills, and they all shared very prosperous herds of sheep, goats, and yak."

"Wait," Big Mike said, "that little lady there, uh."

"Yes," the monk said without batting an eye. "She is very loved and very revered in the family, because they came to a good compromise." His smile broadened as Jose shot Carlos a look.

"Now, dude, for real, how do they work that out?" Rider rubbed his chin and looked at the brothers, who all seemed pleasant and smiled proudly at their prize, Mei.

Monk Lin blushed, but relayed the question. The Tibetan brothers laughed and slapped each other, as Mei retreated to uproarious giggles behind her hand.

"They think you all are foolish, this is why there aren't enough babies in your family. The eldest brother says you have an embarrassment of riches in your family," he added, waving before the women in the group. "He believes there should be fifty children or more."

Inez covered her face and laughed hard, making the others on the team do the same. "Chile, no!"

"The second brother is open for a wife who is strong, as he says he must always wait for his youngest brother—who leaves his shoes outside the tent too long. This is how they compromise. Each man leaves his boots outside, and his time alone with their wife is respected. The others tend to the children so no young ones are hurt . . . uh, while . . . one of the husbands is unavailable."

Damali laughed so hard that she had to turn away as the brothers nodded and gave her shy smiles. "Monk Lin, I've heard enough," she said through the giggles. "We are all up in these people's business and shouldn't press our hospitality."

He bowed and turned to the group of men and spoke to them in gentle, easy tones. But whatever he said made them burst out laughing. Then they offered the men on the team cigarettes and pieces of smoked yak by passing the items first to Monk Lin, a revered holy man, without touching him. Their trust was implicit, so was their generosity.

Carlos shook his head and pounded Jose's fist. "That is deep, man, but would never work in our house."

Jose glanced at Juanita and smiled. Damali nodded and let the tension drop from her shoulders. Juanita let out her breath and moved beside Jose. Peace on the team had been restored just that quickly.

The rest of the team joined in the camaraderie as bits of foodstuff were exchanged, all being careful not to actually touch the gracious herders. Everyone used Monk Lin as a go-between, a cleansing conduit, as not to harm a family that deserved never to have its innocence stolen.

Damali offered an earring from her ear to Mei via Monk Lin, and people gave whatever they had handy to show friendship and appreciation. Children danced by and looked up at the Guardians that seemed to be giants compared to their much shorter fathers. Big Mike's sheer bulk captivated them, as did the younger Guardians that seemed as anxious as the children to run in the field for a quick a game of chase.

"I'm still getting over the shoes thing," Rider said as the team was invited into the huge, yak-hair tent.

A central hole sent a column of smoke up and out, but the rank smell of yak butter used to help waterproof it, and the yak chips added to the fire to help keep the embers going with nominal wood tinder available, made their eyes water. However, it was warm and cozy as they all sat on the floor, and hospitality was hospitality. They shared what food provisions they had, but Mei wouldn't hear of it. She'd prepared butter tea and what seemed like roasted barley, and made her humble offering to the group.

As Monk Lin passed out small bowls of tea, he offered a discreet warning to the team. "The people of the mountains don't have much, and roasted barley flour, *tsampa,* is somewhat bitter. But to decline an offering is to make the offerer lose face." He hesitated until all Guardians nodded, and kept his focus on Kristen and Bobby. "Their sweetener is salt. Sugar is not well known in these parts, so a bit of salt flavors the tea. But the yogurt is freshly made and is very, very tasty."

All heads nodded, knowing exactly what that meant. The tea and the barley was gonna be pretty rugged going down, but chase it with yogurt, smile, and only accept a little bit to show consideration for this woman's large household.

Damali watched with a smile as the noses in the group battled for composure. The moment Jose and Rider brought the cups to their mouths, they paused, tossed it back like it were a shot of whiskey, and winced. Mei nodded and clapped her hands, elated. Marlene sipped her tea slowly to hide a broad smile. Carlos held a bowl with two hands, calmly took a sip, shuddered, and grinned.

"This is good," he wheezed, trying to offer the woman a compliment, even though she couldn't understand him.

Mei apparently did understand a smile, and having a generous spirit, she got up quickly to refill Rider, Jose, and Carlos's cups, much to their chagrin—always offering it through the presiding monk who blessed it first. Bobby looked green, and Kristen was taking teeny sips with shaking hands. Marjorie sipped hers with one pinky out, and swallowed the nasty brew with such elegance that Emily Post would have been proud. Marjorie cast a lethal glare at her children, and they ate without missing a beat. Her husband, however, was having issues, but one glance helped him resolve his resistance.

The tactical sensors were cool, though. Damali watched Shabazz go to some far-off place in his mind and chew in a steady motion like a cow absently munching cud. J.L. fell in line with Shabazz's approach, and shortly thereafter Dan got the hint and was able to hang.

Laughter and banter filled the tent, as did multiple languages and soon after came songs. Monk Lin was the bridge between worlds, filling in the blanks, but after a while much of what was being said required no translation.

From a distance, the young girls and Mei studied the varied types of hair each woman had, marveling at the differences between Damali's locks; Juanita's straight tresses, which matched their own in color and weight; Inez's soft braids; and Marlene's thick silver hair, as well as the color variations of Kristen's and Marjorie's hair, which was like theirs in texture, but the hue fascinated them.

They showed off jewelry, different pieces of turquoise and beads. The men showed off bows and small rifles, and Monk Lin offered the Guardian males a warning via a raised eyebrow not to make the tent lose face by pulling out a bazooka. They drew on the dirt floor with sticks, telling of how they had been blessed with large herds, and how they would go up into the mountains in the summer to further expand the herds. It was rutting season now, the eldest husband explained, and soon the flock would double. All was well in their world.

Damali noticed Rider had fallen quiet, and Mei had, too. Their hostess had sidled up to Monk Lin with a puzzled expression, seeming afraid that she had caused some offense.

"Rider," Damali said quietly. "You okay, brother? The lady of the house thinks something's wrong. Is it?"

Rider smiled sadly and looped the long leather thong over his head that held an old worn eagle feather, a piece of jade, a small turquoise stone, and a bag of magic dust that he'd never understood. He held it out to Monk Lin to give to Mei and bowed his head.

"Tell her this used to belong to my first wife. . . . Her name was Tara, and your people remind me so of her people, this should be yours."

Monk Lin bowed and accepted the gift, spoke in soft tones that stilled the mirth in the tent, and passed the jewelry to Mei. To everyone's surprise, tears instantly filled her large brown eyes. She clutched it to her breast as though Rider had given her a bag of diamonds. She made a gesture over her chest and then in the air toward his and looked down at the bag as her husbands drew near. Her voice was so soft and so sweet that tears filled Monk Lin's eyes.

"She said, man with a good heart, you have come to the

oracle. I cannot hide from you and your family. Old turquoise from the ancients has spiritual value that is without measure. Ask your questions. You are part of her family now. You have passed the test."

Stunned silent, the group looked at Rider.

"What did she call me?" Rider whispered, his voice raw.

"Man with a good heart," Monk Lin repeated.

Rider nodded and drew in a shaky breath. "That's what *she* used to call me."

Mei nodded, not requiring interpretation. She reached for Rider's hands and then clasped them hard.

"Oh, my God—no!" Rider drew back quickly and was on his feet within seconds. "I've just poisoned her house. All of 'em, her husbands, the kids. Jesus Christ, this lady and her family didn't deserve it!"

The team was paralyzed. Monk Lin was also on his feet in an instant and held his hands out for everyone to stay in place and remain as calm as possible. He spoke so quickly and frantically that no one in the tent moved. Mei clutched the bag Rider had given to her chest and smiled oddly. Slowly Monk Lin's expression became one of stunned awe and he sat slowly with a thud.

"How do we fix this?" Damali said fast, her gaze ricocheting to Marlene then over to the monk.

"We can't leave 'em like this," Carlos said, his voice straining to stay even as his gaze bore into Monk Lin's.

Mei held up her hand, her gaze gentle, and she patted the ground for Rider to return to the place before her.

"The damage is done, Rider," Monk Lin said quietly. "Let her finish the divination, and then . . . I don't know."

Mei spoke softly to Rider, while Monk Lin interpreted. Strained gazes holding empathy settled on the woman as Rider simply hung his head.

"Your first wife is in a better place," Monk Lin said quietly, waiting for Mei to speak in slow, calm tones. "You have a large family to care for, much yet to do, and she cannot go where you must . . . but her love lingers forever."

Rider stood and walked out of the tent wiping his face.

Carlos stood to go to him, but Mei held up her hand and spoke quickly, making Monk Lin nearly talk over her to keep up with her flurry of words.

"The spirits will heal him, but you, too, are a man with a good heart. It is different. The spirits are guiding you. What was sickness in you has passed. There were two of you; one side dark, one side light. The Naksong had to be sure of this before teaching you," Monk Lin said, stopping as Mei stared at Damali. "You have lost a child, but it was sick. You will have many in days to come, but not today. Be patient. Be as one. Fight as one. Help fill the tent with goodness and love. The Naksong is ready for you now, because you are ready for the Naksong. My third husband will show you the way."

"But the contagion," Damali whispered, her eyes brimming with tears of compassion. "You have to tell her, Monk Lin. We never meant for this to happen."

Mei sighed and stood, making all eyes follow her as she spoke in a very calm voice and walked deeper into the tent.

"She says you have the tears of an angel," Monk Lin said, his voice hitching with emotion. "May they fall upon you at the Roof of Heaven and never hit the ground."

"Tell her," Damali said, choked up, "that I wish I could find them so I could spread them to save her family and mine . . . everybody's, really. Just tell her how sorry we are." She looked at Monk Lin. "She's an oracle and knows her family is infected, doesn't she?"

"Yes," Monk Lin said, tears shining in his eyes. "She knows and is unafraid. The people here are very philosophical about the whims of fate."

"It's not right, though," Carlos said, swallowing hard and standing. The walls of the tent were closing in on him, and he knew Rider was about ready to pitch himself off the edge of any given cliff. "Tell her we'll all pray for her family, and go do what we've gotta do to keep them whole . . . Tell her, man, that I'd open a vein if I could, if I had silver in it, anything to reverse what just went down."

Mei turned and looked at Carlos and pointed to his eyes.

Berkfield nodded and stood. "I'd open one, too, for this family. I got kids . . ." he shook his head as the Guardians slowly stood. "Any of us would do that."

Mei murmured softly and closed her eyes.

"She says you have the eyes of compassion and good now. There is no more evil within you," Monk Lin said to Carlos. "Your eyes hold silver, their sacred metal." He waited until Mei had spoken again. "She said your brother has the sacred in his veins, and your mother-seer has the salt of sages. Your mate has cried many tears of heartbreak and worry . . . now she will give her tears to replace that."

"Aw, man," Carlos said, rubbing his jaw, unable to look at the family they'd polluted.

Rider stood at the door of the tent. "I'm so sorry, lady."

But Damali slowly broke away from the group and went to Mei. "What did you say?"

Mei held out a small silver container no larger than a pill-box covered in coral and turquoise. Monk Lin rushed over and nearly swooned.

"The tears from Heaven."

The members of the team shared confused glances.

Hot tears streamed down Damali's face. "She said in the greatest temple of all . . ." Damali pointed to the tent door. "Not a man-made structure, but these majestic mountains created by God. That's the most spectacular temple."

Mei nodded and folded the box into Damali's palm, and began speaking quickly.

"Make the antidote," Monk Lin breathed out in a rush. "The tears, the Red Sea salt from Marlene's bag—held by the salt of the earth, wise team mother. Berkfield, get a blade and nick yourself. Do it now, in this tent, heal the team, then this family."

Mei nodded as everyone crushed together to gather around Damali and Mei.

"She had to be sure first that whatever was in Carlos was no longer there. His call for prayer did it. Damali's tears of compassion confirmed it, and they were led there with a man with a good heart and nothing left to give but his heart . . . and he did—Rider. That was the test, and she'd been waiting for a sign."

The group dropped down on the dirt floor and formed a circle while Damali carefully uncapped the delicate container. A thin layer of white substance like confectioners' sugar, barely covered the bottom of the quarter-size silver box. She looked up confused.

"There's so little, just enough to maybe do the people in this tent once we add the other elements—but the whole world out there needs the antidote. How will the Covenant get it out to cure everyone else who has been infected?"

"The antidote was for you so that you could complete the mission that will cure the others, once the dark energies are sealed away and the names released from the book," Monk Lin said, his tone awed and reverent. "They overturned temples and pillaged sacred places looking for this rare element, never seeking the humblest of herders, and a female who resided within the greatest temple of all."

He closed his eyes. "Profound and ironic, but so obvious that a shepherd family should be the keepers of this sacrament . . . people with grace, humility, ordinary weapons, compassion, hospitality, and love enough to even share one another without struggles, so that no man in their group should suffer. This is why the Naksong would not touch you or teach you to find the Chairman's lair until this was learned and the antidote discovered and administered—not even the Covenant could have foretold this. It all depended upon the choices and statements each of you made as one. You all revealed your inner hearts, your willingness to selflessly give what you each had to protect people you didn't know, Mei's family, and did so within her inner sanctuary, the oracle's home. The man with a good heart, Rider, led the way when he parted with magic that covered his heart and had helped him for decades." He bowed where he sat. "I have learned much this day myself."

"Very, deep," Marlene whispered. She looked at Damali. "Do you know the formula, baby?"

Damali nodded and swallowed hard. "Yes, my angel-mother told me."

The group filed out of the tent anointed and considerably sobered. They accepted bits of prayer cloth and tied them to their wrists and hair, anyplace that they would remain fastened. And they waited behind a sinewy young man, whose eyes blazed with an important mission within them. A small caravan of yak lumbered behind the group gently swaying with trunks of highly explosive ammo tied to their sides. Glances of concern were shielded beneath lowered hat brims as each Guardian mounted a horse and nudged the creature to follow husband number three.

Within an hour, one of Mei's husbands held up his hand, calmly stopped, dismounted, and motioned for the others to do likewise. He spoke in an unfazed tone, and began to un-hitch the harnesses on the burdened beasts.

"He says, from here, the yaks cannot pass. The horses have difficulty. It is not the normal grazing lands. But the Naksong is wise."

To their horror, Mei's husband dropped a trunk and wiped his hands on his coat.

Big Mike and Shabazz were off their mounts in seconds, going to help the man before he dropped another trunk. Carlos rounded a huge beast's side with the other men, as Inez and Juanita covered their heads. Marjorie practically fell off her horse, and it whinnied and shied at the affront. Everybody quickly jumped down off the pony they were riding, and glanced around confused.

"He's gonna just leave us here?" Damali couldn't believe it as Mei's third husband smiled, waved, and called to his animals to follow him in the direction they'd just come from.

"He says to take our possessions to the clearing, and it would be best to pitch a tent. Sometimes Naksongs can be fickle, and may decide to change their minds if the signs aren't right."

"Oh, my God," Inez wailed, boxing the chilly temperatures away from her arms. "Monk Lin, tell him to stop playing out here!"

"Be cool, 'Nez," Big Mike said, hoisting down a trunk with care.

Damali went to the top of the ridge. "There's a fairly flat valley here, a pocket we can set up shop on," she said, looking at the small expanse of green around them.

"Lord have mercy," Marlene said with a deep sigh. "All right, folks, we know the drill. Mount up the equipment, we get it over the ridge and—"

"Leave it," a crotchety voice ordered. "It is unnecessary at this juncture."

The team whirred around and a small, wrinkled face popped out from behind a rock. For an elderly man, he moved down the rocks with unusual grace to stand before the team with his arms folded. "You are persistent. I suppose that has merit. At least you have been anointed and cleaned. Humph. Now I can work."

No one moved a muscle as his beady little eyes surveyed the group.

"The first time I saw you, you were blind," Carlos said, half-ready to draw a weapon, his nerves were so shot.

"Yesterday, so were you," the old man said, and smiled. "Things change."

"How do we know you're Zang Ho?" Damali pulled a blade from her hip. "You looked different in the cave, your eyes—"

"You were using only one sense, your eyes. You will learn to use them all. You have been through many shocks, and you are each still purging the infection. In an hour, you will be yourselves. This is why I must work quickly with no arguments to test time or tempt fate." He brushed past Damali and swiped her blade, then stood before Marlene and gave it to her.

Damali stared at her hand and then up at him. "How did you do that? I didn't even feel you take it?"

The Naksong bowed and addressed the team. "Pitch a

tent just over the ridge. I will collect you shortly. There is so much work to do, so little time; so many questions, so many answers." He smoothed his long, white beard and closed his eyes, as though staving off complete annoyance. When he opened his eyes again, they had become cloudy, white cataracts once more, and he pointed a bony finger at Carlos and Damali. "You two. Follow me."

CHAPTER TWENTY

"Where are we going?" Damali called out, trying to keep up with the agile little old man.

"Hey, hold up. Why can't we do whatever we gotta do with the team?" Carlos called out, also finding it difficult to follow the Naksong.

"You ask many questions," Zang Ho said in an irate tone, while stomping on rocks as he climbed higher. "But you ask the wrong ones. You forget true wisdom, but remember what should be forgotten. You fight about nonsense, instead of picking wise battles. You have tested my patience, but you have not tested your own!"

He grunted and slipped over a frigid peak, and Damali and Carlos practically fell over it behind him, sliding down a steep, gravelly incline until they landed with a thud within another grassy knoll.

Thoroughly agitated, they stood, dusting themselves off. Zang Ho folded his arms over his chest and motioned with his chin toward a blanket and two swords lying on the ground near the edge of a cliff.

"Now, we begin," he said.

Carlos and Damali perked up and followed him toward the weapons.

"Observe," the Naksong master said, pointing toward wild sheep grazing in the crags. "It is rutting season, and the males will lock horns, but will not fall to their deaths—most times."

The moment Carlos looked up, Zang Ho rabbit-slapped his face so quickly that his nose began to bleed.

"Yo, man!" Carlos shouted, blotting his nose with the back of his hand. "What was that for?"

"Suck it up and taste the blood. Salty, yes?"

Carlos's eyes narrowed on the old man as Damali chuckled, but a swift pop to the back of her head made her hand go to the place where she'd been struck.

"Ow! What was that for?"

"Pick a weapon," Zang Ho, said, motioning to the swords, "if you can."

Carlos began walking toward the thick, yak-hair blanket that held two long blades. The moment he stepped forward, his feet went out from under him, and he was flat on his face on the ground. Fury roiled within him as he immediately jumped up and made a quick dash toward the blanket, but the blanket moved to the other side of the glen.

"Have I made my point?" Zang Ho asked, studying the sun as he pet his beard. "If you are not the weapon, an external one can always be taken away."

Carlos held up both hands. "All right, all right. Point made."

"You are still not asking me the right questions," Zang Ho said, popping Carlos in the back of his head, without ever nearing him, and making him lurch forward.

"Cut it out, old man. I'm not playing."

"Ah. You have temper. Good. Use it, but use it well." The old man crouched low in a fighter's stance.

"I'm not falling for that," Carlos muttered. "Besides, if we connected, I'd—"

"Hurt me?" Zang Ho shook his head. "Because of appearances, you have made dangerous assumptions." Zang Ho walked away, and turned his back to Damali and Carlos. When he turned around, he became a svelte woman, his robes filling out to assume his new form. "If I were her," he said, making them both squint as his voice remained crotchety, but so different from his body, "you might have other designs on this form than warfare." He turned around slowly and became a snow lion, causing Damali and Carlos to jump back. "Or this might make you feel that victory would be impossible." He returned to his original form.

"That is the smoothest shape-shift I've ever seen," Carlos murmured. "In daylight, too?"

"Now we are making progress," Zang Ho, said.

"You work with energies," Damali said stepping forward. "You use the energy from the Light, like Neterus do."

"That is how I acquired your small dagger," the master said. "Now, when I tell you to fetch a weapon, do not waste time. Materialize it in your hand."

Damali stared at the blanket, focusing hard. They'd tried to teach them this before, but it had been so hard to focus like that lately.

"No. Stop!" Zang Ho ordered. "That is kinetic energy. It requires you to move mass through the air, lift it, bring it to you, but during a battle, you must be one with the blade." He stared at Carlos. "When you were in the shadow lands, did you have to will your teeth to become the dragon's, or was that a reflex response to a sudden threat?"

"It was *all* reflex," Carlos said, his voice containing more reverence. "That is profound."

Zang Ho offered the couple a slight bow. "Before, they taught you to move objects. If a threat occurs, just like his dragon's teeth would appear, a blade should be an extension of your hand, should grow from it. Whatever element is in the universe can fuse with your energy to become your energy. Take it, embrace it, be it." He clapped his hands twice. "Again!"

Damali stood by Carlos's side. Both closed their eyes and opened their hands, but no sword was in it when they opened their eyes.

"Now. What question should you ask me?" Zang Ho folded his arms over his chest.

"Why the sword didn't—"

"No," he snapped, swishing away. "You should ask what stillness must I achieve to obtain this reflex." He walked in a wide circle, first staring at Carlos and then Damali. "They gave you, the male, a shield. Clap your hands, and the shield appears—in an arc. Your line of vision can cut like laser, when provoked. These happen just like the dragon's teeth appear, yes?"

Carlos looked away and shook his head no. "Not lately."

"Ho? What is this travesty?" The Naksong bowed low and walked around Carlos peering up. "Why not? This is old lesson."

"My energy has been a little off center, and . . . uh . . ."

"Hmmm," Zang Ho placed a finger to his lips. "Yes. Something corrupted your energy fields. You need realignment."

"Is it still there?" Damali asked in a worried voice. "Whatever got into his system?"

"The first wise question I have heard this afternoon." He looked at Carlos. "No. It is gone. It fled."

"Did it get into her, somehow?" Carlos glanced at Damali nervously.

The Naksong rubbed his beard. "No. It tricked you, but it was never *in* her. It blanketed her, covered her, but never had permission to enter her. Hmmm . . ." The Naksong smiled. "Very interesting, indeed."

"But I saw—" Carlos attempted to say, summarily getting cut off.

"Your eyes see what you fear, not what is. Your greatest fear is yourself. That keeps you from accepting all elements of yourself. You will need you to fight you. Success in fighting you will allow success in fighting what is not you, but was you."

Carlos scratched his head and nodded in agreement, even though the Naksong had just confused the hell out of him.

"There was something really dark in him, sir, I think," Damali said. "It scared me, too."

"Quite right," Zang Ho said, unfazed as he effortlessly materialized a sword in each hand and leisurely began swinging them at nothing. "It should have frightened you. You should have fought it. Good that you never granted it permission to enter you. But your greatest fear is not what was within him, but what was within you. This is what you also fight. If you did not fear being lost to him, then whatever was there to try to take your freedom and vanquish you could not."

"Okay, now that's deep," Damali said, walking away.

"Look around," the aged master said. "Does the wind seem afraid of the mountains, or the earth afraid of the sun? The elements of the universe do not fear being taken over by the other. They coexist. They know that even if the water overruns the land, the land is not gone, its minerals are within the water . . . and sooner or later the sun will dry the waters, and the minerals will be deposited back upon the earth, perhaps changed into salt. But they never stop existing. So the water never struggles against the sun as it evaporates. Such struggle is all a waste of energy."

Damali and Carlos looked at each other and then at the Naksong.

"I used to be a vampire. That old life—"

"Now you hunt the darkness, correct?" the Naksong swung a blade and merrily leaped from side to side.

"Yeah," Carlos said slowly.

"So, you need a little cunning. You need a little illusion. You need a little blood lust, perhaps a sprinkle of larceny to search for what is in the shadows. If you are not afraid of it still being a part of your nature, it cannot consume you. You control that in the way you use the weapon, the weapon should never control you." Zang Ho flipped a sword to Carlos, who caught it by the handle. "It was there as a part of you, now use it."

The two combatants bowed. Damali stood back to watch Carlos's lesson unfold and to learn from it as well. Zang Ho made the first lunge. Carlos spun away and caught the master's blade against blade, causing steel to collide in hard strikes that drew sparks. Carlos swung harder, and Zang Ho disappeared, then came out of a fold of nothingness in the glen, just behind Carlos, to try to catch him unaware. But Carlos sensed the old teacher coming before he even materialized and spun in time to avoid being gored. Carlos swung again, and Master Ho balanced on the end of his blade, stepped backward onto the air, and gently floated down.

The master smiled and bowed. "You are still fighting me like a man, though there has been a vast improvement. In your earlier incarnation in the shadows, you owned the air, disappearance and reappearance, and you would have had my head rolling along the grass by now."

Zang Ho tossed a blade to Damali, and she caught it with her right hand. "Your lesson is different. You have been taught to shape-shift. You are already a master with a blade. But you hold back. It takes time for you to decide what to become and then make the shift, because it frightens you . . . the power of uncorking true rage."

He smiled and swiped the blade at her. She easily met his swipe as metal made contact with metal. Suddenly the blade fell from his hand and a huge black snake reared up from what had been his sword. Damali jumped back and brandished her blade as the serpent hissed and struck at her. She refused to let go of the sword for a moment, until the thing before her sprouted wings and began to evolve into a dragon.

Still clinging to the sword, she flipped out of harm's way, finally dropped her blade, and became an eagle to fly high above it. Zang Ho sighed and returned to his natural form.

"If this were a night aerial attack, and I turned into a monster, then what?"

"I'd lower a shoulder cannon at you and blow your head off," Damali said, as soon as she touched down and put both feet on the ground.

"That is a good option out here, but in tight confines, you must overcome your fear to use that natural weapon." The master wagged his finger. "You two must be in sync, have complete trust, and be able to match each other's moves, blindly. If he swings in one direction, you must avoid his swing. If she shape-shifts, you must be able to match her new shape with a complimentary choice. Two dragons, an adder and a lion, and so forth. If he arcs a shield, you must be able to use your blade as though one of his arms, and the converse is true." The old master pursed his lips. "Most important, you must be able to know each other by all indicators, not just the eyes. In the heat of battle, you could kill your partner—take the wrong head—and the enemy would laugh at your loss."

"Now *that's* a fact," Carlos said, picking up the abandoned swords and handing them to Zang Ho. "Done all the time. If a vamp gets in a corner, it will cast an illusion to look like someone you know, to make you hesitate, or send a body-double illusion so you don't know which one to stake."

Damali dabbed at the perspiration on her brow. "We just witnessed that back in Lhasa. For a moment, I wasn't sure, then I was."

Zang Ho put his hands behind his back. "There should have been instant recognition or close to it. Sense his energy field. His scent. His eyes. His gestures. Tone of voice. Words. Mood. All these facets should be calculated by your brain in an instant." He looked at Carlos. "You, too. You must *know* her, or one night in battle, you might accidentally kill her."

Damali absently rubbed the side of her face where Carlos had slapped her. Carlos looked away.

"Imposters should stand out without a second guess." Zang Ho walked around Carlos and Damali, making them spin as he circled them. "Why don't you know each other's energy fields? You are newly mated Neterus, soul mates. What has happened here? I am confused. He is about to apex and you two do not know each other? Why not? There is a riddle. There is a block that I do not understand."

"We're not exactly sure, either, sir," Damali said.

Carlos looked away at the cliffs. "I don't, either. It's not her fault, though. I mean . . ."

"There is no fault," Zang Ho said, and fussed, rubbing his bearded chin. "This cannot be. Foul play is at hand. Something more has happened than is apparent. Your quest is to become still and remember what you know." He stared at Carlos hard and squinted farther, then turned, bobbing his head from side to side, studying Damali. "Nothing inside you from the shadows, either. Humph. Interesting puzzle. Come."

The Naksong reached out his hand, the yak-hair blanket appeared in it, and then the swords encased in scabbards slid under his arms. "Any day now. Any day. You could go into apex, which will lure the she-demon, which will draw the male, and you are not ready. Neither of you are. This is bad. She will bring the most feared vampire," he said, then stared at them, halting abruptly. "Dante. The Serpent of the Garden. He is not to be challenged without complete alignment and balance. Your attempt to go after them before you were ready was foolish. Luck and favorable auspices were on your side, but one should not prevail through luck alone. Skill and preparation are the best weapons." He glanced around still seeming distracted, and began walking again.

Zang Ho climbed over a large boulder, nodded, and waved Damali and Carlos forward. He inched his way down a steep incline that gave way to a milder slope, stooped, looked around, and flung open the blanket. "Sit," he commanded.

Carlos gave Damali a sidelong glance. She discreetly shrugged, and they sat down beside each other. Zang Ho slapped his forehead in frustration.

"No! That's not the way two warriors fight, sitting side by side like boyfriend and girlfriend—sit back-to-back." He leveled a blade at them and dropped a sword on each of their laps. "Keep your eyes on the horizon. From the flowers that cover the mountainside in new color, to the sheep that graze and mate lower in the fields, to the birds that circle the cliffs, to the winds that shift the clouds, to the earth's tonal vibrations—hold the sword and feel it all through the sword to become one with the weapon."

He walked around the pair, making their necks crane as they strained to keep eye contact with their teacher. "When you are ready and can feel your partner's energy vibrate through you, through the steel, stand. Remain back-to-back and begin the movements of fighters, slow, controlled, steady, until you can anticipate each other's moves. Keep your eyes closed once you stand. If one of you is not ready, whisper it in your mind; the other must wait. Make your fight pace quicken, until you can move like thought-lightning without injuring each other; then gradually slow your rhythm until you are still enough to again go back-to-back, sit, and breathe as one. That is your exercise for today to align your energies."

"How will we get back to—"

Zang Ho snapped twice and frowned at Carlos, silencing him with a glare. "Still the wrong question. I will go teach the others what I can today. *They* need weapons and whatever else you've brought along, but their generals should not. They require years of training, but we are out of time. I will do the best I can under the circumstances." He clicked his tongue. "So it is." He folded his arms and frowned. "I will collect you just before sunset and rejoin you with your team, and then we shall camp with nomad protectors until you are ready to flush the hunted from the shadows."

Carlos and Damali stared at the Naksong's back, watching him gradually fade away in the mist.

"That was live, D," Carlos whispered, not sure their teacher was gone.

"Shush," she said in a nervous whisper. "What if the old boy is still around? Chill. Do what he said."

Carlos unsheathed his blade and held it at a ninety-degree angle to his heart before him, listening to Damali unsheathe her weapon. After a bit, the blade began to feel heavy, and he shifted position and crossed his legs Indian style, then lowered the blade so that the handle rested on the ground and the tip was skyward. They sat that way, back-to-back, for what seemed like a long time. He watched the horizon and then allowed his gaze to soak in the profusion of subtle colors that carpeted the slope. Damali's natural scent wafted over her shoulders and flowed over him. Soon he could pick out the various wildflower fragrances, discerning grasses from flowers, soil from animal musk, just like he'd been able to before.

The awareness was startling. It was as though something had wiped his mental slate clean, taking away not only the best of his old vampire skills, but all his newly acquired Neteru gifts with it. For months he'd felt like he was living a half-life, where everything was muted, sensations were dulled, his emotions were contained. Shabazz had told him many of the things the Naksong said, but for some reason those truths didn't resonate before. He'd heard them, could intellectually process them, but could never translate them into innate understanding. He'd wondered why that was, what had kept him so separated from what was clearly logical? Now, in the pristine air and sitting quietly, bits of his old self began to slide back into place.

Initially, he'd been so bored that he was ready to just give up, but soon he felt a sense of comfort and listened to Damali's slow, calm breathing. Her back expanded against his, warming it as she breathed in, leaving cool places along his shoulder blades when she exhaled. Her spine nestled against his and there was heat where their vertebrae met. Slowly he became aware that if he listened hard enough, he could feel her heartbeat through her back.

He kept his eyes closed, remembering her heartbeat, how it sounded when he'd laid his head against her chest . . . remembered what it felt like beneath his palm. He remembered her breaths, the gentle expulsion of air when she laughed, or sighed, or her hot breaths of sudden rage . . . or passion. The heat felt good against his neck and face, it was moist heat, similar to, but unlike the sun's. But there was also a breeze, a shifting of air and air pressure, of air temperature. Her breaths made him feel light, and as the wind caressed the mountainside, he imagined the wind to be her whispers. He made a game of listening to it, imagining it as her laughter, or fussing, or crying, or sighing. Was she telling him a secret or calling out his name? He chuckled as he thought about it.

"What?" Damali whispered.

He smiled and kept his eyes closed. "I like your voice."

She smiled. "That's one of the things I love most about you—your voice."

"Really?"

"Yeah," she murmured. "Concentrate."

He opened his eyes using the sense of sight, and stared at the awe-inspiring landscape. There was so much about Damali that was more spectacular than the mountains and contained just as much mystery. She'd healed another family, had healed theirs, too; the angels had given her their tears. He could still feel her gentle rhythm behind him. The wind still seemed to be her voice. The colors now added a new level of awareness, and he definitely wondered how he'd been so blind? For all the ugliness in the world, the world was still going on. Here, sitting at the edge of heaven, never did he dream that both he and Damali would be alive in the same time and space, sharing a yak blanket on the cliffs of nowhere, with stainless steel blades on their laps, watching sheep mate.

"You think the shepherds used to do this?" she murmured.

"Do what?"

She laughed softly. "Sit and try to feel all the elements of the universe while watching rams fight over flocks?"

"I supposed there's not much else to do up here, other than that," he said with a deep chuckle.

She liked the way his laughter rumbled through his body into hers. "We're not supposed to be talking," she said laughing.

"Shush, we're not talking," he said quietly, "we're whispering and laughing. Don't have Zang Ho come back up here and pop you in the head again."

He felt her body shake with giggles and knew she'd covered her mouth with her hand. He could see it without even seeing it, just like he could mentally envision her megawatt smile. Here he was supposed to be a Neteru, and all his senses had been so dull . . . How did that happen?

"You have to go back to making music," he said softly as her giggles abated. "Writing poetry, singing, jamming with the band in the studio, or on the steps. Music is energy, harmonic chords that create positive vibrations. You know?"

"All right, Naksong," she murmured, a giggle in her voice, but with a deep tone of appreciation threaded through it. "I sorta got away from it, because it can be so all-consuming and I didn't want to shut you out."

"Baby, don't give up anything like that for me—music is part of your soul."

He felt her nod and closed his eyes and sighed.

"So are you," she said quietly.

"Same here," he murmured. "You know I would never, ever hit you," he said in the barest of whispers.

"I know you didn't hit me," she said, and then laughed softly, "but you slapped the shit out of her."

He laughed. "I'm sorry. It scared me."

"You know that's only the second time in our lives you've admitted that?"

"You've never told me that," he said, his tone becoming mellow. "I wasn't sure how you'd react, if I ever told you something like that."

"Deep," she murmured. "Then I owe you an apology, because I've been scared as shit for a long time."

"Get out of here, D."

"I'm serious."

He didn't answer for a while, but continued to feel and listen to her breathe.

"The Naksong was right," he finally said in a gentle murmur. "There's no reason we haven't been in sync. No matter come what may, nothing should ever get between me and you. Not even old flames . . . especially not that."

Again he felt her nod, but she said nothing. However, he did notice that her breathing hitched slightly and was no longer deep and even.

"You getting tired?" he asked, wondering if her legs were starting to fall asleep. Discomfort would be the perfect reason for her to tense; at least he hoped that's what it was and not what he'd said. He'd meant every word.

She slowly shook her head no, then took in a deep breath and held it for a second; he could hear her release it through her nose. Then she leaned her head back, slowly, carefully, as though she were falling, and inhaled deeply again as the back of her skull fit against the curve of his neck. Either she was getting sleepy and didn't feel like keeping the rigid meditation posture, or she wanted to stand and move, like he did. He wasn't quite sure, so he gently tested by straightening his legs and then pushing his spine against hers.

Force met force, and there was enough trust that they wouldn't drop each other by pulling up in a sudden move. His knees bent and his feet pushed against the ground; so did hers, until they stood back-to-back, and turned at the same time. He went to the left, she cut her blade to the right, slow motions, moving clockwise and counterclockwise to each other's controlled moves, eyes closed, sensing the motion before it happened, knowing where the other would be, mirror images, moving faster.

He could feel dampness coat his skin, tasted salt as he licked his lips and kept pace with her. The air was cool flowing through his hair; it had dampened, too. She smelled good; he knew where she was at every moment till time stopped, sound abated, nothing existed except the sound of her breaths.

He'd glimpsed her expression from the corner of his eye as they passed each other in a blur of motion. His back slammed against hers. She froze and didn't move. Enough. Time to slow it down, slide back to the ground, and regain their breathing. He was so turned on that for a moment he couldn't will his knees to bend.

She waited, had caught the look on his face. Gooseflesh covered her arms beneath her sleeves. His eyes burned with pure silver light. His Neteru marking on his jugular glowed white hot. He was majestic swinging a blade under the sun. They had to sit down, they had to sit down, they *had* to sit down. All she had to do was simply bend her knees.

She did, and they buckled, causing him to almost plummet, then pause, wait for her, and continue the slow descent to the blanket, adding pressure to pick up the slack when her weight shifted. He was trailing pure male Neteru; she sucked in a huge breath and allowed the scent to coat her tongue and her insides. It was all in his sweat, mixing with rarified air, and flowers, and grasses, and rich, dark earth. She hit the blanket with a thud. He'd stopped breathing for a second. Her blade trembled in her hand, not from fatigue. She was one with the blade, she was one with the blade, she was *one* with the blade. . . . She dropped it. She heard another one thud as it hit the dirt.

"Listen, D—"

"I know."

"You think he's coming back anytime soon?"

"That old dude pops out of thin air," she said after a moment. He nodded, and took in a huge breath of air. "Yeah, I know."

"I think we're synced up."

He nodded and swallowed hard. "Yeah."

She closed her eyes and opened her hand. His filled it, not the sword. He nuzzled her shoulder with his chin, slightly turning. She breathed him in with a shudder.

"You smell so good it doesn't make any sense." She opened her other hand and his filled it.

"I can feel your Sankofa, like it's burning right through your coat."

She squeezed her lids shut tighter. "It's climbing up my back, like you," she said hoarse. She turned her arms inward, but didn't turn to face him as he wrapped them around his waist. She dropped her head back to touch his and pressed her knees together. "You're apexing."

He nodded. "I know. I can barely breathe."

A shudder claimed him as her pulse quickened in his palms. Suddenly he could feel the gooseflesh on her arms. His mouth craved hers like a dying man craves water. It was beyond a thirst, it had become a necessity.

Every pulse point she owned lit within him, fusing his to hers, until he dropped her hands, spun, and took her mouth. His fingers found her hair, a sensation so missed that they trembled in the lush texture. Her skin, her gorgeous, rich cinnamon skin was alive, even the color of it was living heat beneath his palm as it caressed her cheek, and the sound she sent into his mouth made him cover her on the ground.

His opened coat became one with hers, creating a double, moving, writhing blanket of hair and animal skin and bits of crushed flowers. Her voice muffled his as he moved against her, fabric creating friction, heat, resonance on the wind. Sound echoes clashed with the distant, steady, rhythm of rams horns locking in to-the-death imperatives established at the dawn of time.

She looked up into solid silver irises, a safety net catching her before she fell, yet she was one with the elements; yes, free from fear and worry, a hand touched her face in gentle surrender. Hers was covering where a misguided blow had landed, echoing truth from the soul, I'm ready. Just say it. Her spirit understood the slap was for another. Truth permeated it all.

"I love you."

She closed her eyes and felt the brand on his jugular, the heat seal that said he was on her side and in the Light. "I love you, too," she whispered. "But with no intent to carry."

Just say it, her mind called out to him again. She looked into eyes that told her no matter what his mouth said, there was a fifty-fifty chance she'd get up from the encounter planted with life. "Just say it."

"I can't lie to you." His voice was hot and ragged against her ear. "My intent is shaky."

She squeezed her eyes shut. "You're apexing, you know what that means."

He nodded and covered her mouth again, his tongue tangling with hers until she gasped and broke the kiss. "Don't make me make promises I can't keep."

Truth vibrated within his words, truth resonated within her soft moan. Layers of wool now seemed a divide as vast as the mountains surrounding them. Each peeled-away, pushed-up bit of cloth sent shivers. Touched torsos burned skin-to-skin, quaked backbones in jagged shudders. Hands worked fastenings to open hidden caverns and close gaps within the fabric of the universe, still held within the fabric of wool and jeans. Legs shackled to the knees in pants that stopped at boot tops contributed to a blackout-level frustration to connect. Blinding pleasure, wet slide hard arching one with lightning arcs; unsettling nesting birds now taking flight due to the cosmic disturbance.

If he had only known what it would have been like to apex in her arms, he would have never wasted time taking a walk on the dark side. Every touch she landed exploded pure white-light pleasure beneath her smooth caress till it went down to his marrow and resurfaced on his skin. She hunted sensations, trapped them, and knew just where to send them to climb up his shaft.

Oh, God, yes, this woman knew . . . Her hands knew him; she siphoned truth in unintelligible groans of consent. Yes, she could suck pleasure from every pore, making rain with his sweat, hard thunder from his voice, then evaporate it all in a hot-steam bath—she knew how; she knew all. It was her right to open up the heavens and transform stone into pliable clay. She could take his rib and create whatever she wanted, just so long as she didn't stop taking him into her . . . *and she knew that.*

The old man was wrong; he knew the questions to ask. He just couldn't get them out between sobs. *Oh, damn . . .* She was an element, hot wax, fire, oil. You didn't ask the elements, *you begged them . . .* paid homage, made sacrifices, lit butter lamps, left gifts, and prayed hard. Yes, she was one with the universe; he was one with her. Elements fused with known hysteria, because his woman knew him so well . . . *shit.* She felt so good; he knew everything but his name. She knew the hidden mysteries within, and had opened the door to transformation when she'd opened her warm thighs, and allowed him to pour himself into her.

The moment he entered her, she knew. She couldn't breathe. Her hands molded the curve of his ass; she knew the muscle cords under his skin like she knew her name. She knew his rhythm, his pulse, knew so fully that the tips of her breasts stung with remembrance. She knew the thick sinew that created leverage within his thighs, pushed his knees against the earth, sent his hot, staccato pant through her system, chasing deep, subsonic moans up from his diaphragm.

Oh, God, yes, she knew those slightly rough hands splayed wide across her back and behind, a mouth harsh and tender, butter tea sweetened with salt, yet never-bitter. Yes, she knew this man from all imposters, knew him before he stuttered her name, knew how he fused Spanish and English when he was near the edge . . . and knew this time he couldn't thread together a sentence to save his life.

His energy was wrapped around her like his earthy, fabulous, aphrodisiac scent. That's how she knew how to move with him, against him; knew that this apex was making him sob, fight a losing battle with control; it had stolen hers, made her careless, even though they both knew the consequences. There was never any question when her voice rent the air. They both knew a bite was coming that wouldn't break the skin, but would send ribbons of colors to spiral behind shut lids.

Rites of passage, rites of spring . . . seasons blurred. Too much time had gone by, yet not enough time remained in the world. This man, her man, had synced up with every element in the universe. He brought pure thunder to her valley, sudden lightning strikes of pleasure, then rained hard within her, and made her want to be mother earth. For him she would be whatever—she didn't care. Everything within her converged on their sacred central joining . . . his touch, his voice, his ragged breaths, his scent and sweat, until her internal heaven opened and poured forth all she had with her tears.

Yeah, she knew quite clearly that they were both infected . . . infected with each other. . . . That's what had them amid the cliffs losing their minds.

CHAPTER TWENTY-ONE

Breathing hard, sitting back-to-back, they kept their eyes closed and tried to pull themselves together before Bonpo Master Zang Ho, the Naksong, returned.

They heard him before his tiny little feet hit the ground. They knew he was scowling as he swished around them in a circle. It was not necessary to open their eyes.

"So!" their teacher said crisply. "It is near sunset. Have you aligned your energies?"

Damali felt a smile creep over her face and connect to Carlos's. "I think so," she said and offered him a slight bow by tilting her head down while she kept her eyes closed. If she looked the old man in the face, she knew her eyes would tell all and she'd burst out laughing.

"And you?" the master snapped to Carlos's.

"Oh, yeah . . ." he said, his voice slow and mellow. "I'm *real* straight."

For a moment, the Bonpo master didn't respond. He paused, fidgeted a bit, and then began walking again. "Good. Then would you care to demonstrate what you have learned?"

Damali's eyes popped open, she could feel laughter rising within her and connecting to a belly laugh swirling within Carlos. He broke before she did, and it was all over. He fell on his side and shook his head. She tried to keep her stoic facade, but it crumbled and gave way to gales of laughter.

"No, man," Carlos said, wheezing through heavy bursts of laughter. "Some secrets are not to be revealed."

The Naksong walked away and stood with his arms folded. "The swords," he said in a peevish tone. "In your hands. Now!"

"All right, all right," Carlos said, recovering and trying not to smile. "My apologies." He pushed himself to sit up and pressed his spine to Damali's again. He closed his eyes, laughter still erupting intermittently. "On three, baby."

"I got you," she said, unable to swallow away the mirth.

Carlos opened his hand at the same time Damali opened hers, and a sword appeared in both of their palms.

Shocked, they both stared down and marveled.

"That was deep, D," Carlos whispered.

"I know," she said, turning her wrist so the blade caught the setting sun.

Zang Ho rubbed his beard and allowed a half smile. He glanced at Carlos and then began walking. "Your eyes are silver," he said coolly. "I take it that you have been properly realigned."

"Master Zang Ho," Monk Lin said, bowing deeply as the party of three approached the small settlement camp.

Zang Ho frowned and returned Monk Lin's deep bow. "I am done teaching for a lifetime," he fussed as he stood with folded arms. "Incorrigible. Nondisciplined. Unorthodox. Slow to learn!"

"The oxen are slow, master. But the earth is patient," Monk Lin said with a quiet smile.

"They are ready," Zang Ho said begrudgingly, as he eyed Carlos and Damali, and then the rest of their team. The old master walked back and forth in front of the group, which was assembled before a large yak-haired tent. He glanced down at the ammunition trunks on the ground. "It was wise of you not to put innocent nomad protectors at risk."

"Yes, revered one. We let them know our approximate location, but have moved our team away from their campgrounds . . . just in case." Monk Lin smiled and kept his eyes lowered.

"He is apexing," Zang Ho snapped, pointing at Carlos as he walked away. The old man spun and folded his arms again, stopping his agitated movements. "Correction. Apexed. Past tense."

Monk Lin nodded and gave the Bonpo master a slight bow. "I know, esteemed master. We heard it echo through the glen."

She was done. She must have packed and unpacked and checked and rechecked artillery a hundred times, and there still wasn't a good place to keep her line of vision. She wasn't trying to see a single smile or smirk. She didn't want Carlos to say a word to her to make it any worse. Oh, my God, if her team had heard all that . . . no wonder the nomads had picked up tents and rolled.

Damali kept her eyes on the steel blade she was polishing. She'd begged silence in order to so-called concentrate. When she did speak, it was strictly business. Monk Lin, thankfully, was as discreet as ever, and worked at distributing night gear with Rider, whose expression remained unreadable. But Inez's glee was wearing her out. No, she was not discussing this with her girl. Not!

Conversely, Juanita still issued glances that could cut metal. Now that was one heifer that had better stay out of swing range—she was in no mood. Jose remained aloof. Damn. But that was cool. Had to be that way. Big Mike kept nodding to himself and showing off his silver-spiked hiking cleats while wearing a huge smile, and joking about kicking demon ass till it sizzled. He wasn't fooling a soul; Big Mike needed a diversion to allow him to belly laugh at something so they wouldn't take direct offense. Bottom line, though, Mike was *all* in their business. *That* was working her nerves to the bitter end. Bobby and Dan just seemed to walk around bumping into each other, all nervous, while Krissy and J.L. couldn't get out of each other's faces.

Damali let out a breath of frustration as she glimpsed Marjorie from the corner of her eye, noting that in the poor woman's distress, she'd brought some wildflowers into a daggone artillery tent, and was sprucing up the hovel like a spring wedding was in the offing. Berkfield seemed lost, his worried focus on his daughter, who was now clearly in full bloom. Hey, what did the man want? It was springtime in the mountains, and the girl was grown.

Damali let her breath out hard again. Her business was all in the streets. Was it possible to die of instant mortification, she wondered? The only ones who were somewhat cool were Marlene and Shabazz. They simply raised eyebrows with a knowing smirk and kept their conversation on neutral topics. But, that damned Carlos couldn't wipe the smile off his face. He was so cheerful that she couldn't even look at him.

Carlos plopped down behind her. Pressed his back to hers and began polishing his already gleaming blade. Damali laughed softly, unable to help herself.

"Get away from me," she whispered. "Your eyes are still flickering."

He smiled and turned his blade back and forth, catching the dim lamplights and tent center fire in it. "Really?"

"Stop," Damali said, working harder on the steel she held.

"That's not what you said a little while ago," he said under his breath, a low chuckle rumbling through his back into hers.

She had no words.

His laughter abated, but his mood remained light as he began polishing his blade behind her. After a moment, he abruptly stood and walked to the other side of the tent, blade pointed to the ground, studying it. No one paid him any particular attention, but she'd seen his lids lower by a quarter just as he'd turned to walk away. It was the sexiest of nuances, just a slight tremor unnoticeable to the others around them, but unmistakable to her. Then he quickly gave her his full back, as though trying to regain his cool.

In that moment, time seemed to slow down once more. She could feel his energy waft across the interior of the tent, enter the tip of her blade, and travel up the length of steel in her hand as though it were a giant antenna. Soon the blade in her hand became a lightning rod of sorts, picking up sensations that made it difficult to continue to hold the sword and keep polishing it. The more she rubbed it, the shakier his breaths seemed to become. She looked at the sword and stopped polishing it for a second, saw his breath hitch, and mouthed a silent *wow* . . . He was one with the blade. Very, very deep.

She'd promised herself that she would ignore him, but she couldn't help watching Carlos slowly sit on the ground and fold his legs Indian style, take in a quiet but shaky breath, and lay his sword across his thighs. Ever so slowly she noticed a slight mist of color begin to overtake his aura. It was a very deep navy, nearly indigo, that was close to black, with flicks of silver iridescence threaded through the hue. Although she kept the observation concealed within sidelong glances, the entire spectacle was mesmerizing as the vapor emanating from him began to fill the tent and mingle with the plume of smoke coming off the fire, and exiting the center chimney hole above.

Just watching him struggle for composure did something to her. With all the eyes around and the unseen dangers, she knew he was fighting a losing battle between the intellectual and the primal. Zang Ho was wrong, he hadn't apexed; he was apexing. This wasn't something that just happened quickly and was over. It was a process, and took a month to get out of one's system. She'd been there, almost pushed to the brink of her sanity when it had been her ripening time, and there was no one there when it happened . . . no one that she wanted to be with like she'd wanted to be with him.

Carlos's glance caught hers the very second the thought crossed her mind. *You don't know how much I wanted to be there,* mi tresora. His expression was stone serious as he looked away, leaned his head back, and sat as though in deep meditation. *I couldn't. I was injured. I would have changed the fate of the world, anyway, if I wasn't. But, I promise, I'll make it up to you tonight.*

She stared at his back. *I know. But not tonight.* Damali quickly glanced away and returned her attention to the sword that had practically come alive in her hands. Madame Isis *never* did this, she mused. The old girl never had a charge on it like what was running through her palms now. She had to distract herself, had to keep her focus. The brief mental answer she'd given Carlos was all she'd allow for a mind lock with others around. That had always been a volatile connection between them, and in a family tent with no options for privacy, there was no way was she going to keep this up.

You don't understand. The tone of Carlos's mental reply made her drop the polishing rag. The message was urgent, visceral, sent through the steel on her lap as a sensation at one with the thought. *You never opened Pandora's Box, never tasted being with the only one for you while in this state. Damali, you cannot imagine . . .* He took a deep breath. *I have to laugh to keep from crying, right about through here. Once. Once? Baby, that was just enough to make me crazy. I can't stop thinking about earlier today.*

Nope, she was not answering him or addressing what he'd just mentally jettisoned toward her. Yeah, he was crazy. Out of his dang mind. They were not alone! They were in the Himalayas near known danger—uh-uh. The family was at risk if they went off and did anything wild. She focused on the leather bindings that kept sections of the tent wall held together. Thankfully, the team was used to their Neterus sitting alone quietly at times, meditating, trying to pick up vibes, so nobody was in her or Carlos's face.

It was a nice ruse. Something very necessary to allow them to both cool off and recalibrate their nerves. She kept her back to the hubbub of conversation in the tent and to Carlos. He was on the other side of the tent doing the same. Good. Yes, she would mentally talk to him, but a *sensual* mind-lock in full view? Not here, not in front of family, and not with all that was possibly hunting them. On the mountainside was bad enough, where there was no way in heaven that she could have said no. However, that *taste,* as he called it, would have to hold them both for now. She smiled slightly and shook her head no with the barest hint of movement.

Immediately, she felt a hot kiss land on her lips that parted them with an insistent tongue. She almost moaned at the sensation, but sat there, staring at the tent wall, with wide eyes. He could do that—not as a vamp? Shit! She risked glimpsing him, and all she could witness with normal sight was his back slowly expanding and contracting with deep breathing. A sweat-darkened V had formed on his shirt between his shoulder blades. The blade burned against her thighs where it lay, and it felt more like him than metal. Damali closed her eyes. Oh, this was not good.

A few small pebbles slightly stirred on the ground, and made her open her eyes at the imperceptible sound. Mike hadn't heard it. Was it real or happening inside her head? Damali stared at the pebbles that began to move toward Carlos, as though he were magnetic. She glanced up at the hue of the chimney smoke, which was now richly colored with his scent, flickering silver as it made its way out of the opening, but then the dark hue suddenly doubled back, separated from the smolder coming off the fire and wafted in her direction to fill the tent. The fire in the center of the floor sputtered slightly, flaring with small silver flickers. Damali nervously glanced at the others, who hadn't noticed, but were fully engaged in whatever they were doing.

Stop, she mentally whispered, *before you take us both somewhere we can't go.*

I can't help it, I don't know what's happening to me, and I don't have control over this.

The scent of him was intoxicating, made her hands tremble, and made her breathing labor in response. *Baby, you have to just chill. Take cleansing breaths, be still, stop sending thoughts of what you want to do. Don't dwell on it, okay? It'll pass. Remember what you told me when I fluxed vamp and tried to breach daylight to get to you? Focus on that, the impossible.*

Why'd you have to remind me of that morning? Too erotic.

My bad! I meant, uh, focus on what is impossible. Not the incident.

She felt him nod from across the tent, felt it through her back, but also felt his hands cover her breasts in a phantom touch. Oh, no . . . the Naksong had told him to use what he used to know, not to fear it, and bring to it into his Neteru core. If he was bringing his old vamp talents of a mind-blowing phantom caress up in this tent . . .

She shook her head, trying to tell him, don't do it, and stopped breathing for a moment when his forefingers and thumb took her nipples in a slow roll back and forth between them. The sensation created a hard throb in her bud, and then sent a burn to cover her rim until it contracted, needing his entry. She fought not to move, not to arch against the pleasure, and couldn't make a sound, but was forced to sit there, stone rigid, as though nothing was happening at all. *Cut it out.*

Warm hands poured liquid heat over her buttocks beneath her pants, caressing her skin, setting fire to it, and slid over her belly to stroke the insides of her thighs. The blade pressed hard against them, reminding her too much of him. She could feel her inner thigh muscles contract of their own volition as the gentle stroke chased heat between them. For a second, she almost forgot where she was and who was there as a finger slid against the slick, wet folds that had become engorged with want. A gentle suckle played at one nipple while the other was teased with a steady thumb flicker. She bit her lip to keep sound from exiting her mouth. *Stop . . . baby, before we both embarrass ourselves.*

Her eyes literally crossed beneath her lids, as the sensation of his nose dragging along the edge of her shoulder and up the side of her throat stayed her complaint. *Not fair. You know that's my sweet spot. Stop.* Embarrassment made her face warm as she sat perfectly still, trying not to flinch, stifling a moan, and so wet that she was afraid she'd leave a damp mark on the ground.

Although her ears heard nothing but the chatter in the tent, she could separate out Carlos's breaths from that, pushing the noise and movements of the others further and further to the far corners of her mind. She glanced over her shoulder at the same time he did. His eyes were solid silver and he closed them and turned away. Oh, man, this was really bad, and truly tacky. She pressed both hands together, yogi style, and tried to chase away the thick desire that had erupted between them.

I can't, she heard him mentally stutter. *It's worse than earlier today.*

She could feel him about to hyperventilate, which she knew would draw attention. If he started babbling some sexy shit in Spanish, it was over. *Baby, breathe.* But she was the one who was beginning to hyperventilate. It was a slow, steady increase, stilled only by her horror of possible in-front-of-family humiliation.

Damali squeezed her eyes shut and inhaled sharply. He smelled so damned good, his mental caresses with an apex scent spike was blowing her away. She wanted to reach out and touch him so badly her palms ached to just allow her hands to cover his skin, feel the heat that radiated off his body. Her lips parted; she needed to kiss him hard, tangle her tongue with his. She could feel the dip in her lower back pulse with the need to jerk to his thrusts.

The Sankofa tattoo over her base chakra had ignited spinal fluids, releasing mental spasms, as well as every other liquid her body owned. By now the draw to touch him was beyond her ability to resist, so she picked up the sword, instead, and ran her fingers down the edge of the blade. His reaction was a sharp hiss. She opened her eyes and glanced around, but realized when no conversation had abated that, he'd apparently had enough wherewithal to keep that sound a mental one.

Put the blade down, Damali. Once, earlier today, was just a tease. After being apart for months, out of sync, no, once was not enough.

She heard him pause, but didn't stop stroking the metal lying across her lap.

The team is strapped to the gills, maybe . . . for an hour, they'd be all right?

It was surely a tender offer, one nearly impossible to refuse. Maybe, if they took a couple of weapons and a blanket somewhere. . . . She knew she sounded crazy to her own mind, but this was like fighting one's own DNA!

I'm a female Neteru, I have no defense against this, Carlos. You have to be the one to hold the line, or . . . oh, my God, I can't stand it. She put down the blade very carefully beside her and kept her eyes closed, blotting at the building moisture on her forehead and the damp sheen that covered her neck. She could almost feel it pool right in the center of her neck, where her collarbone created a small V. Her shirt was sticking to her; her pants felt like they'd been glued on. She wanted to, had to, get out of her clothes, or she'd suffocate in them.

Oddly, when she opened her eyes, Carlos's image was before her, sitting cross-legged in front of her, both staring at each other, but she knew it was just a vision. Carlos was actually sitting with his back to her, a good fifteen feet across the tent. *Stop,* she mentally repeated. It was bad enough that they'd made love on the mountainside without access to water, and she knew her Guardian brothers with the noses had picked that up. Now she was so wet again that it didn't make sense. The sexual tension between them had literally made the hair stand up on Shabazz's and Dan's arms when they'd walked into the enclosure to rejoin the team. J.L. was practically liquefied by it. No doubt Mike heard it all . . . and anybody else with half a gift had picked up on the deal. If they weren't real careful, in a minute Marlene would be in it with her second sight, and who knew if Marj or Juanita or Inez had that capacity strong enough yet to get in their business? *Now, stop.*

Damali's blade rested beside her leg as she made the request. The sword handle had been too hot to hold, felt molten in her palm. She wiped at another trickle of perspiration that rose on her forehead and slid down her temple. Was

it her imagination, or did the heat in the tent kick up a few
notches? Damn, this brother was drawing in elemental
forces. She turned to glimpse him, and found herself staring
as he slowly got up without using his hands to push off the
ground. Carlos just stood in one lithe motion, sauntered over
to her, garnering temporary glances and wry smiles from
team members, who then went on about their business once
he sat before Damali.

"I can't do this," he said in a low, private murmur. "I can't."

She held his hands as they faced each other, sitting in
meditation position. "Yes, you can. I did. It's hard—"

His sly smile cut off her statement of logic.

"It's difficult," she corrected.

"For me, because of the time I was born, and probably
because of what I'd been before, it gets worse at night."

She stared at him. She'd never considered that. All she
could do was nod for a moment. "It'll pass," she finally said,
trying to put conviction in her tone.

The pain in his expression made her want to look away,
but she couldn't.

"How did you deal with it?" he asked in a low, hard,
whisper, his gaze open, and no games evident in it. The
sound of his voice was so gravelly that it sent a silent tremor
through her.

She couldn't immediately answer the question, or continue staring into his silver-lit eyes. She wasn't sure how
she'd made it through that ripening month when he was supposedly dead. She tucked away a new reality that made guilt
twist the pit of her stomach . . . that was when she'd almost
gone to Jose.

Damali kept her eyes on Carlos's hands. All of it made so
much sense, now. She might be a Neteru, just as Carlos might
have once been a vampire, but at the end of it all, they were
human, flawed, and made of flesh and blood. Desire was a
powerful entity all on its own, and to add a Neteru ripening or
apex spike to the equation, anything could go down . . . just
like adding a little vamp to the mix was a recipe for disaster.

She knew what he was going through. All she had to do was think back on those powerful urges, the procreation imperative that had her up at night, feigning. . . . Yeah, she remembered wanting some so bad she was crying. Hysterics were not out of the question as her body had pressed against the sweat-damped nothingness of sheets and she'd clung to dream sensations in her fitful sleep, days offering no escape, as everything had reference to hot, raw sex. . . . Celibacy had been a true bitch, there was no other way to tell him.

He squeezed her hands tighter, sending the message that he'd heard her. But the look in his eyes begged her to step outside for a little while.

"Where?" she said with a slow smile. "Don't even try it."

When he didn't smile back, the smile slowly left her face, too. Kinetic charge filled her palms through his and raced up her arms like a quick shudder. Suddenly, no one was in the tent. The walls seemed like that of a cave. Beneath them, thick, warm, unidentifiable animal skins covered the cave floor. Dark red, Neolithic rock art was set to glow by a fire, telling a moving story of humanity's struggle for survival against beasts. Stick figures danced across the rough walls, chasing predators with spears, arrows, and bows. The fire in the middle of the floor flared and danced with the moving frescoes. Tinder crackled within the blaze. Bits of glowing ember twigs leapt from it, striking Carlos's bare torso as he sat before her nude, holding her hands, each flaming contact leaving a red brand that went white-silver, marking him in what seemed to be war paint.

Her eyes filled with tears of pure need, the desire was so palpable that her fingers trembled as she touched his face. They left a deep, crimson mark where they'd landed, as though he'd been burned by her caress, and he closed his eyes and touched her face, marking her where his fingers fell.

Then trembling touches became a sudden, violent kiss. Her hair was in his fist, his bare chest pressed against hers, the markings on it transferring to her naked skin, sending white-hot pleasure from every stripe until she

cried out. She immediately knew where she was, she had
gone back to the dawn of time with him. First man, first
woman, that was all that there was . . . the first tribe, cave
dwellers—hunt, eat, survive, procreate—that was all that
there was. He'd apexed and gone back to Adam's beginning . . . just outside the Garden when the true battle began, and where the first male Neteru had to step up. Be
fruitful and multiply.

Carlos flattened her; the erotic scent of him caused instant delirium. She moved beneath him, urgently trying to
get him to enter her. They had to create, stop the burn, and
be as one. But his head jerked up, and he looked over his
shoulder, growled, and stood.

Instantly she was back in the tent, no one else had changed
position, no one had moved, conversations remained unbroken, no one even seemed to notice that Carlos was pacing.

She stood slowly, trying to regain her bearings. Her breaths
were open, ragged pants. Two seconds ago, she wouldn't have
cared less if he'd made love to her in a filled stadium. She was
about to go to him when he held up his hand, breathing in
shuddery gulps, his eyes keen on something outside the tent.
She tried to focus in on what he was sensing. His scent permeated her skin, the animal skin walls of the tent. Small
clumps of dirt rolled toward his feet, magnetizing to his
highly charged energy. The fire sputtered and hissed as though
water had been sprinkled on it, and the air swirled in a lazy
dance around them. He'd inadvertently drawn the elements,
and possibly something else more dangerous.

"I'm worried now," she finally said in a tense murmur,
unable to chase away the desire burn that lingered. She was
angry that she still felt it, angry that they hadn't finished
what they'd started, angry that they'd been interrupted, angry that her focus should be elsewhere, but was still locked
on making love to him—

"I know," he said quietly, scowling at the tent walls and
then briefly closing his eyes. "That is a good way to have the
entire team smoked. I'm sorry, but—"

"No apology required," she said in a quiet, breathy voice. "I'm right there with you, but I don't know what just happened. It was like some kinda dimensional distortion that shouldn't have gone down."

"I know, I know." He bent and picked up her sword and handed it to her. "It was reflex. I couldn't stop what I was feeling, was thinking about it so hard I just projected, I guess. I wanted to be one-on-one so bad that I couldn't shake the image, which could've gotten us all jacked." His voice remained low so only she could hear his words, and his eyes held hers for a moment. "Later."

She nodded and kept her tone private. "Later, but soon, I hope."

He closed his eyes briefly and nodded, sucking in a huge breath, and kept his voice intimate, like hers. "I am really pissed off, right about through here."

"Ditto, but can you sense what's coming?"

He tilted his head, stared at the wall, but a sly smile tugged at his mouth. "Yeah."

"All jokes aside, you just perfumed the entire mountain, brother." Damali pushed the tip of the sword into the dirt so it stood beside her and glimpsed up at the hole in the tent. The remnants of sunset were nearly gone. She raked her fingers through her hair. "If you hadn't pulled up, you would have had me calling your name in front of the team. Now try to think of what made you stop like that."

Part of what disturbed her, beyond the acute ache of the interruption, was that he'd looked up the way master vampires did when interrupted in their lair. She hadn't seen that look in his eyes, or heard that low resonant growl split his diaphragm in a very long time. She'd thought that had completely gone out of his system, and the fact that it was fused with a Neteru love-making dance really worried her no end. So did the time-distortion thing he'd just done. It was as though some of his old master's abilities had come back with the new apex, which *really* worried her.

"I don't know," he finally said in a quiet tone, his gaze slowly moving over the tent wall. "It was a large presence, female, dangerous."

The fact that Carlos's mating vibration was strong enough to produce a virtual hallucination still had her reeling. Her knees still felt like rubber. But it also meant that it was more than a lure to something they had to kill. It was here, somewhere, turned on, and on the move.

Carlos nodded. "I know. Was trying not to think about that." He paused and turned around to completely face Damali. "I thought you might also be worried about something else, too, like getting pregnant again." He stared at her for a moment and then looked away. "Definite possibility tonight. Restraint of intent ain't nowhere in me."

"I *am* worried about that," she said honestly, but kept her voice private and gentle. "But that's something long-term to consider, if we live through this mission. I'm more worried about what we'll have to face, short-term."

She looked around the tent at the team that was still scattered in groupings of conversation, card games, and general relaxed chaos. This was a bad position for any of them to be in, to have both generals mentally compromised by a genetic force, while something serious was on their asses.

"Our timing, once again, sucks," Carlos said, wiping his palms over his face. "I do *not* like being in a situation where my head ain't right. That's a perfect way to get jacked."

"I'm right there with you, brother—we're on the same page. My concentration ain't no better than yours."

For a moment, they both just stared at each other.

You remember how I was when you were ripening and I'd just turned vamp?

She nodded. *Yep, and now I know what you were dealing with, because if you don't stop the mind locks, I will throw your fine ass to the ground in this tent with everyone watching.* "Don't go there, or revisit that." *I'm in a very fragile state—*

horny beyond your comprehension. Just the freakin' memories send chills, you clear! Damali turned away and wrapped her arms around herself and drew in a shuddery breath. But Carlos snatched her arm and turned her around hard, making the others briefly glance at them for the first time.

They both glared at the team, which sent lines of vision away from them. The message was implicit; the argument was private, stay out of it.

Then, don't even suggest something like that . . . Okay? Carlos mentally said, stabbing her mind with a low rumble once the team went back to their own conversation. *Do not talk dirty to me in here, or even think about a ground body-slam, hear! Not right now, because I'm about to take you up on the threat.* He looked at her hard, but there was a plea in his tear-filled eyes that made her measure her words. *Know that I have complete respect for what you went through alone. Get back on the subject.*

Damali nodded, went to touch his arm, but made her hand fall away. "It's on me and you, now," she said in a soft apologetic tone, running her fingers through her locks as she looked up at Carlos. This made no sense, both of them battling to breathe, both sweating like they'd been chased and had an entire team to keep safe, but also having to fight this apex thing going down to twist their brains. "We baited this thing; it's hooked and headed our way," she finally whispered, taking long pauses to collect herself. "I can feel it. We're responsible for what happens to this family."

"You think Zang Ho got the young bucks ready?" Carlos said, his gaze sweeping Bobby and Dan, then over toward Krissy and J.L. His gaze lingered on Marjorie, and then Inez and Juanita. Then he soberly answered his own question. "Yeah, D. This is tight."

Carlos and Damali moved closer together. They both stared at each other, the quiet plan implicit.

"Draw it away from the tent," she murmured.

"Give the family a chance to aim and fire." Carlos glanced around. "Two-by-two detail."

Damali nodded. "Okay, everybody. Listen up," she said, walking away from Carlos and blotting her damp forehead with the back of her wrists. "In about ten minutes, we'll have true nightfall. I want everybody who doesn't have night vision capacity, or a fully developed gift, with goggles on, even in the tent. Your gun is in readiness position, unholstered, safety off, and in quick reach range. Shield bracelets are on. Grenades hooked to your vests. Cold-body indicators are on your hip at all times and set to vibrate. Every person in here should have a Bowie or some type of blade. If it gets ugly, and you get separated from the group, make sure you have heat packs and switch your locators on transmit, because if you do make it to sunrise, we don't want to find you frozen to death. Until we get back down that mountain in full daylight, you look alive and stay alive."

Smiles faded, eyes hardened, heads nodded as the team stared back at her and Carlos, and teammates began to stand and comply.

"Me and D are doing this first night shift. At this juncture, I need to be away from this tent and as far away from any of you as possible. I'm bait, and trailing. So, the last person you get next to if it gets rugged is me. Home to Damali to take cover. Understood?"

Again, heads nodded. Silence made the tent feel smaller. Tension practically sucked the air up and out of the small center hole above.

Krissy slid the bracelet on her arm, lit a beam to surround her body in a shield, and tapped her indicator. "This one is defective," she said, glancing around nervously. "It's already buzzing."

Before she'd finished her sentence, a giant claw ripped through the tent wall where she stood. J.L. flat-kicked her in the chest and she landed by Big Mike as the tent collapsed. Something snatched J.L. out of the torn opening so fast that Carlos couldn't get to him as the heavy folds plumed down on the group.

Pure mayhem broke out as Carlos and Damali cut their way out of the tarp. They heard J.L.'s voice screaming a long descending echo. They glanced at each other; two seconds told them the deal. He was falling. Damali's sword dropped. A pair of eagle eyes replaced hers. Wind rushed beneath her. Talons outstretched. His body was too heavy. He'd take them both down. Zang Ho's voice stabbed at her mind. *Dragon.*

She became huge, strong; her muscles split across her breastbone and wrapped her legs in what felt like steel cable. J.L. was semiconscious; his body rimmed in blue-white light from his bracelet, and was reaching for a vest-hitched grenade. Friendly fire was about to kill them both. She snapped at his arm to send his hand back, circled the mountain, and dropped him as gently as she could near other blue-white rimmed bodies.

"You're ass was lucky," Damali shouted, to make J.L. know not to attack her. "The only thing that probably kept you from being gored was the bracelet. Hold your fire. It dropped you because the UV burned it."

Blue-and-yellow rapid-artillery ejections looked like fireworks from the distance. She left J.L. and circled, trying to find a safe place to come in for a landing without taking a shell. Then something slammed into her midair, a slash sounded behind her, and she ducked a razor-edged tail, but it got her wing.

Tumbling, she landed with a hard thud, rolled, and held her left shoulder. The gash was two inches deep and blood was everywhere. But she had to get back into the fight. It wasn't time to bleed or die. Damali scrambled over the ridge to where the unseen beast had fled trailing sulfur, knowing it was headed in Carlos's direction.

Carlos ran as fast as he could to draw it away from the others. He somersaulted behind a rock formation, but a bolt of black energy smashed it. The blade in his hand had snapped like a twig when he'd swung it with all his might, the beast ducked, and it made contact with stone. Carlos flung the useless handle to the ground. Two huge yellow eyes appeared in a black scaly face and leaned down from its ten-foot advantage, fangs glistening, one wing smoking, but not slowed in the least.

"I believe you were looking for me," he hissed.

Carlos's back was to air, his heels perilously crumbling pebbles. Even with the thunderous distortion, he'd know Dante's voice anywhere.

Claws extended as the beast lunged forward in an open-fisted reach toward Carlos's chest. His golden energy shield rose, blocking the heart-snatch, but he fell backward over the ledge.

He was tumbling so fast that all the air in his lungs instantly exited his body. Then something snatched him and stopped his collision with the ground. His stomach lurched and felt like it was in his esophagus, the change in direction was so abrupt. A long, red tongue splattered with black ooze licked the side of his face and covered his hair in slime. Grayish-green hooked claws held him to a cold, scaly torso with breasts. The thing that carried him was so large that he couldn't see its face. Carlos glimpsed down at the several-thousand-foot drop, then glimpsed up at the entity that clutched him. Options were limited, but it was not about going with her toward the destination of a cliff-side lair.

Carlos opened his hand. A new sword was in it. Death before dishonor. Unable to get a good angle to penetrate the creature's body, he swiped at one of the huge, leathery wings that beat the air.

The creature screeched, but didn't let go. A razor tail slashed at his blade, fending off another stab. The female beast that held him was listing to one side, injured in the joint, not in the webbed leather like the other beast had been. Her hulking body billowed foul yellow smoke, her narrowed gaze sought a landing, when something mounted her back. Carlos was flung against the dirt, his sword lost in the hard fall, and he backed away from the edge of a yawning drop, as two beasts collided midair, one black, one gray, and tumbled in a downward death-struggle.

"Take cover," the gray beast screeched toward Carlos, her eyes glowing black. "You cannot be destroyed. Not now during your apex!"

He didn't wait to watch the outcome, but rejoined the team, running a hundred yards toward the clearing where blue-white outlined bodies could be seen in the darkness.

J.L. was back on his feet. Rider and Shabazz had locked on targets and released cold-seeking missiles. Big Mike had released a shoulder cannon shell that took out a section of mountain over the next ridge.

The team ducked, scattered, and took cover in five directions as the smoking gray beast was suddenly hurled over the edge of the ridge, slid through the tent and equipment, and landed two hundred yards away against the mountainside. Big Mike was trapped as she rose, dashed forward, and snapped at him. But Mike's silver-spiked boot caught the beast's jaw, hurling her back and splattering blackish-green slime at his feet. She reached out with a deadly swipe; Mike ducked and rolled away from the tail that stabbed at him. Inez jumped up, not taking cover, squeezing rounds from an Uzi and screaming Mike's name. Rider opened fire with Inez and Shabazz to give his man cover, allowing Mike to scramble behind another huge rock.

"Lilith, you bitch!" A deep voice rumbled in the distance. "You will never supercede me to make him your heir apparent! Not in his apex, not ever!" Within seconds, the black beast flew over the cliff edge toward the injured one, his black tail swishing in fury as he gained momentum. The gray one tried to lift off, screeching and hissing, and sending a weak arc of energy toward the larger creature hurling toward her; then suddenly the black one ducked, allowed two cold-seeking missiles to pass him, and covered his face and chest with his wings. The mountainside instantly yawned, sending black, sulfuric smoke into the air. Lilith screeched as an unseen force yanked her body into the cavern "Nooo, husband, I beg you!" she screamed. The mountain sealed.

Missiles made contact, missing their target, Lilith. The explosion quaked the mountainside. Clips and weapons flew out of hands as human bodies flattened to the ground from the impact. A slow rumble sounded overhead. The team got up quickly. No one fired; everyone froze, looked up, and began running.

"Avalanche!" Damali hollered.

"It all comes full circle," the huge predator hissed, touching down before them to block their retreat. His focus narrowed on Carlos as he lowered his head. "I'll see you back in Hell, where you were born!"

A black arc snared all gunfire. A sword materialized in Damali's hand. She swung; Carlos pushed her to fall, and made her miss the Chairman's throat by a millimeter.

"No," Carlos shouted. "Not yet!"

"Bring me my book," a low voice rumbled behind the entity that disappeared.

The team's attention immediately shot to the fast-moving white threat behind them. Small knots of humanity fanned out, sought rock formations, anything to get behind as a shield. But there was nothing, simply a flat, two-hundred-yard glen, then they would fall over the edge of the world, pushed by ice, rocks, snow, and dirt.

"Everybody come together!" Carlos yelled.

"Hold the line!" Damali shouted, moving to his side. "Temple formation! Don't separate!"

Bodies slammed against bodies. All eyes turned toward the white-and-brown sea of mother earth hurling toward them. Carlos and Damali stood in a north-south position, back to back with the team between them. He opened his hands; she caught the end of his shield, arcing a dome of golden, impermeable light over the group.

Initially rocks and pebbles leading the avalanche bounced and skittered off the dome, making them cringe, but they all closed their eyes, said a prayer, and braced their bodies for the death impact.

Hundreds of thousands of pounds of ice pushed the dirt

over the dome, making all but the two Neteru's holding the shield, fall. Carlos and Damali could feel the entire team being moved inch-by-inch, backward while they strained to keep their position.

Then, as quickly as it had begun, all motion stopped, leaving the team sealed within an icy white tomb.

Breathing hard, Carlos kept his eyes shut while team members stood slowly, glancing up in disbelief. Damali's head dropped forward, her arms shook from the pressure, and for the first time since the chaos began, her injury started to burn and throb, making her painfully aware it was there.

Marlene's attention snapped toward Damali, as her side of the shield began to give way. "Medic! We've got a Neteru down!"

Berkfield quickly shoved toward her. Carlos peeped over his shoulder and his side of the shield buckled.

"Keep your concentration, man!" Damali shouted. "I'm all right. It's a flesh wound, Carlos."

She lowered her head but kept her arms outstretched, muscles in her arms shook as pain carved at her exposed shoulder blade.

"I'm looking at bone and gristle, hon," Berkfield said nervously, opening his hands and lowering them slowly toward her wound.

"Don't," Damali ordered. "It's a demon nick, Council level or worse. You're a sacred blood healer and the shit will burn like hell." Sweat covered her forehead and she coughed as nausea from slowly setting shock began to claim her.

"Seal her up," Carlos said through his teeth. "That shit will make her sick."

"No," Damali said, her voice losing some of its strength. "It'll fuck up my concentration when the burn goes down. I won't be able to hold the shield."

"You ain't gonna last another five minutes, baby," Marlene whispered, glancing up with the team as the dome began to buckle and yawn.

Bits of ice and rock began to rain inside the dome as Marlene spoke. Carlos's knees bent slightly, and he strained against the fissures like a man holding up the weight of the world. "You've lost a lot of blood."

"It was a vamp nick from the Chairman, not Level Seven. My system will fight it, I'm . . ." Damali's words trailed off as delirium from blood loss began to make her woozy.

"I said seal her up! That's an order," Carlos shouted. "I got this. Heal her."

Still the team hesitated, but the golden light protecting them got brighter. Carlos suddenly dropped his hands and turned, his focus beyond the group. Team members covered their heads in reflex but the dome never wavered. He walked toward Damali, who still had her hands outstretched, her head dropped forward, rivulets of sweat running down her temples and her nose, making her keep her eyes sealed shut.

"You have *got* to trust me," Carlos said near her ear. "Just like I have to trust you. We're both strong," he said, taking her hands within his, as she fell forward against his chest, "but sometimes we have to pick up the slack for one another." He looked at Berkfield. "Heal her."

Carlos handed Damali off to Marlene and walked to the edge of the globe they'd created. Damali's screams almost shattered his concentration, but there was something more important than individual pain: the survival of the family. Damali would live. But the wound had to be cleaned out and sealed.

As Berkfield slit his palm with a Bowie and sent the sacred to chase the unholy out of Damali's wound, Carlos allowed her screams of agony to make him stronger. Berkfield's agonized hiss as his palm's covered Damali's shoulder and the wound opened on his back made it all the more maddening while the healing happened behind Carlos. The sound of Damali's cries, breathing, the smell of blood, the exit of sulfur, the scent of spent vomit, sweat, tremors, tears, wails, pain. Never again.

He remembered it all so clearly now. Her screams of

agony, hysteria, how they'd clawed his seed from her womb. Blackness had entered his lungs, polluting his system, making him a carrier. His vibrations had affected the team, had strained the dynamics for months, adding to the contagion, had threatened his woman's existence . . . had rendered confusion as an illusion. It wasn't a concussion from the car accident. He'd taken the Chairman's throne; it had attempted to take him by force, blood-rape sacrilege. They'd wanted the worst of him to step forward, then as Zang Ho had said, so be it. The head of the Chairman, then the book lodged in his double's chest would expel and open. A simultaneous hit had to go down. He had to kill the worst in himself. As far as Lilith went, he had no choice but to let the Devil deal with his own wife.

Carlos sat slowly on the ground and crossed his legs Indian style with his back to the frightened team and Damali as she recovered. He was cool. He was one with the elements. He was snow—*fucking ice*. He was fire—molten lava. He was stone—a vast cavern of secrets protecting his family under his granite arch. He was the shadow of the night—never to be revealed to the enemy. *He was the weapon*.

Damali stirred slowly, her gaze immediately going to the holding shield and over to Carlos. All eyes followed hers as she sat up.

"He's in deep meditation," Marlene said quietly. "Do not break his concentration, or we'll die."

Damali nodded as she stared at the cold puffs of breaths expelled by the warm bodies around her. Lips were blue; frost had begun to form on people's eyebrows, turning hair white and skin gray. "We have to get out from under the shield and generate heat," she said quietly.

Carlos nodded but didn't turn, however, his slight movements made all eyes instantly land on him.

Fear was etched in frigid relief within all expressions. Damali knew what they were thinking; it was a silent scream at the forefront of everyone's mind. How long would this hold? How long would they be entombed? How long could their bodies withstand the elements before freezing, subzero temperatures killed them? . . . As the bodies dropped, and the days passed, would the worst of human starvation turn them into the beasts they all fought, making them hunger for human flesh to stop the pain?

She calmly crossed her legs where she sat and placed both hands together and closed her eyes. She envisioned an orb of red heat between her palms. Slowly her body began to warm and she offered the gift of heat to the others, becoming one with the elements. She was controlled fire. Her family was warmth, love, hope, joy; all that she had she would gladly share. She was sunlight and fresh air. She was a child of the universe. . . . She was melting snow; she was spring, and dawn, and new rivers that flowed over the golden dome to offer Tibetan valleys the first element, the basis of woman—water.

They sat that way for hours through the night. Her back to Carlos on one side of the dome; his back to hers on the other. Large chunks of snow fell away in thunderous echoes, sliding over the golden circumference, opening the top to new dawn.

Carlos didn't move until enough of the snow had melted away from the edges of the protective enclosure. Everyone understood that soft walls could still pose a danger. No one moved until they heard Rider's "All clear." She and Carlos both opened their eyes, stood up at the same time, and craned their necks to a sound in the distance that even Big Mike hadn't heard.

"Choppers in the distance," Carlos said, stepping up higher in the snow and shielding his eyes to the sun.

"They've picked up our locator beacons," Damali said, facing the direction Carlos stared, watching the new day's light. She glanced at him and kept her words private. "You were awesome."

He glanced at her. "You weren't too bad yourself," he said, returning his gaze to the horizon. "Good teamwork.

Woulda frozen to death without you." He looked at her for a moment. "I couldn't have done it all alone."

She nodded and kept her gaze toward the approaching choppers. "Neither could I have. Remind me to thank you properly, later."

The team stared at General Quai Lou in total disbelief. Damali and Carlos glanced at the two Black Hawk helicopters idling in the distance. Heavy guns were trained on their team; nervous eyes watched for a sign of resistance. Itchy fingers rested against triggers.

"You have destroyed the breeder female our agency was most concerned about. Therefore, it is time for you to go back to the U.S. and to leave China."

Carlos and Damali shared a glance.

"There's another one still out there. The male," Damali said, trying to keep her tone civil.

"We are aware of that, but after the potential reckless endangerment to the natural environment . . . an avalanche almost reached a village. If this had been Beijing, it would have been disastrous. The female is destroyed; the vortexes that Dr. Zeitloff described should be sealed."

"Your weapons caused the avalanche," Carlos protested in a low, threatening tone. "Monk Lin tried to warn you. Up here, conventional weapons wouldn't work. The only reason you aren't picking body parts out of the snow is because of the Naksong's teachings."

"Yeah, you need to recognize," Damali said curtly, her eyes sweeping her team and recounting heads to reassure herself that everyone was still there.

The general placed his hands behind his back. "Your service has been invaluable and most appreciated. The demoness that has been terrorizing our region and spreading infection is no more. The male is on the move and headed back to where you are from. We will assist you in visas, equipment, and reentry into your own country, and wish you well." He turned away, dismissing them with a wave of his hand. His officers dropped rope ladders and there was no more discussion to be had.

"You believe this shit?" Berkfield said, trudging forward.

"Yeah, I do," Carlos said and spat. "That's why I hate working for the government."

CHAPTER TWENTY-TWO

Once the choppers touched down in Lhasa, it was obvious to them all. No one was fooled by the general's cocky display; the U.S. arm of the world organization had obviously levied serious pressure to reacquire its own force.

Marines stood at attention. Two heavily decorated men stepped forward, nodded to General Quai Lou, and approached the Guardian squad.

"I'm General McHenry," the first man said, his hard hazel eyes scouring the group. "This is General Swainkoff," he added, gesturing toward the silent man with a steel gray stare. "You've been briefed. We have a situation."

The team looked at the huge military plane before them and shared glances of concern.

"You suit up on the plane. We have weaponry you'll need. Military-reinforced Humvees will pick you up at LAX, and our drivers will take you wherever you need to go to quell the disturbance."

"What disturbance?" Damali asked, thrusting her chin up as Carlos folded his arms in defiance.

"The gates of Hell have literally opened up, ma'am," General McHenry said; then he and General Swainkoff turned, received a salute from their line, and walked up the steps of the plane.

Carlos leaned forward, his gaze sweeping the marines that never blinked on the team's flank. "Number one, I don't like being in the air at night any more than you do, but if what they say is true, and Highway 405 and the 10 are blocked with multicar pileups and bodies, plus the 110, the 105, and the 101 are all fucked up, I don't see any other way in, except for side streets, which are treacherous." He looked at Damali for confirmation and support. Receiving her nod, he pressed on. "Number two; if downtown L.A. is already burning, it seems a little late. Whatever was there has come and gone, most likely. We've gotta chopper in using Black Hawks, then we'll do this the old-fashioned way, on foot."

"Yeah, but the problem is," Shabazz said, "we don't know exactly what we're looking for. We know it's the Chairman, but how do you find that rat bastard? Lilith was our only way to draw him out when she made a grab for Carlos." Shabazz's cool glare held all eyes.

"We've got one serious demon down, one more to go," Damali said. "It's—"

"We've got two more to go, baby," Carlos said, his gaze raking the team geared in black fatigues and strapped to the hilt with weapons.

"Two?" she said, dropping her voice to pull the team in closer, never leaving Carlos's gaze. "Talk to me."

"Why do you think I blocked your slice at the Chairman's throat?"

Bodies eased back discreetly. Looks of concern rippled down the flight bench. Carlos's eyes darkened.

"You kill him first, and *The Book of the Damned* will open inside the one from Level Seven, and he'll have access to everything in it. You think what the generals told us about was the actual Armageddon?" Carlos shook his head. "This ain't shit. This is practice, a warm-up session for them."

"Then, what do you propose?" Damali said. She kept her gaze focused on Carlos's eyes.

"We have to do a simultaneous hit and make a grab for the book. Both of them have to be in the same location at the same time to pull it off."

"That's the point, dude," Rider said, blowing out a hard breath. "Damali isn't in phase, so there's no draw. You make the males battle nuts, but we still don't own a target location."

"Wait a minute," Damali said, still holding Carlos's gaze. "When the Chairman attacked, he said something about things coming full circle."

"I hear you, and he said he'd meet me in Hell, where I was born," Carlos said, shaking his head. "But this ain't the time to take a squad to a subterranean level, baby."

"Word," Big Mike said, pounding several fists. "Suicide."

Damali's gaze drifted toward the window, manipulating the puzzle pieces in her mind. "That's not where you were born," she said, her voice distant. "At least not to his empire."

Carlos stared at her.

"Where were you born, Carlos?" Damali said, her voice an urgent murmur. "Where did you receive the turn bite?"

Carlos absently rubbed the side of his neck. A shiver of memory made the invisible tattoo over the wound burn. "In the woods . . . when I handed off money to Nuit."

Damali nodded. "But it wasn't Nuit's bite. It was the Chairman's that created the discrepancy with supernatural law. Right?" Her eyes scanned the group. "That's a power center for him and for you, because he turned you instantly, didn't observe the dead-three-nights rule."

"Well, it's gotta be a lucky place for hombre," Jose said with a nervous smile. "One small technicality and our brother would have been locked down for life."

"That's a very dangerous place," Carlos said quietly. "You might stand a better chance underground."

Damali stared at him until he lifted his gaze. "I know that place brings back white knuckles for you, but I've gotchure back out there."

He stared at her. The team passed nervous glances. "You don't want to face him out there."

"We did the chamber and have been to every dark Level, except Seven," she said calmly, holding the line. "We can do the woods topside."

Carlos shook his head. "This ain't like before."

"Why not?" Damali asked, her voice calm but firm as she

covered Carlos's hand with her own. "We'll smoke the bastard, trust me. Just tell me what he looks like?"

Carlos's eyes darkened until tiny slivers of silver could be seen within them. "That's just the problem. He looks like me."

The military cargo plane had to touch down in LAX because of size, but the team didn't care if it landed on an accident-blocked highway, just as long as it wasn't in the air. Several hours from Lhasa, after a brief refueling stop in Manila, twenty-some hours in flight, and almost forty-eight hours with no sleep, the team was nearly ill from inhaling fumes. Pure adrenaline kept them from passing out as they flew from day into night, thirteen hours behind where they'd been, as though flying back in time.

But the moment the aircraft circled the area and started its descent under a sky lit by a full moon, they all pressed their noses to the windows. Billowing black smoke raged from tall buildings. Unmoving fire trucks flashed red lights, and sat abandoned. Cars were smashed and twisted around poles or crunched upon each other. Bodies lay strewn in piles, littering the streets like tiny specs of paper. Damali covered her mouth, unable to fathom mobs of people moving in masses like frightened herds of sheep, a large glob of humanity running one way and then shifting in another direction as something unseen chased them.

"The airport, like the city, is under martial law," General McHenry said over the intercom. "The moment we touch down, we'll cover your team and you head for the Black Hawks."

"Roger," Rider whispered as they got closer to the ground.

The team stared in shock as large were-demons materialized, and they saw what the crowds were running from. Huge beasts stood atop piles of bodies, feasting, lifting their ugly heads occasionally to snarl at each other as they fed. Black shadows darted in and out of bodies, turning frightened civilians on each other in sudden, random acts of violence.

Carlos closed his eyes and lowered his head as he saw a woman fleeing with her baby suddenly drop the flailing infant and stomp it.

"Oh, Jesus," Marlene said, cringing and jerking her sight away from the window. She began rocking. "Now, if ever before, this is a good time for the Twenty-third."

"The Covenant should be here," Big Mike said quietly, wiping his eyes.

"They're where they should be," Damali whispered. "Holding the line in vigil . . . just like Monk Lin had to stay in Lhasa."

"You think Mei's family made it out, if people in the town turned, or anything else came up over there?" Rider said quietly, his line of vision glued to the window as the plane touched down, bounced over bodies, and sucked several fleeing victims into the engines.

"Yeah," Damali said, breathing hard. She stood as the plane screeched to a stop. "We pray. We get out. We do this. Gotta stop the madness."

Carlos stood slowly. He looked at the marines around them. "You all are just babies, no more than eighteen. Probably never jaywalked in your lives, let alone dropped a body or disobeyed a direct order." Carlos took the safety off his weapon and his eyes met confused, disoriented stares. "When your generals and the pilots come out, if their eyes are black—shoot 'em."

The marines were on their feet in seconds, their guns leveled at Carlos. But when the doors to the cockpit blew open and black, glowing eyes stared at them, the Guardian team's sharpshooters did the honors. Rider and Shabazz opened fire in neat, calm, coordinated trigger pulls. Green gook splattered. Two young marines upchucked; all were frozen for two seconds past too late where they stood.

"Mar had you covered in here," Damali said. "She set a prayer barrier for all present. Those guys up front, nonbelievers. You saw for yourselves, the weapons help, but ain't your first line of defense." She nodded at Dan, Shabazz, and Berkfield. "Pull 'em out."

They extracted their dog tags, showing a Star of David, a crescent, and a cross.

"J.L., you got a Buddha on you?"

J.L. nodded and whipped out his dog tags.

Damali's eyes raked each enlisted man. "It doesn't matter which faith, as long as the foundation is about the Most High, the divine. If you believe and haven't already been contaminated, you won't be possessed. If you're not possessed, you've got a fighting chance and can use the conventional weapons to fend off whatever might try to eat you. But don't hold up any of these if you've been bullshitting about having faith. Fangs will take your throat." She spun and looked at Marlene. "Before those helicopter pilots take us up, make sure those boys are straight, Mar. That's all we need is for a chopper to go down. Blowing Harpies out the air will be bad enough."

Damali's lungs felt like they were on fire as she dashed across the runway to the waiting choppers. She took the lead, clearing the way, mowing down anything that lunged or slithered in their path. Carlos had the rear; Mike, Shabazz, and Rider kept flanks clear, while J.L., Jose, Berkfield, and Dan made body shields to protect the team's newbies.

Marlene prayed faster than Damali ever saw her pray, splashing young frightened foreheads with water and oil, and scattering sea salts and herbs on chopper floors, where they were crushed under steel-toed army boots.

The first chopper lifted, tilted, and swayed as something unseen adhered to its side.

"Mike, underneath!" Damali shouted, leaning out the door as the helicopter in front of them dangerously tipped.

Rider hooked his harness to a side rail, leaned out, took dead aim, and splattered a Harpie so the chopper could right itself. Shabazz got two more headed for the blades, splattering vile demon innards on the roof and window. Mike saluted and leaned back. The second chopper went airborne as an ap-

proaching jumbo jet took a nosedive, burst into flames, and
sent fuselage down the runway they'd just vacated.

The team members glanced at one another; the pilots
glimpsed out the window and then never looked back.

Carlos sat immobilized. What they'd witnessed from the
plane was brought to them in full sense-around-sound so
close to the action in a chopper. L.A. International was lit
with military machine-gun fire, sending red-and-blue
streaks through the complex. Smoke was pouring out of
every building orifice, windows were smashed, glass was
everywhere. If this was the airport, East L.A. was gonna
bring him to tears.

His mind kept going over the same thought like a broken
record: the people—and the babies, children, dear God.

Storefronts had been looted and torched. Houses reduced
to rubble. Streets were impassable. They saw it all from the
air. Churches and mosques and temples were on fire—
hallowed ground kept out demons, but there was more than
one way to get to food . . . smoke it out. Carlos closed his
eyes and slowly leaned back against the seat, his ears soak-
ing in the shrill screams and mayhem as the chopper blades
kept a steady beat in the smoke-darkened sky.

Every sense in him told him Damali was right. The
Chairman came here to pick a fight. Right in his own backyard. Just like he'd brought the pain to the Chairman. Fair
exchange was no robbery. He'd desecrated the Chairman's
black hole on Level Six, now the Chairman was back to return the favor.

The most horrifying part of it all was he'd actually helped
the bastard do it. When he'd been taken over, before the black
separation within himself, he'd turned Hell out. Now it needed
somewhere to live. L.A. was a perfect place. There was no such
thing as homeland security. If there was bullshit going down,
anywhere on the planet, you could run, but you couldn't hide . . .
taking out one cell at a time, one level at a time, was futile.

Carlos opened his eyes as he felt the sting on his neck

turn into a throb, then an ache, and then a wet stabbing pain. He looked at his bloodied hand, glanced at the trees below, and signaled to the pilots to touch down in the small clearing that began it all.

"Your neck is bleeding," Damali shouted over the choppers.

"Douse it!" Rider hollered, his eyes frantically going from Carlos's gaping wound to Marlene.

"It's an old scar," Carlos said. "Just chickens coming home to roost." He waved Marlene off and winced, and then jumped down as the Neteru tattoo heated, sizzled, and sealed the old vampire bite.

Damali jumped down behind him, motioning for the team to disembark. "Push those choppers back, but stay near," she yelled over the thudding whirl. "If we have to use explosives, you're sitting ducks." She glanced back at the team. "Goggles, on, all equipment readied."

The pilots nodded and lifted off, seeming too happy to oblige the request. Soon their airborne blades became distant, but the team briefly shut their eyes when a double explosion sounded overhead.

"One of 'em was just a kid," Damali said, not looking back. She glanced at Marjorie's tear-filled eyes and sent her gaze into the darkness. "Rest their souls in peace."

"Ashé," Marlene murmured and began trudging behind Damali saying the Twenty-third Psalm.

"I wish Mar had her stick," Shabazz said in a quiet tone moving forward. "It's been with her since forever. Now it's up in the Tibetan mountains under fifty feet of packed ice."

"Monk Lin will get it," Marlene said absently. "It'll rise and come home, as always."

Rider fingered his dog tag and then dropped it, remembering that his amulet had been given away. "If wishes were fishes, we'd all be free." He said quietly, no sarcasm in his tone. "Just like we all wish D had her long blade out here."

Carlos abruptly halted, and the group stopped forward motion behind him. All eyes except Carlos's and Damali's strained in the dark behind goggles. Ears listened intently. Jumpy nerves made muscles twitch as the slightest movement from the wind and small woodland creatures cut into their senses.

Carlos cocked his head to the side, sniffed and relaxed. "*Que pasa,* man!" He stepped forward toward Yonnie who walked into the clearing. "Damn, am I glad to see you."

Damali's hand landed gently on Carlos's arm as she stared at the expression on Yonnie's face. "You're in apex, baby. Stay downwind from your boy."

Carlos backed up. "Yo, man. It's me. You cool?"

The group leveled artillery as Yonnie's eyes narrowed, glowed solid red, and his fangs glistened. Yonnie was already battle bulked, but Carlos had given the order to stand down.

"Yo, yo, easy. Everybody chill. The brother has been out in this bullshit by himself, my scent is throwing him off, no doubt—"

A black arc knocked Carlos off his feet. When he landed beside Big Mike, his fatigues were smoldering in the center of his chest where the bolt struck. Were it not for Damali's brand, his chest cavity would have been split wide open and his heart would have been lying on the grass. Instantly Carlos raised a small shield in front of him, and then got up slowly with some help from Big Mike.

"Want me to smoke this motherfucker?" Mike asked, his shoulders knitting as he kept steady aim with a cannon.

"No, that's all me, bro," Rider said, keeping a blue light on Yonnie's chest.

"This is between me and Carlos," Yonnie said through his teeth. "No beef with the rest of the family."

Damali shook her head. "Can't let you go there, Yonnie. In a month, all this will be over. He's—"

"I know what he is!" Yonnie shouted. "Go back to your team, Damali, and stay out of it!"

Tara instantly materialized by Yonnie's side and hissed at

Carlos. Members of the squad looked at each other, confused.

Rider kept a beam on Yonnie and walked forward several paces. "Tara, he's not himself, you ain't yourself. Stand downwind from him and both of you will be all right."

"Shut up, Rider!" Tara snapped, her claws growing as she spoke. "After what he did to us, there won't be anything left to stand downwind from."

Before anybody could react, Tara and Yonnie had gone airborne. Carlos's shield blocked the first punch lobbed by Yonnie, but Tara got a good rake at his back. With Carlos in the center of the vicious attack, there was no way to shoot at the fast-moving creatures without risking a mortal injury to Carlos. Damali rushed forward to enter the fray, but a black bolt from Yonnie sent her hurling backward.

She was stunned, but just sucker-punched. The pulse was a weak one, a nice shove out of the way. When Damali flipped herself up, she was more angry than injured. But it was obvious that the beef had to do with more than Carlos's apex scent. The female, Tara, should have had the opposite reaction. Damali could also see Carlos blocking shots, but not landing any. When the vampires retreated for a moment to make another lunge, she was able to get by Carlos's side and unsheathe her baby Isis dagger.

"Hold up! What did he do?"

"Tell her!" Yonnie said, breathing hard and snarling.

"I don't know what you're talking about, man! I didn't do anything!"

"Liar!" Tara shouted, pointing at Carlos. "He won't reveal himself in front of you. He'd never want his beloved family to see the beast he's become." Hot tears of rage filled Tara's gleaming red eyes.

"She's telling the truth," Rider said. "This ain't no scent-induced hysteria. I know my woman."

Yonnie nodded. "Then you won't have a problem with me and Carlos finishing this to ash."

Yonnie was airborne again, but to everyone's surprise, Carlos met him there, no shield in hand as they collided, snapped at each other, and landed, separated by twenty yards.

"Before you try to rip out my heart, you need to at least tell me what I did to you?" Carlos glanced at Tara breathing hard. "I know I never did *anything* to you, girl, but have your back—the whole time when I was a master, and on Council, I never—"

"You tried to rape me!" Tara shrieked, vanishing and coming to Yonnie's side. "He was *your friend,* you made him watch and left him for dead after you whipped him till there was no flesh left on his back!"

Damali slowly lowered her blade as she stared at Carlos. Rider took the laser off Yonnie's chest and put it in the center of Carlos's head.

"Tell them!" Tara screeched.

The agonized, shrill pitch of her voice forced Big Mike to cover his ears, and the goggle-wearing team members had to lift the audio sensors away from their heads as the technology failed. Carlos stood quietly, dazed, shaking his head no.

"I bled out Gabrielle's house to bring him back—that's right, black-blood exchanges with every demon in the house, Mr. Chairman," Tara yelled, sobs breaking up her complaint into raging sputters. "The only one I spared was Gabby, because she's like *family.* You remember family, Carlos? Family! She helped us, gave us a place to hide because of you, you bastard!"

"Not because of what you did to me, but because of what you did to her. . . . I vowed," Yonnie said, his hand stroking Tara's hair as he passed her, the force of his rage ripping up tree trunks and crashing down branches, "that if I ever regenerated, Chairman or not, I would personally rip out your heart or die trying." His voice dipped to a vicious whisper. "Because we *were* family."

"I'll help you," Damali said quickly, thinking fast on her feet. "If you've got the right one."

She watched Yonnie pause. Carlos seemed so pained by the charges leveled against him, she could tell by the look on

his face that he might not have been able to defend himself
to the death. "He's not the Chairman," Damali yelled across
the distance. "There's two of them."

"He has you under an illusion," Yonnie bellowed, swirling up
black storm clouds as his energy gathered for a final beat down.

"He's a liar," Tara shrieked, taking a battle stance.

"I didn't do you like that, man. Would never . . ." Carlos's
words trailed off as Yonnie shot the images into his mind.

Damali caught them, too, and she turned her head for a
moment. But a flicker of movement caught her peripheral vision. "Yonnie, get down!"

Yonnie ducked and yanked Tara low with him. A black
bolt split a tall redwood, and the team opened fire toward the
blackness. The Chairman materialized, his tail slicing bramble out of his way.

"You fools," he snarled, and sent an arc at Yonnie and Tara.

From some reservoir of memory, Carlos flipped, vanished, and his shield caught the bolt, placing him between
Yonnie, Tara, and the Chairman, but his back was dangerously exposed to two predators that wanted his head.

"Do you think I would allow him to waltz into Hell and
simply take my throne by sitting his unworthy carcass in it?"
The Chairman seethed, his voice so low it echoed like distant thunder and quaked the ground. "There is only *one
name* that has *ever* been etched into my seat of power since
the dawn of time—since *the Garden,* just like there's only
one book! Mine. But the hand of a Neteru must release it
from the current abductor, because a *Neteru* stole it. Kill
him, and then this Carlos later, after he returns what is
mine." The Chairman paced and then turned his gaze on
Damali and her team.

Snap instinct kicked in; she knew the Chairman was going for a hostage. If the team opened fire, Carlos was again
on the wrong side of the heat. She reached out her hand
without thinking about it. The Isis long blade filled it, replacing the baby Isis that hit the ground. She grasped
Madame Isis, feeling its power coil up her arm and connect

with everything Neteru within her. The gleaming silver edge deflected the Chairman's black magnetic bolt. Her team scrambled and took cover.

Slow clapping in the darkness ceased all action. Human and demon eyes alike turned toward the dark figure walking out of the brush. Damali's jaw went slack as she looked at a very dark version of Carlos with gleaming black eyes. Hearing about it and seeing it were definitely two different things.

The body double seemed amused as he straightened his custom-tailored suit. Yonnie and Tara backed away, their gazes jettisoning between the Carlos with the shield that protected them and the one that they now understood had tortured them without mercy. The Chairman bulked another head taller. The Carlos in a black Armani suit studied his manicure, unfazed.

"All this drama for nothing. A waste of precious energy, just like all that chaos in L.A. is a waste. I'll have to clean that up later." The dark Carlos smiled at Damali. "Sorry about what happened back at your place, baby, but if you would have relaxed, you would have enjoyed it more."

The Carlos she knew narrowed his eyes. Damali was sure something crazy was running through his head when he lowered his shield and it disappeared. Her man was two seconds from old-school, hand-to-hand combat at a very inopportune time. The team couldn't move; black paralysis suddenly held them where they stood. Shabazz's weapon melted in his grip; his yell echoed through the glen and connected with the screams of pain from the team. Dropped weapons became molten steel and useless, causing Shabazz and the others to forcibly disarm or lose a limb.

Yonnie and Tara were covered with a red, sizzling light that made them yell out in pain, but kept them caged. Giant iron shackles simultaneously lurched up out of the ground and clasped the Chairman's thickened ankles. It all happened in milliseconds. The Chairman hissed and twisted in outrage, darkening the already pitch-black sky. His fury turned the moon bloodred as he strained his wings against the air, only to lift a few feet and land again hard. The struggle the Chairman put up as he yelled and bellowed shook the trees and opened a wide cavern around his feet, splitting the earth and sending Harpies over the edges of it to claw at his huge legs.

"He is also my father!" the Chairman shouted. "I will not be disinherited in the final days! I was first!"

"And the first shall be last and the last shall be first," the dark Carlos said with a smug smile. "You should read *all* the books." He shot an appreciative gaze toward Carlos. "Knowledge is power, right, hombre? Thanks for keeping a brother in the know. You had a lot in your head worth taking, especially her."

The dark Carlos chuckled and pointed at the Chairman as he surveyed the team. "Look at him, crying and whining about his father, when he should be ashamed that his mother was a *real* bitch. What was she, man? Hellhound, Harpie, some stray female demon shit around at the beginning before Pop had serious options? At least I can say Lilith was fine." The entity looked at Carlos. "Your mother was pitifully human. That's the difference between me and you—no backbone. It's all genetics; Darwinian Law. The survival of the fittest."

Carlos stared at the evil version of himself, controlled fury unlike he'd ever known roiled within him. But this abomination of all that he was had let on to a profound truth. It was about what was locked within genetic code. The Naksong had been right; integrate oneself. Embrace it; use it, transform it into power. Be the weapon. He was darkness and light, vampire and Neteru, a hybrid fusion that had never been before. Just like the dark half even knew about the Good Book he'd read, that also meant the converse. He knew everything this dark side of him knew. But just like he never knew a vamp-Neteru fusion was possible before he sat on the Chairman's throne, this sonofabitch didn't know that fact now.

Therefore, ergo, Carlos reasoned ever so quietly within the black box of his mind, the differential in the match was only about one thing: which of the two had the stomach to go the distance. His palms burned as he felt magnetic force traveling up his arms and connecting to his spinal column. He had no fear of the darkness; he'd already taken a walk through the Valley and had been the baddest mutha in it— and would drain that bastard pretending to be him of power. All he had to do was think about what his body double had done to Damali within her house. The violation spiked stroke-level rage through every cell. The image of his other self, naked and heaving, dick dripping, on top of his woman, trying to get her to give him permission to enter . . . aw, shit . . . *It was on!*

"Damali, give me your blade," Carlos said low in his throat. "Now." He kept his eyes on his body double, silver from his glare lighting a hot path toward his darker self, burning grass in its wake.

"D, *mamacita,* I was hoping you'd finally get yourself together and find your Isis. Lop off this sonofabitch's head, for me, won't you, baby?" the dark Carlos murmured in a sensual tone, and then nodded toward the Chairman. He spat fire and cleared his throat. "This apex thing that other punk bastard is going through is fucking with my sinuses, though." The entity glared at Carlos and blew a kiss toward Damali. "It's making him cocky and stupid, and he's pissing me off. After I do him, maybe me and you can go get a bite to eat? Or, we can stay right here and gorge." He glowered at Carlos, taunting him, baiting him into a no-win physical struggle, using Damali as a lure.

All the locks in her mental tumblers turned within the split second it took her to lunge. She glimpsed the bad Carlos, her memory snapping back as she hurdled forward. The visions returned with it. She'd seen this in her backyard. She also saw how the Carlos she knew had been attacked in Council Chambers. The throne. The porch. The confusion. The clothes that didn't burn. Juanita. In her house! The hotel-room incident. Nightmares. Her man's skull being split open and his memory dredged out.

The good Carlos lunged at the same time she did, as though they were welded to the same nervous system. But it wasn't about ever letting go of the Isis again in the heat of battle. A tiny voice inside her head became a Neteru Council's battle cry. *Never release the Isis.* Something was wrong with both Carlos images, and she wasn't sure what it was; the blade stayed with her.

This entity before them was fast, agile, like air. They both landed on their feet, side-by-side but frustrated.

"I *am* the prince of the airwaves," he said laughing, reading the thought Damali and Carlos shared with a glance, and dodging them again.

Damali stopped moving. Carlos stood away from her breathing hard. For her, blind rage was not an option. Be strategic. She could still move, so could Carlos. There was a reason why—there was something in their makeup that the bad one couldn't jack with. The Neteru-infused elements. Be air.

This time when she came at the dark Carlos, she caught him with a solid kick to the midsection. She flipped away from his snatch, just as her Carlos landed a jaw blow that sent him sprawling. The dark one was back on his feet in seconds, eyeing them both, deciding which one to attack first. Good, they'd pissed him off and made him show fang. But what was happening to her Carlos slowed her roll. He'd bulked slightly, the dark Carlos glimpsed it, then bulked into full battle mode.

They both went at each other like released tigers. Hands around throats, the dark entity's claws drawing blood, a spin roll near the Chairman's feet, landing both of them in danger range of an infuriated, chained beast. The dark Carlos was immediately stabbed in the thigh with a slashing tail in an odd turn of events. Her Carlos backed up, the slightly injured one now furious, leaking black blood and hissing.

One pair of eyes gleamed black, another pair was solid silver. Fire and dark lightning ejected from one hand to match hot silver laser from the other. A parting, another lunge, two bodies airborne and no way to get between them. Black ice keeping Carlos's silver gaze from severing limbs, a gold shield turned breastplate making a heart snatch impossible.

Black blood mixed with red-silver blood; both semi-winded, they separated. Eyes narrowed and they came at each other again, fusing strategic martial arts with primal fury blows. Tree branches were down, the earth was ripped up, Harpies went scrambling for cover, but the huge beast pinned to the ground by shackles was the only thing that didn't give way.

Red cages of heat around Tara and Yonnie sputtered and weakened, releasing two vampires into the fray. The dark Carlos was clearly getting tired, and he was pulling back evil energy that had been used to contain the others in order to both fight Carlos and chain the furious Chairman, while also defending against two strong, airborne vamps with a grudge. Holding the line alone was siphoning him dry. Yonnie and Tara circled for an opening. The dark arc around her team began to dissolve, but she watched her man in horror as the earth opened beneath them and both Carlos bodies rolled over the edge into the chasm.

Before anyone could get to the edge, something massive flew up out of the new ground that moved so fast it swept her Carlos up with it from the sheer updraft. The force of the earth's ejection toppled Tara and knocked Yonnie back. Fire pushed her team out of position as it scorched the grass around them. Rounds on the ground discharged from half-melted weapons, sending the human team for full cover. Smoke from the holy water and hallowed earth mix made Yonnie and Tara back off farther. The Chairman was on his knees, fighting against the gases hazardous to his kind.

Damali was partially blinded by the combination of white smoke and sulfuric plumes, but could hear her Carlos gagging. His body hit the ground, she heard bones snap, and this time he didn't move. She swung wildly, saw Carlos open his eyes where he lay, his eyes intermittently flickering red and silver. Then he sat up. She paused for a beat. He should have been dead. Which one was it? Shit. Carlos leapt up. The other one could have taken on his clothes to cause confusion. Illusion. Both now stood facing each other, dressed exactly the same.

"Do him," they both said in unison, breathing hard.

One Carlos looked at the other. "Your biggest mistake was messing with my woman!"

She saw a dark current exit both bodies. Both Carloses bulked to master-vampire stature with Council-level powers as the link continued to connect them. Both had fangs. Both had red eyes. Both swiped at each other in a mirror image, ripping away black fatigues. Both turned and reached for her blade. One had a hint of silver in the red of his eyes. . . . One had a tattoo lit on the side of his neck. . . . Only one had her brand over his heart.

Damali swung, still half-seeing, aiming for the dark Carlos, the Isis ringing as it connected to the Chairman's neck. The blow sent vibrations of satisfaction up her forearm, into her biceps, into her shoulder as her throat released a warrior's battle cry. A thud sounded, a head rolled at her feet. The Chairman's body exploded, sending ash and cinders into the air. Tears stung her eyes; she'd missed. The blinding smoke . . . She watched the wrong Carlos expand, get taller, and begin to crush the Adam's apple within her man's throat. A dark book burned inside the cavern of his barrel chest, creating a red outline, pushing against his scaled skin from the inside out, the crest on it living and moving as his laugh thundered.

The evil, stronger Carlos threw its head back and laughed harder. Life began to slide away from her man. As her blade was about to leave her hand in a desperation toss to the dying Carlos, instinct held it to her. A power grab would take it midair. But the strangling Carlos opened his hand and it was there. Just as the growing entity looked up, for a split second their eyes met, her Carlos smiled a half smile, swung, and the dark one's head rolled.

Her Carlos fell to the ground clutching his throat, coughing from being strangled. A duplicate of his head rolled to

Damali's feet and stared at her glassy-eyed. A dead ram's head replaced the Carlos look-alike and turned to ash that blew away.

Cinders made the team hack and cough as Damali rushed to the surviving Carlos's side. A beam of white light opened in the sky, a heavy breeze blew the smoke away, and they watched in awe as the writhing ashes of the dark entity exposed a burning book cradled in the middle of its rib cage.

Heaven lit; the book lifted and vanished. Meteors fell in a natural fireworks display. Carlos flung a golden shield away from his body like a discus and covered Yonnie and Tara beneath it. Holy water rain blessed with angel tears poured down to wash the foul earth. Damali sat on the ground in the mud as her Carlos slowly pushed himself up to sit beside her. The team gathered around within the blue white circle of light that bathed them. Yonnie and Tara's eyes shone from deep within the forest behind a protective globe. A torrent of clean rain became a curtain around them. Harpies squealed, crackled, and burned trying to escape the Light.

The earth sucked in a pair of shackles with charred sections of skeletal remains crumbling and breaking apart as ash while the wounded earth resealed itself. Trees righted, time stopped for a moment, two choppers approached, and everything went back to the way it had been. A pair of friends nodded in the darkness and vanished as Carlos's shield lifted.

Carlos and Damali looked skyward with the team.

"You weren't supposed to throw me your sword. I was supposed to earn the right to borrow it."

"I know," she whispered. "Baby, I know."

EPILOGUE

"I still can't believe how they put a totally untrue spin on everything," Damali said, leaning up to peek at the news. "That is pure propaganda! How in the world can they say it was civil unrest and rioting over gas prices that blew L.A. up like that? Not to mention, all those eyewitnesses, and—"

Carlos leaned up and kissed her, clicking off the plasma screen TV across the room, and stopping her words with his tongue at the same time. He stroked her hair as she returned her head to his chest. He sighed with utter contentment as she curled up near him in their most favorite place in the whole wide world—next to each other in bed.

"But then how do you discount landslides, avalanches, meteor showers, freakin' sand storms in Arizona? Is it me, or am I crazy?" Damali sat up, waving her arms in the middle of the king-size bed as she spoke. "People are crazy, Carlos. They don't know how close they came to the big one. There's still stuff out there, some of that mess on the streets got away and sunk beneath the earth. How can people go back to business as usual after a major catastrophe? We still have crime, global warming, ecological damage, economic problems, war . . . Really, this just makes me wanna scream. They aren't tapped into what's going on, what's important."

His gaze slowly raked her. He loved the way the white silk sheets moved when she moved, caressing her skin as they fell away from her body. Seeing that always did something to him. He was just glad that she didn't have a problem with him having a little bad boy still in him. "Yeah, baby, I know," he murmured, thoroughly enjoying the sheen that post-lovemaking perspiration and sun left on her buttery soft skin.

"We have to do something. Be involved. Take a stand. Speak out about how the story wasn't told right and the world governments covered it all up—they are altering history, and the real stuff going on behind the scenes should be documented and chronicled."

He just watched her naked breasts sway as she got herself worked up about things beyond their control. She had beautiful nipples.

"It's probably being written in one of the big books as we speak," he said stroking her hip. "Marlene's got it." The news be damned. It was what it was; the struggle between good and evil wouldn't be over until the last days . . . which were not today. At least not at the moment, while he was in bed with this gorgeous, sexy woman he loved. Priorities. Everything was a matter of perspective.

"You're not fazed at all, are you?" she said shaking her head and reaching for the remote.

He smiled and held it away. She opened her hand and had it.

"Aw, girl," he said rolling over on his side to capture her. "You have to be nice; I'm still going through changes." He smiled and showed her a hint of fang, knowing what that did to her. "I can't do stress right through here while I'm still apexing."

She chuckled and dropped the remote on the floor, then kissed the bridge of his nose, and watched his dark lashes lower, hiding a hint of silver flickering with a little red in his irises. Well, maybe she wouldn't worry about all that at the moment . . . not while sunlight bathed him, and just like everyone else, only gave him a rich, golden tan. It seemed like he'd beaten the system again, coming out holding aces . . . seeming more like a daywalker than a Neteru, but who was she to judge?

This sexy, incorrigible hunk wouldn't live forever, either. So why waste precious time? She kissed him again more slowly, appreciating this vast natural resource she held in her arms, who was her best friend, an excellent lover, an in-the-trenches partner, but was also more mortal than anything else, just like she was. Guaranteed, mortal or not, he'd be around working the system for a very long time, just like she had a very long time to collect the rest of the stones she was supposed to have.

What he was, exactly, she just wasn't sure, but she had given up trying to figure it out . . . just like the powers that he had finally given up trying to understand. Her man defied definition, didn't fit into a nice, neat category. He had pulled a little of his old self back into him to beat the worst of what he was . . . but not too much, just enough to give him a little edge . . . and a nice hint of fang when he was in a particularly amorous mood. But she could deal. He worried both sides, the Dark and the Light, though, on account of the fact that he had a little of both all up in his DNA. He made the governments crazy and didn't show up on their radar—did wonderful work for them when absolutely necessary, but always on his own terms. He had shown her how to hide in plain sight . . . very cool. Still a master of the game who had his good days and bad days, like anyone else, he was the last brother on the planet you wanted to find in a foul mood.

She laughed and just gave up as his kisses trailed down her neck. Tell *him* no? How? It was a stalemate, always, and they both won when the shoutin' was over. Damali sighed.

Like hers, his was a strange truce with the universe, and all sides had taken a pause to figure out what to do with him—or her, for that matter. In the meanwhile, if something went bump in the night and messed with an innocent, they handled it nice and smooth. At least the blood hunger didn't rule him, except when he was particularly turned on . . . not that that was such a bad thing . . . oh, no, not the way *he* served a siphon. She had what he needed. It was all good, indeed.

"The beach can wait," he murmured with his eyes closed, reading her body, not her thoughts.

"Ya think?" she said in a hot whisper near his ear, allow-

ing her hand to slide farther down his belly. She chuckled.
"Never mind. I have the answer to my own question."

"You just have to know the right ones to ask." He smiled
and lazily stroked her back with his eyes still closed. "You
still gonna treat me this nice when I'm out of apex?"

"No," she snapped and laughed, making her voice approximate the Bonpo master's. "That is *not* the right question. The question should be . . ."

She ran her fingers through his hair, nuzzled his forehead,
and kissed him there, opening his third eye so she could tell
him more secrets and pour sensual images into his mind.

"Oh, *yeah,* you know me," he said on a shudder as she
sent a wickedly delicious request into his senses. "Or a
daylight-inspired V-point?" He laughed as she nipped his
shoulder. "Maybe later. I like your idea better."

"Good, 'cause you don't need permission to enter." She
breathed in deeply, inhaling hard against his neck, and then
trailed her nose across his collarbone, loving how his tremors
always released the fading hint of apex that she was surely
going to miss until his next phase. "Standing invitation."

He flipped her on her back and pinned her, nudging her
head to the side with his jaw so he could study her jugular.
"Uhmmph, uhmmph, uhmmph . . . you gonna make me act a
fool up in here today, girl."

"Like you already haven't?" She laughed deep and sexy.

"Yeah, but that was last night . . . do my best work when
its dark, but might have to pull out all the stops this morning,
if you keep making wicked mental suggestions like you just
did." He suckled the tender side of her neck.

"It's broad daylight," she whispered with a sly grin. "And
turn on your silver."

"You sure you want me to do that, or you wanna go au na-
turel?" He kissed her forehead. "Just once?"

"With you, there is no, 'just once,' and you're packing too
much heat—and you know it." She laughed as his smile
widened and let her hands find the dip in his spine.

"Umm-hmmm . . ." he said, opening the window from

across the room without moving to let in the ocean breeze. "Can't blame a brother for trying. But if the lady wants da silver to help her relax . . . hey."

Yes . . . the lady wants the silver," she murmured, warming under his attention.

"Just remind me when I get real close. I don't think I wanna turn it on just yet. I like the way you feel without it." He breathed her in and shuddered as his hands slipped under her backside.

"Turn it on," she whispered without resistance, and then gasped as his lips slowly found her breast. "Okay," she finally breathed, "but how close?"

He chuckled and rounded her taut nipple with his tongue. "When I'm *falling*."

She laughed and tried to push him away. "That's too damned close."

"I know, but it makes things exciting." He found her other breast and paid it tender attention.

"You like living on the edge, don't you?" Her murmur was so conflicted and what he was doing felt so good that she closed her eyes.

"No," he said in a hot breath, sending ripples of pleasure into her navel. "I like living over the edge . . . with you. Tumbling . . . falling . . . out of my mind," he whispered kissing down her abdomen on each word, saving the last one to send as a heat-laden sensation against her mound. "Ain't nothing like it," he added, claiming her bud.

She arched, unable to respond with anything coherent beyond a moan.

"You know," he whispered, his voice low-rolling thunder vibrations against the soft folds of her, "since we're synced up . . . the next time you go into phase, I'll be in apex."

She nodded as the crown of her head dug deeper into the pillow. "I know . . . no silver, then, all right?"

He stopped what he was doing and set his chin on her belly, then smiled as she looked at him with a pained expression. "You serious? Is that a deal?"

She laughed and tried to sit up, but he blanketed her and found her neck.

"Stop messing with my mind, Carlos."

"I wasn't. I was messing with your body."

She closed her eyes. "Then why'd you stop," she whispered hard into his ear. "I was right *there*."

"Hmmm . . . because I thought I heard a tender offer. Maybe a sweet promise. Must be losing my touch," he said, his smile fading slightly as he entered her slowly and closed his eyes.

"You haven't lost anything," she said between a gasp and a moan. "What you've gained drives me crazy. Oh . . . God . . . You smell *fantastic*." She dragged her nose up the side of his throat and teased his tattoo with her tongue until it lit in her mouth, coaxing his hips into a deeper thrust. "If you pull out, I'll make the other one light up, too . . . if you want."

"No, baby . . . just don't stop . . ." he said between his teeth, throwing his head back with his eyes closed as he moved against her with more force. "It's already lit real, *real* good . . . you have no idea *how damned good*." He dropped his burning forehead to hers. "Mali, it's always so good."

She moved her hips in a lazy circle, dipping away from his slow thrusts. "Then you gonna stop messing with my mind?"

"You win this round," he murmured against her hair, and increased his grip around her waist. "But I ain't *never* gonna stop messin' with your mind . . . oh, *baby*, if it makes you do *that* . . . right there, oh, God . . . like that," he said in a rush, wincing from pleasure as she brought him into her harder.

"You, *Carlos* Rivera, are a dangerous combination of things," she whispered on a quiet gasp as he nipped her neck and poised a passion-length fang over her jugular sweet spot.

"I *love* the way you say my name when I'm inside you, *corazon*." He gently knocked her jaw back with his.

"You still worry me, though . . . got a lotta bad boy still in you."

"Yeah . . . you bring it out and that's who I am, baby. Somewhat reformed but not completely recovered. Can you live with that?" he whispered hard against her throat, lowering himself to fully enter her before he bit her.

She arched and found his jugular sweet spot. "Yeah, *oh, yeah* . . . Car . . . los . . . I think I can live with that."

Turn *the page* for a sneak peak at the next Vampire
Huntress Legend novel

The
Forsaken

Available in trade paperback
from St. Martin's Griffin

To beg her husband to relent was futile. His rage knew no bounds. Lilith stared at his large black glistening hooves as she huddled on the searing floor of his pit and waited for the stomping to begin again.

"You allowed my son to be baited to his death by a Neteru! *My son?*" he bellowed, causing a thunderous wind to sweep across her exposed vertebrae and ignite them in flames. Vermin that had nested in her hair squeaked at the violation of their feast. "They took Dante's head, Lilith! His head by an Isis, which means that *even I* cannot raise him from the Sea of Perpetual Agony!"

She wailed from the excruciating pain and dissolved into sobs without tears, her will to survive fractured. His litany had been a monthlong refrain with each tail lash. The beast would not be appeased this time. In her mind she begged for him to turn her body over to the Harpies.

"The Harpies shall not have you, for you have taken my greatest source of torture pleasure from me—*Dante!*"

She covered her head with a remaining arm and immediately felt it ripped from her body; the dull thud of flesh striking the wall converged with the convulsions that jerked her limbless torso.

"Husband, please. I swear to you—"

"That you had been fucking my firstborn son for years was of no consequence to me. I enjoyed watching. That you would try to create another through a stolen half-vampire–half-Neteru embryo, I found delightful, sensually ruthless. . . . I wanted to see what it would become; the experiment was intriguing. But you failed."

"That's why I did it, my love . . . for you," she whispered, begging on a strangled swallow and choking on her own black blood. "*Anything* for you, *everything* for you, my all. I knew you would cherish the child since nothing like it had ever been created. It was a gift, a surprise for you, darling. Please let me make it up to you, my dark essence, please. . . . Just *please* stop the torture. I'll do anything; just command it so."

"You were always my most treacherous and favorite, Lilith. How could you betray me with such a loss? Had you not set the strategy in motion, Dante would still exist." His anger seethed forth, and, baring his hooked teeth, he bent down to snatch her by her throat and then held her above his head with one clawed talon.

"I'm the only one left who has interacted with the Neteru males to know their weaknesses and vulnerabilities!" she shrieked, forestalling his blows.

He paused and stared at her for long tense seconds. "Talk to me," he said, his tone deadly.

"I was Adam's first wife."

There was silence, and her mind scrambled to make her case within milliseconds.

"It was I who tricked the newest and most aggressive, Carlos Rivera, to descend to Dante's throne briefly—only I did that. I even made him ignore the warnings of warrior angels! Dear husband, please consider the possibilities as you rightfully rage against me."

A cool wind blew, and her body began to knit itself back together and heal.

"Husband, my love, I was able to act quickly and rationally at a time of great chaos to snatch the embryo from the carnage of the female Neteru's womb . . . the millennium slayer. If you let me survive, I know another way to raise Dante."

"Continue," his disembodied voice said as the Unnamed

One disappeared into the shadows, considering her offer. His eyes glowed red, then went black within their slits. "Bargain with me, Lilith. You know that's my favorite game."

Hot tears coursed down her face as she tried to speak quickly to him in Dananu. "As long as Dante's firstborn male from his original bloodline exists, all that he was can be summoned forth. It's in the DNA, as always. There is only one other who can sit on Dante's throne to replace all that Carlos Rivera had the potential to be. He is Rivera's exact match, perhaps stronger."

"The one you speak of is in a place that our realms cannot penetrate." Her husband's low, growling voice thundered quietly through the darkness.

"Your month of exacting torture against me has ripped the fabric between the dimensions," she whispered, shivering and holding her arms around herself, braced against a possible sudden blow. "The subterranean disturbance has—"

"The one you speak of still resides within a realm that we cannot breach," he said evenly. "Do not toy with me, Lilith, for if you fail, I will blot you from all existence . . . slowly . . . with excruciating horror."

She shook her head. "Neither you nor I can breach that realm, but a living Neteru can. I've been around them and know their weaknesses."

Again, her proposal was met by silence.

Panic-stricken and yet filled with hope, she pressed on. "The one we seek has the mark of banishment from the One that we never name, but a Neteru can bring him forward through the barrier if the veil between worlds is weakened. You just did that, my beloved. You weakened the veil as you raged beneath the earth. Torturing me was wise, dear husband, and most appreciated, for it created another opportunity that we may have missed."

When her husband didn't answer, Lilith's voice became strident. "I know Rivera's greatest weakness, his insecurities, because he sat in Dante's throne. It's still there; I can still taste that essence," she said, speaking quickly and bar-gaining for her life. "Therefore, knowing *his* shortcomings, I also know the female Neteru's greatest weakness as well, be-cause they are linked at the heart chakra, they are *soul mates*. Fracture the soul mates and you will have your re-venge, which will be no less catastrophic to mankind than what happened to Adam and Eve."

The lack of response made her tone urgent as she contin-ued to speak in a flurry of Dananu. "Husband, your righ-teous fury thinned the veil between worlds. Time stopped, a rip occurred; therefore I can siphon the past to the forefronts of their minds. I can delve into the darkest crevices of what they have forgotten, what has been forsaken. After that, all we have to do is sit back and watch as their love implodes, taking their team of Neteru Guardians with it. Unprece-dented. The Covenant will wobble and fall. There will be no earthly protection for humankind. The past will feel like the present, the present like a faraway thing of the past. Let me work unhindered, beloved. You have seen my best efforts, and I have only failed you this once."

A low, threatening chuckle filled the cavern.

She bowed and then fell to her knees, going prostrate in submission as tears of relief ran down her cheeks. "Let us turn our combined outrage to the more important matter at hand rather than my continued torture. . . . I know and re-spect that you have the Armageddon to concern yourself with as a priority to your magnificent master plan. I could assist you in creating chaos among the young Neteru so that distrust, dishonor, fury replace their love for one another. . . . And just like the fragile balance between dimensions, per-manent fissures among them will allow one of them to call your grandson from his banishment. The female Neteru's weakness is one of your most irresistible wiles, and it was encoded in your grandson's natural lineage. All is not lost; his torture may even be greater than Dante's. Through this new vessel, your firstborn can live again—if you allow me to correct the error I've made. It will even cause disarray among the Neteru Councils and thus the angels above them—something we've never been able to achieve. Imagine how strategic that could be so close to the big war."

Silence made her swallow hard and shudder with anticipation, knowing his decision could go either way.

"You were always my favorite, my most shrewd bitch."

She remained cowering on the pit floor as the slow clatter of hooves began a threatening circle around her body. Lilith closed her eyes, but dared not shield her body with her arm again. The situation had surpassed volatile; he could be thoroughly enraged that she'd devised a logical plan and he hadn't—or he could be temporarily mollified. His power charred her skin as he moved around her, thinking, but she didn't even breathe, much less cry out.

"I will install him on a dark throne," she whispered to the bloodied floor, her eyes shut tightly. "I will lead him by the hand to Dante's power vessel."

"If you fail—"

"I will not fail you, will never fail you," she murmured.

READING GROUP GUIDE

1. *The* theme of relapse and redemption is explored here in depth. How do you think it is possible for a person to beat a substance abuse issue that clings to them if they briefly relapse into an old lifestyle?

2. *What* do you think about Yonnie and Carlos's friendship? Discuss the fact that while Yonnie was still in the old lifestyle, he encouraged Carlos not to relapse. What are some possible consequences if Carlos had relapsed? How would it have affected their friendship?

3. *What* are some daily issues in your life that cause your "dark" and "light" sides to battle, (just as Carlos struggled in the book)? How do you reconcile the two sides?

4. *Was* Damali's intuition that something was wrong justified? Do you think that after all she and Carlos had been through together, she was right to hold herself apart from the unseen, nagging issue that she felt—or should she have accepted him "as is"?

5. *What* is your take on all the house drama among: Yonnie/Tara/Rider; Juanita/Jose/Carlos/Damali; and J.L./Krissy/Dan? Also consider Berkfield's reaction to his daughter's suitors; Marlene/Kamel/Shabazz; and Inez and Big Mike's infection.

6. *Explore* the role of The Convenant and how the team was "called back" during this time of crisis because they, too, were compromised. What are some possible scenarios in which religious leaders are ineffective because they are overly compromised? What are the consequences, and what should be done?

7. *As* the team evolves, and the relationships change, what do you see as the next major hurdle(s) for the Neterus and Guardian team in this series?

**For more on the Vampire Huntress Series,
visit www.vampirehuntress.com**

For more reading group suggestions visit
www.stmartins.com/smp/rgg.html